Incidental Fate

Book 5

Moments in Time

Summer Leigh

Also by Author Summer Leigh:

Incidental Fate™ Series, books 1-6 & GAVIN

Romanoverse® Spin-Off Series: LUCA, SOFIA, STEFANO & GIORGIA.

Social Media: @AuthorSummerLeigh
@IncidentalFate
www.AuthorSummerLeigh.com
www.IncidentalFate.com

ISBN: 978-1-7372724-6-5

CONTENTS

One World.

Two Series.

Twelve + Books.

Incidental Fate™ + Romanoverse®

Author Summer Leigh

6 MONTHS LATER

"Ready?" I asked, rushing out the door into the garage where Gavin was bending over the stroller, buckling the babies in. It never failed, my heart skipped a beat every time I saw him. He was always handsome, always sexy, but now he was more. There was something about seeing him with our babies, the way he smiled at them, the way he held them, hearing him speak Italian to them, and knowing how much he loved them.

He finished with their buckles, his face rising, finding me, which made his smile grow even wider. "Wow, I haven't seen those shorts in a while."

I ran my hands over the flimsy fabric barely covering my thighs. "I haven't been able to fit into them in a while. But they're my favorite running shorts."

"Mine too!" He flashed me that devilish grin, arched brow and all. Then he was jiggling the stroller, checking to make sure it wouldn't move before charging to me. "Let's go back inside, Baby." His hands swooped to my ass, grasping it hard, but I wasn't about to let him distract me, again. I needed this run. I needed to prepare for this week, and *their* arrival.

"No!" I shook my head, trying to convince myself as well. "Babies are strapped in, and I need to run!"

"I have ways to relieve your stress too, Baby." Those dark eyes were staring deep, pulling me into his trap.

Focus, Sadie. I lifted my hand to his arm, grazing his bicep. "I'll probably get pretty sweaty on this run, which means I'll need a nice, long shower when I get back, which also happens to be the babies' nap time," I hinted. "You'll be sweaty too, so you might have to join me."

His eyes lit up, smile twisting wickedly at the edges. Shower sex was his favorite, and we still had so much time to make up for. "Andiamo!" he yelled. "Let's go!" He smacked my ass before grabbing the stroller. "How about we put the twins to bed early tonight?"

"Grant's coming by, remember? You promised to help him set up his portfolio."

"Fuck," he groaned. "That's right."

"He's serious about going into investing. Maybe one day the two of you will have your own company, Romano and Sons Investing," I teased; he rolled his eyes.

"You think you're funny, Mrs. Romano? You know I can easily close this garage and throw you down onto my workout bench."

Oh. The flash of heat was instant, the memories vivid, sending my gaze to the bench that he'd worked me out quite a few times on that thing. Oh. No! I dashed to the garage keypad, jabbing my finger against the button to close the garage. "Time to go, Papà!"

I took my place next to him, walking at his side while he pushed the double stroller down the street. When the babies were infants, he had no choice but to always push. Now he insisted on it. He was so proud, always smiling and boasting when neighbors stopped to ask him about the twins. Not to mention Mamma liked the view of his flexed biceps as he pushed. He was a very hot papà.

"My family's not that bad."

Huh? I blinked, shaking out the thoughts of those arms wrapping around me. "No, that's not what I was thinking about, although..."

"It was your idea to name them godparents, Baby."

That it was. I had said it in jest, delusional from the pregnancy. I never thought Gavin would actually insist on their baptism, or the naming of their godparents. He said it'd make his parents happy, so how could I say no to that. "I'm excited for them to come."

He looked down at me, smiling. "I've held them off as long as I could. They're coming whether we want them to or not."

And it was time. The twins were six months old, and they needed to meet the family too. Gavin had been such a nervous wreck for the first few months after they were born, working himself to the bone taking care of all three of us while still working for the company. I had offered for him to call Sofia or Giorgia to come help, but it was too much for him. It wouldn't have mattered anyway. Gavin wasn't the guy who let someone else take care of his family, he had to do it. He wanted to do it.

His arm swung over my back, holding me with one hand while his other pushed the stroller. "They're really excited to meet the babies and to see you again."

"I'm excited they'll be here for our anniversary! We can get a night away!" I went in for a kiss, but he went silent. A silence I knew too well. "What, Gavin?"

He shrugged, dropping his arm from around me and pushing it back to the stroller. "I don't think we should leave the babies. Piccolina's used to me rocking her to sleep every night, and they're only six months old. It's too fucking soon! They don't know my family yet. They'll be scared."

"This is the perfect time for the twins to get to know them!" I tugged at his shirt, making him look my way. "We've stayed home for six months!" I met those deep brown eyes, pleading with them. "For Valentine's Day, your birthday, my birthday. We can go out for one night, just you and me."

He rolled his face back towards the sidewalk. "We have a big ass house! We don't need to fucking leave." He veered the stroller through the neighborhood gate to the beach sidewalk.

I knew Gavin would be a protective dad, that was his nature. But after everything that happened in the hospital he became a little too overprotective. I loved my babies more than anything, and I'd been with them twenty-four seven for the last six months. It was time for a night with just my husband. I wanted to get dressed up, go out, and enjoy Gavin and Sadie for just a night. "We could have dinner at the hotel, maybe get a room and room service, some champagne." I wiggled up next to him, shimmying.

"Maybe," he mumbled, but I saw the way his lips twitched up at the edges.

I stretched my arms up and out. "I'm going to run. I'll meet you on my way back!" I pushed up on my tiptoes to smack his cheek with a kiss before hopping to the front of the stroller. I knelt down, meeting Nora and Vinny's smiles, their two bottom teeth in full view as they babbled and waved their arms. "Mamma loves you two! I'll be right back." I pressed a kiss to Nora's forehead, then Vinny's, and then I straightened, meeting the giant behind them, the one with the same dark eyes as my babies. "I love you too, Papà."

"Don't go too far, Baby." He reached to the cornicello around my neck, adjusting it.

"Never."

CHAPTER 2

I tipped my head back under the shower, closing my eyes while running my hands through my hair to rinse out the sweat from the long run. Then I heard the glass clank, the chill from the outside air hitting my wet skin, nipples immediately perking. He was here. "Welcome." I swung my arm back, twisting on the second showerhead. "Are you rethinking our anniversary plans? We could have fun in the hotel shower."

His dark eyes met mine for a split second before rolling down to my chest, my stomach, my legs. "Our shower's bigger, Baby." He stepped over, pinning me back against the stall. He looked down into my eyes, his dark, eager ones blinking the water away as the steam rose between us. "You looked sexy running." His hands dropped to my breasts, capturing them, kneading and pinching the tight buds before his hands relaxed, sliding down my wet stomach, dipping between my legs. "I like when you're wet."

His fingers gripped my thighs, lifting me, slamming me down his hard, long. "Oh! Shit! Gavin!" I took all of him at once, the strike intense, sending my eyes rolling back and whimpers of pain and pleasure bursting from my lips.

He groaned, fingers clawing my sides, pushing me up the wall, emptying me only to pound me back down, filling me until I was bursting. He paced faster, harder, his chest tight against mine, dragging my breasts with his thrusts, the friction almost unbearable. "Fuck, I've, missed this, Baby." His chest flexed, arms tightening with each thrust, face tensing with his grunts. "See, Baby. I don't need a hotel room to fuck the shit out of you."

My fuse was lit, building, sparking the impending orgasm. "Gavin!" I met his eyes, his grin turned wicked, his grip strong, lifting me off of him, my feet hitting the shower floor. He bent me over; my palms smacked the glass, water dripping down my face as he stepped behind my thighs, ramming back inside me. Fuck. Fuck. Fuck. I gasped, desperate for air, shaking, climax rendering me breathless, speechless, weightless.

He pounded one last time, releasing, finally dropping his hold of my hips, but my legs buckled, refusing to hold me up, sending me stumbling forward. "Fuck!" He dove, hands clasping around my waist, catching me before I fell and holding me up, locked to his chest.

Damn. I rested back, letting my breathing calm. "I'm okay now," I whispered, and he spun me around in his arms, his proud smile falling to mine, but I turned my head away. "I was hot when I got into this shower; now I'm overheating. I'd probably pass out if you kissed me right now."

He laughed, running a hand up my arm to my face, gliding his thumb across my bottom lip. "We don't have to go anywhere to get you hot."

"A hotel would get me hotter," I attempted to flirt, but he shook his head no as he elbowed the glass door open and grabbed us some towels. Then he stalked off to his closet while I walked into mine, pulling out a sundress.

"I like that one."

Shit! I jumped, my heart racing, my hand clutching my heart. "You've got to stop doing that!"

"Watching you get dressed, never," he teased.

"Sneaking up on me!"

He flashed me a wry smile as he turned to walk out, only to still, mouth agape, eyes on my closet wall. "What the fuck is that?"

I followed his stare to the giant canvas hanging in the open space of my closet, and the dark eyes, wave of black hair, and delicious smile printed on it. "Oh, you haven't been in here in a while, I guess."

He looked at me, then to his face on the wall. "Why?"

"So I can see my sexy husband whenever I want!" And I looked at it quite a bit. "It's my favorite picture of you, although I do wish you weren't wearing that suit, would make for much better eye candy."

His eyes went wide, studying me, his cheeks blushing. "I didn't know you had this in here."

"It's not a big deal." I tugged the dress over my head. "I like reminding myself how lucky I am."

"Fine," he sighed. "We can go out for our anniversary."

"Fine?" Seriously. "It's our one-year anniversary, Gavin! And you're taking me out to what? Appease me?"

He stepped over, swinging his arms around my back. "I'm nervous, Baby."

"Then we'll stay in," I relented. The last thing I wanted was a nervous, antsy Gavin.

"I didn't mean—"

A cry echoed into the room, so I pushed out of Gavin's hold, checking the baby monitor on my way out the door to the nursery. I cracked the door open, seeing them both sitting up in their cribs. "How was your nap?" I flipped the light on, walking over to Vinny, whose black hair was wild from sleep and whose big eyes matched his smile.

Gavin shuffled in behind me, picking Nora up and following me and Vinny downstairs.

"Grant should be here soon," I reminded him.

He veered into the office, sweeping his arm across the desk to clear the space, only then all you saw were my nail marks. "No! You can't work with him in here."

"I can't work with him... in my office?" he clarified.

I waved over his desk, specifically the nail marks. "It's too weird! Those are obviously claw marks, and those are fresh!" I pointed to the ones at the edge from the other night. "It's too weird having him in here with this."

"I told you not to claw my desk, Baby."

"It was your fault!" I countered, laughing now. "You gave me no choice!"

He rolled his eyes, gesturing me back out into the hall. "The dining table then," he suggested.

"Hmm." I gave him a knowing look, reminding him of our dessert adventures just last night.

"Fuck," he grumbled and chuckled as we continued to the kitchen. "In here then."

I looked around the space. This would work. "Okay. Just don't sit in your chair." Gavin had a habit of waking up early every morning and sneaking downstairs to drink his coffee, in only his boxers. And Mamma had a horrible habit of following him down and ending up on his lap. "You know! I should buy a table that's strictly a no-sex table!" I could look into one today, have it here tomorrow.

But Gavin started chuckling again. "Baby, I'd fuck you on it the second you brought it home."

The doorbell chimed; I gave Gavin my 'be on your best behavior' glare before hurrying down the hall to open the door.

"Grant!" I went in for a hug while Vinny practically jumped from my arms, so excited to see his brother.

"Hey, buddy!" Grant set his laptop on the entry table before taking Vinny and following me to the kitchen.

"You and Gavin can work in here at the table." I waved towards the chair, but Grant wasn't moving.

"Here?" He looked between Gavin and me. "But he's got that giant desk I can spread all my papers out on."

He *did* have a giant desk, but it wasn't paper that was usually spread out over it. "I'm going to make dinner for us! And there's no eating on Gavin's desk." I shrugged to Grant while raising my eyes, meeting Gavin's devilish grin behind him.

"Really?" Gavin growled, eyes darkening. "That's not what you said last—"

"Gavin!" I warned. "Give me Nora so you two can get to work." He handed her over, and I met his teasing stare. "Best behavior!" I mouthed as he puckered, blowing me a kiss.

CHAPTER 3

An engine roared, the floor vibrated, which meant, they were here. I lifted Vinny in one arm, Nora in the other, adjusting her pigtails and his Yankees jersey as I trudged to the front door, barely keeping my hold of the babies. Gavin made this look so easy, tossing them up and carrying them around like it was no big deal. But then again, he carried me around like it was no big deal either. I swung the front door open, watching the car park, and meeting the rush of Romanos.

"Sadie!" Sofia shouted, tears escaping her eyes as she rushed over, lifting her hand to Vinny's face. "Bellissimo! So handsome!"

"Hi, Sofia!" I *had* missed them.

Giorgia followed, throwing me into an embrace.

"Wait!" Gavin yelled, pushing forwards. "Wash your hands before touching them."

Sofia rolled her eyes, wiping the stray tears from her cheek as she addressed Gavin. "They're six months old, Gav. They're not infants."

He still pushed in front of her, plucking Nora from my arm, noticing her hair. "What's this?"

"Pigtails! Doesn't she look cute!" I replied, watching his smile spread into his cheeks. Vinny was Gavin's boy, but Nora, Nora was his piccolina. She made Papà's eyes light up, and she already had him wrapped around her tiny fingers.

"Let me hold her!" Luca demanded, pushing up next to Gavin, arms outstretched.

But Gavin rebuffed him, shouldering him away. "You especially need to wash your fucking hands. Forget soap, put some fucking gloves on before you touch my babies."

"Watch your language in front of your kids!" Luca barked back. "What the fuck's wrong with you!"

"May I?" Sofia asked, hands out for Vinny.

"No, Paulo?"

"He's away," she sighed, eyes locked on Vinny.

Stefano walked up behind them, tossing an arm around my shoulders. "You've shrunk, Patatina."

"So then you can stop calling me potato," I insisted.

"Nah," he teased, his grin curling cheek to cheek. "I like patatina."

I hadn't really spoken to Stefano or Mark since New Year's, and I had no idea if they were still talking. "Are you bringing anyone to the ceremony tomorrow?"

"No," he mumbled, eyes downcast.

"Zio Stefano!" Sofia chirped, interrupting us. "Come meet, Vinny."

He stepped over, and Vinny lunged at him, lifting his little arms up for Stefano. "That's my boy!" Stefano took him from Sofia, letting him nestle against his chest.

"Nora!" Giorgia squealed as she and Sofia swarmed Gavin and Luca. "She's beautiful!"

"Yeah, don't worry," Luca grumbled. "Zio Luca and Stefano will fuck up anybody that comes near her."

That's if anyone made it past Gavin. He was protective of me, but I had nothing on his piccolina.

"Her dress!" Sofia cooed, running her fingers over the dress she'd bought back in New York. "Can I hold her?"

Gavin and Luca were too busy making Nora laugh, so Sofia reached right over, tugging Nora away.

"Where's Piccolo?" Luca yelled again, pushing his way towards Stefano.

"With his favorite zio," Stefano boasted.

"Second favorite," Luca scoffed. "And a Yankees jersey! You're raising him right! Vinny, come to Zio Luca!"

Vinny lifted his head from Stefano's chest, appraising Luca, but seemingly unimpressed, so he dropped his face right back against Stefano.

"My boy's fucking smart!" Gavin elbowed Luca before reaching his hands for Vinny. "Vieni da Papà. Come to Papà."

Vinny smiled, lurching forward into Gavin's arm. Then Gavin raised his free hand to the sky, rounding up his family. "Va bene, andiamo dentro ora. Everybody inside."

Giorgia hopped over to me, hooking her arm in mine. "Last year you were walking down the aisle! Now you're baptizing the babies!"

I had walked the aisle to Gavin with no idea that Vinny and Nora were walking with me.

"I'm envious," she mused, looking off in the distance.

We trailed the family in and out the back doors, where Gavin was gushing about the view. "La spiaggia è proprio lì," he said, waving his arms towards the ocean before turning back and meeting my eyes. "The beach is right there," he translated for me. "E il giardino di mia moglie," he continued, pointing to my garden. Gavin had insisted my garden be in the back because I tended to fall asleep in the grass when I was supposed to be gardening.

Then Sofia started for the door. "Ora, vediamo la stanza dei bambini! Sadie! I want to see the nursery!"

"Upstairs," Gavin answered. "Luca and Stefano's rooms are up there too. Sofia and Giorgia are downstairs."

I walked into the kitchen, watching the family head down the hall, and listening to their footsteps shuffle up the stairs. Then I heard them shuffling back down, all roaring into the family room to play with the babies.

"Sadie," Giorgia yelled over. "Where are you and Gav going for your anniversary?"

I shrugged. "Gavin wants to stay home."

"But I said we would watch the gemelli!" She looked over at Gavin, then to me. "I'll watch the twins!"

"I told him," I mumbled back.

"Gav!" Sofia sighed. "Devi uscire, è il tuo anniversario!" She focused on me next. "You have to go out! It's your anniversary!"

Tell me something I didn't know.

Giorgia elbowed Gavin. "Quando è stata l'ultima volta che hai portato Sadie fuori?" Her eyes were on him, but he took too long to answer, so she turned to me. "When's the last time he took you out, Sadie?"

"New Year's," Gavin answered, waving at the babies. "Siamo stati occupati, non possiamo lasciare i bambini."

"Non puoi dimenticare di tua moglie!" Sofia snapped, eyes landing on me. "Sta per uscire dalla porta!"

I couldn't stand when they went off in Italian because I had no idea what they were saying. Well, I had things to do anyway. "I'll be right back!" I walked down the hall, throwing the front door open, hearing a boom of laughter as I shut it behind me, en route to the mailbox. I'd been waiting on the gift I ordered Gavin for our anniversary, but the mailbox was empty.

"Hey, excuse me!" A car slowed, the driver waving. "Are you number 28?"

"Yes," I called back.

"I have a package for you. It was delivered to our box. Give me a minute!" He pulled into the driveway three houses up while I waited on the sidewalk. "Where are the babies?" he asked with a smile, box in hand. "I see you out with a stroller a lot."

"They're inside." *With their people.*

"I'm Chris, by the way. My wife is Delaney."

"Nice to meet you. I'm Sadie," I replied, but his eyes rolled up, watching something behind me. "And this is my husband, Gavin." I pointed over my shoulder just as arms wrapped around my waist.

"Nice to meet you," Chris greeted him too. "We should all hang out sometime! I'm sure my girls would love to play with the twins!"

"That'd be great!" I took the package as he gave us a wave, starting back towards his driveway. "What are you doing out here?" I spun in Gavin's arms, watching his eyes follow Chris away.

"What was that about?" he asked, stare falling to me.

"He had a package for me."

"Excuse me!"

I held up the box. "It was misdelivered."

"I'm sorry," he said, pulling me against him.

"Packages get misdelivered all the time. No big deal."

He chuckled, squeezing me in tighter. "No, about being such a dick about our anniversary. I want to take you out, Baby. We never get another first anniversary. I want to do it right."

"So your siblings convinced you they could babysit?"

"Something like that. Let's get back inside." He led me to the door; only I stopped him before he could open it.

"Baciami!" I demanded, puckering my lips as I tugged his shirt.

"Sempre, Baby. Always."

CHAPTER 4

I hurried down the stairs, meeting the family who was gathering their stuff at the door.

"Wow, you look good, Mamma!" Gavin took my hand as I hit the bottom step, whirling me to him.

"I haven't dressed up in a while. I miss it!" I had missed dressed up Gavin too.

"Ready?" Sofia entered the hall, holding Vinny in her arms, while Stefano stepped up beside her holding Nora, whose long white gown draped over his arm. All the Romanos seemed so proud, beaming over the babies as if they were their own. But the proudest stood at my side, hand wrapped in mine, with his natural smile plastered across his face. This was a big deal for him.

"Let's go!" I insisted, and Luca swung the front door open, ushering us out. "The babies can drive with you."

"What?" Gavin slammed to a stop, already shaking his head no. "No, we all drive together!"

"You can't fit everybody in your car."

"No, Baby." He was stern, yanking my hand over as he leaned to my ear. "I want you with me." He unlocked the car, directing the guys to the third row before they loaded the twins.

"Okay." I climbed into the passenger seat, watching the car fill behind me, and then we were off. Gavin's hand squeezed mine tighter and tighter with each passing mile. "Are you okay?" I whispered, seeing the tense smirk that had replaced his proud smile.

"I'm nervous," he whispered back.

"I'm sure your parents have big smiles right now. Think of them."

He nodded, pulling my hand to his lips, kissing my knuckles.

We arrived at the church, and everyone piled out of the car, with Luca taking the lead. He walked into the church, down the aisle to the front pew, guiding us to sit. It was such a strange feeling, not that I was back in a church, or the fact that I wasn't even catholic, but that Gavin and I were here together, dressed up and holding our babies for their baptism.

The music started, the priest walked out, addressing the parishioners, making it all real. What were we doing here? What was I doing here? Stefano's elbow suddenly jabbed me, gesturing towards the priest whose eyes were on us, beckoning us to come up. Here we go.

I stood with Nora, following Gavin, who led the way with Vinny. We stopped aside the priest while Luca and Sofia made their way to Gavin's side, and Stefano and Giorgia took their spot on mine.

The priest spoke to the parishioners, then to us, asking a series of questions that everyone around me answered before he addressed Gavin and me directly. "You have asked to have your children baptized today. In doing so, you are accepting the responsibility of training them in the Catholic faith. It will be your duty to bring them up to keep all God's commandments as Christ taught us, by loving God and our neighbor. Are you in agreement with this?"

"We are," Gavin replied, stare not wavering from the priest, who now turned to address Luca and Sofia.

"Do the godparents agree to lead these children in their spiritual growth and show by example righteousness with a strong moral compass?"

My gaze went to Luca as I stifled a laugh. This was my idea. I had chosen Luca to be the moral and spiritual compass for my child, that is what being crazy pregnant and living off chocolate did to your brain. I half expected Luca to say something like 'Fuck, yeah' but he didn't. He was actually very stoic, taking all this seriously. He rested his hand on Vinny's leg while addressing the priest. "We do," he and Sofia said in unison.

The priest gestured for Gavin to lower Vinny, signing the cross on his little forehead before he scooped a cup of water. "Vinny Diego Romano, I hereby baptize you in the name of the Father, the Son, and of the Holy Spirit," he recited as he poured the water down his hair, making Vinny wiggle in Gavin's arms. Then the priest promptly turned towards me, repeating the same sentiments to Stefano and Giorgia, who said "we do" in unison. "Nora Elise Romano, I hereby baptize you in the name of the Father, the Son, and of the Holy Spirit." He poured the water over her hair, causing her to cry out, sending all arms reached for her, each Romano trying to soothe her, but her little arms only reached for Papà, so Gavin handed Vinny to Sofia and lifted his piccolina, instantly calming her. There was such pride amongst the siblings right now. A pride I didn't really understand because I was raised so differently. They were all smiles and wet eyes, watching the priest dab oil and light a candle.

We returned to our seats, Gavin immediately throwing his arm around me, curling me to him and Nora. "Thank you, Baby. This meant a lot to me and my family."

"Of course. Although I'm a little worried about Vinny and his new moral compass."

Gavin's chest rumbled with his laugh. "Luckily, we live three thousand miles apart."

I nestled into him, my mind wandering off as the priest continued. Today was all about the babies, but tomorrow would be all about Mamma and Papà. A year ago, we had our own ceremony, and ever since then, I've had to share him. It was time for a few hours of just Sadie and Gavin, getting out and losing ourselves in each other. I rubbed my hand over his suit, feeling the muscles that stretched the fabric. He looked and felt so good in a suit. I leaned up to his ear, brushing my lips against his lobe. "I want you to wear this tomorrow night."

"Jesus fuc—Baby, we're in mass, please tell me you're not thinking about—"

Shit. I mean, crap. Ugh. What was wrong with me? "I'm not!" I lied, in church. Dammit. I forced naked Gavin out of my thoughts while raising my hand, attempting the sign of the cross.

"You did it backward. Now I know you were having impure thoughts, Baby." He arched a brow as I slouched into the seat, feeling the heat in my cheeks. "But don't worry, Baby. You can confess those thoughts to me later, and I'll make sure to bless you."

CHAPTER 5

I examined the black dress, twisting it front to back. I barely fit into my old clothes, but I wanted to look good tonight! It was our first date in six months, and it was our anniversary. Here goes nothing! I stepped into it, tugging it ruthlessly up my thighs and over my ass, sucking in as I yanked the zipper up. It was on! I did it! I spun to face the mirror, immediately laughing at the ridiculous cleavage pressed up to my neck in the too-tight dress. Good thing Gavin liked boobs because this was ridiculous. I grabbed my stilettos on the way to the door, checking my hair and makeup one last time before leaving the room. I looked like I was ready for a night out in Vegas, not just dinner, but it didn't matter. I felt sexy, and I hadn't felt that way in a while. I danced down the stairs, running into Luca stepping out of Gavin's office.

He stilled, that Luca smile curling up his face as he looked me over. "Gav's such a little shit."

"Why?" I glanced down the hall. "What happened?"

"Nothing." He walked past me, stopping halfway down the hall. "Gav, don't make your moglie wait!"

"Shhh!" Gavin roared back from the other room. "Don't wake the fucking babi—" he stepped into the hall, gaze landing on me, jaw dropping. "Holy shit." He plowed past Luca, charging towards me. "Fuck!" His arms flew to my waist, stare dropped to my cleavage. "You look fucking amazing, Baby!"

"Thanks!" I felt amazing. "Same to you!" He was in his black slacks and that navy blue collared shirt, perfectly fitted to his muscular arms and chest.

He swung one arm back, grabbing the keys to his car before bolting forward, dragging me out the front door, kicking it closed behind him, and whirling me up against the wall, mouth crashing to mine. "I forgot how fucking sexy you are, Baby." His husky rasp hit my ear, sending a shiver down my spine. "How about we drive to a parking lot and—"

A parking lot! I pushed him back. "You want to go to a parking lot on our first anniversary?"

"Oh fuck," he sighed, shaking his head no. "No, shit, of course not. Sorry, this fucking dress and your fucking tits. I, fuck, let's get going."

It was funny how a tight black dress and stilettos could make a man lose his damn mind.

He opened the garage, hurrying to my side to grab the car door before racing to his side. I hadn't driven in this car in forever, but the sexy memories were still so vivid. Maybe a parking lot wasn't so bad.

He dropped into his seat, that devilish grin curled up as he revved the engine, and he slammed the gas, reversing out of the driveway, zooming away. Papà was gone, and Gavin was behind the wheel, cruising down the highway, while his hand inched up my thigh.

We drove up to the hotel's valet, and Gavin hopped out, dashing to my door to take my hand. His eyes never left my chest, blatantly eye-fucking me, and I couldn't be happier. I had missed this. Gavin always wanted me, and he always wanted sex, but the look in his eyes tonight was different—it was wild lust.

His hand gripped mine hard, locked, melded to mine as he led us into the lobby, the two of us immediately drawing attention. Apparently, Gavin wasn't the only guy who liked tight dresses and massive cleavage, and I wasn't the only woman who liked six-foot men with dark hair and bulging biceps.

"Fuck," he bellowed. "I forgot about this shit." He let go of my hand to drape his arm around my back instead.

"What shit?" I laughed, looking up at his tense face.

"That everyone fucking looks at you, fucking stare as if I'm not right next to you!" He suddenly pulled to a stop.

"I don't—"

His body slammed into mine, lips attacking my mouth, his tongue halfway down my throat before I knew what hit me.

I gasped, throwing my hands up in surprise, then dropping them to his sides, falling into the kiss.

He was ravenous, passionate, hands sliding across my back while his kiss grew deeper. I was just as needy, losing myself in his scent, the soft scratch of his stubble, strong arms locking me tight to him, the steam between us rising. Oh! That wasn't the only thing rising. I broke the kiss, the connection, taking a step back while looking at his growing pants, and trying to quell the heat under my dress.

He drug his mouth away from mine, eyes still closed, and then he grabbed my arm, jerking me in the opposite direction of the restaurant, straight for the registration counter instead. "I need a room!" he demanded, yanking out his wallet and tossing his license and credit card to the man behind the counter.

Room? "But I didn't bring my stuff."

"We're not staying, Baby. I only need the room for an hour or so."

Oh my god. I slunk back behind him, hiding behind his broad frame to avoid the look I'm sure I'd be getting from the clerk.

"We have a few rooms," the man started.

"I don't care," Gavin snapped, sending a hand back to me, rubbing over my dress. "Just give me a fucking key."

I felt like a cheap date, a quick thrill, kind of dirty, and I liked it.

I was being yanked away again, Gavin's hand dragging me towards the elevator, whirling me right inside.

"Hold that, please!" A woman called, rushing towards us, but Gavin smacked his hand over the 'Door Close' button.

"No!" he apologized, eyes black and bold as he turned from the door to me, raking me over from heel to hair, his hand flying to the back of my neck, tipping my face up, lips smacking mine, rough and hungry. All his layers peeled away, papà, husband, provider, protector, leaving just Gavin, raw and wild.

The door slid open, and he was full steam ahead, key in the lock, kicking the door open, spinning me in, and pinning me up against the wall. "Fuck, Baby. You are so sexy." He dropped his hands to his belt, ripping it loose, black leather slapping in the air, drawing me to it. Then his face was diving into my chest while he ripped the dress down, so he had full access to my chest, filling his palms with my breasts. It felt so good to be ravaged, to be groped.

His hands slid down my stomach, my thighs, bunching the hem of the dress in his hands, lifting it now, searching for panties that weren't there. "I'm not wearing any," I confirmed, meeting his hungry gaze. "Easy access."

He slipped his hands between me, eyes rolling back as his fingers rolled over me. "Fuck." It was a grunt, his hands tightening with it, lifting me, only he stopped, dropping his hand to mine instead. "I want to watch us, Baby." He led me to the bathroom, flipping on the light while pressing my back tight against his chest. He stared, studying my body in the reflection, watching me as his hands crept up my sides, cupping my breasts, kneading, caressing, toying with my nipples. Then his lips hit my ear. "Bend over."

I flung forward, palms down to the counter, ass arched, desperately waiting, rubbing back against his erection, watching his hands slither away, disappearing, only to be felt between my thighs, grazing my wet center.

"Fuck, I've missed you, Baby!" He smacked my ass, his hips thrust, his dick slammed inside me.

"Oh, fuck!" I grasped the counter, clawing it as he filled me, working himself deeper, watching himself while I watched him, watched every muscle he had flex with each jolt, ripping through his shirt.

He knew this position made me weak, that he could destroy me so easily, pounding until I hit my breaking point. "Gavin!"

"Fuck, Baby!" His pace quickened, thrusts drilling into me as his fingers dug into my hips.

My face fell like a brick against the counter, held up by legs shaking so violently under me. My body was reeling from the implosion of pleasure. Then his hands slid under me, lifting me from the counter and tossing me up in his arms, whisking me out to the room to the bed. He was all smiles, his sexy hair messy now, his eyes bright, staring at me as he stepped into his pants and reached for his belt.

"I like that," I choked out, my chest still trying to sync with my breathing.

He chuckled, a sexy strained laugh. "What?"

"Your belt is sexy."

He immediately stilled, stretching the belt in his hands. "It's sexy, huh?" He started towards me, kicking his pants right back off.

"We can't." I shook my head, seductively wiggling my body over the sheets. "We have dinner downstairs!"

"Scoot over, Baby," he instructed, gesturing me to the edge of the bed.

"Why?"

"Because there's nowhere to tie you up over here. Now scoot to the post."

I laughed, but he was serious, so I complied, scooting until I was in line with the bedpost. "Now what?" I asked, and he dropped the belt to my foot, dusting it along the inside of my thigh, teasing my center before dropping the cold metal clasp against my breasts.

"Don't worry, Baby. I'm not gonna do anything crazy." His hands fell to my wrists, pulling them up and over my head and looping the smooth leather belt around them, knotting it tightly onto the bedpost behind me.

I instinctively tried to wriggle my arms free, but they were locked. "What are you going to do?" I was tied up, exposed, watching his pupils dilating.

"Dinner downstairs," he teased, climbing over me, his fingers latching to my nipples as he slid down, eyes meeting mine one last time before disappearing between my thighs.

Holy hell! His tongue shot out, taking my clit hostage, sending me arching off the bed, arms jerking but bound too tight to move. The pressure was back, building too fast, too intense. "Oh, fuck, Gavin!" I writhed against his mouth, reeling from his lips, that whipping tongue, his hot breath blowing into me in spurts and waves, driving me fucking crazy. I yanked my arms again, desperately arching under him.

His hands shot up, slamming my hips down, holding me in place, taking me prisoner while he devoured me. Fuck! I needed my hands! I needed to pull him away, push him deeper, grasp his wild black hair, claw into something, anything! "Gavin!" I was on overload, still not recovered from earlier, still sensitive—he didn't care.

"Untie me!" I screamed, breath uneven, panting, the orgasm right on the precipice. His face shot up, taking his tongue with it. "No! Don't stop!" I yelled, and he fell back between my legs, sliding his hands down, hooking his arms under my thighs, pushing his face even deeper, licking me that much harder. "Fuck!" My lips quivered, eyelids twitched, chest heaved. Then his mouth was gone. "Gav—"

He bulldozed, arousal ramming inside me, his scream meeting mine.

He groaned, thrusting fast, fucking hard until he fell over me, mouth landing at my breast, sucking my nipple as he pulled out. "Oh, fuck!" His face sprung up, meeting my eyes as he licked his lips.

"What?" I was paralyzed, euphoria slowly dissipating, taking my climax coma with it.

"I just got a fucking drink," he chuckled, shooting out his tongue and licking his full lips once more. "Your milk, Baby. Fuck, what if the babies wake up hungry!" And just like that, we were back to Mamma and Papà.

"I put bottles in the fridge and showed Giorgia where their food was."

He rolled over, landing on the bed beside me. "Do you think they're okay?"

"Yes," I assured him. "But, Gavin?"

"Yeah, Baby."

"Can you please untie me?"

CHAPTER 6

I tried to fix myself up before dinner, combing through my hair with my fingers before swiping under my eyes. "How do I look?" I asked Gavin, who had his back to me.

"Beautiful," he replied without looking.

"Gavin!" I laughed, causing him to turn around, eyes raking over me while he finished latching his belt.

"Beautiful," he repeated with a teasing smile. "Also, like you've just been fucked."

"I've heard that before!" I waltzed over, gaze locked with his. One year, how did I get so lucky? "You ready?"

He reached for my hand, taking his time to intertwine each finger. "I love you, Baby. Happy anniversary."

"I love you, too! Now take me out on a proper date," I teased, meeting his devilish grin. "Sex is supposed to come after dinner. We're always doing stuff backwards."

"Can't have dinner without an appetizer. And don't worry, Baby. You'll come after dinner too."

I bumped my shoulder into his, the two of us staring at each other as we made our way down to the lobby and to the restaurant, laughing and smiling so big it hurt.

"Romano," he informed the hostess while slipping her some cash. "Sorry we missed our reservation. We were, tied up." His gaze flicked to mine, eyebrow arching.

"Not a problem!" She giggled, blushing up at Gavin. "This way." She led us into the crowded restaurant and to a small candle-lit table sitting against the glass, facing the waves on the other side.

Gavin pulled my chair, waiting for me to sit before taking his own seat, and a second later, a server was there, filling our wine glasses.

He raised his glass, eyes focused so intently with the most sincere smile. "Per cent'anni."

"Only a hundred years?" I balked playfully. "Cheers to eternity." I tapped his glass, keeping my gaze on him as I took the sip.

He set his glass down, pulling a jewelry box from his pocket. "Happy anniversary, Baby." He handed it over with the proudest smile, and I wrapped my fingers over it, smiling as I flipped it open, to sparkling jewels.

"Gavin!" The candlelight hit each stone, reflecting the brilliant purple and green. I tugged the stacked stone ring out, studying the four bands. The first three each featured a glistening amethyst, while the last held a single peridot.

"It's for your right hand," he gushed. "I had it custom made. The four bands match your wedding ring. The amethysts are for the babies and me. I didn't even realize our fucking birthstones were purple!"

I did. "I love purple even more now!"

Then he gestured to the last band. "And the green one is for—"

"Grant." He had remembered Grant, and his birthstone. I slid the ring onto my finger, wiggling it. "Thank you!"

He stretched his hand across the table, squeezing mine. "I'm glad you like it, Baby."

"But it makes my gift to you seem so small." Gavin was the king of flashy gifts, but I wasn't wired that way. I never had the luxury of flashy, and I never knew what to get him, he had it all. I lifted the 4x6 box from my purse, presenting it to him.

He unwrapped it, laughing at the photo immediately. When I gave the babies food for the first time, they'd both smeared it across their faces, so I smeared some over mine too, and we took a picture. The babies had inherited Gavin's beautiful face but Mamma's messiness. "Since you love messy faces so much," I teased, and he gave me his sincere smile. "You can add it to your collection." He had a row on his desk—my messy face from our first date, me at our wedding with cake on my nose, one from May's party with my little pregnant belly on display, and now he had one of me with our babies. "Another chapter."

He ran a finger over the glass. "It's perfect, Baby." He set the frame on the table, staring while the candlelight reflected off the tears his eyes were welling with.

"Gavin?" I slid my hand to his, squeezing it to make him look at me. "What's wrong?"

He lifted my hand to his lips, kissing my knuckles while whispering against them. "I have everything I've ever wanted."

"A messy family?" I joked, making him crack a smile.

"But it's mine," he boasted. "My messy family."

We lost track of time, ordering, eating, laughing, and loving. We were lost in our own little Sadie and Gavin world until he finally pushed out of his chair, helping me up next and leading us out of the restaurant. Except I wasn't done with sexy Gavin. I missed this, and I wanted just a little bit more before it hit midnight and he turned back into Papà. "We still have the room upstairs," I hinted, leaning into his side. He didn't reply or react, just swung his arm over my back, leading us right past the elevators towards the valet. "So, that's a no."

He rolled that serious gaze down to me. "We've been gone a long time, Baby, and— "

And he missed his babies. It was the first time he had ever left them, and honestly, this Gavin, the one wanting so badly to get back to his children, was just as sexy as the Gavin tying me up. I stepped in front of him, resting my hands on his waist. "It's okay. I had an amazing night."

The valet pulled up with his car, we drove home, and the second he hit the brakes, he was bolting. He rushed into the house, with me two steps behind him, laughing under my breath. And as expected, the house was dark and silent.

"Everyone's sleeping," he whispered.

"See, all is well."

He let out a content sigh as he grabbed my hand, taking me to the kitchen. "To finish the night," he continued whispering, opening the fridge door and pulling out a plate with the top tier of our wedding cake sitting atop it. "It's tradition, Baby."

I grabbed a fork from the drawer, following him up the stairs to our bedroom, quietly closing the door behind us. He continued to his side of the bed while I sank onto the edge of my side, flipping the lamp on while removing my rings. Then he was back in front of me, his belt level with my eyes. "Dessert," he called, reaching his hand for mine, but my focus was on his belt and zipper, and dessert.

My hands hit his pants, whipping the belt free, sliding the zipper down, yanking his pants to his knees, making him stumble in surprise, gasping as I freed him from his boxers. "Shit, Baby."

I sat back, nudging the straps of my dress down until my entire chest was on display, giving him a quick show before clasping my hands around his thighs, drawing him closer, hearing his groans already starting. "Time to come after dinner." I opened my mouth, flashing my eyes up to his as I flicked my tongue out, slapping against his tip, my lips following.

"Fuck, cazzo, fuck," he yelped, grunted, hands weaving through my hair, pulling and twisting, holding on while I dove faster, filling my mouth with him. "Baby."

I bobbed faster, taking him deeper, his stare rolling from my face up to the ceiling, gasping. It was my mouth causing his undoing. He was at my mercy, and I wanted more! I dug my nails into the back of his thighs, pushing him into me, down my throat, cheeks hollowed as I deep throated.

"Sadie!" he screamed my name for once, and now, the icing on the cake. I relaxed my hold, sliding him out just enough that I could fit my hand around his base, making sure his inked name on my finger was visible, and only inches from the mouth he was inside. His eyes shot to his name, watching me blow him with his name front and center. He bucked, hips jerked, coming. "Go." He nodded his head towards the bathroom sink, but I shook my head as I slid him out.

"I swallowed."

He pounced, broad chest smashing over me, his hips against mine, and his revived erection already digging between my thighs. "Fuck, Baby! I want to see my name again," he demanded, so I threw my hands to my breasts, clutching them as he railed into me. God, he knew exactly where to hit. My body instantly succumbing.

"I love you," I gasped, his lips falling to mine at that moment, smacking a plump kiss while he came.

He rolled off of me, reaching to his bedside table for the cake. "One year ago, Baby." He sat up, resting against the headboard while I wiggled up next to him. Then he cut a piece, pushing it to my lips first before cutting himself a piece. "How is it?" he asked, waiting for my answer.

It was gross. I laughed. "It tastes like cake that's been sitting in a freezer for a year." I watched him chew it and promptly spit it back onto the plate. I nestled into him, resting my hand on his thigh. "Did tonight change your mind about hiring a babysitter?"

"Nope," he sighed. "I'll have my family come out when we need a date night."

"So I have to have a house full of Romanos to get a night alone with you?" I rolled my eyes teasingly. "I'm going to change." I started away, but his arm shot out, holding me back.

"No, Baby. I'm not done with you yet."

CHAPTER 7

I heard a faint cry, instantly ending my good dreams, and sending my arm out for the monitor, seeing Nora on the screen, squirming in her crib. I powered it off and slipped out of bed, trying not to wake Gavin as I padded out of the room. I continued down the hall, leaning my ear to the nursery door, hearing a shushing sound in lieu of Nora's cries.

I opened the door, finding Luca in the rocking chair, holding her against his chest. "I'm sorry she woke you." I walked to Vinny's crib, lifting him out and sinking into the chair beside Luca.

"I was awake," he spoke in an uncharacteristically quiet voice as he rested his head over hers. "You two have fun last night?"

We had fun over, and over, and over again. "It was nice getting out for a bit. Although, it probably won't happen again. Gavin doesn't trust anyone with them."

"Good," he agreed. "They shouldn't be left with anyone but famiglia."

Of course. "How'd it go here?"

He smiled with a shrug. "I chilled with Vinny."

"Does that mean he likes you now?" I teased.

"Of course he fucking likes me. I'm Luca Romano."

"Hey, moral compass, can you chill on the language," I asked, sliding my eyes to his.

"Sorry," he chuckled.

"Speaking of which, how are you doing?"

"I'm not smoking."

That was a start. "Drinking?"

"Less."

"A girl?"

"Many," he countered.

And this was the reason my husband didn't know how to date. Luca had also been Gavin's moral compass.

Nora lifted her face from Luca's chest, her big eyes up on him. "Zio loves you, Piccolina," he cooed, melting over her smile the same way Gavin did. So Luca had a soft side, who would've thought. "It's like looking in a fucking mirror. Actually, it's like staring down at Gav. How's he doing with all this?"

"Amazing." I didn't even have to think about it. Gavin was so incredible, not fazed by anything. He handled the good, the bad, and the ugly. "He's the best papà."

"I figured he would be," he sighed, stare still glued on Nora. "I'm kinda pissed we're leaving today. I like these two. Thank you for giving them to us."

"I'm not giving them to you," I laughed. "But you can borrow them on date night." I noticed a flicker from the corner of my eye, catching the babies' camera panning. Someone's awake. I stifled a laugh at the eavesdropper. "He's watching," I whispered to Luca, gesturing towards the camera on the wall, and Luca quickly transformed back into his loud, obnoxious self. Then he leaned over towards me. "You know," he almost yelled. "If Gav won't take you out. I will! I'm older, wiser, and if you think the youngest is good, wait until you try the oldest."

I shook my head at him; both our smiles curled up so tight they were about to burst. "Five, four, three—"

The door swung open, a sleepy-faced Gavin storming in, black hair wild, eyes fuming. "Che cazzo è questo!" Gavin snapped, making Luca and I crack up laughing.

Gavin rolled his eyes, muttering under his breath. "It's too early for this shit!"

"Go back to bed, Fratellino!" Luca tightened his arms around Nora. "Sadie and I've got this."

Gavin studied me holding Vinny, then Luca holding Nora beside me. "Get out of my fucking chair!"

"Seriously!" I warned him. "Language."

"Sorry, Baby." He walked over, bending to press a kiss to my hair before turning towards Luca, arms out for Nora, but Luca ignored him, bravely tempting Gavin. "Adesso!" Gavin snapped.

Luca pushed himself up and handed Nora over. "Sei un uomo fortunato, Fratellino."

"Lo so." Gavin smiled as Luca walked out the door.

"What'd he say?"

He took Luca's seat, then took my hand. "That I'm a lucky man, but I already knew that."

"They leave in a few hours."

"Yeah," he mumbled, gaze drifting away. He'd been so nervous for them to come, now he didn't want them to leave.

"But they'll be back for Christmas!" I tried to cheer him up, only he just shrugged. Oh, man. I had to do it. I couldn't stand when he was disappointed. "You could invite them down for Halloween, if you wanted to. That's only two months away." Why, Sadie, why!

His eyes lit up with his smile. "Really?"

"Why not," I laughed. "They're your family. You can have them visit however much you want." I had grown fond of them too. "We can have another date night."

"I didn't hear you complaining last night in our room," he teased, cocking his eyebrow up with his sexy grin. "Well, I guess you *were* whining."

"Stop!" I smacked his arm, still laughing.

Suddenly Vinny started crying, whimpering to be fed, so I automatically slid my strap down, freeing my breast for him, but it was Gavin who jumped up, hungry eyes on me before racing to the nursery door. "Will you guys watch the twins for a bit?" he yelled out, stare flickering between us and the stairs.

"Of course!" I heard Giorgia call back.

"Um, Gavin!" What was happening? "He just started eating!"

"And Papà will finish!" He stepped out with Nora, handing her over to Giorgia before returning to the nursery.

Then another set of footsteps pounded down the hall, Luca swinging in, stilling in the doorway, eyes on my exposed chest. "This a buffet? I'm next in line."

"Jesus Christ!" Gavin belted out. "Get the fuck out of here!"

"They told me to grab Vinny!" Luca started towards me, smiling way too big. "Sei un uomo fortunato, Fratellino," he repeated the same phrase he had earlier, and Gavin knocked into him, grabbing his shirt and shoving him back out the door.

"Here." I pulled Vinny from my chest and handed him over to Gavin, who was now grumbling and rolling his eyes on repeat. "There's a bottle in the fridge."

"Put your shirt back on," he instructed before squeezing out the door.

He was back in a flash and I was being dragged down the hall to our room. "Ready for round two, Baby?"

HALLOWEEN: 1

"Knock, knock," I announced myself as I turned the knob of the office door, stepping in and catching Gavin face down in his palms. "You okay?"

He slid his hands away, fingers now rubbing his temples ferociously. "Where are the babies?"

"Sleeping."

He slapped his fist to the desktop as he flung himself back in his chair. "This fucker is killing me," he bellowed, sinking his eyes shut. "God, I fucking hate dealing with this shit."

"Isn't he one of Luca's clients? Why do you have to deal with him?"

He sighed, tossing his hands up as he shrugged. "It's too much stress for him, especially after the heart attack."

"So now, you're stressed and taking it out on us." Luca was still going out and partying; he could easily keep this client and deal with it himself. "I'm going to talk to him when they get here!" He and Stefano would be arriving tomorrow, and I had no problem discussing this client.

"No, Baby. I'll handle it," he insisted with a stern tone, warning me. "Don't get involved."

Don't get involved! It was my husband who had been a jerk all week because of this client. I had the right to get involved.

"I just want to have fun this weekend," he continued. "Go out with them tomorrow night. Then take the babies trick or treating," he smacked his screen down. "I'm sorry for being a dick all week."

Maybe this time with his brothers would be a good thing, distract him. "I hate seeing you like this, especially when Luca is perfectly able to handle this client."

His finger suddenly shot up to silence me while he snapped up his vibrating phone, pushing it to his ear. Back to work. I reversed out of the room, closing the door behind me, hearing Gavin's raised voice echoing down the hall. Then his doors boomed back open, angry feet stomping down the hall, growing louder as they made their way towards me in the kitchen. "Fuck!" he barked, marching right to the fridge, tearing the doors open, only to slam them back shut. "They want impossible fucking returns!"

I hated seeing him like this. He was a perfectionist, and this was Luca's client, which meant he put double the stress on himself. "Can't you just drop him? You have plenty of clients."

"No, Sadie!"

Sadie. Oh, he was pissed.

"He," he snapped. "They're not a client we can drop."

I stepped over, raising my hands to his chest, feeling the heavy rise and fall from his angry breathing. "Is there anything I can do? I hate seeing you so stressed out."

"No," he answered without hesitation. "Just put up with me, Baby." He shook me off, then he took off, stomping back to his office.

I caught the time on the oven clock. Babies would be up in thirty minutes, which meant I had time to either clean up for our guests or help my husband relax. Relax it was. I padded up the stairs, hurrying to my dresser, searching for my sheer red lingerie. I'd never done anything like this, but I knew it would help to de-stress him or at least relax him for a minute. I squeezed into the lingerie, tugged my ponytail out, shook my hair loose, and padded back down the stairs, stopping in front of the closed glass doors.

His eyes were on his computer screen, slowly drifting up, finding me, studying me, then lowering his screen and standing from his chair.

I opened the door, meeting him halfway. "Are you sure there's nothing I can do for you?" I asked as seductively as possible.

He grunted, hands flying to the lace over my nipples, while mine ran down his stomach, unhooking his belt, en route to his zipper, taking that with me as I dropped to my knees.

But his hands swooped down, taking hold of my hair and yanking it, forcing my eyes up to his. His lips parted, closed, looking as if he wanted to say something, but wasn't. "What?" I asked, mouth inches from his firming arousal.

"Nothing," he lied.

"Gavin!"

"Fuck, Baby, can you bend over the desk instead? Let me fuck you. Really fuck you."

I gripped his hips, using them as an anchor to pull myself back up. Then I stepped against his desk, palms flat on the wood, ass arched, already feeling him press in behind me.

"This is sexy, Baby." His fingers danced down the lace. "Haven't seen this in a while, since you asked me to fuck you in Roma."

"Now, I'm asking you to fuck me at home-a." I laughed, hearing his slight chuckle behind me, the deep vibration inciting a chill, followed by a wave of heat.

His hand continued over the lace, dragging down my ass, sweeping over my wet center. "Fuck!" It was a grunt, a bang, a hit, his tip jabbing.

He struck hard, shoving deep, hands now digging into my hips. *Oh, god.* My nerves screamed, I screamed, yelping from the blow, the impact.

"Gavin," I begged, willing him to go harder.

And so he did. His hands bunched the lace, yanking me back, his hips pounding, thrusts to furious rams, unleashing his stress, taking me to my breaking point.

"God," I screamed, clawing into the wood, adding to the nail marks littered around my hands. "There, fuck, there!" I clenched my thighs, the burn eating away at me, his dick battering the fire, sending the surge erupting. I was there, oh, god. I rocked back as he fucked me harder, my body under his control, his hands fisting the lace like reins. "Gavin!" An ice wave prickled my skin, a heatwave took me down, my lips parted, panting, eyelids fluttering, legs trembling, the flood of relief sending my shaky arms collapsing

"Fuuuck!" His hands smacked my ass, fingers dug into my skin, holding me steady while he bucked hard, fucking fast to finish us both off. Then he collapsed over my back, heaving against me while his arms slid down my sides to my stomach, holding me. "Fuck," he muttered, breath like waves rolling across my neck.

He lifted, taking me with him, turning me to face him and hugging me, holding me again while burrowing his face into my hair.

"Do you feel better?" I asked, steadying myself on my wobbly legs.

He let out a weak laugh. "Yes, Baby, very."

"Why don't you call it a day," I suggested. "We can go to the beach with the babies. You need a break, Gavin. You don't want to be an ass when your brothers get here."

His hands clasped my waist, lifting me off the ground and setting me onto the top of the desk. "So—" he leaned in, kissing the lace over my chest. "Are you gonna come by my office like this every time I'm pissed? Because—" he smashed another kiss over my nipple, whipping his tongue over the bud. "If that's the case, then I'll take on all of Luca's clients."

"No." I kissed the top of his hair while sending my hands to his face, stroking his cheeks while he nibbled on me. "I just don't want my husband in a bad mood on Halloween, especially when I show him his costume."

His face tipped up, brows furrowed. "My what?"

I knew it'd be a fight, but it was our first Halloween, and I wanted it to be special. "The twins are Pebbles and Bamm-Bamm, and we are Fred and Wilma," I told him, meeting his blank expression. "You know, from the old cartoon The Flintstones."

He immediately shook his head. "I'm not wearing a fucking costume, Baby!"

I had expected this. "It's the twins' first Halloween!" I pleaded, pouty lip and all. "Mamma will be very happy."

"Cartoon? Flintstones?" he repeated, agitation evident. "What kind of shit is that anyway?" he huffed, his smile from the sex gone. He needed a break, a real break.

"Let's all go out tomorrow night! I'll get Grant to come over when the babies go to sleep, and we can head to a bar with your brothers. Luca can be the driver." I laughed at the thought of a sober Luca.

"Grant?" he mumbled more to himself. "To watch the babies?"

I captured his hands. "They'll be fast asleep."

"He's too—"

"Young," I finished his thought. "You need to get out; we both need to get out!" And if push came to shove, then I'd stay back with the babies, so at least he could get out.

"I don't know."

I released his hands, dusting my fingers up his arms instead, all the way up to his slightly parted lips. "You haven't had drunk Sadie in a while, and she hasn't had drunk Gavin in a while." I slipped off the desk, falling to my knees, face up towards his. "Is there anything I can do to convince you?"

HALLOWEEN: 2

The floor rumbled, followed by the roar of an engine pulling into the driveway. The guys were here. I opened the baby gate, watching Vinny and Nora's eyes light up at the thought of freedom. They crawled out and down the hall, making it halfway before the door swung open, and three strapping Italians barged in.

"Piccolo, Piccolina!" Luca boomed, dropping to meet them, with Stefano right behind him, both of them with their arms out for the babies, who were high tailing it forward, climbing straight into their laps.

"Welcome back," I greeted as Gavin closed the door, his entire face smiling.

"Okay," he called down to the babies. "Time for Papà!" He crouched to the floor, arms open for the twins now crawling to him.

"How old are they now?" Stefano stood, arms open for me.

"Almost nine months." I met his embrace, hugging him back. "They might be walking when you come out for Christmas."

"That's crazy," he sighed. "They're growing so fast."

"We don't get to see them enough!" Luca stood next, adjusting his suit jacket.

"You were just here like two months ago, and you'll be here again in two months, and then a month after that for their first birthday!" We'd seen them plenty.

Luca pushed Stefano away, wrapping his arms over me, giving me a... tighter hug. "How are you, Sadie?"

I was fine; it was my husband who was not. I looked down at Gavin with the twins, debating if I bring up the new client, but didn't want Gavin to get upset. "I'm good, you?"

He dropped his arms, continuing towards the kitchen without answering me.

"And how are you?" I walked back to Stefano, meeting his eyes. I wanted to really know how he was, especially after his last trip out.

"Fine," he mouthed back, eyes flashing down to Gavin. "Maybe we talk later."

I nodded just as Luca stalked back into the hall, bottle of water in hand. "You need to move back to New York, so we can see the babies more. This isn't working for me."

Move! I looked behind him to the ocean just minutes away, then around him at my dream home, and then to him, a Romano that conveniently lived thousands of miles away. "Nope."

"No," Gavin answered at the same time, tickling Nora and Vinny, who were climbing over his face.

"But you," I continued, eyes still on a laughing Gavin and the babies playing over him. "Are welcome to move—" I bit my tongue, the words *'to California'* almost slipping out. No, no, no.

"Don't worry, Patatina." Stefano patted my shoulder. "New York's home. We're not leaving."

I felt a pair of tiny arms wrapping around my leg, making me automatically bend down, scooping Nora up while Gavin lifted Vinny. "We were thinking about going out later," I told them.

"All of us?" Stefano asked, gaze on the babies.

"No!" *Just adults.* "To a bar, after they go to bed."

Luca stepped over, hands out for Nora, who sprung to him. "Who will stay here? With them?"

"Grant. You know, my son."

Luca's eyes flicked to Gavin, then to Nora once more. "I don't really know him; have him stop by before we leave so we can talk. What's his social? I'll have my people run a background check."

"What?" I started laughing, but he was stone-faced. "I am his background, and his mother, and their mother."

"Va bene," Gavin sighed before looking back at me. "It's fine. I already talked to him."

Noo. But he was stone-faced too, he had. Of course, he had. He, they, were acting as if we were leaving for days, not a few hours, in which the babies would be sleeping the entire time. I looked from Luca holding Nora to Gavin holding Vinny, to Stefano standing between them. Poor babies. I had to deal with an overprotective Gavin; they'd have to deal with an overprotective Papà, Zio Luca, and Zio Stefano. "Go play," I instructed them all, shooing the babies and their keepers to the family room.

The sun had set hours ago, and Grant would be here any minute. Then we'd be on our way out, my first night out since our anniversary, and even then, we'd spent most of the night in the hotel bed.

I strummed through the closet, grabbing up my tightest jeans and catching that black bodysuit, the one I hadn't worn since girls' night almost two years ago. Perfect! I ran to my vanity next, blow drying my hair and slapping on some makeup before stepping into my knee-high boots. I'd gone from Mamma to Sadie in ten minutes flat. I loved being a mamma and being home, but getting dressed up for a night out was good for the soul.

I took the stairs two at a time, excited to start this night, which I would be starting right now! I went straight to the kitchen, swiping the opened bottle of wine off the counter and chugging it straight. Mamma was off duty, let the pre-party begin.

"Slow down, Patatina!" Stefano shouted over.

Shit, I didn't realize I had an audience. I set the bottle down, feeling the heat in my cheeks as I faced the guys, all of whom were staring at me, including mine whose eyes were already storming. "It's been a long week." *Month, year.* I shrugged, fingers sneaking back to the bottle, snatching it up and pushing it to my lips.

Gavin then hoisted the babies up from the floor, so I walked over to meet him and my babies. "Goodnight, my loves," I sang, rubbing my nose to each of theirs. "Mamma loves you." I rubbed my nose against Gavin's, too, before he took off down the hall and up the stairs to put them to bed. Then a knock hit the door. "Grant!" I hurried down, swinging the door open. "Hi, Sweetie!"

"Hey, Mom!" He hugged me. "Who's the muscle?"

"What?" I spun around to Stefano and Luca standing in the hall behind us, arms crossed over their chests, glaring.

"You guys remember, Grant." I gestured between them. "Isn't it nice that he's going to watch the babies? My *son* doing us this favor."

Luca started fidgeting with his sleeves, adjusting his cuff links while he glared at Grant. It didn't matter that Grant was my son or the twins' half-brother; he wasn't a Romano, and those babies were the heart of the Romano clan. "You know how to take care of babies?" Luca asked.

"Do you?" Grant asked right back, rolling his eyes.

Gavin was right back down the stairs, marching over. "Call us if they wake up, and don't try to carry them, or feed them, or anything," he rambled to Grant. "Just call."

"I appreciate this." I leaned over, giving Grant another hug, whispering against his ear. "I owe you."

"Have fun, Mom."

"Come on, let's go." I started for the door, hearing them trailing.

"Is Vinny eating pizza yet?" Grant called from behind us. "He's got what six teeth now? And if they do wake up, can they walk down the stairs by themselves? Or should I roll them down? Or send them down the banister?"

Gavin whipped back, Stefano and Luca following, all seething and scoffing under their breath.

"I'm joking!" Grant laughed. "Jeez, *Dad,* relax."

Gavin suppressed a laugh. "I swear to god, Grant." He cracked a smile. "Your jokes are just as bad as hers."

"Hey!" Mine were funny!

"Thanks, Grant," Gavin conceded, ushering us all out.

HALLOWEEN: 3

Gavin zoomed into a spot along the street downtown, elbowing his door open, all of his following his lead. I stumbled down, surprised by the wine buzz, a happy surprise.

Arms captured my waist, a spicy scent bombarding my senses as my husband lowered his face to the crook of my neck. "You look fucking good tonight, Baby. We should hang back in the car for a minute."

"Only a minute?" In fact, his car was the one place we hadn't christened yet. "Ask me again after a few drinks." I tipped my face back, looking to his, but his eyes were staring deep into my cleavage.

"This shirt's fucking sexy," he growled into my neck.

"It's not a shirt," I whispered. "Hopefully, this time, you'll be able to figure out how to take it off."

He was quiet, hands running over the fabric. "Holy fuck, that lingerie thing." His feet slammed to a stop, holding me back while his brothers continued across the street. "We'll meet you guys inside," he yelled over his shoulders, already groping me.

"Gavin!" I swatted his hands away. "He's joking!"

"No, I'm not," he rasped, hands jumping right back.

"Gavin!" I yanked him forward, dragging him across the street to meet his brothers and the crowded bar.

Luca plowed through the door with Stefano at his side while Gavin stepped behind me, locking me to his chest, hands sneaking up my top once again.

"Gavin!" I warned, but he simply tried to yank my top up, attempting to cover the cleavage. "That won't work. It's stuck that low."

He rolled his eyes, releasing me so we could follow his brothers through the wall-to-wall swarms of people, most of whom were screaming, pushing, and shoving. I hadn't been to a bar like this in a very long time. My fingers automatically tightened with Gavin's, keeping him close as we made our way through, finally landing at the bar counter and squeezing in.

"Three shots of vodka, whatever label you've got," Gavin ordered, releasing my hand to reach into his pocket. "Fuck, my wallet's in the car."

"I'll pay," I teased him. "I'm used to it."

"Jesus Christ," he grumbled playfully as the bartender dropped the shots. "Here." Gavin slid a glass to Stefano beside him, then raised a glass to Luca on Stefano's opposite side. He denied it, so Gavin handed it to me. I was going to stick to cocktails tonight, but why not. We each raised our shots, cheering before downing them.

"Baby, stay with Luca," Gavin insisted, gesturing for Stefano to follow. "I'll be right back. I'm paying this time." He and Stefano took off through the crowded bar.

I spun back to face the bar. "Another!"

The bartender slid the next shot over, and I looked to Luca, offering it to him, but his stare darted to my side, eyes wide, eyes narrowed—then he lunged, flying at me, pouncing, hand grasping my arm too tight, shoving me aside, throwing me back.

Fuck. I went stumbling, almost falling, arm throbbing, catching the flash of Luca—attacking some guy. Oh my god! Glass smashed, shattering across the counter, the floor. Luca's fist was up, pummeling the guy's face, then his hands locked around the guy's neck, choking him, screaming in his face. What the fuck was happening?

"Luca!" I scrambled forward, grabbing his arm, trying to pull him back, watching the poor guy he was attacking, wailing his arms for help, succumbing to the power of Luca's chokehold.

Luca elbowed me off, still screaming. "Ho intenzione di cazzo di ucciderti!" He wasn't stopping, voice like venom, eyes a solid black, no emotion. He was going to kill him.

His arm suddenly swung back, snatching my shot from the bar while his other hand pried the guy's mouth open, forcing him to drink it, then slamming his hands over the guy's lips, locking his mouth shut. "Figlio di puttana!" He dropped the shot glass to the floor, adding to the mounds of shattered glass.

"Luca!" I clawed at his shirt, trying to pull him back.

He looked over, eyes meeting mine.

"What the hell are you doing? Stop Luca!"

He held my stare for another second, then leaned down to the guy's face, whispering something while grabbing the guy's shoulders, shoving him down to the floor, his foot kicking the guy's face into the broken glass.

Oh, my, god.

My cheeks were soaked, heart racing, afraid of the man in front of me, and afraid for the man under him. I was trembling, choking on my own breaths. "Luca, please!"

Black stone eyes rolled from the guy on the floor to me, then he stepped away, hand hitting my back, shoving me forward.

"No!" I yelled, shaking, skin prickling from his touch. "What the hell just happened?"

"Go!" he demanded, voice a bitter bark and his hand that much rougher, pushing me away.

"Luca!"

He bent down, swinging an arm under my ass, hoisting me up against him, carrying me out against my will.

"Put me down!" I screamed, eyes blurring from the tears. I batted his shoulder, kicking my legs against him, which only made him grip me tighter. "Luca!"

He slowed, the chaos of the overcrowded bar thinning out, but I was still batting, thrashing for him to put me down.

"Put me down, Luca!" I didn't want him touching me! I didn't know where he was taking me or what had come over him."What the fuck's going on!" I pushed back, my palms against his chest, trying to get away.

He rolled his rage-filled eyes to mine, still holding me against him, not giving way. "He spiked your fucking drink, Sadie!" he spat back. "He must have seen Gav and Stefano leave and thought you were alone!"

What? "No!" Luca was as paranoid as Gavin. That type of thing only happened in movies.

"I saw it with my own fucking eyes, and I'm sober. I know the shit I saw! I've been around the fucking block! I know a fucking dirtbag when I see'em."

That's why he forced the shot down the guy's throat. "Put me down! Please."

He lowered me just as Gavin and Stefano came into view, their eyes growing wider with each step. Shit. I looked around, seeing the women's restroom behind us.

"Don't say anything to Gavin!" I begged, wiping the tears from my cheeks. "Tell him we're going home and that I'm sick! Just don't tell him what you think you saw!" I raced off into the bathroom, squeezing past the door, falling against the counter, meeting my reflection. Shit. I took a deep breath, steadying my shaky legs. What had just happened?

I splashed some water over my face, dabbing it dry why taking long, deep breaths. I didn't want to go back out, but I didn't want Gavin to sense anything, and he was probably pissed that Luca was holding me. We needed to leave, go home, get the hell out of here. I braced the counter one last time, forcing myself calm before pushing off of it and spinning towards the door.

I stepped out, running into Stefano, who was hovering at the door, alone. I looked past him, no Gavin or Luca in sight. "Where's Gavin!" I asked; he didn't reply, so I stepped forward.

He met my step, keeping me back. "Where's Gavin!" I strained my neck to see around him. "Where are they, Stefano!"

He closed in, his hand cuffing my arm, keeping me in place. He really wasn't holding me back, was he? "Let's go outside, Sadie."

Sadie. No Patatina. I dug for my phone, but his hand swooped down, plucking it from my fingers, shoving it into his pocket. "Stefano!"

"Outside!" he snapped, dragging me towards the door.

"Stop!" I yanked my arm free, stepping away from him. "What did Luca say? Did he say something to Gavin?" I prayed they were tucked in a corner or outside, Gavin telling Luca not to touch me, but I knew otherwise.

"They're handling it." His eyes were as black as Luca's, his tone was just as cold. "Outside, now!" He seized my arm.

I yanked it right back. "Handling it?" Luca almost killed him! And Gavin, I spun towards the bar, but once again, an arm was around me, locking over my waist, lifting my feet from the ground, carrying me out the doors.

"Stefano!"

He didn't stop until we were outside, then he lowered me down to the ground. "I was told to keep you away; let me do my fucking job!" he yelled, angry at me.

"How could you have let him go back?" My husband was in there! And I had no idea what was happening!

"How could I?" he roared out an evil, dark laugh. "I'm pissed I can't fucking be back there myself."

The doors suddenly flew open behind us, Luca and Gavin rushing out, and I didn't have to ask to know what went down; their disheveled hair and red scraped fists spoke volumes.

"We gotta get the fuck out of here!" Luca raged.

"Why Gavin? You promised me no more fighting!"

"It wasn't a fight!" Luca huffed. "It was a beatd— "

"Enough!" I yelled, focusing back on Gavin. "You can't do this anymore! You're a father! What if he fought back? What if he had a weapon? What if you got hurt? What if you got arrested? We have babies at home!"

Gavin's eyes narrowed, dark, lips twisting, maniacal, lost in his rage, letting out a condescending laugh aimed at me. "You want to play the fucking what-if game, Sadie? I handled it, so there won't be any more fucking what-ifs for you or any other fucking chick in there tonight."

"But we could have called the cops and walked away!" I searched his face, all emotion was gone.

"We did call the cops," Luca belted out. "Taught him a quick lesson first."

They didn't care. This wasn't a big deal to them. "Why can't you ever walk away? You promised me no more fighting. Luca already handled it!"

"No!" Gavin spat, no remorse whatsoever. "I *promised* to keep you safe, and you were out here with Stefano."

"This has to stop! You need to act older than twenty-four! You're a father now! Violence isn't the answer! You need to grow up!"

"There's a right and a wrong kind of violence," Luca shot back. "He deserved what he fucking got. Hell, I'm tempted to go back in, but the cops are on their way."

"Grow up," Gavin repeated, chuckling, hands on his stomach as his fuming eyes stared blankly into mine. "So I can be so fucking righteous like you, because you're so fucking old and wise."

Old. *Fucking* old. The words hit like a slap, making me stumble back. Why was this an attack against me? A taxi pulled up behind us; I ran, ripping the door open and crashing into the seat. "Go!" I screeched, hearing the yells outside as I slammed the door, and the taxi sped away.

HALLOWEEN: 4

Old, no, I was *fucking* old. Gavin knew it was my weak spot- he knew it would burn. He'd been an ass all week, and tonight was just the grand finale. He was yelling at me like I was at fault. I didn't do anything! I was held back, detained while my husband, papà to my children pulverized some guy. Luca should have known Gavin would want blood. No, he did know. The Romano boys were loose cannons that the slightest spark set off. Their pride, passion, and protectiveness created the perfect storm of emotions, and Hurricane Romano was a bitch.

"Where to?" the driver asked, waking me to reality as the car drove through downtown.

"I don't know." I rolled my face to the window. I had nowhere to go but home. "Twenty-eight Playa Pointe."

Gavin was lost in his rage, so pissed that he wasn't even calling me. My phone was silent... my phone... I smacked my purse. "Shit." Stefano had it. Gavin was going to be livid, beyond livid. I took off without a phone, again. But this was his fault. He didn't know how to walk away, and he wasn't a talker. The only remedy when his emotions flared was sex or a fight. Always physical.

He had to stop this. He couldn't be a knight in shining armor nor a personal vigilante. I couldn't be the reason for his violence. I wouldn't be able to live with myself if he got hurt because of me or arrested because of me. He had to learn to walk away. We had two babies at home that had to come first, two angels sleeping in their cribs while their papà beat the shit out of some guy. It was wrong, no matter how right it might have felt.

The driver pulled up to the guard gate, so I waved to the guard, who, in turn, opened the gates. I didn't want to go home. I knew Gavin would be raging, and I wasn't ready to deal with his wrath.

The car turned onto my street; Gavin's car wasn't there, but Grant's was! "Shit." I forgot he was here. I needed him gone before Gavin showed up and unleashed his tirade. "This is fine!" I handed the driver some cash, reluctantly stepped out, and marched to the front door. *Breathe.* I wiped the stray tears from my cheek as I opened the door, following the light to the family room, hearing the little giggles. Oh no.

"Hey!" Grant greeted, holding onto the babies that should have been asleep, but instead were climbing over him, pulling at his hair. "You're back early!"

"Why are the babies up?" They couldn't see Gavin like this, all the brothers like this.

He shrugged. "They were crying, and when I went in, they wanted to play. Where are the guys?"

Good question. Probably en-route here to find me. "Bar hopping. Why don't you get going."

"I'm having fun. I can hang with you."

As much as I wanted to believe that Gavin would come home all smiles and apologies—I knew better. I knew his temper; I knew what was about to happen. "No! I'm tired. I'm going to put the babies back to bed." I fake yawned. "We have a big day tomorrow. You're still coming over?"

"Yeah, Danica and I will be here. She's insisting on dressing up, got us K-pop costumes."

"K-pop? Is that like cereal?"

"Oh my god," he gasped. "You're so old!"

Old. Jeez, twice in one night. "Leave!" I could feel the hysteria and tears rising. "Sorry, I'm just overtired."

"Okay," he lamented, lifting the babies off him as he stood up. "I'll see you tomorrow. Love you guys."

"Love you too, and thanks again." I watched him walk to the door, and the second it closed, I crumpled to the floor, wiping the new tears away. How had everything gotten so out of control? Nora and Vinny charged over, both climbing onto my lap, snuggling into me.

I felt the rumble, heard the roar, brakes screeching to a halt in the driveway. Shit. The front door boomed open, banging against the wall, then slammed shut, shaking the whole house.

"SADIE!" Gavin's angry scream echoed down the hall. "SADIE! I swear to fucking god, you better be here! What the fuck is wrong with you!" His venomous scream grew louder, his footsteps heavier, sending my hands over the babies' ears. "SADIE!" He stepped into the room, mouth open to scream, but his glare fell to the babies in my lap, whose ears I was covering. "Fuck!" he screamed, turning right back around and stomping away.

I listened to his footsteps pounding up the stairs, our bedroom door slamming, followed by pounding footsteps above me. Then the front door swung open again with more pounding footsteps charging down the hall. Luca stalked in; eyes zeroed in on mine. "Jesus Christ, Sadie! What were you fucking thinking!"

I had no words, only tears.

Stefano stepped up behind him, flashing me my phone before dropping it onto the counter, glaring at me like it was my fault.

"You're the one who took it from me!"

He didn't reply, didn't even bother looking at me, just marched over, arms open for the twins. "Come to Zio Stefano," he whispered, demanding them, so I released my hold, letting him take the babies.

I stood back up, trying to compose myself as I walked away, but Luca's hand captured my arm, stopping me. "Stop!" I shouted at him, the force unleashing another stream of tears. "This isn't my fault! Why am I being attacked! That's why Gavin can't do this, right there!" I swung my arm back, pointing to the giggly faces climbing over Stefano. "He's not the same Gavin you used to party with. He can't be."

Luca dropped his hold of my arm. "You don't fucking care what the bastard was trying to do to you? Or the fucking pocket of shit he still had if it didn't work out with you? There are fucked up people out there, Sadie!"

No shit. I'd dealt with my fair share. I stormed past him, charging down the hall and up the stairs, my pace slowing with each step closer to the bedroom door, my resolve turning into hesitancy as I twisted the knob.

The shower was pattering, so I stepped in deeper, just enough to catch a glimpse of Gavin. He had his head down, arms stretched, palms flat against the stall, bracing himself while the water poured over his black hair. I reversed to the bed, taking a seat on the edge, waiting until the pattering stopped and the glass door clanked.

He stepped out, head immediately tilting back, his face on the ceiling, letting out a loud aggravated exhale before he reached for a towel, wrapping it loosely around his hips before turning and spotting me. "Go," he snapped, tone more than bitter.

"Excuse me?" He had never told me to leave before.

"Leave me alone, Sadie!" He tossed the towel to the counter on his way into his closet. "I need to calm down, and I don't wanna say any more shit I'm gonna regret. I need you to fucking leave."

I stood up, starting towards his closet just as he stepped back out in his pajama pants. "You want me to leave?" I repeated, trying to meet his gaze, but he refused to look at me.

He flung his hand to his face, rubbing over his eye for a minute before actually looking at me. "You're not gonna get a fucking apology if that's what you're here for. I'm the one who gets the apology this time! I wanna be alone, go." His arm shot out, pointing to the door while those emotionless eyes glared at me. Fine. If he wanted me to leave, then I would leave. I left, smacking the door shut behind me, hearing *'fuck'* echoing under it.

I wasn't even to the stairs before the door swung back open, Gavin's pounding steps charging out. "Get in here!" he demanded, but I stood my ground, not budging an inch. "Don't do this right now, Sadie!"

Then I heard a faint baby giggle echoing off the stairs, my feet automatically walking me towards the door so we wouldn't make a scene.

He took off past me, pacing across the floor. "What the fuck do you think you were doing earlier? You don't just fucking take off like that." He was livid, arms flailing in the air as he lectured me, still no remorse whatsoever. I'd had enough.

"What the *fuck* did you think you were doing fighting someone while your brother held your wife back!" I screamed back. "While your babies were at home waiting for their papà! I was scared! I watched Luca attack that guy! I saw the blood, heard the screams, had Luca pick me up and carry me out without a word! I had no idea what was happening! Then I lost you!"

He opened his mouth, but I beat him to it. I was fired up and not about to be intimidated, no matter how many F-bombs he threw at me. "You didn't ask if I was okay, you didn't wait for me, you just disappeared with Luca! Did it occur to you that I was scared! Really scared! I needed you! You should have thought about me."

He stilled, eyes going wide. "Are you fucking kidding me!" he yelled, shaking his head wildly back and forth. "You were all I was fucking thinking about."

"You always act on impulse, Gavin."

"He got what he deserved."

"Of course he did. Luca had already handled it. It didn't need to be at your hands!"

"Yes, it did!" he spat back. "I needed to handle it!"

Neither of us was willing to concede. We'd passed the point of reason and were running on emotional fumes. "Shut the door on your way out," he barked, throwing his arm up, dismissing me once more.

"Fine!" I started towards the door. "Gavin." I turned back around to face him. "Never scream at me in my own home! I don't care if you're scared, mad, worried, frantic, or irate with me." I tried to force the new tears away. "You can't scream like you did earlier, especially not in front of *my* children!"

His stare fell to the floor, face finally softening. "I didn't realize they were awake."

I reached for the door. "It shouldn't have mattered. I don't want our kids hearing you scream at me. That's not okay."

"I wasn't screaming at you," he mumbled, rolling his gaze back up.

But he did. I lunged to the bed, grabbing my pillow before stalking out towards the stairs, then veering to the nursery. I didn't want to be alone tonight, or away from my babies. I dropped the pillow onto the chair, setting up my makeshift bed.

I finally made it back downstairs, finding Luca holding a sleeping Nora while Stefano held a sleeping Vinny. "Will you carry them upstairs for me?" Almost in unison, they rose from the couch, silently trailing me up the stairs to the nursery, lying the babies down in their cribs. "Thank you." Luca stopped at the door, holding it for me.

"No. Just close it."

He didn't say a word, closing the door like I asked, while I slumped into the chair. And almost immediately heard our bedroom door whip open, Gavin's footsteps pounding down the stairs, Italian yelling back and forth between the brothers. Then a few minutes later, the loud boom of metal hitting the floor repeatedly, echoing up the stairs every time he dropped his weights to the floor. He was angry. I was angry. And there was nothing more to do. So I closed my wet eyes, forcing myself to fall asleep.

"Sadie."

I gasped, springing up, blinking my mascara glued lashes apart.

"It's just me," Luca whispered from the rocking chair beside me. I was in the nursery. That's right. I looked towards the window, meeting the sunlight streaming through the cracks of the shutters. It was morning. Gavin and I had slept apart by choice for the first time, ever.

"What are you doing in here?" I yawned, looking between the cribs and my two sleeping babies. "I can't listen to more yelling."

"Gav's been downstairs lifting weights like a fucking madman all morning, and I had a hunch you never left this room last night." His face was calm, no more anger in his eyes.

"We needed space." I shrugged, nestling back into the chair.

"So you're pissed he was protecting you?"

"No. I'm pissed he wasn't protecting himself."

"Just so you know, I tried to tell Gav to stay back. I was more than willing to fucking handle it myself."

"But, you *had* already handled it, Luca."

"I wasn't done. I just had to get you away first before I really handled it. No one's gonna fuck with you, Sadie, and get away with it."

"Why does everyone feel the need to protect me? I'm pretty damn tough, and I've been through a lot of shit. Do I look incapable?"

"Not incapable," he sighed, his eyes holding my gaze. "You—you underestimate how much you mean to me, to Gav. You saved my life. I'll be damned if I'm gonna let anyone fuck with yours. I don't care how fucking capable you are—no one fucks with la mia famiglia. Whether you like it or not, you are under our protection, and we are fucking ruthless."

"So I saw." I rolled my eyes away from Luca, staring instead at the closet. "I've been on the receiving end of that kind of violence." The words were out before I could stop them.

"Gav would never touch you."

"I know." I never worried about that. It was more the flashbacks and the paralyzing fear that shot through me when he got aggressive. "It's still scary to see him in that state. And I never want him to be the victim. I don't want him to get hurt. You either."

"Go talk to him, Sadie."

"I'm not ready." I didn't know the right words. I had messed up too. We never fought like this. This was new territory. "I think I'm going to go for a run."

"You like to run away, don't you."

"Go for a run, not run away," I clarified, knowing he was referring to New York.

"Running is running. You run; we confront head-on."

I'd never thought about it like that. Running *was* my escape. If you ran, no one could catch you. "Can you and Stefano watch the babies? Otherwise, I'll take them with me."

"I got it. Go ahead." He nodded towards the door, so I pushed off the chair, sneaking out to my room, hearing the metal clanking downstairs in the garage, each drop rattling the house. He was still so angry. I walked to the shower, needing to rinse yesterday away.

I stepped in, closing my eyes, letting the hot water rush over me while instinctively twisting the handle as far as it could go, the scorching water lashing against my skin, clearing my head. The pain turned unbearable, my skin prickled with welts, the heat overwhelming, so I shut the water off, sinking to the shower floor.

Suddenly, the glass door flew open; I whipped my face up, meeting Gavin's eyes running over my welt-covered body. Great. "Can you hand me a towel?" I wrapped my hands over my legs, blocking his view while the red swelling faded.

He yanked a towel from the rack, holding it up for me, but I tugged it away, drying myself. "We need to talk!" he demanded, gaze still lingering on my patchy arms.

The steam cleared, bringing his face into focus. He had dark rings around his eyes, a stark contrast against his unusually pale face. "I'm going running." I passed him, making my way to my closet.

He stepped in behind me, not saying a word. So I didn't either. "Sadie," he finally said.

I finagled on my shorts and sports bra. "Luca has the babies. I'll be back in a little bit." I stepped past him again, continuing out the room, down the stairs, and out the door.

HALLOWEEN: 5

I wiped the sweat from my brow, slowing my jog to a walk as I shoved the neighborhood gate open. I'd been running for who knows how long, and could barely feel my feet. I stepped off the boardwalk and back onto my street, every emotion still churning the pit of my stomach. My heart ached for Gavin. I hated this rift. I married him knowing how he was programmed, and I couldn't expect him to change, at least not so fast. Every time he fought, it was because of me. I was his trigger. If I wanted it to stop, then I had to remove myself from these situations. We needed to go on a bar hiatus. I continued up our street, seeing his car parked along the curb and our garage door open, and I expected to see him working out; instead, he sat on his bench, eyes on the street before spotting me.

He shuffled to his feet, clutching a bouquet of roses, his tired eyes focused on me as I continued towards him. He bought me flowers. "I'm sorry, Sadie," he sighed, arm out, handing me the bouquet. I grabbed them, pushing the blooms to my nose, inhaling their strong scent as tears blurred my vision. This was a big gesture for him. His arms were suddenly around my back, making me weak in the knees, causing me to fall into him, inhaling him instead. "I'm sorry for taking it out on you," he whispered against my hair. "I was too wound up. I was angry, but not with you, Baby."

Baby... A wave of relief rolled through me, that single word melting away the pain.

"I'm not sorry for what I did, though," he continued. "And I'd do it again, but I'd make sure you were really okay first. I'd handle it differently. I know you want me to walk away and to ignore shit, but I'm not wired like that. I've told you before, you're my everything. You're my whole fucking fire, Baby, my whole world. I'd protect you with my fucking life."

I had so much I wanted to say, to explain, to argue, but this was who he was. He was a protector. I nestled into him closer, his arms tightening in response.

"Do you think I scared Piccolo and Piccolina?" he grumbled, lips pressed against my hair. "I can't shake the way they looked at me last night."

"No." It was the truth. "I think you just surprised them. They've never heard their papà raise his voice before."

"I'm so sorry, Baby. I was just so fucked up from earlier, and then you took off, and Stefano had your phone. All I could think about was that fucking guy, and then you were gone."

"I'm sorry, too." I tipped my face up, meeting his now wet eyes. "I still haven't broken my old habits either. I'm sorry for running away."

"I never want to spend another night alone, Baby. This was our first and last fight, period." He shook his hair out of his face, those deep, dark eyes on mine—longing, love, and remorse filling them. "I needed you, Baby." His face fell, lips brushing mine, asking for permission.

"I needed you, too, Gavin."

Our lips crashed, sweet and soft, needy and ravenous, melting together, our spark igniting. My tongue struck his, the emotion making me gasp, the touch welding us together, our flame spreading like wildfire.

His hands gripped my thighs, fingers sending a current across my skin, both of us gasping, panting. I was up, our mouths locked while he carried me away, closing the garage door. "Don't scare me like that again, Baby," he spoke against my lips.

"Same," I whispered, holding on tight as he backed to his workout bench.

The bouquet fell from my fingers, my hands landed on his cheeks, gliding along the stubble up to his wild locks. "Baby," his rasp echoed across my lips while his hands trailed to the seam of my sports bra, tugging it up over my head, breaking our kiss for a second before smashing his lips back into mine, and sending his hands to my bare breasts.

His arousal was hard under me, so I lifted, tearing my shorts down with one hand while sliding my other under his waistband, his flesh rising to meet my touch. The anticipation of him being inside me was almost as intense as him actually being inside me. I spread my legs, his tip jabbed my center, the two of us moaning as I sank over him.

It was a rush, an intensity I wasn't expecting. His lips crashed to mine again, our kiss following the rhythm of my hips. It was as if I hadn't been kissed in weeks, hadn't been touched in months, and hadn't been fucked in years.

The surge started, my legs trembling, hips rocking faster, thighs bouncing in spurts, making him hit the spot. It had only been one night apart, one fight, but it was too much for us. I felt it now—my frantic desperation, my mouth clinging to his, taking in as much of him as possible, riding him hard, chest smothering chest, hands grabbing recklessly.

"I love you!" I gasped, eyes closing, grinding to a finish.

"Baby, look, at, me," he demanded, so I opened my eyes to his dark ones, rising and falling while our kiss started back up again.

"Fuck!" I screamed unwittingly, nails clawing into his neck as the orgasm unleashed, taking me down limb by limb until I collapsed against him.

"Never again, Baby," he breathed into my hair. "I can't do another night without you in my arms."

I looked up, shaky arms bracing him. "Never again."

We rested there, locked in each other's embrace while our breathing calmed. I didn't want to let him go, but we had two babies inside. "Let's go see Nora and Vinny." I peeled my chest off him, meeting a pair of worried eyes.

"What if they're scared of me?" His voice wavered. "I haven't been able to face them."

"You haven't seen them at all today?"

He shook his head no, eyes dropping to the floor. "How could I?"

I plucked my sports bra off the ground, pulling it on, then reaching for the bouquet. "They need to see their papà!" I waited while he adjusted himself, then led him inside, following the noise to the backyard, where Stefano and Luca were rolling a ball to the babies. And the second we stepped out, the twins came bounding over.

Gavin dropped to the ground, arms out nervously for the babies, who, of course, crawled right onto his lap, smiling. He let out a sigh of relief, pressing a kiss to each of their heads. "I'm sorry," he whispered, giving each of them another kiss.

All was well. I turned to head inside to put the flowers away, only Gavin's hand locked around my leg, holding me back. "Stay, Baby," he insisted, gesturing me to sit beside them, so I did.

HALLOWEEN: 7

It was almost dark, which meant we were only minutes away from the babies' first time trick or treating. I brushed Nora's hair up into a high ponytail then snapped the bone clip over it. My heart melted from the sight of her little ponytail sticking straight up in the air with her little green tank and blue diaper cover. She looked just like Pebbles. Next, I clipped Vinny's hat to his hair, my heart melting all over again from him in his Bamm-Bamm costume. "Smile for Mamma!" I snapped some pics before adjusting my costume, a white dress. We looked cute. It reminded me of when Grant was little. We matched, until he got too cool to match his mommy. "It's time!" I scooped Nora in one arm while haphazardly lifting Vinny in my other. They were getting too big, too fast. Another month, and I wouldn't be able to carry them like this. I headed out and down the stairs, following the noisy banter towards the kitchen, seeing Luca standing in front of the bar, immediately noticing us.

"Flintstones!" he roared with a big smile. "Haven't seen that shit in a while. Damn you guys look fucking cute."

Stefano, Gavin, and Grant rounded the counter, smiles lighting up their faces when they saw us.

"I think we're ready for our first Halloween!" I wiggled the babies in my arms, and Gavin rushed over, bracing their backs to help me hold them.

"Fuck. I had no idea they were gonna be this cute—" his gaze flickered from them to me. "Mamma looks fucking cute, too."

"You all do look *cute,*" Grant mocked, laughing. "But Gavin's too cool."

I looked at my husband in his normal shirt and jeans. He had been adamant about not dressing up, and I didn't want to push it after everything earlier. "Yup. It's just the three of us tonight. Ready?"

I turned for the door, passing the bowl of candy on the floor. "Grant, Danica. Candy's at the front door. We won't be gone too long."

"Have fun!" they yelled back in unison before laughing at the other.

"Wait, Sadie!" Luca yelled, so I slowed, spinning back to face him and the phone in his hand. "Let me get some pics to send the girls."

I lifted the babies higher and Gavin reached for Vinny, taking his place at my side.

"No, Fratellino!" Luca bellowed, waving Gavin away. "Get out of the picture! Just the three of them."

"Yeah," Grant laughed. "You look like a photo bomber."

Gavin backed away while Luca snapped some photos.

"I'll take Piccolina," Luca insisted, shoving his phone back into his pocket before reaching his arms for Nora, who jumped right to him. "You're killing me, Nora. Way too fucking beautiful."

"I'll take Vinny," Stefano insisted, stepping towards me with his arms out for Vinny, taking him without another word.

Then we shuffled out the front door to the sidewalk with Luca and Stefano taking the lead holding the babies while I automatically waited for Gavin, but he was gone. "Wait!" I yelled to the guys. "We can't go without Papà."

Luca and Stefano turned right as the front door swung open. Oh, Gavin! My tall, gorgeous husband was dressed as Fred Flintstone. Gavin Romano was Fred Flintstone.

The roar of laughter from his brothers was immediate, loud enough for all of San Diego to hear, and Gavin met my eyes, shaking his pouty face. "Why? Of all the fucking costumes, you had to choose this."

I tried to stifle my laugh. "I wanted a family costume, and Nora and Vinny made perfect Pebbles and Bamm-Bamm. You didn't have to wear it. The three of us were fine."

He shook his head no. "I don't ever want to hear *the three of us*. It's always all or nothing, Baby, the four of us. No one's gonna push me out of a family photo again!"

"Fratellino!" Luca roared, still laughing hysterically. "Now that is fucking cute!"

Stefano stepped forward, swiping at his eyes with one hand, laughing so hard he was crying. "That's the shit that happens when you move to Cali!"

"Fuck off!" Gavin spat back as he stalked over to them, ripping Vinny from Stefano's arms before stepping to Luca and nabbing Nora.

"No," Luca kept chuckling. "That's the shit that happens when you're pussy whipped."

Seriously. "Language!" I stepped next to Gavin, draping my arm across his back, nestling into his flexed bicep.

"Now, take another picture!" Gavin demanded of Luca.

"Oh," Luca roared. "How could I not!"

"Fuck," Gavin grumbled. "But this only goes to Giorgia and Sofia! No stupid shit Luca."

"Non ti preoccupare, don't you worry, Fratellino," Luca lied. "I don't do stupid shit." He pulled out his phone, and Stefano did the same. "Smile."

Gavin grumbled under his breath, only half smiling. "I can't believe I'm fucking doing this."

"Welcome to fatherhood!" I smiled up at him before looking towards the camera. It was the first concession he'd really made, wearing a costume to appease his wife.

We started up the sidewalk towards the first house. "I can hold Vinny!" I offered.

"They cover my costume," Gavin laughed, pulling both babies tight against his chest as we headed up to the door.

We let the babies knock, waiting while the door swung open to an older couple smiling ear to ear at us.

"Say it, Fratellino!" Luca goaded, nudging Gavin with his elbow.

"Trick or treat," Gavin mumbled with the brightest red cheeks.

The older woman smiled, looking us all over. "What a beautiful little family."

I looked up at Gavin just as he looked down at me. We did have a beautiful family and apparently very sweet neighbors.

"And Fred Flintstone never looked so good!" She eyed Gavin as she continued, handing him a piece of candy.

Excuse me! Or maybe not such sweet neighbors.

"Thanks," he mumbled as I grabbed his arm, yanking him away.

"Damn, Gav!" Stefano started laughing again. "You've got a cougar next door."

"And one in his bedroom," I said under my breath.

"What, Baby?"

I shook my head, laughing. "Nothing, next house," I directed them, pointing up the street. "You guys go. I'll hang back here."

The guys walked the path to the next house, knocking and chuckling before turning back with more candy. It was so strange to think that just last night, Gavin and Luca were raging; now they were laughing, and Gavin was dressed as a cartoon character, holding our babies on their first Halloween.

I watched them walk back, Gavin's muscular chest stretching against the fabric as he walked, his strong arms looking even bigger against the cut of his costume, and those same strong arms wrapped tightly over the twins.

"Why are you smiling like that, Baby?" He was in my face, breaking my reverie.

"You look sexy," I replied honestly.

"Yeah, sure," he scoffed, rolling his eyes. "Real fucking sexy in this shit."

"Strong arms wrapped around our babies, a papà dressed to match his family. This is the Gavin I love the most."

He dipped his mouth to my ear. "Funny, I remember you saying how much you loved the Gavin that was fucking the shit out of you in the shower earlier."

"Gavin!" I smacked his back, trying to ignore the heat rising inside me and the immediate wetness between my thighs.

"We've only hit up two houses! You two already calling it a night?" Stefano yelled over.

"The kids don't even eat candy." I shrugged back while running my hand up Gavin's biceps, tracing his tattoos.

"One more house," Gavin sighed, although his sigh sounded more like a moan.

"I'll knock this time," I teased, pushing forward in front of the guys to knock on the door.

It swung open, with our neighbor I'd met once before, greeting me with a big smile. "Sadie, right?"

"Yes, good memory and um, Chris!"

He smiled back. "Wilma Flintstone! You look great!"

"Thanks, not everyone was happy with the choice," I laughed while swinging my head back, meeting the three brooding Italians glaring at the neighbor with the candy dish. "Anyway, trick or treat!"

"How about a treat," he laughed, causing Luca to step up to my side.

"How about I fuc— "

"Luca!" I snapped, grabbing his arm. "Thank you!" I said to Chris while shoving Luca back.

"You know, I think Delaney and the girls are probably hitting up your house right about now."

"I'll be sure to say hi to your *wife* if I see her! Have a nice night!" I waved before turning around, shooing the brothers down the walkway.

"How'd he know your name?" Gavin huffed, eyes still on the house behind us. He had apparently forgotten that he had met him before as well.

"I swear I can't take you guys anywhere! Nora, Mamma apologizes in advance for Papà and your zios."

"I think," Gavin started, but I jumped in front of him, shutting him up.

"Calm down, Papà. I need you to save your energy for later. We spent an entire night apart, which means we have lots to make up for tonight."

His smile was immediate, his eyebrow arching. "The garage, the shower, the closet weren't enough for you? How many times are we going to make up?"

"I'm saving the best for last."

HALLOWEEN: 7

"Babies are asleep." I walked into the bedroom, closing the door behind me. "Did Grant and Danica take off?"

"Yeah," he called from the bathroom.

I continued over, meeting his reflection in the vanity mirror, watching him laugh as he studied the costume he was still wearing. "Last night, you were screaming at me to leave, and tonight you're wearing a cartoon costume."

His eyes found mine. "I said I'm sorry, Baby."

"I'm not looking for another apology," I assured him. "You're just a complicated man, Mr. Romano."

He turned around, holding my gaze for a minute before dropping his hands to the bottom of his costume, ripping it up and over his head, leaving him in nothing but his black boxer briefs. Fuck, he was hot.

I was walking forward, feet on autopilot, my body not informing my brain of its intentions, arms flying to his chest, fingers running over his tight abs. He felt just as good as he looked. I pressed in closer, kissing his chest, but it wasn't enough, and, I owed him. I parted my lips, sucking instead.

He groaned, trying to back away, but my mouth wouldn't relent, not just yet. I sucked harder until I left a tiny purple bruise.

He puffed his chest out, so he could see what I was looking at. "A hickey?"

"That's right!"

"I don't want any hickeys, Baby."

"I owed you for the display you made on me back in New York," I reminded him. "Do you want me to forgive you or not?" He rolled his eyes, a slight chuckle escaping his lips as he watched me. "Now, let your wife suck on you."

His erection shot up, stabbing me through his briefs. "You can't say shit like that, Baby!"

"I can't?" I dropped my hand to his shorts, rubbing over the bulge, slowing my thumb when it reached his tip, tracing his edges as I dropped my lips back to his chest, marking him once more.

"Get on the bed!"

"No," I whispered against him. "I'm in control tonight." Tonight he was getting a lesson in patience, and for once, I was taking control. I stepped back, dancing my fingers down my dress, curving them under the jagged hem of the costume and cinching it in my fingers, tugging it inch by inch up my thighs, over my panties, up my stomach, watching his eyes as I pulled it over my chest, feeling my breasts bounce out before tossing the dress to the floor.

His hands shot up; I slapped them away, continuing to my panties, hooking my fingers under the silk, dragging them down my legs, still watching him as I bent over to step out of them.

"Fuck!" His hands shot out again, but I shook my head no, straightening up, watching him eye-fuck me, over and over again.

"Where's your belt?"

"No, Baby," he groaned, eyes still wild. "The belt is only to be used on you. I don't get tied up."

"Then keep your hands to yourself." I closed the space between us, arching my chest so my nipples flirted with his skin. "I'll let you know when you can touch me and when you can fuck me."

"Fuuck," he sighed, tilting his head back, eyes on the ceiling as he inhaled and exhaled.

I underestimated how hot being in control was. I drug my hard nipples against his stomach, pressed my mouth to his abs, swirled my tongue before latching my lips, sucking his skin once more.

"Fuck," he grunted, hands straining at his sides.

I released my bite, kissing the bruise I'd left behind. Then I flashed my eyes up to his while sinking just a bit lower, hands gripping his legs as my mouth hit the spot where his briefs hit his thighs.

"Baby," he exhaled a grunt. "I said sorry, stop punishing me."

"Punishing you?" That's not what I was doing. "I'm just having fun with you!"

"Your mouth is an inch from my dick—you're fucking punishing me."

Was I now? I straightened, just enough to be eye level with his hard, stretched briefs. "You prefer my mouth on your dick?"

"Holy fuck!" His hands were flying down, yanking me up. "You never fucking talk dirty like that!"

"I said keep your hands—"

His arms flew around my waist, hoisting me up in the air, rushing me over to the bed.

"Hey! I'm in control tonight!" I batted against him, but he tossed me down, pinning me to the sheets.

"Not when you say shit like that!" He kicked off his briefs, strong arms bracing my sides so I couldn't move.

"Fine," I relented. "You can fuck me now."

He rammed inside me, no warm-up, just a hard pound, grunting through gritted teeth as his hands anchored my shoulders, thrusting, plowing.

"Gavin!" I tilted my hips, driving him deeper, his face tensing, pace quickening.

And then he collapsed over me. "Fuck, I'm sorry, Baby."

"Already? I... I didn't finish." And I needed to finish!

"Oh, Baby. I'm not done with you or your dirty mouth yet." His lips attacked my breasts, his dick hardening inside me as he rolled us over, so I was mounting him. "Take control, Baby."

My eyes throbbed from the sunlight shining directly on them, and my body throbbed from the night of make-up sex. I wasn't ready to wake up. I automatically reached for the monitor, seeing only two empty cribs. "Gavin!" I shook him. "Wake up!"

"Nooo." He pushed his face back into the pillow.

"Babies aren't in their cribs!"

He shot up, reaching over me to grab the monitor. "Luca and Stefano probably got'em." He dropped it back down then plopped back down himself.

"I'm going to check, you sleep," I leaned over, pecking his forehead as I threw the covers off my legs.

"I've gotta get up anyways to drive them to the airport," he grumbled, pushing himself too.

We crawled out of bed, both padding to the dresser where I threw on a T-shirt and leggings and he stepped into his flannel pants. Then we started for the door, but he stopped me, entwining our fingers. "I love you, Baby."

"Love you, too."

We followed the stairs, then the hall, hearing the guys with the babies in the kitchen. "There they are," Luca chuckled.

"I'm sorry!" I walked right over, arms out for Nora, but Luca shook his head no. "I didn't even hear them this morning."

"Well, at least someone got some sleep," he continued chuckling.

"Why? Did they keep you up?"

"Not them," Stefano sighed. "You guys have a big ass house, but it's not soundproof."

"Huh? Oh, OH!" I inadvertently squealed, feeling the heat in my cheeks as I slunk behind Gavin's arm. How embarrassing.

"Yup, heard that last night too!" Luca teased.

"No, no, we were sleeping," I lied. Shit. We were so lost in each other last night that I forget we had guests.

"Yup," Gavin grinned back to his brothers. "We were sleeping, all, night, long!"

"Gavin!" I swatted his back. "Isn't it about time for you guys to get going?" I looked at the clock, gesturing them all to the time.

"I don't know. Is it Gav?" Luca grinned maniacally, arching his brow as his voice grew higher. "I mean is it, Gavin, Gavin, oh GAVIN!"

Ah! No! The guys started laughing; Gavin's smile grew way too big for his damn face, while I was mortified. "Oh my god!"

"Think you screamed that too," Luca chuckled.

This was not happening. I walked over, yanking Nora from his arms and heading towards the family room.

"I'm gonna get changed," Gavin tried not to laugh. "I'll be right back down."

"I've got to grab my bag too." Luca followed Gavin up, leaving only Stefano and me.

He joined me in the family room, taking a seat on the floor with Vinny. "So are we cool?" he asked. "You know I was trying to keep you out of it the other night."

I shrugged. "I was disappointed. I expected that from Luca but thought you'd be more a voice of reason. You were as bad as them. What if it was Mark?"

He studied me for a minute, looking lost in thought. "Then I'd have fucking killed the guy. And you're lucky it was Gav who went back. Luca would have never stopped if Gav wasn't there, and trust me. I'm no fucking voice of reason."

"I just assumed you'd have more tolerance."

"Why? If someone deserves to have the shit kicked out of them, then I'll be the first in line. I'm still a fucking Romano, wired the same as my brothers. I just have a different preference about who's on my arm and in my bed. That's it." Vinny nestled into his lap, and Stefano wrapped his arms over him, pressing a kiss into his hair. "Look, Patatina. I'm sorry things got so heated, but you see why we had to protect you, right?" He looked down at Vinny, then to Nora reading her book. "These two right here, plus you got Gav to dress up as a fucking cartoon,

Gav! He'd do anything for you. I know you think last night wasn't a big deal, but for Gav, dressing up like that, in public, fuck."

"Well, don't ever get between my husband and me again. I don't want to have to hurt you."

He chuckled, nodding his head yes, before patting my shoulder. "Okay, Patatina."

"Let's roll!" Luca roared, charging down the hall with Gavin behind him, so Stefano and I stood to meet them. "I need to get home and get those pictures printed! Might be the only evidence we have of Gav ever dressing up! I think Gav put a stop to all that shit last night."

Oh god.

Gavin grinned, eyes rolling to mine. "I'm dressing up every fucking year. Whatever she wants, *she's* in control."

Oh god.

"See," Luca yelled over to Stefano. "Pussy whipped!"

Oh god. "Okay! Time to go! Bye! We'll see you soon!" I waved them goodbye.

"Ah, Patatina. I know you'll miss us." Stefano threw his arm over me before kissing Nora and Vinny.

"I'll be back in an hour, Baby."

"Bye, Sadie." Luca laughed. "You gave me memories that'll make me smile for a lifetime."

"Eww!"

"Shit, not you and Gav! Gav wearing that costume—" he rolled his eyes. "By the way, that's some kinky fucking shit, Fred Flintstone."

"Bye, Luca!"

"Nora and Vinny," he continued. "Zio Luca loves you, and I'll see you for Christmas." He bent down, pressing a kiss against each of their foreheads before straightening to me. "If anyone gives you hell, or you need anything, call me. I'm forever indebted."

"I think I'm good." I was good on favors from Luca, actually. "Luca, wait!"

"Always something," he chuckled.

"Anything?"

"Yeah," he answered wearily.

I stepped in closer, looking down the hall to make sure Gavin was outside. "I want you to take back that client you gave Gavin."

"Oh, I can't," he started, but I stopped him.

"You said anything, and that guy is really pissing Gavin off. Also, Gavin asked me not to get involved, and he's very smart, which means you can't say anything and you can't just take the client back; Gavin will know. So, I want you to give him another high profile client, an easy one, and tell him you're taking the shit client back so he can focus on the new client."

He grumbled. "Jesus Christ, anything else."

"Text me those photos from last night, and have a safe flight."

"Sure." His smile went mischievous again. "I mean, yes, yes, oh, YES!"

CHRISTMAS: 1

I grabbed the babies' coats before hurrying down the hall to the kitchen, finding Gavin washing out his coffee mug.

"What?" he asked, shaking out the cup and setting it on the rack.

"You drink more coffee than I do now," I laughed.

"Two babies and a demanding wife will do that to you!"

"Demanding!" I jumped my fingers to his side, but he twisted away before I could tickle him.

"You were last night," he teased, grin growing wider, brow arching.

I looked to the family room to ensure we didn't have an audience, only to catch Nora standing against the couch, smiling at us. "Gavin!" I yanked his arm. "Look!"

Nora's big eyes were lit up as she turned, leaving one hand on the couch as she took a step.

"Holy shit," Gavin whispered, both of us watching her giggle. She took another step, dropping her hand from the couch completely, taking a full step on her own before promptly plopping to the floor, giggling away.

"She walked!" Gavin's eyes were still wide, so proud.

"They're ten and a half months. It's about that time."

"What about Vinny?"

"He'll come around," I assured him. "He just needs to process how he feels about walking." Nora was Gavin, impulsive and impatient. She was the first to roll, crawl, and eat solids. She didn't think first, she just went for it. But Vinny was me, he stewed. He watched Nora crawl, then tested it for a few weeks before giving in. He liked to take his time to process just like I did.

"I can't believe Piccolina's walking. They're growing up too fast," his voice wavered, eyes softening as he watched her.

"Let's get going before you start to cry," I teased.

"What!" he scoffed, shaking his head. "I don't fucking cry! I have allergies."

"Sure." I lifted on my tiptoes, pressing a kiss to his nose. "We've got a Christmas tree to pick out." We headed for the babies, each of us scooping one up on the way to the car. "At least it's colder this year!"

"Seventy degrees, Baby," he chuckled, rolling his eyes teasingly. "Still sunny, and we're still getting a tree from a parking lot."

"Well, maybe we take the twins to New York one year."

"No!" he belted out. "No snow, seventy degrees, and a parking lot's fine by me."

We strapped the babies in before taking our seats. Last year we'd gone to this same Christmas tree lot with Nora and Vinny in my belly, and now Nora was walking.

We parked, Gavin loaded the twins in the stroller and wheeled them right into the lot while I started appraising the trees. I circled each of them, picking at the branches quickly, knowing that Gavin had no patience for this, so I had to act fast.

"No," he shouted, pushing the stroller towards me. "Too small."

"Too small?" I laughed, flashing my eyes up to his.

He handed over the stroller; then took off to the back of the lot.

I hurried after him, watching as he ripped the strings from the trees, shaking and studying them, all the while, working up a sweat, and wiping his brow, yanking his sweater off, tossing it to the top of the stroller.

"It needs to be bigger."

"Oh, I think it's big enough." I focused on his biceps as he shook the tree again, definitely big enough.

He looked at me, shaking his head. "Seriously? You're pushing the stroller, Baby. Stop thinking dirty."

Fine. I flicked my wrist, waving for him to continue, just so I could watch Lumberjack Gavin and his muscles. Ahh, the joys of Christmas. "That looks good."

"I'm not sure," he sighed, spinning the tree slightly.

That's not what I was referring to, but okay. "I thought you didn't care about trees?"

He shrugged, staring down at the twins in the stroller. "That was before we had one in the house, and it's their first Christmas. It has to be perfect! I think we should get an eight-footer! We have tall ceilings." He walked to the next stall, lifting a giant tree, immediately ripping the strings away, shaking it out.

"I like that one! What do you think, babies?" I stepped in front of the stroller, meeting their toothy grins and rosy cheeks. "Looks like they approve!"

"Me too," Gavin agreed. "Let me get someone to help."

Help? Oh, no, no. "I think you can carry it," I insisted, stepping back behind the stroller while my eyes lingered on his bulgy arms.

He leaned into the tree, gripping the trunk firmly, his arms and back stretching his shirt, giving me a glimpse of his boxers as he attempted to lift the tree.

"Earth to Mamma! Baby!"

I rolled my eyes back up, lingering on his flexed arms before meeting those dark eyes and the matching dark hair that was now dangling over them. Lumberjack Gavin was sweaty.

"Jesus Christ, Baby."

"Huh... what?" I shook myself out of the daze. "Did you say something?"

"I said it's too big. I need you to get someone to help."

Too big was right, and I did enjoy helping.

"Sadie!"

"Yeah, yeah." I threw my hand up in apology as I spun the stroller, taking off towards the front. I rushed to the trimming center, inhaling the freshly cut trees, clearing my mind before grabbing one of the workers to help us.

They trimmed and wrapped the tree, then followed us to the car to secure it to the roof.

Gavin finally climbed in, double-checking the babies in their seats before giving me a look. "Is this gonna happen every time we get a tree, Baby?"

"I don't know what you're talking about. I just haven't had my coffee this morning."

He chuckled back, wrapping his hand up in mine as we drove off. "I can't wait for Christmas. I'm really excited! The babies, this tree, my family!" He was smiling ear to ear. "Santa, all that shit. I want to do this right!"

"I'm excited too!" This was my first big Christmas. It had always only been Grant and me. But this year, I'd be waking up to the twins, Gavin, Grant, and the rest of the Romano family. "Let's put the babies to nap first so you can setup the tree without four little hands trying to get to it," I suggested as we pulled up into the driveway.

He parked, beelining for Nora while I unlatched Vinny, and he followed me up, leaving both babies with me, so he could return to the car. I got them ready and put them to nap before padding down the stairs, meeting Gavin, leaning against the doorway with no tree.

"Where's the tree?"

"I figured you'd want to watch."

"I always want to watch." I fell right into him, kissing those perfect lips.

Gavin poured me a glass of wine, handing it to me the second I entered the kitchen. "Twins are finally to bed!" I let him know while happily plucking the glass from his hand. "They loved the tree." I smiled from the memory of them with those giggly, curious faces with wonder-filled eyes exploring the tree. "I can't wait until they wake up tomorrow morning and see it lit up and decorated."

"Why didn't you want to decorate it with them today?"

I took a long sip of my wine, lost in old memories. "I always did this with Grant. He went to bed with a plain tree, and when he woke, the house was decorated and all lit up. I told him the elves did it, a little Christmas magic."

"Then let's get to it!" He took one last swig from the bottle before taking my hand, leading me to the family room. He dropped me at the tree while he headed for the closet, pulling out all my boxes and stacking them across the floor.

"You hang stockings," I directed him. "And I'll decorate the tree."

He popped the lid off the first box, lifting out the new stockings one by one. "Papà, Mamma," he read the names aloud as he laid the stockings next to him. "Vinny, Nora, Grant," he chuckled, then his eyes fell to the box, stilling a minute before he smiled again. "Luca, Stefano, Giorgia, Sofia, Paulo. You got my family stockings too?"

"Our family," I corrected him. "And I wasn't sure if this was their only Christmas here or if this was the first of many."

He suddenly pounced, arms swinging around my back, capturing me against him. "I love you so fucking much, Baby!"

"No!" I twisted my face away from his incoming lips. "If you kiss me, then we won't be able to stop, and I want to decorate! Now, take those hooks and stick them to the fireplace."

He didn't balk, he was too happy. "On it!" He scooped the stockings up and headed for the fireplace.

Now for the tree! I sorted through the ornaments inside the box, carefully selecting just the right branch to hang them on. Tonight was perfect, well, almost. I swung back to grab the remote, powering on the TV, turning it to the holiday station. "And while you're over there," I called to him. "Start a fire, please." I felt my smile, warm from the wine, the now roaring fire, and the carols filling the air while my husband meticulously hung the many stockings across the fireplace mantel. "Can you help me with the star, Papà." I shook the step stool out, and he stepped over, securing the star to the top of the tree. "It's perfect!" I followed him back to the fireplace, sipping the last of my wine as I appraised the ten matching stockings. "Santa needs to go shopping."

He chuckled. "Santa's only got a few more days before my family gets here."

"Feels like they just left." Halloween had been fun, and the almost two-month recovery was even better.

His hands clasped my waist, spinning me towards the tree. "Where are the lights, Baby?"

Lights? Lights! "Shit," I laughed, jumping over to the boxes to dig out the lights. I knew it was too easy. I pulled out the first strand, unwinding it while draping it across the branches. Gavin followed, grabbing another strand and layering it on the higher branches, circling the tree opposite me.

We crossed paths, so I blocked his way, but his hands swooped under my arms, lifting me aside. "Hey!"

He lifted me back up, my legs wrapping around his waist while he carried me towards the fireplace.

He sank to the floor in front of the flames, taking me down with him, his hands sliding from my thighs to my hair, entangling his fingers in my locks. "This is amazing, Baby. I never knew how happy this shit could make me."

"It only gets better." I tipped my face to touch his, our lips brushing.

"Tu sei il mio tutto, you are my everything." His lips pressed into mine, smacking me with a plush kiss. "Want to go upstairs?"

I didn't want to go anywhere. "And waste this perfectly good fire?"

He didn't hesitate, lowering my back to the floor, only then he stood, racing to the wall to shut down the lights, so all we were left were the flames flickering in front of us, dancing off our skin, shadows reflecting on the walls around us. Then he was on top of me, heavy breathing rivaling the crackle of the fire, and the heat rivaled by the chill his hands induced as they slid under my shirt, inching it up and over my head.

His lips dove to my breasts, loud kisses and wet licks overtaking my skin, devouring my chest while his fingers coasted down my stomach. His lips slowed, face rising, eyes finding mine, his reflecting the flames beside us.

"Baciami!" I whispered, demanding a kiss, and once again, he didn't hesitate.

Our noses brushed, his stubbly chin swept across my cheek, then those full lips flattened over mine. His kiss still held so much power. Our touch was always intense, but tonight our kiss was everything. I don't know why it felt so powerful right now, so different. Maybe it was the fire crackling in my ear, or the flickering orange glow that illuminated us in the dark, or my typically impatient husband kissing me with slow abandon, a tenderness that didn't come naturally to him.

Suddenly slow turned to ravenous, two sensual bodies grinding, desperate, dancing tongues to dueling tongues, soft touches to wild hands—our fire ten times hotter than the one burning beside us.

CHRISTMAS: 2

"Papà's going to be home any minute, and he's bringing all your crazy uncles and aunts with him," I teased Nora, who was practicing standing, one arm on my shoulder as she teetered beside me. Then I looked over at Vinny, his curious eyes studying her, watching her walk, but then he shrugged and went back to the toy he had been fiddling with.

The doorbell chimed. Weird, I hadn't even heard the car. "They're here!" I hurried to the front door, swinging it open, to Grant. "Hey, Sweetie," I greeted automatically, noticing the duffel bag in his hand. "What's going on?"

He smiled as he pushed past me, dropping his bag next to the stairs. "I told you I was staying here for Christmas."

"Christmas," I repeated. Christmas was days away.

"Christmas break," he clarified. "Everyone left campus for the holiday. Obviously."

"Ohhh." Obviously. We had three guest rooms and six guests.

"I'm going to run my stuff up to my room!" He grabbed his bag back up. "Where are the twins?"

"Um, family room." I pointed down the hall while he started up the stairs.

And almost immediately, Luca was charging through the still opened front door, following by a thundering boom of Italians. Breathe, Sadie, breathe.

"Ho, Ho, Ho!" Luca roared, arms flying up for a hug.

"What," Stefano shouted, shoving him aside. "Those three chicks in your bed last night."

"Coglione!" he barked back before pulling me into his arms. "Sadie! Where are my babies?"

"In the back."

"Patatina!" Stefano was right behind him, hugging me after Luca. "I've missed you. It's been what eight weeks," he chuckled.

"Six and a half." *Not that anyone was counting*. "And can we drop the whole potato thing?"

"Nah," he said with a smile as he trailed Luca to the family room.

"Sadie!" Giorgia squealed. "It's so hot! This isn't winter! You can go to the beach in December!"

"Hi, Giorgia!" I hadn't seen her or Sofia since August.

Sofia walked up next, rolling in two giant suitcases. "Sadie!" she greeted, walking in with Gavin, who shut the door behind them.

"No Paulo?"

Her gaze rolled to the floor for a second before giving me what seemed like a forced smile. "He's working."

"Let's go!" Luca boomed, his feet stomping behind me, causing me to automatically spin around, seeing him and Stefano holding the babies.

Then Sofia took off up the stairs. "Give me a minute to grab their outfits!" she insisted, rushing up to the nursery.

"Gavin?" I looked up at him, but he just shrugged.

"It's time to go see Santa!" Luca announced.

Santa? Now?

"That cool, Baby?" Gavin asked, but he was wearing that happy smile, and there was no way I could say no.

"Mom!" Grant called from the top landing, sending all eyes to the stairwell, watching him bounding down. "Oh, hey everybody."

I turned to address Gavin. "Grant's staying here as well for Christmas break."

"What!"

"Great, let's go, kid," Luca yelled up at him, snapping his fingers and pointing Grant to the door. "We're going to the mall."

"I'm good," Grant chuckled, hopping down the last few stairs. "I'm going to eat and watch TV."

"No, you're going!" Luca insisted, stepping across the hallway to block his path. "We're all going! Capisci?"

"What? I don't want to!" Grant shrugged, trying to push past Luca, unsuccessfully. "I'm cool watching TV!"

"You're her kid, and we're not leaving you out. Head to the fucking car!" he demanded. "Family time."

"Dude!" Grant snapped, reaching for Nora. "And watch your language! They're going to be talking soon!"

Luca stood there, his face twisting in anger as he looked at his piccolina, who Grant had just stolen from his arms.

"This Burberry is perfect!" Sofia sighed, hurrying down the stairs, and once again, all eyes whipped in the other direction, watching as she ran straight to Grant, plucking Nora from his arms. Then she beckoned Stefano to follow her to the family room.

Grant looked at me, eyes widening with his smile. He was the only one in this room who truly understood me. Gavin could read my moods, and he knew me, but not the way Grant did.

Sofia and Stefano rounded back into the hall, my stress fluttering away from the sight of Nora in her plaid dress and Vinny in his matching suit.

"Perfezione!" Giorgia sighed. "Perfection."

Gavin walked towards Nora, but Luca stepped in front of him, grabbing her away, so Gavin turned to Stefano, who also rebuked him, walking straight out the door.

I stifled my laugh, watching Gavin roll his eyes as he grabbed his keys.

"I'll drive with Grant," I told Gavin. "We'll meet you guys there."

"Baby," Gavin warned.

"Go, Grant!" I tugged his arm while I grabbed my keys, pulling him along with me to the car.

"I didn't realize the Italian mafia was staying here too," Grant chuckled as he slammed the door.

"You always did want a big family Christmas," I teased, starting the engine and waving goodbye to the family.

"I don't ever remember saying that."

"Let's just pretend you did," I laughed.

"Wait, Mom. They're not really Italian mafia, are they? Because that would explain the money."

"No!" I replied automatically, but... "Well, I'm not sure about Luca, actually I'm not sure at all." Hmm.

"You know, I could have driven alone." He reached for the radio dial, turning the station.

"I know. I needed a quiet car. You have no idea what it's like driving with a car full of Romanos."

The mall was packed, leading me to circle the lot a few times before finding a parking spot. Then we trekked to the entrance, seeing Gavin pulling up to the mall valet.

"Good timing!" I watched them pile out while waiting for Gavin, who was handing his key to the valet.

"I missed you, Baby." His arm swung across my back, leading me forward.

"It *was* a long ten minutes," I teased.

Luca and Sofia were holding the babies, disappearing through the mall doors ahead with Stefano, Giorgia, and Grant right behind them. So I hurried Gavin along, trying to keep up. "Grant!"

He slowed, waiting for us. "Shouldn't you and Gavin be holding the babies? Or a stroller?"

"You didn't know? The twins are community property," I joked.

We followed the family to the center of the mall, taking our place in the Santa line, causing quite a commotion. Every woman, and man, around stole glances at the three Italian men fussing over the babies and the two women dressed like they just stepped off a runway.

"Next," a young girl in an elf costume called robotically, her eyes flashing up to Gavin and Luca, doing a double-take. "I mean, welcome to Santa's Workshop! Who do we have here?" she gushed, overly interested in Nora. Then Stefano stepped forward with Vinny. "This way," she tried to flirt, forgetting that she was dressed as an elf with giant plastic ears.

The guys placed the twins on Santa's lap while Sofia fussed over Nora, and Giorgia adjusted Vinny's suit, making that happy elf seemingly annoyed.

"Smile for Mamma!" I crouched next to the cameraman, who began snapping photos.

"Grant get up there!" Luca shouted, pointing Grant towards the jolly Santa.

"What! No!" Grant snapped, looking at me.

"You're her kid!" Luca belted back. "Get up there with the kids," he repeated. "All the kids in the photo!"

"No!" Grant yelled back. "I'm twenty years old! Mom!"

Luca reached into his pocket, pulling out his wallet, and thumbing through it, flipping out a hundred-dollar bill. "Here, now go sit on his lap."

Grant looked at Luca's outstretched hand. "You're giving me a hundred bucks to go sit on an old man's lap? You see how creepy that is, right!" Grant looked at me for support, but I couldn't help laughing, so he rolled his eyes, stalking over to Santa and lifting Vinny, taking his place on Santa's knee with Vinny now in his lap.

I smelled a hint of spice before I felt the strong chest and arms wrapping around me. "He's going to hate me, you know," I whispered to him.

Gavin chuckled. "He owes you."

The cameraman started flashing again as Luca stepped forward, smiling at the kids. "Say cheese!"

And Grant looked at us, then straight at Luca. "Cheese you motherfuc—"

"Grant!"

He stormed off the second the cameraman was done and I charged right after him, swinging my arm over his shoulder to slow him down. "You know how I always give you two hundred for your Christmas gift?" I nudged his side, trying to get him to smile. "How about I bump it to five hundred this year, as a token of my appreciation."

"So you're going to pay me off, too?" He laugh-scoffed. "I knew they were mafia."

"We're going home now, and I promise you no more Santa and no more drama!"

"Grant!" Someone yelled, drawing both our attention to the two guys walking right for us, their smiles on Grant, and then me.

"You spoke too soon," Grant bellowed.

"You and Danica break up?" The taller one asked, eying my arm draped over Grant's shoulder.

"No, she just went home for Christmas. This," Grant sighed, rolling his eyes. "Is my mom."

"Whoa!" the guy started, then slowed, eyes rolling up. "I know you!"

I felt Gavin step behind us, towering over both Grant and me. No Gavin, walk away. I looked at Grant, shaking his head; an annoyed grumble escaping his lips.

"Gary," the guy continued. "No, Gavin! You graduated a few years ago, right? You were a legend!"

A legend, huh? I tipped my head up, meeting Gavin's smug smirk as he nodded what's up to the guys. Quite the ego for a man who just shed a tear when his babies sat on Santa's lap.

"A legend?" Grant mocked.

"Yeah, a fucking legend! You remember him, Grant."

"How could I forget," Grant mumbled.

The way the guy was saying legend inferred one of two things, one, Gavin had slept with a lot of girls on campus, or two, he had slept with someone newsworthy outside of campus, like an older woman, like a mom, and I had a hunch which one he was referring to.

And as if answering my question, Gavin wrapped his arm around my waist, curling me into him. "Come on, *Baby*."

"Oh shit," the guy screeched, gaze flying between us.

"Gavin!" I warned him, pulling myself out of his grip as Grant stomped off in front of us. "A legend?" I huffed, taking off after Grant, leaving Gavin's fan club behind.

"I've been called worse," he laughed, cocky smile still bright while Grant sulked away. The one thing that made Gavin the proudest made Grant the most embarrassed.

"How about I take the babies home, and you hang here with your family? The twins need to nap anyway." And I needed to spend time with Grant.

"You sure?"

"Yeah! Grant!" I called, and he reluctantly turned back. "Grab Vinny," I insisted.

We said goodbye, headed for the car, and buckled the babies in. Grant's smile finally returning.

"They're mostly okay." He laughed, staring at me as we drove off. "Except for Luca."

"You know he raised Gavin."

"That explains a lot," Grant continued laughing.

"Gavin lost everything and then had Luca to comfort and raise him. Luca!"

"That sucks."

"Yeah, it's complicated. Luca—" I couldn't believe I was saying this. "Is actually a good guy, with a good heart. He's complicated too."

"Well, I guess I got a hundred bucks out of it today." He shrugged, pulling the cash from his pocket. "Plus, the five from you! Not bad for an hour." He tucked the hundred back into his pocket.

"And I'm sure you can milk him for more," I teased. "He feels protective of you, oddly, and sitting with Santa was his way of including you."

"You know, Mom. We've had more drama in the last two years than I've had my entire life!"

I met his smile, both of us cracking up laughing.

I eventually pulled up into the driveway, unloading the babies with Grant following me upstairs, playing with the twins for a bit before helping me get them down for nap.

"I'm going to my room to call Danica," he said as we exited the twins' nursery. "I'll be down in a little bit."

"Okay." I padded back down the stairs, hearing some chatter in the kitchen, finding Giorgia and Sofia sitting at the kitchen table. "You all are back already? Where are the guys?"

"They left as soon as we got home," Giorgia answered, her usual chirpy voice now dull.

"To where?"

"Luca said something about lights," she sighed, looking off towards the window.

Neither of them seemed very chatty, so I walked back down the hall for the stairs, only something caught my eye out the window. I saw a group of women gathered down on the sidewalk in front of our house, all pointing up and smiling at something. That's weird. I opened the door, waving to the group on my way down to them.

"Just admiring your lights!" One of them gushed.

My what?

"I already have my lights up, but I'd tear them down to hire them!"

Them? I turned around, looking up at my house, my gaze landing on Gavin, balancing on the second story balcony railing, his back to us, his shirtless back. Stefano stood at the opposite end of the railing, also shirtless, also flexing, stringing the lights after Gavin, and above them, Luca, standing on top of the roof, his eyes on his audience as he tugged his shirt over his head. Good lord.

"Where did you find this company?" Another woman practically moaned. "I want to hire them too! Who cares if Christmas is only days away!"

"I didn't hire them." I rolled my eyes while watching the three handsome men bending and stretching, putting on a show for every woman on my street. "I married one, and the other two were just part of the package."

"Oh!" One of the women gasped. "One of them is your husband?"

"Yup, and his brothers." I turned to face the women, effectively shutting down the Romano show and sending them all scattering away.

"What are you guys doing?" I yelled up; Stefano looked down.

"All your neighbors are decked out for Christmas! You and Gav have nothing out here!" he yelled back.

"Well, let me know ahead of time, so I can charge for admission!"

"What?" he called back, completely oblivious to the adoring audience they had.

"Forget it. Keep up the good work." I returned inside, walking to the kitchen, meeting the girls who still sat at the table. "Your brothers are hanging Christmas lights." I grabbed a water from the fridge, then took a seat across from them. But they suddenly got quiet, both so serious. "I'm sorry, did I interrupt something?"

"No," Sofia sighed.

"Sadie," Giorgia started. "How did you know Gav was the one? That you really loved him?"

What? I looked between the sisters, watching Sofia glance over at Giorgia. "I don't know. I never *had* to think about it. We had a connection." No matter how hard I'd tried to fight it, there was always something so strong between us. "I felt complete with him. I guess I never really knew if he was the one, he just was. And as for really loving him—" I laughed. "My heart was his since the moment I stared into his eyes. It was like my heart had a space waiting for him before we ever met. There was no big event or a series of dates to get to know and understand each other. We were connected, a wildfire that couldn't be contained."

"But you and Gav are so different," Giorgia mused, staring down at the empty glass in front of her.

"I don't think that matters. Your soulmate is a deeper connection, a stronger feeling, nothing else matters. You have a connection that makes you feel whole." I spun my wedding ring, seeing the black ink that spelled his name. "He was my destiny. My Fate. There was a greater force at work when we met, and for once in my life my heart was in control, not my brain."

They both watched me, though neither were smiling. "Why?" Now they were starting to worry me. "Did Gavin say something?"

"No," Giorgia assured me. "I was just curious."

"What about you, Sofia?" She was also married.

She smiled back, eyes distant. "My answer is nowhere near as beautiful as yours."

"Baby?"

I whipped my face back as Gavin stomped into the kitchen, still shirtless. "Hello!"

He continued to the fridge, wiping the sweat from his brow before pulling out some water bottles, then stepping over to the table, stopping right behind me, so I tipped my face to meet his. "Love you," he whispered, pressing a sweaty, upside-down kiss to my lips.

"Love you, too. Please be careful up there." I watched him walk away, right out the front door. Sweaty Gavin looked good. "It's a beautiful day!" I pushed out of my chair. "I'm going to the front yard and enjoy the view."

"Isn't the view better in the backyard?" Sofia asked, looking towards the ocean.

I shook my head no. My husband was outside working, shirtless. "Not today."

CHRISTMAS: 3

I stared at the mirror, bating my time as the commotion grew louder downstairs. They'd all be at the door, ready to leave. But I was in my pajamas, giving myself one last final pep talk before heading down to break the news that I wasn't going. I didn't want any drama so close to Christmas which meant I had to step back and remove myself so that there'd be no jealous or overprotective Gavin. He could just enjoy the night with his family and not worry about me—no fights, no drama.

"Baby!" Gavin's voice echoed into the room. It was time. I walked out to the stairs, watching Gavin below. "Why aren't you dressed?" he asked as I started down.

"I'm going to stay home tonight. To spend some time with Grant." I stepped off the last stare, ignoring his glare that was now on me. "You all go! Have fun!"

His eyes bored into mine as he swung his hand out, grabbing my arm. "Go change," he insisted. "You're going with us, Baby."

"No," I replied, staring into his eyes to let him know I was serious. "I want to stay with Grant. Enjoy this time with your family. They're only here a few days." I looked to my arm, gesturing for him to let me go.

"Grant?"

"That's a good woman," Luca roared, making his way over towards us. "Let her hang with her kid, Gav."

But Gavin shook his head no. "I'll stay home too then," he grumbled. "I'm not going out without you."

He had been at my side since the hospital, and I loved how much he loved me, but he needed to love his family too, and he needed to let me have some space. "No, go." I reached for his hand, squeezing it just as Luca grabbed his arm, tugging him towards the door.

"Baby—"

"I'll see you later. I love you!" I lifted up on my tiptoes, smacking him a quick peck before starting down the hall.

Grant was slumped on the couch, surfing channels on the TV, so I sat next to him, setting the baby monitor on the table at my side.

"You know I'm fine here alone."

"I know, but I've missed you!" I leaned over, bumping his shoulder with mine. "Gavin needs to learn how to play with others too." I knew he'd have a good time, they always did. "Want to watch a movie? I'll make popcorn." I hopped up, heading straight to the kitchen to start the popcorn. "How's Danica?"

"Good," he called back. "I miss her."

"When does she get back?"

"New Year's Eve."

There goes our babysitter, but I was happy he'd have her back. They'd been together a year and a half, and Grant seemed so happy. "That's great." I returned to the couch, plopping down next to him. "I'm glad you're here. We haven't spent time together like this in a while."

He smiled back, nestling his head against my shoulder. "I've missed you, Mom."

He was twenty now, but he still felt like my little guy. He held a piece of my heart that nobody could ever fill. I rested my head against his, watching the movie he put on, my eyelids slowly growing heavier and heavier.

"Isn't that fucking cute."

"What the fuck is this."

"They're all cuddled up."

"Baby, Baby."

"Leave her here. Let them have their fucking moment."

"Get the fuck out of here, Luca."

I felt a jolt, my eyes springing open, body jumping in surprise, staring up at the five Romanos hovering over me. I lifted my head, realizing Grant was fast asleep on my shoulder, and I instinctively pressed a kiss to his hair before sneaking a pillow under him and stepping away. "What time is it?" I yawned, stretching the kinks out.

"Two," Sofia whispered. "We'll see you in the morning." The girls headed to their door while the guys started back towards the stairs.

"Goodnight." I leaned into Gavin, wrapping my arms around his waist. "You guys have fun?"

"I text you!"

"Oh, sorry. We put on a movie, and I must have fallen asleep. I don't even know where my phone is."

"Fell asleep like that?" he huffed, nodding to Grant. "You ditch me to fucking cuddle him!"

It was too early for this, or too late for this. And he was too drunk. "It's late. Time for bed." I tugged him to the hallway, shutting the lights off as we hit the stairs.

"I don't like this," he grumbled again.

"The dark?" I teased, still pulling him up the stairs. "But most of our fun is had in the dark."

"You know what I fucking mean."

I drug him through our door, shutting it softly behind us before wrapping my arms back around my drunk, brooding husband. "Gavin, we've talked about this." And I didn't want to talk about it again. So I tugged his shirt, pulling him down until his face was level with mine. "I missed you tonight." I stuck my tongue out, hitting his lips, tasting the whiskey that had stained them. "Are you ready for bed?" I slipped my hands to the top button on his shirt, but he was sexy like this, so I dropped my hands to his belt instead.

"Baby," he groaned. "I don't—"

"Shh," I whispered, rubbing my palm over his zipper while tugging it down. Then he grabbed me, slamming his lips into my neck as he lifted me to the bed. This was the drunk Gavin I loved—starving lips, uncontrollable hands, and such urgency.

He dropped me to the sheets, climbed over my body, resting himself on all fours, his face hovering over mine. "I don't like when you're not with me, Baby. I don't like when I call and text you, and you don't reply, and I don't like being at a bar without you by my side."

"That's a lot of things you don't like." I pushed my hand to his chest, unhooking a button. "Instead, why don't you tell me some things you do like."

He sat back, eyes drifting down.

"Do you like... my tits?" I grabbed the hem of my shirt, wriggling it up over my head, enjoying the way his jaw dropped. "Let me tell you something I like." I reached for his hand, tracing his fingers. "I like your talented fingers, and I've missed them."

His eyes flashed to mine. "Talented fingers?"

I released his hand, and it immediately hit my stomach, fingers dragging down under my waistband, inching to my clit, rubbing away. "Shit!"

He arched back, sliding down while taking my shorts with him, his face then falling between my thighs. "I have many talents, Baby."

Suddenly he was inside me, thick fingers curling into that spot, plunging—then a lick, his tongue flat against my clit.

"Ooh!" His fingers were hard, his tongue was hard, his chin and knuckles, all smashing against my center.

"I," he hissed, sending hot air streaming against me. "I like that you're always so fucking wet for me, Baby." He drove his fingers harder, then faster, while his tongue focused solely on my clit.

"Gavin! Fuck!" Oh my god! I threw my hands to his hair, lips quivering, eyes rolling back from the intensity of his greedy fingers and his hungry tongue. "There! There!"

"And I like when you scream my fucking name, Baby!"

He was up, fingers out, tongue away, body arching, his pants flying in the air; then he was falling back against me, his rock-hard erection banging its way between my thighs.

"Gavin!" I yelped, smacking my hand over my mouth, holding in the screams as he pounded. "Now! Now!"

"Fuuck," he let out a deep groan, coming, collapsing.

"Gavin?" I was pinned under him. "Gavin?"

A grunt rumbled over my chest, then another before his breathing steadied. He passed out, drunk snoring, and drunk Gavin did not wake easy. "Shit, Gavin! I can't breathe." I batted at his chest. Nothing. Fine, have it your way. I danced my fingers up his sides, digging into his ticklish spot, making him jerk away, rolling off me and onto his pillow.

I gave him a quick kiss, staring at the man who drove me crazy in both a good and bad way. "Do you want to know what I like the most? You."

CHRISTMAS: 4

I heard the chatter from the baby monitor, the babbling waking me from a very good dream. I opened my eyes, nestling my face against Gavin, who I was still draped over. He hadn't moved since he passed out and was still fast asleep. He needed the sleep more than I did. So I slid my legs off the bed, the rest of my body following, taking me to the dresser to get dressed.

The house was quiet as I padded down the hall, passing Luca and Stefano's door just as it opened, with Luca stepping out, shivering in surprise when he saw me. "Did they wake you?" I whispered.

"No," he yawned. "Stefano's fucking restless, talking in his sleep. I don't know what's going on with him."

"I'm sorry you have to share a room, and that one of you is on an air mattress." I gave him an apologetic shrug, and he waved his hand with another yawn, gesturing it was okay. Then I opened the nursery door to two happy babies jumping in their cribs. "Want to help me?"

"You don't even need to ask." He went right for Vinny while I grabbed Nora, the two of us carrying them down.

"Hey, Mom! Hey, Luca!" Grant looked up from the table, spoon in hand with a mouthful of cereal.

"Good morning!" I walked over, kissing the top of his head as Luca took the seat beside him, dipping his head for me to kiss it too, but I shook my head no. "I'm going to walk the babies. Want to go?" I asked Grant, who nodded yes. "Okay, I'll get them ready while you finish eating."

"Sadie," Luca called, twisting his face over his shoulder. "Where's the espresso?"

"In the invisible box next to the coffee machine," I laughed while plucking Vinny from his arms, carrying both babies away to change them.

I loaded the twins in the stroller, and Grant met us in the garage, taking my side down the driveway. "Want to push?" I veered the stroller in front of him, and his hands immediately latched to the bar. We used to walk, rather run together all the time back in Arizona. But since college and Gavin, we hadn't. "You know, we should go running later! We haven't raced in a while!" I elbowed him, making his smile curl up into his cheeks.

"You'd win," he conceded. "I eat pizza two meals a day at school."

"Maybe we should bet on it?" I teased. "If you win, then I'll add another hundred to your Christmas present."

He chuckled. "Okay, moneybags!"

My wallet was stuffed with cash, and now I had good use for it. This was the first year I wasn't struggling to save up for his gift. In fact, I had more than enough.

We continued to the top of the street, then started back, eventually making our way up the driveway and into the opened garage, where a dismayed Gavin stood, leaning against one of his machines, glaring at us. "What the fu—where were you?"

"Walking, obviously," I teased as I walked up to him, swinging my arms around his back. "You were sleeping, so Grant and I walked the twins this morning."

His lips pinched, his face dipping towards his chest for a second. "That's our thing, Baby. We walk the babies every morning."

"I didn't want to wake you." I leaned up, waiting for a kiss, but he wasn't lowering to meet me.

"You should have waited for me," he mumbled under his breath.

"It's fine, Gavin, relax. It was one morning." I stepped back, grabbing Vinny while Grant lifted Nora, following me past Gavin into the house.

"Nora! Vinny!" The girls gushed, immediately rushing over and swooping the twins away.

"Good morning, Giorgia, Sofia," I laughed on my way to the kitchen.

"Morning," they called back in unison on their way out to the backyard.

"Want to go race now?" I goaded Grant. A run sounded good, a race sounded even better.

"Let me change," he sighed with a mocking smile.

"Me too." I jogged up the stairs, straight to my closet, changing into my running shorts and sports bra before zooming back down the stairs, where Gavin, Stefano, and Luca were at the kitchen counter, eyes flying to me as I raced by. "We'll be back in a bit!"

"We'll?" Gavin repeated. "Where are you going?"

"Mom!" Grant shouted from the stairs, hurrying down the hall right behind me. "What's your record again?"

"Four and a half!" I boasted to Grant. "We're going running," I then called back to Gavin.

"I'll go too," Gavin insisted, reaching out for my arm, but I was too excited to slow down.

"You don't run," I reminded him, laughing over my shoulder.

"Then stay here with us, Grant," Gavin shouted. "We're heading into the garage to lift."

"No thanks," he laughed, sticking to my side.

"You sure?" Gavin snarled. "Because you could really stand to bulk up."

He didn't! "Gavin!" I snapped, whipping back around, glaring. "Let's go, Grant."

Gavin's lips were tight, a flat line, eyes narrowing as he watched us leave. He was too much sometimes. I gave Grant a playful push out the garage door, and then we were off, sprinting down the driveway, racing down the street, and through the gate to the boardwalk.

"Sprint?" I yelled over, ready to ramp up this run.

"Sure, if you're up for it," he teased, tone mocking me, sending us both flying down the sandy walkway.

My legs moved as fast as they could, spinning under me while I half-watched Grant from the corner of my eye, falling behind me. "I'm winning!"

"Mom!" he yelled, but I saw it too late, my legs moving too fast to stop, bumping right into the large rock, sending me stumbling, tripping, sliding palms down, leg skidding across the concrete.

"Shit, Mom!"

Ouch. The sting burned from my knee to my ankle.

"Mom? Are you alright?" Grant dropped beside me.

I pushed up on my palms, flipping to sit. "I won." I smiled up at him.

"Jeez," he bellowed, rolling his eyes. "That doesn't look good."

I followed his stare to my bloodied, skinned-up leg. "I think I'm okay." I pushed up again, trying to stand, but my foot throbbed, pain immediate, causing me to fall right back down. "I rolled my ankle. I think it's sprained."

"Here," he sighed, reaching for my hand to help me up.

I finally made it to standing, hobbling on one leg. "The way home will be a bit little longer," I laughed.

"I can carry you," he offered; I laughed, continuing to hobble up the boardwalk.

"Seriously," he scoffed. "You don't have to be jacked to lift you. I can lift Danica."

"You can?" The snide response flew out before I could stop it. I was shocked that Gavin could lift me and Grant was half his size.

"Jeez," he grumbled. "Don't act so surprised."

"Sorry. I'm not surprised. I—" I guess I was surprised. He was only a few inches taller than me.

"Uh, huh," he mock-laughed. "Can you get up on that bench?"

"Maybe? Or maybe you should just call Gavin."

"Mom, I can handle it."

"Okay."

He helped me over to the bench, and I hobbled up, then onto his back, his arms hooking right under my knees.

"Are you sure you're okay?" I asked to verify. He was huffing pretty heavily, pushing me up every few steps.

"How small do you think I am? I'm not like six-four or however tall Gavin is, but I can carry you."

It wasn't about strength. I just didn't want to hurt him. "Okay, but we can rest if you need to!"

He didn't reply, just kept trudging along, making his way back to the gate and onto our street, the final trek taking him ten times longer. We finally made it to our driveway, and Grant sucked in a deep breath, panting his way up to the opened garage.

Gavin and the guys were there working out, all lifting weights, subsequently all dropping their weights when they saw Grant carrying me up. Then Gavin's stare found my banged-up leg, his eyes flaring, wide, black, angry. "What the fuck happened!"

Stefano and Luca stepped up beside Gavin, all those dark eyes on me. Here we go.

"I—"

"What the fuck did you do to her!" Gavin cut me off, yelling while storming towards us.

"I tripped!" I assured him, raising my voice to calm his rage.

"Yeah, relax," Grant huffed, half out of breath. "It wasn't my fault." He bent down so I could slide off his back.

I landed on one foot, keeping my other up, hobbling once again.

"Holy shit! What the hell happened!" Gavin yelled, eyes on my legs. "Why didn't you fucking call me to help?"

"I had Grant. He helped." I watched him, watched his pupils dilate and darken.

"This is reckless fucking behavior!" he finally snapped, his tone a bitter bark. "You take off with him—"

"With Grant!" I snapped back.

"Now you're all fucking cut up and limping!" His glare flew between my scraped-up leg and my ankle, his chest rising so hard with each breath that it looked like it was going to burst. He couldn't handle seeing me hurt.

"We were running! Not reckless. Accidents happen." I realized my poor choice of words too late, but it didn't matter. He was too far gone.

"This is your fucking fault!" he spat at Grant.

"No, it's not!" Luca boomed, wedging himself between Gavin and Grant.

This was getting out of hand way too fast. "Gavin! Can I talk to you upstairs?" I more demanded than asked. He needed to calm down before he did something he'd really regret.

"No!" he belted out. "You can talk to me right here."

"Check yourself, Gavin," I warned, meeting his eyes, letting him know how serious I was. "My leg is bleeding, and I need to ice my ankle. If my husband won't help me, then I'll find someone else who will. Do you understand!"

"Fuck," he groaned, shaking his head as he continued over, hands capturing my waist, swinging me up in the air and into his arms, cradling me against his chest as he stalked back into the house.

He was silent, stalking through the house to the stairs, taking them up to our room. "Reckless behavior?" I repeated to him. "Really!"

He kicked our bedroom door closed behind us, then marched straight to the sink, plopping me down on top of the counter. "I don't fucking like this," he grumbled under his breath. "And now, you're all bloody and can barely walk."

"All this? All this… time with Grant?" He couldn't be serious. Between Danica, school, and our life, I hardly ever saw him. "Well, if he doesn't go to Texas and Florida like he did last summer, then he'll be back here again, so I suggest you chill. It wasn't his fault that I fell."

He ran a washcloth under the faucet before pressing it to my leg, studying the scrapes in silence.

This was ridiculous. "If I would've known there'd be a fight anyway, then I wouldn't have skipped out on last night!" Oh, shit. I squeezed my eyes shut, praying he didn't hear, or wouldn't read into it.

His eyes flashed to mine. "What?"

"Nothing." I shrugged, pretending to focus on my leg, but he backed away, tossing the washcloth at me.

"If you would've known there'd be a fight you wouldn't have skipped out," he repeated. "What the fuck does that mean? I thought you stayed home to hang with him."

"Grant, not him." So irritating. "And... yeah I did."

"I'm losing my fucking patience, Sadie!"

Fine. "I thought it'd be better if I stayed back while you went out. Every time you get in a fight or get mad, it's because of me. I didn't want a fight at Christmas."

"Last time," he started, but I lifted my hand to stop him.

"I mean, the other times. You get jealous or protective, and I didn't want to take a chance, not so close to our first real Christmas."

His face twisted into a scowl, his face nodding slowly. "So, just so I fucking understand, you're not going out because you're afraid that I, your *fucking* husband, might overreact if some douchebag gets close to you," he spat before promptly storming out of the room, slamming the door in his wake, leaving me up on the high counter.

CHRISTMAS: 5

"Gavin! Gavin!" I shouted, looking down at the floor that seemed so far below me. I'd have to jump, land, and balance on one foot. Dammit, Gavin. "Gavin!"

Suddenly there was a knock, the door squeaking open. "Patatina?"

"I'm in here," I called out, watching Stefano search the room before finding me.

He laughed. "Are you, uh, what's it called... an elf on the shelf,"

"Very funny." I stretched my arms out for him. "Can you help me down?"

"Gav left you up there?"

"He did. Is he downstairs?" My guess was he probably stormed into the garage to work out.

"He left."

"What?" I met his eyes as he clasped my waist, lifting and lowering me to the floor, helping me to the bed.

"He grabbed his wallet and keys and took off."

"Shit." Gavin never left.

"Why is he so pissed? He's been bent out of shape all damn morning."

"Gavin being Gavin," I sighed. "And Sadie being Sadie."

He chuckled, his smile inducing mine. "He laughed."

"Guess I might need an X-ray for my ankle, and I just so happen to know a good radiologist. Want to take me to him?"

He smiled. "You know the best," he beamed. "But I bet he's up north with his sister who just had a baby."

"So you two *are* still talking."

"Yeah," he said through a smile. "He's got his life down here; I've got mine in New York, but it works."

"Absence makes the heart grow fonder," I sang.

"It does. Except in Gav's case, absence makes the heart go fucking crazy."

"In only Gav's case?" Sure.

"I hate the distance," he admitted. "But it's safer, I mean, better this way."

"When are you going to tell *them*? Assuming they still don't know."

"Soon. I have to, for him." His eyes were deep, looking so much like Gavin's.

"I think I messed up. I think Gavin's really pissed." I didn't want Gavin thinking his wife lied so she wouldn't have to go out with him. I needed to explain myself.

"Hold that thought, Patatina!" He straightened, heading to the sink, wetting and ringing out a washcloth before returning, dabbing the cloth on my leg. "Continue."

"Nothing," I sighed mostly to myself. "Just the jealousy and overprotectiveness get a little too much sometimes."

Stefano met my eyes, a smile instantly on his face. "You married the wrong man if you don't want to deal with being protected. Sadie, we've lost a lot, and I understand how Gav feels now. All we have is our family, and all he loves is you. We tend to protect our world because what would we do without it? And as for the jealousy, I'm not that guy, so I can't relate, but I can guarantee you've got another decade before he calms his ass down."

I tried to hold my laughter in. "You're not the jealous type?" Liar.

Just then, the door swung open, Gavin rushing in, stare on Stefano.

"That's my cue." Stefano stood, handing me the towel before squeezing past Gavin and out the door, closing it behind him.

"Where'd you go? You left me up on the counter!"

He didn't reply, simply swung a bag that was hanging on his arm as he knelt in front of me, immediately taking the washcloth and rubbing it over the scrapes. Then he dumped the bag onto the floor, reaching for the antibiotic cream that was inside it.

"Wait," I insisted, causing his dark eyes to raise to mine. "I need to shower first to get all the sand off before you put on the cream and bandages. Can you help me?"

He stood up, and I stretched my hand for his, but once again, he ignored it, his hands cinching my waist instead and carrying me over to the shower door. He lowered me onto the mat, releasing his grip, only I wobbled a bit, causing his hands to fly right back to my waist to steady me. He still wasn't saying a word, which meant he wasn't mad, he was hurt.

I didn't know what to say either, so I grabbed at my sports bra, tugging it over my chest and tossing it to the floor, making his fingers dig into my waist even tighter.

Then I bent for my shorts but couldn't get them with his hands still holding me. "Can you help me?" I rested back against the glass while he hooked his thumbs under the waistband, dragging them down my legs, over my feet.

"Thanks." I stretched my hand to the shower lever, then held the wall to steady me as I lifted my sore leg in, trying to balance under the water.

He muttered under his breath, suddenly yanking off his shirt and shorts, stepping in behind me, and wrapping his arms around my waist to steady me once again.

I slumped into his chest, his arousal shooting up in response, jabbing my back. "Fuck, I'm sorry," he finally spoke. "He's used to fucking you in the shower." He backed away a little, enough for me to spin in his arms to face him directly.

"I'm sorry, Gavin."

He ran his hand up to my face, wiping my hair away from my eyes, his face softening as he met my stare. "It's okay. I understand."

He... what... "Wait? Really?"

He nodded yes, the motion sending water droplets streaming down his face. "Baby, the three of you are all I have. I almost lost you once, so if someone threatens to hurt you or take you from me again. I'm gonna unleash hell. I just wish you would have talked to me instead of trying to avoid me. That's the part that fucking hurt."

I hated this. I hated when his dark eyes looked sad or when he felt hurt, especially when it was my fault. "I didn't want you to get mad."

He cracked a smile, his fingers still weaving through my hair. "And how'd that work out for you?"

"Backfired. My husband stormed out, left me stranded on the counter."

"Damn straight, I did! I was fucking livid. My wife is all torn up and limping, telling me she doesn't need me protecting her, and that I'm fucking drama." He laughed, rolling his eyes. "I left before I said shit I'd regret. I went to get stuff for your leg."

"Speaking of which, I should probably bandage it now."

He reached behind me, cranking the shower off before reaching for a towel and draping it over my shoulders. I started out, but he clasped my waist, lifting and carrying me back over to the bed.

He sank to his knees, patting the scrapes on my calf dry while his towel unraveled, exposing his thighs, and more. "You need to put pants or boxers on, something!" I tried but failed to keep my eyes off his lap.

He rolled his eyes playfully as he stood up, giving me a quick wink before strutting to the dresser and grabbing out some boxers. He dressed and returned, lowering back down and squeezing some cream onto his finger, rubbing it over my cuts before covering them with the bandages he'd bought. "I wasn't sure if you needed this." He pulled out an ankle wrap.

"I do."

"Do you need to go to the hospital? We could make it a tradition. Last year Luca, this year you." He was smiling as he unraveled the bandage.

"No!" I laughed. "I just need a wrap and ice. I'll rest it tonight while you all go out."

"I'm not going out tonight, Baby."

That's why I didn't talk to him first. "Gavin—"

"We can do something together. Luca shouldn't be at a bar anyway. It's Christmas, Baby. I want to be together."

"Even Grant? You know you don't need to be jealous of him."

He stopped wrapping my ankle, looking up at me with wide eyes. "Jesus Christ, Baby. I'm not fucking jealous of Grant!"

Could have fooled me. "You seemed like you were."

He sat up, snaking his hands up my thighs, wrapping them around my waist. "I... I don't like feeling like I've been replaced."

"Gavin!"

"I'm not used to having another man in my house that you give so much attention to. I know he's your son, and you two are close, but I only see him a couple times a year. He's still new to me." He sank back, continuing to wrap my ankle. "I don't like to share. It's hard for me, my head always goes to a bad place, and I tend to—" he met my eyes once more. "Overreact."

"I'm sorry you felt that way. I wasn't replacing you."

"I know, Baby. I have a rational brain. It's my heart that likes to fuck with me."

"I've missed him," I told him honestly. "And it was fun spending that time together. He's only here for the week."

"I know." He clipped the wrap, then climbed up onto the bed next to me. "Adjusting is never easy for me, but I'm working on it. I'll apologize to Grant."

"So, what are we *all* going to do tonight?"

He swung his arm over my shoulders, pulling me into him. "What would you usually do on the night before Christmas Eve?"

"Hot cocoa while looking at Christmas lights!"

"Then that's what we do, Baby."

"Help me up?" I held out my hand; he sprung up, reaching for my arm, my towel conveniently dropping to my feet.

He stilled, looking my naked body up and down.

"What?"

"I think you have a few more scratches I didn't see."

I looked down at my legs, then back up to him, meeting his devilish grin.

"I think I need to properly look you over, Baby," he continued, his chest brushing mine while his hands found my ass.

"Oh yeah?"

He lowered his face, lips pressing into the hollow of my throat, kissing their way down to my breasts. "Yes, Baby. I need to look over every last inch of you."

CHRISTMAS: 6

"Cold," I emphasized with a fake shiver to Nora and Vinny, who were poking the bag of ice on my ankle.

"Be gentle with Mamma's foot," Gavin warned them, attempting to lure them away, but they were too excited about their new discovery.

"It's fine," I assured him, squeezing his hand that was tight with mine. "So, when do you think they'll be back?" Everyone, including Grant, had left to grab coffee hours ago while Gavin stayed home with me.

"I don't," he started, only to be interrupted by the door booming open and boisterous screams filling the hall.

"Sadie! Gav!" Giorgia raced in with an armful of bags, piling them onto the bar counter. "We stopped at Target! Have you been?" She was giddy, eyes bright, smiling like a kid in a candy store. "It was incredible!"

"You've never been to a Target?" Not surprising.

"No!" she squealed. "I'll be right back! I have to help them unload everything."

Everything. Oh god. I handed the ice to the twins, then gestured for Gavin to help me up. He promptly hooked his arm around my waist, helping me past the gate to the end of the hall. "Holy shit!" I gasped from the sight, the loaded front porch stacked with bags and the entryway currently being filled. "Is that a playhouse?"

"Mom!" Grant bounded through the front door, smiling wider than I'd ever seen. "Luca bought me a PlayStation!"

I looked up at Gavin, laughing once more.

"Gav!" Stefano yelled as he and Sofia stepped over the bags lining the hall. "We got the babies a climbing thing, a house, tons of shit for Christmas."

"But Santa already got them—" They pushed by me, piling the bags in. They bought the whole store.

"That store was interesting!" Sofia mused. "Nothing designer, but it had all the little things you never think about."

"It sure does," I suppressed a laugh.

"Fratellino," Luca roared from outside, stacking another box onto the porch. "Look at this Christmas inflatable shit for your yard. You're gonna have the craziest fucking house on the street!"

"Fuck, yeah!" Grant shouted back to Luca, stepping beside him while proudly holding his PlayStation box. "This is gonna be the best fucking Christmas!"

"Grant!" Oh my god! The last thing I needed was Grant turning into a mini-Luca. "Gavin!" I tipped my face to him, watching him try to contain his laughter.

"That's great, Luca." Gavin nodded, cheeks tight with his smile. "Let's get it set up because tonight we're going to look at Christmas lights."

"Where?" Sofia asked, turning towards us. "Are there department stores around?"

"Just the neighborhood," I informed her. "You know, we'll drive around and look at the decorated houses," I explained while they watched me, looking confused. "It's what we do out here, it's Christmassy! And tomorrow's Christmas Eve."

"Sounds perfect, Patatina," Stefano answered for all of them, nudging Sofia with his elbow, making her smile as well. Giorgia and Sofia then collected a bunch of the bags, walking them to the family room, where the babies were still playing.

"Nora!" Sofia gasped, clasping the bags. "Vinny!" She and Giorgia started unpacking the toys for the twins while Grant stomped up the stairs excitedly.

Gavin's lips tickled my ear. "I'm gonna go outside, light this house up," he chuckled. "What do you want to do?"

"Couch!" I looked up just as he bent down, sweeping me off my feet and into his arms, carrying me to the sofa.

I slumped into the cushions, watching Nora holding Sofia's shoulder, her little legs wobbling, and then she let go, stepping the few feet over to me, clapping for herself. "Good job, Nora." I leaned over, pressing a kiss to her button nose. "Mamma loves you, baby girl." I noticed Vinny sitting behind her, with mounds of new toys surrounding him, but his sole focus was on the bag of melting ice in his hands. "Vinny, bring Mamma the bag," I asked, pointing to the bag he was holding. "Bring it to Mamma."

He flipped down to his hands, crawling to Sofia, then grabbing onto her and lifting just as Nora had, pulling himself up to standing. "Vinny!" The scream burst from my lips, making Nora swivel back to see too.

He had the biggest smile on his face, his big brown eyes on me as he dropped his hand from Sofia, taking a step, wobbling, then falling with a laugh and crawling the rest of the way over.

"Yah, Vinny!" I kept cheering, clapping, welcoming them into my arms. "Mamma is so proud of both of you!"

Giorgia and Sofia were clapping too, gushing over the twins. "All these new toys, and they just want to be with you!" Giorgia sounded stumped, waving her arms over the toys spread across the floor.

That's because they were just like their Papà, ruled by their hearts and wanting to feel loved and connected.

"Okay!" Stefano's yell shot down the hall. "It's getting dark!" He popped into the family room. "You girls ready to go?"

"Let me go unpack my coat," Giorgia laughed. "It's the first time I might actually need one." She scurried away with Sofia while the twins continued to use me as a jungle gym.

I laughed, tickling the little bodies climbing over me, suddenly feeling someone's stare on us and catching Gavin from the corner of my eye. "You guys ready out there?" I called over, laughing with my giggling babies.

He continued to the couch, perching his head above mine, causing both Nora and Vinny to jump over me, clamoring to get to their papà. "Ow," I laughed, causing Gavin to immediately scoop them both up in his arms. "Their jackets are in the closet," I told him. "I'll have Grant drive my car, and we'll follow you guys."

"What? No," he balked. "Our whole neighborhood's lit up, Baby. We'll just walk."

Umm... I pointed to my bandaged ankle. "Walk?"

"I'll carry you," he said with a completely straight face-like it was no big deal.

"Gavin—"

"Baby," he demanded right back. "It's all or nothing. I'll get coats on the twins and load them into the stroller."

I nodded yes. "Okay, Papà."

He took off as the girls shuffled back out in their heavy coats and as Luca walked into the kitchen, giving me a random thumbs up before heading right back outside. I didn't even want to know what that was about.

"Let's go, Grant!" Gavin's shout came from the front. They were all already outside, without me. I braced the armrest, pushing myself up from the couch, hopping on one foot to the hallway just as Grant zoomed down the stairs and out the door. Never a dull moment.

Gavin raced back in, seeing me and shaking his head. "Baby, don't try to walk on that!" He bent down, waiting for me to climb on, and I knew better than to fight it, so I fell over his back. His arms flexed under my thighs while mine draped around his neck as he carried me out.

"Hey!" Giorgia whined the second she saw us. "I want a piggyback ride, too!" She turned to Luca expectantly.

"Me?" he huffed, shaking out his coat. "You're not a kid anymore, Sorellina!"

Giorgia's eyes grew even wider, her bottom lip jutting out, staring up at Luca.

"Unfuck—" he grumbled, bending down to let her hop up on his back. "See what you started, Sadie." He hoisted Giorgia up, rolling his eyes. Then Sofia looked at Stefano; he laughed in reply, then hunched down for her. "Only in fucking California," Luca groaned. "Are we ready yet?"

All three of us girls were on the guys' backs, and all of our smiles turned to laughing fits.

"Sorellina," Luca huffed again. "You need to lay off the fucking lasagna."

"Stronzo," she laughed, slapping the back of his head.

Stefano slowed beside them, twisting his head back to meet Sofia's. "Sof— "

"Sta 'zitto!" She snapped, pointing her finger playfully in his face to shut him up.

I couldn't stop laughing, watching our caravan mosey down the driveway behind Grant pushing the stroller.

"Our house is obviously the best one on the fucking street!" Luca announced, stopping on the sidewalk to face our front yard.

"*Our* house, huh?" I repeated, still laughing into Gavin's ear. Then I looked at our front yard. "Oh, my, god!" The red and green Christmas lights ran haphazardly across the roof and sides of the house while a giant inflatable Santa, Christmas tree, and reindeer covered our grass. It looked like Christmas had thrown up on my front yard.

I literally had no words. I glanced down at the twins beside us now, both their faces awestruck, giant excited smiles strung cheek to cheek. Then I looked up at Luca, who was smiling with so much pride as he watched the babies' reaction. "Our house is definitely the best! You guys did a good job!"

"Andiamo!" Stefano urged. "Let's go!"

Grant pushed the stroller, all of us following his lead, laughing incessantly over the lights and the men carrying us. We didn't need cold weather or the glitz of New York to have a perfect Christmas—we just needed each other.

CHRISTMAS: 7

We were finally home, all of us yawning as we waited for Gavin to unbuckle the twins from their car seats. It'd been a long day and an even longer Christmas Eve mass. Gavin lifted a sleeping Vinny first, handing him to Luca before rounding to the opposite side to get Nora, holding her with one arm while using his other to help me to the front door. I disarmed the alarm, unlocked the door, all of us shuffling in. "Wait a minute!" I called to Stefano and Grant, who were starting for the stairs. "Just because mass is over doesn't mean the night is. Grant, what happens when we leave on Christmas Eve?"

"Oh jeez," he laughed. "Are you still doing that?"

"Me?" I shook my head no, playing aloof. "I don't know what you're talking about."

He rolled his eyes, smiling. "Santa's elves come while we're away and leave us a gift under the tree, which are always pajamas."

"Then go get your PJs, kid," Luca chuckled. "I'm tired."

He wasn't getting off that easy. "I think we should all go to the tree," I urged everyone forward, herding them down the hall towards the family room lit up from the lights on the tree, perfectly illuminating the nine wrapped boxes under it.

"Us as well?" Sofia asked.

I shrugged back, playing coy as Gavin helped me to the couch, helping me down and handing over a still sleeping Nora. Then he bent down in front of the tree, grabbing up the first box. "Grant," he announced, tossing the box over before grabbing the next. "Luca."

Luca walked over, sinking next to me on the couch with Vinny against his chest, and Gavin handed him his box while Sofia and Giorgia knelt by the tree, reaching for their boxes and handing Stefano's up to him.

"And Mamma and Papà." Gavin smiled, stacking the last four boxes in his hands. "The babies will have to open these tomorrow."

Everyone opened their gifts, lifting out the matching red and green Christmas pajamas. "They're all the same!" Giorgia laughed, scanning everyone else's hands.

That's right! "We all wear them tomorrow morning."

"Christmas morning?" Sofia clarified, eyes wide as she examined the festive pajamas. They were a stark contrast to the pencil skirt and stilettos she was currently wearing.

"We have to wear these?" Stefano flipped the shirt front to back.

"Yep! Wearing matching pajamas is a tradition in my family."

"This is fucking great!" Luca spoke over them, giving me a nod of approval. "And the twins are matching, too?"

"Of course!" I tightened my arms around Nora. "Now, everybody can go to sleep."

The girls took off to their room while Stefano and Grant started for the stairs, and Gavin grabbed Nora from me, gesturing Luca to follow him upstairs. "I'll be right back, Baby."

"Okay, Santa," I smacked him an air kiss as he left the room.

The house was finally quiet, it was time. I limped to the closet, unloading the boxes of gifts for the babies.

"Baby," Gavin gasped. "Let me help!" He hurried over, snatching the box from my hands. "Matching pajamas?"

"Yeah, should be cute."

"Are you gonna make me dress up every holiday now?"

"Not on Valentine's. I dress up that night!" I puckered, demanding a kiss. "Although, I do love you in a suit." Our lips brushed, that burst of love hitting hard. "Do you want to do stockings or presents?"

"Is doing Mamma an option?" he rasped, lips dragging over mine.

"Later, Santa. Christmas first!" I pecked his lips one last time before pointing him to the tree.

He popped the lid off the first container, appraising the presents. "Now, what?" he asked, standing there holding the wrapped gifts, looking clueless.

"You put them under the tree. Do what Santa does."

He nodded, sorting through the gifts, placing them meticulously under the tree. I'd been doing this for almost two decades and forgotten what that first Christmas felt like. This was old to me, but new to him. I hobbled to the tree, bending to the floor beside him to watch. "The other box has stocking stuff."

"Okay," he replied, too busy sorting and analyzing the presents and their placements.

He arranged, rearranged, taking it so seriously. And when the last present was placed, he hopped up, circling the tree in deep thought. "This is cool." A proud smile lit up his face.

"You did a good job! I think the twins are going to be very excited about what Santa brought!"

He opened the next container, pulling out the stack of thin boxes. "What are these, Baby?"

I didn't want to tell him. Santa needed to keep some surprises. "Names are on the label. Just stuff them in the stocking."

He matched the packages to the names on the stockings while I sprinkled candy into each stocking to top them off. "That's it!" I clapped silently. "Now, we hide the boxes and call it a night."

He tossed the containers into the closet, pivoting right back, capturing my hand, half-carrying me to the couch. "Can we sit a minute, Baby?"

"Of course, Santa." I curled onto his lap, staring at the tree, the presents, the mantel.

"I can't wait to see their faces tomorrow," he whispered, lips brushing my hair. "This is amazing."

"Well, they'll probably be more interested in the paper than anything," I laughed, remembering Grant's first few Christmas. The boxes and paper were his favorite gifts. "Next year, they'll really understand presents."

"I've missed Christmas," he sighed, resting his head against mine. "It felt good last year, but this feels fucking incredible."

"You know what else feels *fucking* incredible?" I hinted, teasing him. "Sleep."

He laughed. "Not until Mommy kisses Santa Claus." He slid his arms under my legs, lifting me into his arms.

"Happily!" I clasped my hands around his neck, kissing him while he carried me upstairs.

He elbowed our door open, taking me straight to the bed and laying me down before continuing to his closet. The bed felt good. I nestled into the pillow, the sheets, eyelids growing heavier by the second...

"Gavin!" I gasped, rolling over to his side, sliding my hand over where he should be, except the bed was empty. "Gavin?" I heard a bang, no, banging. What the heck? I slid off the bed, limping to the window, squinting to see in the dark, spotting Gavin and Luca in the backyard building a playhouse. I reached for the balcony doorknob but didn't want to disturb them, so I hopped back to the bed. I'd let them do their thing. I flipped my phone, 3:02. I dropped it back down; the flash of light illuminated an envelope on my bedside table. Huh. I sat right back up, switching on the lap, reading the envelope. "Mia Moglie." That was me. I tore the seam, sliding out the card that had gold letters reading, *My Greatest Gift*.

Buon Natale, Amore Mio! Merry Christmas, My Love. I started writing this last year but couldn't find enough words for you then, and I won't repeat everything you've already seen.

I barely remembered the words from that email now and wished I *could* read them again.

But that's okay because I have the words now, Baby. First, I want you to know how much I cherish you, how I don't go a day without realizing how lucky I am. That I have two babies that have my eyes, that hold me tight, and know I am their papà because of you. You almost lost your life to give life to them, and I will never forget that Baby.

I am in awe at your selflessness, it never stops and I'm damn proud of your heart, Baby, especially because most of the time it's putting up with me, and the other time you're giving your all to our babies.

I already knew you were going to be an amazing mamma, hearing and seeing the sacrifices you made for Grant, but nothing prepared me for how incredible you'd actually be with our babies. How am I ever supposed to compare when Mamma's around? I'm no match for your love, your patience, or your heart.

I stretched my hand for the box of tissues, ripping one away and pressing it to my wet cheeks.

I love you so much, Baby. Thank you for giving me this Christmas. You have no idea how happy it makes me to have everyone I love staying here together in our home.
Here's to a hundred more Christmases together.
Love always, tuo marito, your husband,
your Gavin

I stuffed the card back into the envelope, immediately pushing another tissue to my face, blotting the tears just as the door opened and Gavin's surprised face met mine.

"Shit, Baby! You okay? Why are you awake? Crying?" He hurried to the bed, plopping down at my side.

I waved the envelope up at him. "I'm sorry if you wanted me to wait until morning." I set the envelope down on my table. "I had to read it."

He stood back up, chuckling as he tugged his shirt off over his head. "I wanted to give it to you earlier, but you fell asleep."

"Sorry," I yawned almost on cue. "What were you doing downstairs?"

He crawled under the covers, throwing his arm open for me, so I turned the light off and nestled into his chest. "I couldn't sleep," he whispered, coasting his fingers up and down my arm. "I was too fucking excited. So I woke Luca to help me set up the house they bought the twins the other day."

"You were too excited," I repeated, kissing his chest.

"Yeah, my first Christmas as a papà and Santa. I didn't think it'd get me like this."

I lifted my face, focusing on his moonlit eyes. "I still owe Santa a kiss."

"Can we talk instead, Baby?"

"What?" I watched him, waiting for the dirty joke.

"I, um," his voice faltered as he looked towards the window. "Can I tell you some stories from when I was a kid? About our Christmases." He was sincere, opening up to me.

"Of course." I draped my arm over his chest, holding him as tight as he was holding me.

"My mamma and papà..." he paused, breathing shakier.

"It's okay. Take your time. We have all night."

CHRISTMAS: 8

The sunlight hit the windows, gradually lighting the room. It was finally Christmas. I sat up, looking down at Gavin's handsome face, his flexed bicep locking over my thighs. "Merry Christmas," I whispered, dropping my fingers to his arm, tracing his tattoos, dancing my way up to his crazy morning hair.

He nestled his face in my lap."Buon Natale, Baby."

"Get your pajamas on, and we'll go grab the babies."

"You're serious about the pajamas?" He threw the sheet off, springing from the bed excitedly.

"I am!" It wasn't just the twins who were excited for Christmas.

He opened his box, changing into them with a laugh before tossing me my box. "Thank you!" I caught it with two hands, unfolding the pants inside. "You know, you're exactly what I was hoping to find under the tree, Mr. Romano."

He ignored me, too excited, tugging his festive top on. He laughed, walking over to face the mirror. "Where do you even find shit like this?"

"Me? You mean Santa's elves." I changed in the bed, waiting for him to help me out.

He clasped my waist, lifting me to standing. "How's your ankle, Baby?"

"Still a little sore."

He leaned back, appraising us. "I can't tell if matching is cute or fucking ridiculous."

"I think we're cute!" I tipped my face to his for a kiss, but apparently, our kiss had nothing on Christmas. He tucked the twins' pajamas under his arm before banging our door open.

"Buon Natale!" he shouted, voice echoing and rattling the walls. "Get your pajamas on and get downstairs!"

"Warn me next time," I laughed, pressing my hand over my ear. "Maybe Santa needs another kiss to calm down."

"Someone say Santa?" Luca stepped out in front of us wearing his matching pajamas, and holding a Santa hat.

"Jesus, Luca," Gavin chuckled, yanking the hat from his hand. "There's only one Santa in this house!" He kept charging, plowing through the nursery door with Luca. "Buon Natale Piccolina e Piccolo!" Then the guys carried the twins out in their matching pajamas. "Cute!" Gavin smiled as he passed me. "Definitely cute."

Stefano stepped out of his door next, yawning. "Buon Natale, Patatina."

"Merry Christmas, Stefano."

Grant's door was next, opening on the other side of the floor with him walking out in his pajamas, too. "This is so embarrassing," he grumbled, reluctantly meeting us at the top of the stairs.

"Take it up with the elves," I teased, throwing my arms around him. "Merry Christmas, Sweetie!"

"Merry Christmas, Grant!" Gavin was right behind me, hands clutching my waist to help me down the stairs.

"Where's—" I started, only to see Stefano now holding Vinny. Oh, I smelled coffee, and fire.

"Buongiorno!" Sofia chirped, waltzing into the hall to meet us, somehow making red and green pajamas look like they belonged on the runway. "Buon Natale!" She hugged one sibling to the next, even Grant.

"Merry Christmas, Sofia!" I kissed her cheek, seeing Giorgia bounding up behind her. "Merry Christmas to you too, Giorgia!"

"Look at us!" Giorgia squealed, phone already in hand. "I love this!" She snapped pictures while we continued towards the kitchen.

"Holy shit!" What happened to my family room? There were stacks of presents everywhere. Apparently, another Santa had stopped by last night.

The twins followed my stare, immediately thrashing against the guys, tiny fingers pointing to the tree, then the fire, then the presents.

"Look!" I exclaimed to the twins. "Santa was here!" I nodded for the guys to put the babies down, so they started into the family room with all of us trailing behind. "Stockings first!" I insisted, limping my way to the mantel.

"Stockings," Stefano sighed, crouching to the floor with Vinny. "I haven't had one of those in—"

"Eleven years," Giorgia answered for him.

I passed the stockings out, watching them pull the thin boxes and start unwrapping. I'd gotten them all matching picture frames with a photo of each of them holding the babies at the baptism.

"Oh!" Sofia gushed, running her fingers over the glass. "È bellissimo, beautiful."

I walked over to Luca, leaning into him. "I know you don't do pictures," I tried to whisper. "But I thought this one was special."

He shrugged. "I have one up now. This will go next to it."

Gavin's arm captured my waist, pulling me onto his lap as he opened his picture, one of his entire family and him with the twins. "I love it, Baby."

"Now presents!" I nudged Gavin, and he picked the first gift, handing it to Nora, who shook it, then chucked it at Vinny's head. "Nora!" I lunged, trying to block Vinny. Then Nora picked up another and threw it again.

"Shit, NO!" Gavin told her, trying to sound stern, but he was smiling. "Not funny, Piccolina!"

"Come on, Vinny. Zio Luca will help you!" Luca pulled Vinny onto his lap, handing him a present.

"What's this?" Grant chimed from the other side of the tree, causing all of us to look over at him and the card he was holding. "It's just a paper with an address on it."

"That's your new condo," Gavin called back.

His new what?

"What?" Grant took the word right out of my mouth.

"Escrow closes in twenty-eight days," Gavin continued. "So you'll be moved in by spring break. When the dorms close, you'll have a place to go."

"Gavin," I whispered over my shoulder. "Why didn't you tell me?" Twenty-eight-day escrow! He bought it two days ago, and didn't even discuss it with me. He was so damn impulsive.

"I told you I was going to buy an investment property when my condo sold," he answered casually, because of course buying a condo for my son was no big deal.

"Are you serious?" Grant yelped, suddenly frantic. "My own place? Me? You bought me a condo!?" He searched my face, and I nodded. "This, thanks!" He pulled out his phone, immediately typing.

"We'll talk about this later," I whispered to Gavin.

"Now," Grant bellowed dramatically. "If only I had a brand new car," he said more to Luca. "Even the babies have Ferrari's."

"Grant!" I warned.

"What?" He laughed. "They do."

Giorgia suddenly sprung up. "We need a family photo!" She set her phone on the mantel, angling it on us before grabbing Nora while Sofia lifted Vinny, and we all stood, smiling at her phone.

Everyone then found their place on the floor, or the couch, opening presents, but it was time for me to get started on dinner. "I'm going to start prepping the food," I announced, making my way to the kitchen.

"You're cooking?" Giorgia asked.

"Of course! I'm making lasagna!" An easier Italian meal that I'd hopefully not mess up. "I'm making everything from scratch, too. A real homemade Italian dinner."

All eyes were on me, but no one said a thing... perhaps Gavin had warned them about my cooking.

"I'll help!" Stefano hopped up, following right behind me. "Luca and I used to make the lasagna with Mamma every Christmas."

They did? I immediately focused on Gavin. I had no idea this was her tradition; I'd just chosen it because it was one of the only Italian dishes I knew.

"I'll help, too!" Luca boomed, shuffling to his feet.

Gavin's stare drifted to the gifts ahead, but he wasn't really looking at them. I knew that look.

"Gavin never helped your mom?" I whispered to the guys.

Stefano shrugged back. "He was too little."

"Gavin!" I called to him, breaking his trance. "Can you help me? My foot's a little sore."

He gave Nora and Vinny a quick kiss, then hopped to his feet, meeting us in the kitchen.

"I was going to follow a recipe, but why don't you two show Gavin and me how the Romano family does it. That way, we can pass it on to Nora and Vinny."

"Recipe?" Luca groaned, shaking his head no before turning towards the cabinets. "Gav, grab the flour!"

"Buon Natale," Luca toasted, raising his glass to meet all of ours. Stefano then sliced the lasagna, scooping it onto our plates.

"The twins' first Italian food," I announced to the group, chopping some of mine onto their plates. All eyes were on the babies poking the noodles cautiously. Then Nora picked some up, chomping down, Vinny following. Then they both shoved the rest of the pasta into their mouths, making everyone clap excitedly.

"True Romanos!" Stefano boasted.

The rest of the dinner was just as I'd hoped—good food, great wine, and an abundance of laughs and memories. The girls insisted on cleaning the table since the guys cooked, and finally, we gave our last Christmas greetings before Gavin and I carried the twins upstairs for bed.

"Buona notte, Piccolina," Gavin whispered, laying Nora in her crib. "Buon Natale. Ti voglio bene. Papà loves you." Then he met me at Vinny's crib, rubbing his hand over Vinny's thick black hair. "Buon Natale, Piccolo. Ti voglio bene. Papà loves you too."

I took his hand as we snuck out of the room, entwining our fingers. "Merry Christmas, Papà. I love you."

He lowered his face, the stubble of his chin scratching my nose before our lips smashed.

"So, thanks again, Gavin!"

I blinked, letting the voice register in my brain, Grant! I pulled away from Gavin, finding Grant standing at the top of the stairs. Embarrassing.

"It's from us," Gavin choked on his words as he tried to catch his breath. "And, no problem."

"That's really cool of you guys!" Grant smiled. "Merry Christmas. I'll see you in the morning." He made a beeline to his room before I could say a thing.

I forgot about the condo. "I can't believe you bought him a condo without even telling me! Did you buy him that so he doesn't have to stay here?"

"That's not why I did it," he countered.

"You bought it two days ago!" I laughed. "You're right, you're bad at sharing!"

"Nah, I just needed a Christmas gift for him."

I laughed, giving him an exaggerated roll of my eyes. "You know you're a bad bullshitter!"

"Luckily," he growled, snaking his arms back around me. "I'm good at other shit." He led me into the room, closing the door behind us, fingers already sweeping under my shirt, touch sizzling across my skin. Then I saw the Santa hat from earlier. Ohh... I broke his grip, lunging for the hat and pressing it over his thick hair.

"Hey, Santa. I think it's time for your present." I pounced, falling to my knees, unbuckling his belt and sliding his zipper down. "What view would you like?"

It was a grunt, eyes darkening, legs still shaky from the surprise.

I palmed over his boxers, inducing more grunts. "On my knees? Over you on the bed?"

He stumbled back, hitting the bed and falling over it, scooting himself up to the top, laying there naked, except for the Santa hat. And my top was off, all my clothes were off, and I was climbing over him. "What view would you like?" I asked again, sliding my hand up his inner thigh, exploring his package before clasping his arousal. "Want to watch my mouth or my ass while I blow you?"

"Oh, fuck." His dick jerked in my hand, his grin curling wickedly up to meet his black dilated eyes. I'm guessing that means ass. I crawled around him, bending over his chest, ass arched in his face while I sank my mouth down.

He grunted again, hands flying to my ass as my tongue ran with my lips, up, down, breathing through my nose, choking him down, rocking to give him both a show and a performance. "Cazzo, fuck, Baby!"

Music to my ears. I bobbed deeper, his hand suddenly sliding down my ass, two fingers plunging inside me. Oh god. I tried to go down on him, to keep my pace, but his fingers were hitting harder, getting deep, his heavy breathing hitting my ass that was in his face. "Fuck! Gavin, you can't—" but he wasn't stopping. "I—" his other hand grasped my hip, yanking me back closer to him, and suddenly his tongue was licking places it usually didn't. Oh, oh! "I, can't, finish, you." I tried to pump him, but his tongue, his fingers. Then his tongue drug away, his fingers slipped out, and he rolled up, keeping me on all fours as he squared up behind me, thighs and erection against my ass.

"Now!" I arched, gasping for breath, throwing my head back.

He caught my hair, wrapping it up in his fist.

"Fuck! Now, Gavin!"

"You know what those words fucking do to me, Baby."

"Yes, and that's exactly why I said them! Fuck me now!"

FIRST BIRTHDAY: 1

"Mom! Do you have Nora's shoes?" I rushed down the hall, finding her in the front room with Nora in her lap.

"Yes," she answered, not bothering to look over. "I put them on the entry table."

I wheeled around, bumping into Grant, who was flying through the front door carrying a case of water bottles. "Grant! Have you seen Grandpa?"

"He's in the backyard teaching Vinny how to golf."

"And Gavin?"

"Setting up the tables," he replied over his shoulder on his way to the back.

Gavin's family, and the guests would be arriving any minute. "Danica!" I called, and she popped her head in from the front patio. "How are the balloons looking?"

"I'm almost done. Dan's going to help me set up the gift table in the back, next." And just as she mentioned him, he pushed past her, carrying in beer.

"Thanks, Dan!" I stepped out, looking at the balloon arch and the birthday sign hanging over the balcony announcing the twins' first birthday. Then I saw a black

SUV driving up. They were here. I hurried back inside, grabbing Nora up on my way to the backyard. "Gavin! Grab Vinny! Your family's here!" We walked out just as the car pulled to the curb, doors swinging open with Luca hopping out first, sending the twins into a frenzy, running excitedly towards the car.

"Sadie!" Giorgia rounded the trunk, with Laurence.

"Laurence!" I screamed, running down automatically, surprised and excited to see him. "Welcome!"

"Hi, Sadie!" He wrapped his arms over me, giving me a tight hug just as a third arm gripped my back, pulling me away.

"Laurence," Gavin greeted, draping his arm around me while looking at Laurence, surprised to see him too.

They were finally back together, and Giorgia looked so happy. "So, you two..."

She snuggled into him, placing her left hand over his chest, the diamond on her ring finger on display.

"Engaged!" I pulled away from Gavin, jumping back to her and Laurence.

"I thought you broke up," Gavin grumbled behind me, making Giorgia roll her eyes.

She ignored him, focusing back on me. "I want you to be a bridesmaid, Sadie, and Gav obviously a groomsman. And Vinny and Nora, ring bearer and flower girl," she squealed.

"Of course!" I squealed right back, just as excited.

"The wedding is booked for December in New York! Right before Christmas!" She was smiling ear to ear; her bubbly self was back.

"We can't make it," Gavin snapped.

I whipped my face to meet his. "Of course, we can!" I corrected him. What was he thinking!

"No," he repeated, grumbling under his breath before storming up the lawn into the house.

"Excuse, Gavin," I apologized to them. "He's, well, he's just Gavin," I laughed, waving them to follow the family that was heading into the house. "Giorgia, if you could show Laurence around. I'll be back down in a few minutes." I hiked up the stairs, pushing through our bedroom door to Gavin sitting at the edge of the bed, resting his head in his hands. "What was that about? You don't like Laurence that much? You were so rude to Giorgia!"

He rolled his face up, his features soft. "I don't want to take the twins to New York, and definitely not in winter. Why would she even say that shit today? Knowing what this weekend is."

This weekend? Ah. It wasn't just the babies' birthday; it was also the anniversary of his parents' death. I sank next to him, taking his hand in mine. "She's excited. She's getting married! You can't let your parents' accident scare you from taking the twins to New York. You have to get over this fear. They're getting older, and I want to travel just like you did as a kid. We can't stay cooped up in San Diego forever, and we can't miss your sister's wedding."

"Fuck, I know. I'm just, fuck. I was thrown off guard. You know this time is hard for me. My head's already in a bad place. I mean, what if something happens!"

"If it snows, we'll stay inside, but we're going, and you need to apologize to Giorgia. You made it sound like you don't support her marriage."

"Why is there always so much drama?" he huffed.

"I don't think the drama's following you," I teased him. "I think you're the source."

He rolled his glare down. "You think you're funny," he laughed, shooting his fingers to my sides, but I jumped away laughing.

"Come on!" I demanded, hand already on the door. "We've got a full house downstairs and more guests on the way. Plus, I want to formally introduce my parents to your—oh, shit!" I ran down the stairs, out the back, seeing it before I could stop it.

"Florida? Jesus Christ, it's fucking hot down there!" Luca roared. "I've been a few times but couldn't handle that shit!"

I flashed my eyes from him to my wide-eyed, horrified parents.

"Sadie!" he boomed. "Where the fuck's Gav?"

Oh god. I walked over to meet them. "He's inside. Go find him, please."

Luca took off, leaving my parents pale and speechless.

"That's Gavin's eldest brother. You remember him from the wedding? He, um, I have no excuses. He's just Luca."

My parents gave each other a look while I turned back towards the house, catching Stefano down the hall with Mark coyly following. Mark!... with Stefano! "Stefano!" I took off, racing up and enveloping him in a hug. "I'm so happy to see you and—"

"Is Luca and everyone here?" he cut me off, scanning the house.

"Yeah, in the back." I stepped over to Mark, hugging him as Stefano disappeared, taking off without a word. "What's he—no!" I looked from Mark to the door. He still hadn't told them. "Not yet?"

Mark shrugged, exhaling a heavy breath. "He hasn't found the right time."

"It's been what, a year since you two started dating."

"A little longer," he sighed. "Off and on."

"That doesn't bother you?" That was a long time to be hiding.

"Of course it does." His stare lingered on Stefano in the distance. "But, it's hard to stay mad at... that," he laughed, leaning against my shoulder.

Yup, I knew exactly what he meant. One grin from Gavin and I melted, no matter how mad I was. "May will be here soon, so you'll have someone to hang with."

"Are those your parents?" He nodded his head to a couple cornered by Luca, their faces even paler now.

I laughed. "Luca's playing the 'how many times can I say fuck' game with my Bible Belt parents."

"And I see you have lots of alcohol, which will most likely be needed," he teased.

"Yep! How else do you expect us to make it through the day with the Romano family, Jones family, and everyone in between."

He stared out the window, laughing under his breath. "Who thought a First Birthday could be so entertaining. Shall we?" He started out, so I followed.

The minute I walked out, I saw May walking in, with a guy. "May!" I yelled, waving her to the backyard.

She dropped some presents to the table, then hurried our way. "They're so big now! Happy birthday, Nora and Vinny!" she sang down to the twins who were running in and out of their playhouse. "Sadie, this is my cousin Will. He and his girlfriend just moved here."

"Nice to meet you!" I shook his hand.

"And this," May started, rolling her eyes. "Is Mark. He works with us at the hospital."

"Hey," Mark greeted. "Where'd you move from?"

"Just up north, Sacramento area," her cousin replied.

"Me too!" Mark screeched, hopping right over to his side. "I'm from Roseville."

"Folsom," he laughed. "And I'm already impressed with San Diego. It's only rained once this whole winter."

I looked between them, catching another interested pair of eyes watching from across the yard, and suddenly Stefano was making his way over, glare on Mark. He stepped up right next to me, awkwardly hovering behind Mark and Will, trying his best not to seem interested in what was happening.

"If you need a tour guide, let me know," Mark offered.

Ohh... I looked at Stefano, face tensing, eyes narrowing.

"Mark," Stefano seethed, causing Mark to turn around, seemingly surprised Stefano was there. "They need your help in the kitchen!"

"Who are *they*?" Mark asked, such a smart ass, straining his head to see inside the house.

Stefano grunted. "If you don't wanna fucking help, then fine, stay out here. It doesn't fuc—"

"Stefano!" I warned, gesturing down to the babies who were right under us. "Watch your language!"

Stefano looked between Will and Mark, letting out a big frustrated sigh before storming off into the house. So I stepped to Mark's side. "Luckily, Stefano's not the jealous type. At least that's what he told me."

"No," Mark exaggerated. "Not at all. And luckily, I'm not the petty type who uses that to my advantage."

"Me neither." I smiled as he addressed May and Will.

"I better get to the kitchen," he laughed. "Nice to meet you Will, and I'm sorry again."

"For what?"

"That you're related to her," he teased, rolling his eyes at May as he walked away.

"He's damn lucky, and he knows it," she laughed.

I saw Gavin across the yard talking with Dan, and he must have felt me staring because he glanced up, smiling when his eyes met mine and gesturing me over. But Luca and Sofia suddenly blocked my view, Luca stepping right in front of me to pick up Nora while Vinny, in turn, reached up for me. "I'll be right back!" I swerved around Luca and Sofia, making my way to Gavin, but my parents stepped in front of me, blocking me once more, babbling away to Vinny.

"Come to Grandma." Mom clapped, sending Vinny lunging for her.

"I've got to get to Gavin, but Nora's with Luca if you want to grab her too."

"She's with him!" Mom bellowed, horror flooding her eyes. "But his language!"

Dad instantly stormed off, walking right up to Luca with his arms outstretched for Nora, but Luca just looked down at him, shaking his head no. Dad was no match for Luca, who towered over him, so he turned away, walking back defeated, grumbling under his breath.

"Sorry," I apologized. "He's very protective of her. She's his daughter, too."

My parents' eyes rolled in slow motion to mine, horror taking over their faces... oh... "Shit!" Fuck. "I, mean, no, no!" Why! I was constantly slamming my head against a wall with them. "Not actually his daughter, he just acts like she is." Oh, forget it! I smiled politely before darting over to Gavin, letting his strong arm wrap over me.

He chuckled. "How's it going?"

"Well, my parents are probably never coming back!" Oh, shit, again. Wrong choice of words. "I meant, oh, forget it." I wiggled out of his grip, heading straight for the alcohol, pouring myself a double helping of wine.

"Easy girl!" May bumped my hips. "It's only noon!" She stood in front of the table, hand roaming over the bottles.

"Only?" I groaned dramatically.

Luca's arm suddenly shot in front of May, obnoxiously pushing past her, making her stumble back as he reached for a drink. "Excuse me!" she snapped. "I don't care how fine your ass is, you will use manners like all the other civilized people here and say excuse me."

"Huh," he muttered like a caveman, arm retreating. She smacked her hips against him, knocking him out of the way. "Fine, excuse me," he huffed, throwing his hand up, looking all put-out.

"I'm picking out my drink. You can wait." She turned her back to him, blocking his access to the table, giving me a smile as she slowly mulled over the drink selection. She finally turned on her heels, giving Luca some side-eye before walking back to Mark.

He reached blindly for a soda, huffing and puffing his way back to the family.

"Need a refill, Baby?" Gavin's arm swooped over my shoulders, curling me into his side with a kiss.

I looked down at the full glass I had just poured, which was somehow already empty. "Please!" I raised my glass.

"So," he whispered, looking around before continuing. "Danica's moving in with Grant this summer."

Danica's moving... I wriggled out of his grip, tipping my face up to his. "What!"

"Dan said she's leaving the dorms and moving in with him. Apparently, they're pretty serious."

He was moving in with her? They were in college! This was too serious. Moving in! "He's too young!"

"He's a senior, Baby. He's gonna be twenty-one." He shrugged like it was no big deal.

"Exactly! Way too young to be so serious! And way too young to be living with her!" He was still in college. He needed to live his life before settling down. I looked up at Gavin, his pursed lips and wide eyes meeting mine.

"I was a senior too, Baby."

"Shit, that's right." I shook my empty glass, desperately needing more. "We're horrible role models!"

His face panned around our yard, our house, then over to the babies. "I'd beg to differ," he countered.

"That's not—" Forget it.

"This party is beautiful!" Giorgia stepped up; her arm hooked with Laurence's. "Purple is growing on me."

"You're empty," Laurence said, eying my glass. "Want me to get you a drink?"

Gavin immediately blocked Laurence, handing me water instead. "Come on, Baby. Time for cake." He pulled my arm, giving me a good yank. "I can't believe he's still trying to give you drinks."

"You still remember that?" Only Gavin.

"Like I could fucking forget."

I stopped him, taking his hands in mine, pressing up on my tiptoes to give him a kiss. "I'll grab the plates while you round up the twins and get them in the high chairs," I instructed, handing him back the water. "Let's sing happy birthday to our babies!" I rushed inside, beelining for the garage door, swinging it open. "Oh my god!" My eyes! I wanted to look away. I couldn't. My feet were frozen in place, my eyes locked on a shirtless May straddling Luca on Gavin's bench. "Oh, my, god!" They both looked over, chests heaving. "Luca, no! She's my friend! Why?"

He grinned over. "I'm going for a two-night stand. Like you told me."

What was wrong with him. "No, this, no! Not what I meant." Not her, not my garage, not on Gavin's bench. Good lord. I couldn't deal with this right now. "You've got this May? You can handle this?" I averted my eyes, desperately trying to erase the image of his hands firmly gripping her ass through her jeans.

"Oh yeah," she boomed. "I'm gonna handle this."

Oh god. I stepped back, letting the door slam in front of me. We would make do without the plates.

"Baby!" Gavin called over from the kitchen, and I slowly turned to face him. "You get the plates?"

"Wine!" I willed my legs to move. "I need more wine."

FIRST BIRTHDAY: 2

Nora and Vinny sat in their high chairs, batting at the purple and blue balloons tied to them. Where had the time gone? How were my babies already one?

Everyone gathered around, waiting as Gavin placed a mini cake on each of their trays. Then he stepped away, arms engulfing me as the cheers rang out.

"Happy Birthday," Grant started the song, everyone joined in, singing to the twins, who were laughing at the show in front of them. I opened my mouth to sing, getting a rush of tears instead. It was too bittersweet. Time was moving too fast. I leaned into Gavin's arm, discreetly wiping away the wetness.

"You okay, Baby?" His whisper hit my ear.

More than okay. "Thank you," I whispered back.

"For what?"

"For them. I can't imagine not having this love. Thank you for giving me what I never knew I needed."

He pressed a kiss to my hair while we watched Nora lick the frosting from her finger, smiling immediately and smashing her face right into the cake. She proudly looked up, smiling with frosting smeared all over her cheeks. "She's definitely your daughter," Gavin chuckled.

"Yeah, she is." Except she was looking more and more like Gavin every day. She had his brown eyes, so dark they looked black, and that same thick, jet-black hair.

I looked to Vinny beside her, his matching dark eyes appraising the cake, his finger hovering right above but not yet touching it. He looked over at his sister, a giggle immediately escaping his lips as he watched her. He might have Gavin's eyes and hair like Nora did, but he had my smile.

"Piccolo!" Gavin started for Vinny, and I knew what he was going to do.

"Gavin!" I tried to warn him.

"Provare la torta, Piccolo," he insisted, stepping up to Vinny's high chair and pushing Vinny's hand right into the cake. "Try the cake, Piccolo."

Oh, no. Vinny looked up at Gavin, eyes growing wider, lips quivering, a cry shooting from his mouth to match the tears. Gavin dove down, rubbing Vinny's back, trying to calm him. "No, no, Piccolo. Papà's sorry, shit!" His eyes flashed to mine for help.

I walked over, leaning down, pressing a kiss to Vinny's forehead as I pushed my hand into his cake too, showing Vinny my matching frosting covered fingers, laughing and wiggling them at him before smashing my fingers to his. "Squishy!" I made a funny face, making him laugh, his tears instantly drying up. Then he poked his finger back in the cake, all smiles as he played. "You can't push him, Papà," I whispered to Gavin hovering over us. "He has to do it on his own time." I straightened up, reaching my hand to Gavin's face, rubbing some of the frosting over his nose.

"He's definitely your son," he laughed, simultaneously letting out a sigh of relief.

"Yes, he is!" I smiled down at Vinny as Gavin crouched down beside him, smashing his own hand in the cake and pressing it to Vinny's hand, both of them cracking up.

"Pahpah," Vinny laughed, and now it was Gavin's eyes going wide, lips starting to quiver, tears brimming.

"That's right," Gavin choked out, blinking back the tears as he pressed a kiss to Vinny's hair. "Papà loves you so much, Piccolo." He stepped away, letting everyone get their photos while pulling me aside. "He called me, Papà," he sniffled.

"Yeah," I laughed, wiping one of his tears away. "That's what we call you."

"We say it, Baby. I've never heard my child say it. He knows I'm his papà. He said my name."

I kept laughing. "You've got a thing for people saying your name," I teased, swinging my arms around his back meeting his big grin. "They love you, Pahpah. We all love you, Pahpah." His face lit up, reveling before leading me back to the babies.

"Dad," I called over to my parents while grabbing the smashed cakes from the babies' trays. "Will you grab the wipes off the kitchen counter?"

"Sure, Honey," he replied casually, making me almost drop the cakes. He hadn't called me that since I was sixteen. After I had Grant, I was just, Sadie. I steadied myself, following in behind him, dropping the destroyed cakes into the trash while he grabbed the wipes. Then he stopped, turning around to face me. "You know Vinny's already got quite a swing. I think he might be a natural golfer."

At the age of one... "Oh yeah." I wanted to smile and cry at the same time. All these years as strangers, so much resentment, and now, maybe, we were finally healing.

"Maybe on our next trip out, we can take the kids to the golf course. Nora might like it too, and Grant says he's up for learning. Gavin could help teach them."

Next trip? As a family... "You want to teach all three kids how to golf? With Gavin?" I repeated; he nodded yes. He wanted to spend time with all my children and my husband. "I think that'd be great."

"Someone say golf!" Luca shouted, charging into the kitchen with a way too happy smirk. "I'm pretty damn good, won a few tournaments. You golf?"

Dad looked Luca over before turning back towards the door. "No, I don't." He walked outside, while my laughter hit so hard it brought tears.

Luca rolled his eyes, tossing an arm over my shoulders, making me laugh even harder. "Any more hot friends I should know about?"

"Eww, and no!" I laughed, shoving him away. "All my good friends have already hooked up with a Romano!"

"What?" He chuckled back. "Who else?"

Oh shit! I automatically focused on Mark outside, and Stefano who was standing a little too close to him.

"That guy!" Luca groaned, following the stare I didn't realize was so obvious. "Fuck. I recognize him! Giorgia fucking hook up with him? I'll fucking kill him!" He puffed his chest, glaring at Mark.

"No, no!" I assured him, feeling the weight of his flexed, angry arm over me.

Gavin was suddenly there, stepping to his side. "Giù le mani da mia moglie!" he spat out. "Hands off!"

"Rilassati, Fratellino." Luca rolled his eyes yet again. "I was just telling Sadie how much I like her friends." He dropped his arm, strutting back out to the backyard while Gavin swung his arm around my back.

"What was that about?" he asked, voice still edgy.

"Nothing," I started to laugh. "But you should order a new workout bench."

"Huh?" His nose scrunched, waiting for clarification that I was not about to go into right now. Then his face relaxed, a smile forming. "He called me, Papà."

"He called me, Honey."

"What!" he yelled, pulling his face away.

"My dad!" I laughed even harder. "Not Luca. He hasn't called me that since I was a teenager."

He pressed a kiss to the tip of my nose, then we were hand in hand, heading out to the backyard. Sofia had already cleaned up Vinny, so Gavin lifted him into his arms as Mom finished cleaning up Nora, and the second she was done, Stefano picked her up.

I walked to the back of the yard, sitting on the bench, taking everything in, especially my husband holding our baby. He had the widest smile on his face, babbling down to Vinny wrapped up in his flexed arm. Two years ago, he was slamming me up against the glass in Vegas, last year, he was by my side in the hospital, and now he was here, looking sexier than he ever had.

"Hey!" Mark blocked my view, sinking beside me. "He's good with them."

"Gavin or Stefano?" I asked, the two of us staring at the guys. Stefano was at Gavin's side with Nora, laughing with her too.

"Both," he sighed, smiling.

"What's going on?" Now, it was May squeezing down next to us, following our gaze to Gavin and Stefano, and Luca walking over to join them.

"It's getting hot." I couldn't take my eyes off Gavin's sexy smile, or his biceps, or any of him.

"Sweltering," Mark added, stare locked on Stefano.

"Burning up," May gasped, adjusting her shirt.

"Think I need a tall drink of water to cool me down," Mark teased, glancing at the two of us.

"Maybe some ice cream." I smiled to myself, picturing Gavin's tongue.

Then May turned her hungry eyes back on Luca. "Nah, I like it hot."

FIRST BIRTHDAY: 3

"Babies are asleep!" I announced, shuffling down the stairs to an awaiting Gavin.

"And everyone's almost gone except for my family and a few of your friends." He reached for my hands. "Which means it'll just be you and me tonight."

"And your family," I reminded him. "They're coming back for dinner."

"Fuck," he grumbled. "They're always here."

"Tell me about it!" I teased, and he lowered his face, lips brushing mine.

"Today was incredible, Baby, and there was no drama with our families."

"Jesus Christ!" Luca roared, instantly causing Gavin to pull away. "Are you two always fucking on each other?"

I rolled my eyes at Luca, seeing May and Will coming up behind him, then squeezing past him.

"Speaking of which," Luca spoke to her now. "I'm here another night."

May stopped in the doorway, turning to look back at him. "Okay, anything for the boss."

Oh, god. "Boss," I laughed under my breath.

Mark then walked up behind them, following May to the door, Stefano, of course, lingering back next to Luca. Then May threw her arm over Mark's shoulders, whirling him back to face us. "We all work in the Romano wing," she sassed, giving me a cheesy wink. "And we're all sleeping with a Romano!"

Oh, god... Oh, shit! I whipped my head up to see Luca's face, his smile turning flat. Then I looked at Stefano, the panic raging across his face.

"You slept with my fucking sister!" Luca spat, taking a step towards Mark. "I fucking knew it!"

"Your sister?" May started away, leaving Mark alone at the door. "Your brother!" she yelled back.

Stefano bolted forward, smacking his palm against the front door, sending it slamming in Mark's face.

"Stefano!" I screamed, hearing and feeling the boom.

"Oh fuck," he bellowed, eyes flashing from the door to Luca and Gavin, his face twisting in panic the same way Gavin's did. Then he took off, storming down the hall.

"What the fuck was that about!" Luca yelled, sharp and deadly.

"Excuse me," I whispered, squeezing out the door to catch Mark, who was almost to his car. "Mark!" I darted across the street to get to him. "I'm so sorry!"

"Yeah, I didn't see that coming," he muttered, resting his back against his door. "May outing us, or the door in my face."

"It was going to happen sooner or later, the outing, not the door. He can't hide you forever."

"It's complicated, Sadie. Trust me, I don't like doors being slammed in my face or having to stay ten feet away from him when his family's around, but Stefano's been closed away for years. He works everything up in his head."

That I understood. Gavin was the same way, getting lost in his head, always imagining the worst. "Do you want to stay?"

"No. He has to work this out on his own. The bandage has been ripped, so hopefully, he just yanks it off."

"I don't know why this is such a big deal." Stefano was in his mid-thirties; his family loved him.

"Sadie, you remember how it was when we were growing up; it wasn't like how it is now. He grew up surrounded by guys like Luca. He's still surrounded by guys like Luca."

And jerks like Adam.

"He was raised in a devout Catholic home, full of pride, superstitions, reputation, ego's galore. He's never been in a relationship before, ever."

This was the softer side of Mark I hardly ever saw. "Old Mark used to be feistier." I elbowed his side, teasing him.

"Old Mark had never cared for anyone the way he does now. Despite *that*—" he waved towards the house. "Stefano has a heart of gold. He's really special."

"I think that door hit you a little too hard," I teased. But I understood what he was saying. Gavin was complicated too, but special. "I know he's a good one."

He let out a heavy sigh. "Text me later, fill me in on the drama, and let Stefano know I was incredibly mad, and I'm rethinking everything. Oh, and that Will was here to comfort me."

"Welcome back, Mark!"

He laughed, pulling his door open and sinking into the driver's seat. "Hey— " he started the engine, talking out the window. "What did May mean by, we're all sleeping with the bosses? Who is May sleeping with?"

"Use your imagination." I waved goodbye, watching him speed away, just as a car pulled up to the curb, and Luca charged out the front door, stampeding down the grass, ripping the car door open, and immediately taking off. What? I walked back to the house, pushing through the door, jumping out of the way of a now charging Stefano, flying out the front door like a wild bull.

"Gavin?" I continued down the hall, spotting his sisters and Laurence outside, so I opened the door to meet them.

"Sadie! This sunset is gorgeous!" Giorgia gushed. "I'd be out here every night watching it."

"It's so peaceful," Sofia sighed, taking a sip of her wine.

What the hell was happening! I looked back in the house, seeing Gavin pacing the hall inside. "I'll be right back." I excused myself, squeezing back through the door, closing it behind me. "What's going on?"

He tossed his hands up. "Luca and Stefano got into it, then Luca took off, then Stefano."

"Meanwhile, your sisters are drunk and cooing over the peaceful sunset in the backyard. Totally oblivious."

"Good," he huffed. "I'm glad they didn't hear that shit."

"Does Luca know now?"

He shrugged. "They were screaming in the garage. I couldn't hear what they were saying."

The back door screeched open with Giorgia, Laurence, and Sofia all walking back in, smiling away. "The car is on its way," Sofia said. "We'll be back in a few hours for dinner."

"Where are the guys?" Giorgia asked, straining her neck to search the house.

"They, left, to, get ready, for, d-dinner," I stammered as they continued to the door, Gavin closing it behind them.

I walked over, hugging him. "So much for no drama. Do you think Luca will come back for dinner?"

"Don't know. What should I order for dinner, Baby?"

"Wine. We need more wine."

It'd been hours, the sun had set, and still no word from either brother. Gavin had been pacing, phone to his ear, then typing, trying to find Luca, and trying to get a hold of Stefano. He couldn't handle any uncertainty, any rifts, he needed everything to be okay. I zoomed a car to Vinny just as Gavin walked back into the family room, dropping to the floor beside me, dipping his head back against the couch. "I'm guessing Luca still hasn't answered."

He squeezed his eyes shut while Nora crawled onto his lap, resting her head on his chest, his hand rising to her back. "Nope," he mumbled. Gavin was dealing with this, his parents, and the twins' first birthday. He was a six-foot storm about to crash.

"I'll go to the hotel and see if he's there." I knew that's where he would be, the bar specifically.

He rolled his face over, shaking his head no. "You're not going to the hotel to find Luca."

I stretched my hand to his, squeezing his fingers. "He'll talk to me. You wait here for your family and try to get Stefano over. I'll find Luca."

"No, Baby," his voice was just as strained as his face.

"Trust me!" I insisted. He knew Luca would talk to me and that I was our best chance at bringing him home.

He groaned, shrugging, okay. "But, Baby. Don't get in his face if he's pissed off or if he's drunk. *Trust me*."

"Okay." I kissed him on my way up, making my way to the front, grabbing my purse on the way to my car.

I drove the familiar route, pulling up to the hotel valet, hearing the beep from the message on my phone, Gavin had sent Luca's room number. But I knew where he'd be, and it wasn't his room. I continued through the lobby to the bar, scanning the tables and chairs, finally seeing the wave of black hair and broad figure at the end of the bar. "This seat taken?" I sat on the stool beside him, hearing the disappointed grumbles from the women eying him.

"Go home, Sadie." He twisted his face over, dark eyes sliding to meet mine as he pushed a beer bottle to his lips.

"Let's get out of here." I gestured him up. "Go walk on the beach. You shouldn't be drinking anyway."

"With my fucked up heart?" He chuckled darkly. "This is only my second." He pushed the beer back to his lips, guzzling it before setting it onto the bar and standing from the stool. "After you."

I led him out and to the automatic doors that opened to the boardwalk, following the moonlight to the water. I veered off the walkway to the beach. "This is better. Sit!" I insisted, lowering to the sand, patting next to me.

He obliged, sinking to the sand. "I'm an asshole." He snapped up a rock, chucking it into the night sky. "Gav, Giorgia, now Stefano."

"Giorgia?" What did he do to her?

"You too," he grumbled, ignoring me.

"You *used* to be an asshole." I looked over, but his stare was on the waves ahead. "But you're not anymore."

He laughed to himself. "I'm the head of this fucking family, and all I've done is fuck them up." He chucked another rock at the water. "Gav's fucked up because of the shit I did and didn't do. Giorgia broke up with Laurence because I fucking told her to." He turned to face me, his dark eyes soft under the moonlight. "I didn't realize what I was fucking doing. My own heart was so sick of my shit that it gave up on me," he chuckled. "And you had to save me, you don't know the fucking irony. Then you make me godfather to the twins." He kicked his feet into the sand, shaking his head with a stifled laugh.

"Gavin's okay," I dug for a stone, tossing it towards the water. "Giorgia's back with Laurence. All is well. Stefano, I'm not sure about. Why did you storm out earlier? What happened with him?"

He stared ahead. "Did you know?"

"Yes," I answered truthfully.

"Ever been in a fight? Where the guy throws the first punch, catching you off guard, throws you into a fucking freefall, a panic, fight or flight, and you start pummeling without a second thought? That's what it felt like. How was I supposed to take that fucking news? We're closer than brothers, he's my migliore amico, best friend. He sits at my side at work, meetings, bars, strip clubs. I've seen him with chicks, heard him with chicks, fuck, at least I thought I had. And he fucking hits me with this—he's with a fucking guy. I never thought, never thought my fratello was a fucking—" he chucked another stone. "We got into it. He brought our mamma into it. I, fuck, I overreacted. I said fucked up shit. Told him I disowned him, my own fratello."

I could only imagine. All three of the brothers reacted on impulse, no control whatsoever, and they used words like swords, in Luca's case punches. "I understand shock, and a Romano overreacting isn't that much of a surprise." I stood up, he followed, the two of us walking down the sand. "I bet he's hurting right now, and as you've said, you only have each other."

"I know, but I got fucking railroaded. There's so much shit I have to handle now. Starting with Stefano."

"What does that mean?"

"He's been fucking hiding for years because he thought I'd disown him and not protect him, and I did exactly that. Like I said before, I'm the head of this fucking family and all I've done is fuck them up."

"So remedy it." I swiveled my feet in the sand, turning back towards the hotel. "It's okay to apologize. Stefano needs your affirmation; they all do."

"They don't need my affirmation."

"Of course they do. They need you. Don't act like you don't know that and use it to your advantage."

"Do the girls know?"

"I don't think so, but I know they'll look to you for your reaction first."

"Gavin?"

I nodded yes.

"He told Gav before me? How'd Gav take it?"

"He already knew, one less guy that he doesn't have to worry about hitting on me.

He grunted under his breath. "My fratello is in love with a fucking dude. What a trip."

"It might take some getting used to." I stepped in front of him, searching in the dark to find his eyes. "Just like it did for Grant when I told him his new dad was only four years older than him."

He laughed. "Fuck!" He tipped his head up to the starry sky. "When did this famiglia become such a fucking soap opera?"

"I don't know." I playfully bumped him as we walked. "Maybe they'll write about us one day."

"So, what are you doing here? Came to tell me what to do next? Yell at me?"

"No, I came because I was tired of changing diapers," I laughed.

"Gav, let you come alone? He knows where you are?"

"He's worried. He doesn't know what's going on. Gavin doesn't like when things break."

He swung his arm over my shoulder, still laughing as we stepped onto the boardwalk, heading into the hotel. "Can we fuck with him? Send him one text, tell him—"

"No!" I yelled, elbowing his side. "I'm not about to have him storming the lobby with the double stroller."

We both started laughing, so hard tears streamed down our faces. "It's time for dinner," I laughed one last time, wiping my cheeks dry. "The family's waiting."

"I'm not sure I'm ready to accept it."

"Stefano or Mark?" I asked, focusing back on him.

"Laurence." He met my eyes, wry smile widening. "He's a fucking Mets fan. That shit's unforgivable, cardinal sin."

I rolled my eyes, laughing under my breath. "Romano," I called to the valet.

Luca smiled sincerely now. "I think you were meant to be a Romano."

GAVIN'S 25th BIRTHDAY: 1

"Happy Birthday, love," I whispered, rolling next to my sleeping husband, who was finally a quarter-century old! Twenty-five, which was basically thirty. I slid under the sheets, feeling him stirring. No boxers, lucky me. I ran my hand over his morning wood, sinking my lips over his tip. God, he tasted good. I slathered his dick, lapping him up, lips spreading wide, sucking him in, exhales steaming under the sheet, starting his birthday right.

He arched his hips, jabbing inside my mouth, filling me cheek to cheek. I sped up, working my tongue with my lips. I liked waking up to this too. A hand hit my hair, the covers being ripped away. "Ohh, fuck, Baby!" His stare was on me, watching me devour him. "Fuck!" His eyes rolled back, hips arching as he came, coating my mouth. "Fuck, I've missed that."

I pressed a final kiss to his tip before looking up at his very satisfied grin. "Happy birthday!"

He had a lazy, satisfied grin. "How about we stay in bed all day?" He kept that sexy stare locked on me while I rested my chin against his thigh.

"And the babies would go where?" Maybe now he'd reconsider a babysitter. "I thought we could drive up to the mission today, and then, Mamma has a very special night planned for Papà."

"Special night?" His semi-hard length hardened right back up. And my face was once again an inch from his hard-on.

"He's happy this morning."

"He's not used to your mouth being so close."

"How about we go to the mirror? I want to see how much you've aged."

He slid his legs over the edge of the bed, but I hopped from the sheets, jumping in front of him, giggling as he chased me. "I've missed this too, Baby." His warm breath hit my neck; his chest hit my back, his erection hit my ass. "This is a great way to wake up."

Yeah, it was how we always woke up. "We have sex every morning." My laugh turned to a gasp, feeling and watching his fingers slide over my hips, snaking up my stomach, greedy hands clutching my breasts.

He dropped his face to the crook of my neck, nuzzling his lips into my morning hair. "Bend over, Baby."

Yes! I smacked my palms to the counter, arched back, grinding into his arousal, staring at his sexy hair stuck up in every direction, his chest and arms flexed, and deep, dark eyes analyzing every inch of my body. "You look older."

"Baby, I told you—age doesn't mean shit!" He rocked, shoving right inside me, no warm-up, no fingers.

"Fuck!" I gripped the counter, nails instinctively trying to claw into it, my insides churning, the burn consuming me. Then I was empty. He was out, hands on my waist, flipping me to face him, lifting me, slamming me back against the wall.

"I wanna kiss you, Baby." His lips smashed mine, hard and hungry, his body pinning me to the wall, revving my back against it. I was up, I was down—filled to the brim, the breaking point, my gasps suffocating as he pounded in and out.

My hands were in his hair, our kiss just as hard as he was fucking, our tongues colliding, melding as one. The heat too much for me. "Gavin!"

"Fuck!" His hands clasped the back of my head, pulling me in deeper, our mouths one, not even the tiniest space between us.

Each kiss, each thrust, each heavy pant growing faster, sloppier. He finally hit the target, the pressure exploding. "Oh, god! There!" I yelped, heat instant, a cloud engulfing me.

"Fuuck!" His groan filled my mouth, his body slowing, a few last rocks to finish him off. "I could kiss you forever, Baby."

"I hope you do." I tried to catch my breath, holding him tight as he lowered me down to the floor. Then I wobbled to the counter, holding it while the shakes subsided. "Are Nora's shoes still in the car?" I breathed up to him, his brows immediately furrowing.

He shook his head. "I think they're in my car, Baby, and remember we used the last of the diapers, so you need to repack the diaper bag." He walked over, wrapping me up again.

"Shoot!" I danced my hands up his arms. "I forgot to order them."

"We can stop by the store."

"Good idea." I smiled up at him, finally regaining my strength. "Do you want to get the babies while I shower? Or do you want to shower first?"

"Hmm?" His devilish grin weaseled its way up as his fingers tickled my stomach. "Shower together?"

"I think the twins are awake." I looked towards the monitor on the table.

"They're in their cribs." His fingers continued to my breasts. "They're not going anywhere."

Round three? This man! He was getting older, and his stamina was getting stronger. "It's your birthday. Your wish is my command."

"Oh really." He dropped his hands, stepping back to the shower, popping the door open. "I have a few wishes."

"Pahpah!" Vinny's voice rang from the monitor, causing Gavin to immediately let go of the door. "PAHPAH!" he called again, sending Gavin rushing out, tripping to get into his flannel pants.

"They're in their cribs," I repeated his words, laughing. "They're not going anywhere."

Gavin looked from me to the monitor. "Papà's coming, Piccolo!"

GAVIN'S 25th BIRTHDAY: 2

We hadn't made this drive in a while. The last time we were here, he was down on bended knee, asking me to marry him. My hands crept to my ears, rubbing over each of the swallow earrings. I hadn't taken them out since I opened them the night before our wedding. We were these two birds. No matter what came between us, we always found our way back home to the other.

"Are you crying?" Gavin parked, glancing over at me while he elbowed his door open.

"No," I answered automatically, only to then feel my wet cheek. "We have good memories here. Our first real date, you proposing."

His smile turned mischievous real fast. "I have good memories here too, Baby. Especially in this parking lot."

"Stop!" I shoved him out his door, but he sprang back, smacking me with a kiss.

"You know," he growled. "It is my birthday."

"We're not alone anymore, Mr. Romano." I twisted my face back, meeting the two smiley faces behind us.

We both stepped out, grabbing a baby, loading them into the stroller. I took my place beside Gavin, draping my arm over his back as he pushed the stroller onto the grounds, heading straight for our fountain. We lifted the twins out of the stroller, letting them toddle around and chase the butterflies.

"Last time we were here, I was proposing, right?" He sank onto the carved-out bench in the fountain, hand out for mine, pulling me to his lap.

"This exact spot." I nestled my head back against him while he wrapped his arms over me, both of us watching Nora and Vinny playing and giggling.

"Piccolina, Piccolo," Gavin called. "Vieni da, Papà!"

The babies ran right over to us, crawling on our laps. "A picture," he said, stretching his arm towards the sky, phone on us. "Sorridi, smile!" He laughed as I kissed his cheek.

The babies crawled back down, toddling off, hands up to catch the giant butterflies fluttering above them. Who would have thought we'd be here today, all of us. A train whistled in the distance, the babies and me looking back in its direction. "Want to take the twins to see the train?"

He was the only one not looking back, wouldn't even meet my eyes now. "No," he mumbled, shaking his head. "I'd rather keep it to good memories today, Baby. Not the shitty ones."

The flashes of that day came back, the fight, him taking off to New York, the earthquake. "Okay."

He reached for my ear, tracing the tiny swallow earring just as I had earlier. "I love you, Baby."

"I love you, too." I stood from his lap, tugging him up too. "We have some babies to chase!"

We chased the twins, we chased butterflies, we stole kisses every few minutes in between, and we shared our spot with our babies. And when the sun started to set, we loaded the kids into the car and drove off hand in hand. Today was an amazing day; tonight would be even better.

Gavin had gone upstairs to shower once we got home, giving me just enough time to set up the cake. "It's time to sing Happy Birthday to Papà!" I cheered to the babies, herding them into the kitchen. "Papà!" I heard the heavy footsteps shuffle down the stairs, down the hall, then that handsome smile as he walked to us at the kitchen table. "Ready," I encouraged the twins. "Happy birthday to you," I started singing, bending down between the kids, trying to get them to sing along. "Happy birthday, dear Papà, happy birthday to you."

He flashed his eyes behind us to the chocolate cake, his sweet smile turning sinister. "Yum, this for now or later?"

"Both, Papà," I teased back.

"Bedtime babies!" he roared, scooping Nora right up then pushing past me to grab Vinny.

"It's a little early," I laughed, chasing after the wild-eyed monster stealing my kids away. "They didn't even get a piece of cake."

He swung his face back, eyes black as coal. "They can have some tomorrow! It's late; they're yawning anyway, and, it's my birthday. My wish is your command, right?" He winked before continuing down the hall with Nora and Vinny in his arms. Good thing I'd already fed them dinner.

"Fine," I laughed. "Since, it is your *thirty-fifth* birthday."

He looked back over his shoulder, rolling his eyes dramatically. "Only your Mamma." He chuckled to the babies. "Papà needs to teach her yet another lesson about age."

Teach me, huh? I listened to his footsteps up the stairs, waiting until I heard the nursery door close, then I rushed up the stairs myself, sneaking into our room. I raced to the closet, digging out my new lingerie. I bought it just for tonight. It was different, but something told me he'd love it. I held up the black patent leather straps, by far the sexiest piece I'd ever put on.

I was quick, tearing my clothes off and finagling the X-straps over my breasts, barely covering my nipples. Holy hell! I tightened the two thin straps that crisscrossed over my stomach, connecting to the patent leather thong. Then I ripped the ponytail band from my hair, shaking it out into loose waves as I stepped into my stilettos. Good lord! I looked like I should be holding a whip or dancing on a stage. Well almost. I hurried to my vanity, blushing from my own reflection while searching for the red lipstick, slapping it on with a heavy hand. Now I really looked like I should be holding a whip or dancing on stage.

I started for the door, cracking it open, hearing him still in the nursery, so I snuck out and down the stairs, straight to the kitchen for the cake, then back down the hall to his office. Now what? I flipped the light on, illuminating his office, making sure I'd be in full view. I hopped up onto his desk, setting the cake beside me, then crossing my legs seductively towards the door, waiting.

His footsteps hit the stairs, growing louder, closer. He was almost here. His arm swung through the doorway first, smacking around to find the light switch before stepping inside, finding me. His arm hung suspended in mid-air, his jaw dropped, mouth agape, eyes widening as they ran over me- stilettos to red lips.

"Sadie?" he choked out, still not moving a muscle.

"Gavin?" I flirted back, watching his emotionless face, and his eyes running laps over me.

"Did, I, I fall? Hit my h-head?" he stammered, arm still hanging in the air. "Um, fuck, am I, am I fucking high?"

"I don't think so." I uncrossed my legs, spreading them so he had a better view.

He clamped his jaw shut, his arm finally dropping to his side. "Fuck, weren't you just in the kitchen, jeans. How the fuck did you get—" he parted his lips again, his eyes studying my body. "My desk."

I scooted to the edge, spreading my legs even further, arching back, breasts bulging out the sides of the straps. "You said you needed to teach me a lesson, aren't desks where lessons get taught?"

His mouth was moving, but nothing was coming out. "Fuck," he finally muttered.

I slid off the wood, stilettos clanking against the floor. "I thought you'd be a little more excited." I stepped closer, eyes on his. "I wanted to give you a very, happy birthday. Your wish is my command, remember?"

"I'm, uh, I'm processing." His voice was low, husky. "This shit's intense."

I took another step, but he moved back. "Back to my desk, Sadie."

There he was. I turned on my heels, tracing his desktop with my fingers.

"How the fuck am I supposed to work in here now?"

"Tonight." I ran my finger across the cake, pushing the frosting to my lips. "I can be the one who works."

"Holy fuck!" He charged, mouth attacking mine, licking the chocolate from my lips.

I twisted away, palms to his chest, pushing him down into his chair, meeting his eyes, blacker than they'd ever been. "What lesson would you like to teach me first, Mr. Romano?"

NEW YORK: 1

"Delayed!" Gavin groaned, huffing and puffing behind me while I pushed the stroller past airport security. He'd been an ass all week, his nerves about this trip consuming him, until I'd finally lost my temper last night, screaming and locking him out of our room. I hated fighting with him, but sometimes he was just too far gone to see reason and needed a hypothetical slap in the face. And he was still so anxious, the sun had barely risen, the twins and I were still yawning, and the last thing I needed right now was Gavin's rage.

"It'll be fine," I assured him, reminding myself that he'd calm down once we were in the air. I took a seat in one of the chairs at our gate, pulling the stroller to my side while Gavin sat down next to me, immediately pulling out his phone, scrolling to the weather.

"No snow," he sighed, tapping his foot against the floor.

"Gavin, breathe!" I pressed my hand over his shaky knee, stopping his rattling. "We're only going to be there a couple of days; everything will be okay."

"I know, Baby. I know." He stretched his hand to my neck, adjusting the cornicello. "Put up with me, please."

My gentle giant had such a worry-filled heart. "Focus on Giorgia's wedding. Your family, friends. It'll be great."

"No, Vinyee!" Nora yelled. "Mine!"

"Vinny!" I shook my head no, and he handed the toy car back to her. They had a month and a half until their second birthday but the terrible twos were already here.

"Now boarding First Class for flight Two-twenty-eight to New York," the speaker announced over us.

I stood; Gavin followed, tense face and all. "Hey," I whispered, tugging his shirt for him to lean down. "Want to meet me in the lavatory or ask for an extra blanket?"

He finally cracked a smile, releasing the tension in his face. "Very funny."

"Sorry I can't help you *release* your stress this time," I teased once more, bumping into his side while we started towards the gate.

"Me too, Baby."

We walked down the bridge to the plane, unloading the stroller and placing Nora on my side and Vinny on his. It was the first time we had an aisle between us.

The doors finally closed, the plane rolling towards the runway. Here we go. I stretched my arm across the aisle, meeting Gavin's hand, squeezing it in mine before letting go, only his fingers locked, not letting me leave. "I love you, Baby," he whispered, letting me go.

I reached for Nora's hand next, rubbing her little arm, watching her sleepy eyes grow heavy, and by the time we hit cruising altitude, she was passed out. I rifled through the seatback pocket, pulling out a magazine, starting to flip through it.

"Hey," Gavin whispered.

I looked over, admiring his sexy eyes and handsome face. "Hi."

"You look really good," he continued whispering.

Good? I was in leggings. Only Gavin. "Sorry," I teased him. "I'm married." I wiggled my ring finger, sliding the bands up to flash him his name. "Although my husband *has* been an ass lately."

He chuckled, dropping his head back against the seat. "I'm sorry, Baby. Glad that ink's permanent, you're stuck with me."

I met his eyes again, the black fading to a dark brown. His moods were so volatile, one minute raging, the next laughing. And we were heading to a place that made his passion that much more intense. "I don't want to see asshole Gavin in New York, okay?"

He shook his head no. "You won't!" He reached over for my hand, but I held it back.

I tried to hide my smile. "Because Giorgia said there are lots of kind, well-behaved, single groomsmen."

He rolled his eyes, chuckling to himself, that devilish grin curling up his face. "That's okay. My girl's not into well-behaved."

"Uh, huh," I laughed, reaching my hand for his now. "No, she's not."

He kissed my knuckles before releasing my hand, and I tucked the magazine away, closing my eyes for a second.

Something hit my cheek, then my chest... stirring me. I peeled one eyelid open, getting hit with something again. What was happening? I pushed my hand to my forehead, grabbing the wet pretzel that smacked into it.

"Mamma, more," Nora giggled beside me, waving a pretzel in her hand.

"She's been throwing those at you for like ten minutes!" Gavin chuckled behind me.

I rolled my face over, meeting his and Vinny's smiles. Then I looked back at Nora. "No thanks, baby girl." Only another hit my hair, a half-eaten one. Gross.

I was suddenly hit with another, only this time it came from across the aisle, so I turned back around to Gavin's mischievous face. My husband used to fuck me on these flights, and now he threw pretzels at me.

He chuckled again. "Whatcha thinking about, Baby?"

"Well behaved men," I teased. "How long was I asleep?"

"You two were out a while. My girls were tired."

"Ladies and Gentleman," the speaker roared above us. "This is your Captain speaking. We'll be arriving at JFK shortly."

"Quite a while," I laughed back over to Gavin. I slept the entire flight. "So, are you ready for New York?"

He studied me, eyes lost on something. "I don't think I'm ever ready."

NEW YORK: 2

I clasped the ruby necklace around my neck, draping it over my cleavage. "Okay! Mamma's ready!" I waltzed back into the main room, spinning in my dress on my way to Gavin on the couch. I missed dressing up.

Gavin glanced over his shoulder, lips curling up at the edges, gaze sliding down my dress. "Wow!" He jumped right over the back of the couch, rushing for me. "You look beautiful, Baby." He dipped his face to my neck, soft kisses smothering the thin skin, sending a wave of shivers over me. "How about we step back into that bathroom?"

"Mamma!" Tiny arms suddenly wrapped around my tights, squeezing my legs.

"We're not alone," I reminded him. "And Papà forgot to reserve cribs, so tonight, we also won't be alone."

"Fuck," he whispered into my hair. "I don't think I can go three days without you, Baby. Especially not when you're dressed like this." He dropped his hand to my cleavage, a feather-light touch dusting across the top of my dress. This would be a first; we'd hardly gone a day without sex since the twins were born.

"Absence makes the heart grow fonder," I teased.

"It's not my heart I'm fucking worried about, Baby." His stare dropped to my chest, that sexy grin immediately flat, and I knew why.

"Don't!" I warned, raising my hand over my neck, blocking his view. "I can't wear that necklace all the time."

"It's not a fuc—it's not a necklace. It's a cornicello."

Yes, I know. I had to wear it every day. "It's still on me," I assured him. "You just can't see it." I slid my hand down the tight dress, letting his imagination figure it out.

"Fuck," he muttered, eyes rolling back. "Five minutes in the bedroom, Baby! That's all I need!"

I laughed as I bent down to pick up Nora, who was still clinging to my leg. "No baby gates, no cribs, *no* Papà."

He shook his head in exasperation before stomping over and scooping up Vinny. Then we started for the hotel lobby, en-route to the banquet room for the dinner.

"Gav! Sadie!" Sofia greeted the second we stepped into the room.

"Zia Fia!" Nora screeched, practically leaping from my arms.

"They look so beautiful!" Sofia gushed, lifting Nora from my arms, covering her face with kisses. "Her dress!"

"You bought it!" I automatically ran my hand over her sparkly black sequined dress.

"And Vinny!" she mused, sighing dramatically.

I looked over at my boys, Vinny in his tiny slacks and matching dress shirt, looking just like his papà; even their hair was gelled the same.

"Gav!" The roar made me swing around to find Luca. "Sadie!" He pulled me into a hug, reaching for Gavin too, yanking Vinny out of his arms. "What's up, Vinny!" He poked Vinny's side, tickling him.

"No, Zio Lewcha," Vinny squealed, wiggling in Luca's hold.

"Where's Giorgia?" I scanned the room, searching for the bride to be.

"In the back," Sofia answered, gaze still down on Nora in her arms.

"I'll be right back!" I made my way to the other side of the room. "Giorgia!"

"Sadie!" she squealed, rushing over, throwing her arms around me. "I'm so excited you're here!"

"We just got in a few hours ago!" I looked back across the room, seeing Gavin laughing with Luca.

"Sadie!" Laurence walked up with the biggest smile I'd ever seen, happily throwing his arms up for a hug.

"Hi, Laurence! Congratulations!"

He released me, swinging his arm right over Giorgia, wheeling her around to the group of guys behind him. "Hey!" he shouted, getting all their attention. "This is the other bridesmaid, Sadie."

It was smile after smile, all of them turning to face us, moving our direction. Ah yes, the wedding meat market. I had forgotten about this. "Nice to meet you," I greeted, smiling politely.

"Sadie is Giorgia—" Laurence trailed off, gaze over me.

"Sadie is... Gavin's wife," a voice huffed behind me as a flexed arm hooked around my waist, pressing me back into the hard chest.

I laughed, reaching out my left hand for them to shake, but Gavin slid his other hand over my arm, pushing it back down to my side.

"And Gavin," Giorgia laughed too. "Is my brother."

The guys' greeted him, but, of course, didn't reply.

"Sadie," Giorgia snickered, trying to suppress a smile. "See that tall one?" She pointed to one of the guys in the group that had just turned away. "That's who you'll be walking down the aisle with."

Gavin's arm clenched around my waist, pressing me deeper into his chest. "No, she's fucking not," he growled, making her laugh hysterically.

"Fratellino!" she insisted. "Don't be so crazy!"

"She's not fuc—" he started again, as if 'she' wasn't right in front of him.

"I'm joking, Gav! She's walking the aisle alone! All my bridesmaids are!"

I tipped my face to his, watching him roll his eyes, grip tightening even harder. "Gavin!" I called, and he dropped his chin down, meeting my eyes. "Too tight! I can't move."

He furrowed his brows, looking down at me confused. "Oh, shit." He dropped his hold, freeing me.

I spun around to face him. "Get me a drink, please," I insisted, watching him eye the guys before stalking away.

"I want to see the twins!" Giorgia tugged Laurence with her, all of us starting towards the other side of the room.

"They're so big now!" Laurence gestured to Vinny.

"Almost two!" I replied as Gavin walked up, handing me a glass of wine.

"Stefano!" Sofia exclaimed, immediately taking off with Nora to meet an approaching Stefano, who walked in with a wave of guests.

"Finally!" Laurence waved to someone behind Stefano. "The snow slows everything down."

Gavin immediately looked towards the doors. Oh no. "It's not snowing!" he practically yelled at Laurence.

"It is," Laurence countered. "Started about an hour ago. You know, New York, weather's crazy. From a chill to a blizzard in minutes!"

Blizzard, the word was a trigger for Gavin, and it hit immediately, his body stiffening, eyes empty black orbs.

"Pierre!" Laurence shouted again, waving over a taller version of himself. "Pierre!" He hugged the guy then spun him towards us. "These are Giorgia's brothers and sisters! This is my brother, Pierre!"

His brother smiled up at the guys, gaze slowly falling to me, lingering on my dress, then my eyes. "Pierre," he greeted me directly, reaching for my right hand, my ringless hand, and pulling it up to his lips. "Ç'est un plaisir de vous rencontrer, pleasure to meet you. Wow," he sighed, his intense stare moving from my hand to my eyes. "T'as d'beaux yeux, you have beautiful eyes."

Whoa... Italian was hot but French, his words rolled off his tongue like butter. "Sadie," I replied automatically.

"French!" Luca spat, breaking me from the daze I didn't realize I was in. "Laurence is fucking French!" His glare flickered between Laurence and Giorgia. "French, and a Mets fan!" His lips pinched, a heavy exhale streaming from his nose before he darted away.

"Drop, her, hand!" Gavin's growl sent a shiver down my spine, his voice bitter, deep, an angry warning. And I realized my hand was still resting in Pierre's, inches from his lips. Shit! I ripped my hand away, raising my left purposely, wiggling my ring as I pushed the glass of wine to my lips, guzzling it down. I didn't even want to look at

Gavin right now, so I searched the room instead, spotting the babies.

I stepped forward, only to get pulled back. Gavin's hands curled over both my dress and my arm, dragging me back out and through the door, straight out into the hallway. "Gav—"

He spun me, pinning my back to the wall, his dark eyes stormy, body falling flat against mine, breath striking my face in waves. I knew this look. I was either going to get kissed or lectured.

His lips sealed, eyes roamed my face, my cleavage, his hand captured mine, tugging me forward, dragging me down the hall, passing a restroom.

His feet slammed to a stop, backtracking to the door, kicking it open, and peeking inside, empty. He charged in, straight to the back hall.

"What—" I started, but he smacked the lock behind us, immediately rushing me to the wall, pinning me once again. His hands flew under my dress, fingers racing up my thighs, stomach, gripping over the tights, ripping them down, fingers now dragging up my skin. Then his mouth crashed furiously into mine, lips hard, tongue frantically parting my lips, furiously whipping inside my mouth. I held on tight, my tongue, my lips dancing with his—a frantic, sloppy kiss that lit everything inside me on fire.

I flung my hands to his belt, unlatching it, forcing his zipper down with my palm, fingers curling over his flesh, stroking him against my panties, my gasps and moans filling the air.

"Oh, Baby," his groan echoed with mine; his fingers swept under the lace, sliding inside me. Finger fucking me with all his might, flexing with every plunge, banging my back against the wall while keeping his lips locked with mine. Then he tensed, hands retreating, sliding to my thighs, spreading them as he hoisted me up, my tights stretching, his body pushing in between my legs, his erection teasing me. "Fuck!" His nails dug deeper into my thighs, gripping tighter, driving me higher up the wall.

I turned my face away, breaking the kiss. The heat surging too fast, the need begging to be hit, the euphoria and anticipation too much. He arched his hips, pounding me down while he thrust up, the force stealing my breath, pleasure almost unbearable. "Harder! Now!" I was there, it was coming, I was coming. Almost... "Say something in Italian."

His face sprung up, dark eyes on mine. "What?"

"Say, something, in Italian," I moaned, clenching my thighs, demanding he finish me.

"Why?" It was a grunt, his hips nailing faster, deeper thrusts. "Because, that, fucker spoke French to you?"

"What, no!" I clawed his shirt, grinding over his lap, but he stopped, heavy breathing smacking my face.

"Are you thinking about him while I'm fucking you?"

I gasped for a breath, meeting his wild eyes as I shook my head. "No! Of course not!" But his eyes were black, face like stone, hands rough, gripping my waist, shoving me away and against the wall as he pulled out. "Gavin!" I stumbled up. "I just wanted to hear you talk dirty. Your Italian always comes out in New York!"

He was staring right at me, but he wasn't seeing me. "You wanna hear some Italian, Sadie?" he spat, kicking the stall bathroom open behind him. "Vaffanculo!"

NEW YORK: 3

Gavin barreled out of the restroom, leaving me panting against the wall. What the hell just happened? "Gavin!" You asshole! I stumbled forward, smacking the stall door shut, falling against it, wiping the tears leaking from my eyes. Seriously, what had just happened? I straightened, tugging my tights up, readjusting my dress while forcing the tears away. How could he have done that? How could he have left me like this? How could he have said that to me! I'd heard him yell, snap, but this—this was different. I knew what vaffanculo meant. He told me to fuck off. Or maybe it was fuck you, or go fuck yourself. How could he! I stepped away from the door, letting it open, walking to the sink, meeting my tear-filled eyes in the mirror.

Dammit! He was such an asshole sometimes. Four hours! We'd only been in New York four hours, and here he was accusing me of thinking about another man, leaving me half-fucked, and telling me to fuck off in Italian. I wiped the mascara runoff from under my eyes, ran my hands through my now messy hair, all the while trying to steady my breathing and calm my shaking hands. I wanted to run, disappear, scream, cry, except I couldn't. Dinner was about to start, and I didn't want to ruin Giorgia's night. I had to put on a happy face and ignore the asshole who left me here.

I opened the door slightly, peeking out, finding it just as empty as it had been earlier. Thank god. I fought with my teary eyes down the winding corridor to the banquet room door. No more tears, smiles only. I pulled it open, sneaking back in.

"Mamma!" Vinny was toddling at full speed towards me, arms wide, so I lifted him while discreetly scanning the room, no Gavin.

"Vinny!" Luca shouted, chasing after him. "Little guy's fast!"

The tears welled up, dammit. I needed another minute. "Will you take him? I'm going to grab a drink before dinner."

"Of course!" He reached for Vinny, eyes on me. "You okay?"

No. I didn't bother replying, just bolted straight to the corner bar. "Red wine, please."

I sank away from the group, scanning once more for Gavin, seeing the door swing open, my heart beating out of my chest as I watched him stalk in. The anger struck like a match, heat burning from the inside out. Fuck. I turned towards the wall behind me, trying to calm down before I did something I'd regret.

"Sadie!" Giorgia beckoned, forcing me back around. "This is Stella, and this is Maria. You met them here a few years ago."

"I remember!" I smiled back politely.

"And Gav is," Giorgia started, twisting back to scan the room. "Right over there. Gav!"

Shit. I saw the flash of him heading in our direction. I couldn't face him right now. I'd scream. "If you'll excuse me," I spoke to the floor, avoiding their eyes. "I've got to check on the twins." I hurried in the opposite direction to Luca, Stefano, and the babies, reaching for the twins as glass started clinking, drawing everyone's attention.

Laurence stepped to the middle of the room, glass in hand. "If everyone could take a seat," he announced, waving everyone to the long table.

Great. I couldn't do this either. I didn't want to be anywhere near Gavin. I looked at the guys beside me. Stefano would move if Gavin asked, but Luca wouldn't. I stepped over to Luca's side. "Will you sit next to me?" I whispered to him while plucking Nora from the floor, holding her tight against me. "Please."

He stared down at us, nodding his head, yes, waving me forward. So I started for the table, keeping my head down, following the feet in front of me, trying my best to avoid Gavin.

"Papà!" Nora yelled, bouncing against me excitedly just as his feet stopped in front of mine.

I gasped from the fear, the pain, anger, disappointment threatening to unleash. I didn't look up, simply opened my arms, letting him take her and hurrying away the second he had.

I took the seat next to one of Giorgia's friends, and Luca took the chair beside me. Then I heard Nora's giggle, my eyes automatically looking up, meeting Gavin's on the other side of the table. I looked away, catching Stefano with Vinny on Luca's opposite side, then Sofia, taking the chair next to Gavin. I was surrounded by him and his family. Once again, I was alone in New York. I glanced down at the plate in front of me, studying the nothing that was on it. I didn't want to look at anybody.

"Welcome!" Giorgia sang from the head of the table. "Thank you all for being a part of this special day, grazie, merci."

"Jesus Christ," Luca grumbled under his breath, my elbow automatically jabbing his side to shut him up.

"I'm especially excited to have my nipoti here, my niece and nephew! Nora, our flower girl, and Vinny, our ring bearer." She pointed towards the twins in Gavin and Stefano's arms. "It seems like yesterday that I was at my brother Gavin and his wife Sadie's beautiful wedding, filled with so much amore."

It was too much. I had too much anger and too much hurt festering inside me to listen any further. I scooted my chair out, folding my napkin over the table. "I'll be back," I whispered to Luca before escaping to the door.

I stumbled into the hallway, inhaling the recycled hotel air, but still couldn't breathe. I needed to escape, to run. I raced to the lobby, out the doors into the cold night air. Breathe. I watched the flakes of snow drifting under the street lights. But I couldn't go any further because I'd already probably caused a scene, so I inhaled the frigid air and walked right back inside.

I continued to the banquet, slowing when I saw Gavin leaning against the wall, blocking the door, watching me. I walked right past him.

He grabbed my arm, his touch unleashing every pent-up emotion.

"Get your fucking hand off me!" I yelled, hands shaking once again.

He relaxed his fingers, dropping his grip. "Don't leave like that."

He couldn't be serious right now. "You're one to talk!"

"Excuse me?" His eyes were still dark, still glowering at me, angry with me!

"No!" I snapped, lips quivering, tears threatening to burst. "You don't get to treat me like this! I'm not an outlet for your jealousy, or worry, or whatever the hell that was about!" I took a step back, putting more space between us. "I'm your wife and mother to your children! How could you tell me to fuck off? Or was it fuck you? Or did you tell me to go fuck myself? How could you say that to me! ME!" I blinked back the tears, tipping my face up to the ceiling before rolling back down to meet his eyes. "I didn't do anything! I've never thought of anyone else when I'm with you! How could you even accuse me of that! I've got your name permanently on my finger; my children have your face. I've given you all of me, every inch, every ounce! You think because some guy held my hand and whispered some French that I'm picturing him fucking me! Is that what you think of me! After everything, is that what you think of me, Gavin? Of us?"

He stood there, back pressed against the wall, staring down at me.

I wiped my cheek dry. "I wish I could be petty and tell you that now that you've accused me of it, maybe I'll picture someone else, but I can't. Not because we're married, but because I'm still so in love with you. That you're the only man I've ever thought about since the day you stepped in front of me. That all day I've been staring at you, just waiting to get you alone. Sex is you, Gavin. It's not the act, it's me being with you. When I think of sex, I picture your face. How could you do that to me?" I met his gaze one last time before pushing through the door, heading straight to my seat.

"Mamma!" Vinny clapped, already walking over Luca, falling into my lap.

"You okay?" Luca mumbled beside me.

No. I looked over, nodding yes. Only then he lifted his hand, fingers brushing a tear from my cheek. He studied me, opening his mouth to say something, but the servers bustled in, plates in hand.

I focused back on Vinny, watching everyone dig into their plates, eating, chatting, lost in conversation. Then there was me, using all my strength to bury the emotions away, counting the minutes until I could cry or scream in private.

Giorgia and Laurence were suddenly behind us, all of us turning to face them. "Sadie!" she exclaimed. "We're all staying in my suite tonight! Join us! It'll be so fun!"

Staying with the girls tonight, yes."I think that'd be good," I answered automatically. I couldn't even imagine having to sleep next to Gavin.

"No!" Gavin snapped from across the table. I hadn't even realized he was back. "What about the babies!"

"I'll help you, Fratellino!" Luca offered and insisted.

"Perfect!" Giorgia clapped. "Tonight's gonna be so fun!"

I felt Gavin's glare on me; I ignored it, pressing a kiss to Vinny's head instead, inhaling my baby to calm me down.

I never touched my plate, just waited patiently until the party finally called it a night, and everyone began saying their goodbyes. Then I was out, holding a sleeping Vinny against my chest as I rushed through the crowd, straight to the elevators. Luca jogged up beside me, keeping my pace, thankfully not saying or asking a thing, even when I attacked the elevator button, jabbing my finger against it so it'd open before Gavin got here.

The bell chimed and I stepped forward just as footsteps stomped up behind me. Shit. I prayed they didn't belong to him, but I knew they did. I continued into the elevator, staring at my feet as Luca stepped in, standing on my left, then Gavin followed, standing on my right.

"I can handle it tonight, Luca," Gavin groaned. "You can go."

No. I tugged Luca's jacket, willing him to stay. I wasn't ready to be alone with Gavin right now.

"It's cool, Fratellino. It'll be fun."

The elevator doors opened, all of us walking in silence to the hotel room, waiting while Gavin slid the room key in, elbowing the door open.

I rushed to the bedroom, pulling the blankets from the bed to lay Vinny down. Gavin followed, laying Nora in bed next to Vinny. Then we moved some chairs, pushing the backs up against the bed so they wouldn't roll off.

"Can we talk?" Gavin reached for my hand.

I flinched, ripping it away.

"No!" I grabbed my bag, hustling out to the main room. "I'll see you guys tomorrow." I didn't wait for a response, blowing right through the door.

"Sadie!" Gavin ran out behind me.

I didn't want to turn around, but I did. "Text me when they wake up, and I'll come down."

He grumbled under his breath. "I don't want you to leave. I—"

"I don't want to stay!" I cut him off, not wanting to hear what he had to say. "I have two beautiful children in there that I can't bear to look at right now because all I see is their papà, and all I hear is him yelling at me to fuck off. You were right, Gavin. We shouldn't have come." I took off, rushing for the elevator.

NEW YORK: 4

I knocked on the suite door, hearing the commotion on the other side before Giorgia flung the door open. "Sadie!" She immediately handed me a champagne flute. "I'm so happy you're here!"

"Me too!" You have no idea. I dropped my bag to the floor to hold the glass. "But I have to leave first thing in the morning. Then I'll come back with Nora to get ready for the ceremony!"

Sofia walked up behind Giorgia, her smile instant when she saw me. "Sadie! How are Gav and Luca handling the babies?"

"Twins are asleep." We were all exhausted. We were up at 4 am, took a cross country flight, had dinner, then the fight, now this. I pushed the glass to my lips, watching Sofia. Wait... "I didn't see Paulo at dinner." I had been so distracted by Gavin that I just realized his absence.

"Working!" Giorgia answered for Sofia.

Sofia flashed her eyes to the floor before meeting mine. "He's in the process of a buyout. He's been flying back and forth between here and Gioia Tauro. Work is his baby, not nearly as cute as Nora e Vinny," she said, forcing a laugh. "He'll be back for Christmas."

Christmas? "He's not coming to the wedding?"

She shook her head no.

Giorgia snatched my hand, dragging me to the couch. "We've missed visiting Cali!"

"We've missed having you!" Our house was so quiet lately, and I couldn't remember the last time Gavin and I went out on a date.

"Sadie," Sofia sighed, taking a seat beside me. "How about I keep the babies tomorrow night, so you and Gav can go out!"

It was like she'd read my mind. Only being alone with him was the last thing I wanted right now. "No, it's okay."

"Are you sure? I can stay in your room or in this suite. You and Gav can have a night alone."

"No, it's fine," I assured her.

A bang hit the door, all of us twisting back towards the string of knocks as Maria danced over, opening the door to Laurence, Pierre, and another groomsman. Oh, great.

"Laurence!" Giorgia sprung from the couch, leaping into his arms. "What are you doing here?"

He lifted her, swinging her in his arms while the other two guys walked towards us. "I couldn't stay away from you, Ma Belle!" Laurence cooed, obviously drunk, and obviously not one for tradition, like Gavin.

"Dibs on Pierre!" Stella whispered to Maria.

Gavin would be so pissed if he knew the guys were up here. It would escalate everything even more, and we had a wedding tomorrow. I stood from the couch, skirting the group. "I have to grab something from the room," I lied to

Sofia. "I'll be right back." I dug a credit card from my bag, stuffing it into my bra as I slipped out the door.

I needed to waste an hour, or at least until the guys left. I continued to the elevator, taking it to the lobby, then to the only place still open. The bar.

It was loud, crowded, eyes following me as I made my way to the counter, taking the only empty barstool in the place. I raised my hand, waving for the bartender. "Red wine," I ordered automatically before remembering I was alone. "Actually, do you have coffee?" I asked, he nodded back. Then I noticed the garland and twinkling Christmas lights lining the bar. "Actually," I started again, sending him swinging back, head tilted to the side as he waited for my order. "Do you have hot chocolate?"

"Hot chocolate?" he repeated, chuckling. "You realize this is a bar, right? Do I need to card you?"

Please. "You'd be my favorite person if you did!"

He rolled his eyes, smiling. "Hot chocolate coming up."

"Hot chocolate?" The guy beside me laughed. "Must have been a really rough night."

"Yeah, and not in the good way," I mumbled.

"Well" —he lifted his beer— "welcome to the club!"

"Rough night for you, too?" Not that I had to ask with the way he was staring off and swirling his beer.

"Rough few days. Been trying to apologize for being an ass, but, uh, she won't give me the time of day. Not that I blame her."

"An ass?" Sounded familiar. "Must be something in the water."

He shook his head, still staring at the wall. "I said some shitty stuff," he grumbled. "Found out I was completely wrong about all of it, which made me an even bigger ass.

Although, I never should have said any of it in the first place." He threw his hand up in apology. "Sorry for cursing. It's been a long week."

I hadn't even noticed. I was so used to hearing cursing that I hardly recognized it anymore. "It's fine. So why did you say it?"

"The curse words?"

"No," I laughed. "The shitty stuff."

He looked over, bright sky blue eyes distant in thought. "I was a dumbass. I didn't hear what I wanted to. I was mad; heat of the moment." He pushed the bottle to his mouth. "One stupid asshole remark, and I lost her, after waiting years to find her."

"Girlfriend? Wife?"

"Neither. It's complicated."

"Jealousy? Another man?" Those were always Gavin's triggers.

He chuckled, gaze dropping to the bar. "Nothing will make you lose your shit faster."

So I'd seen. "My husband..." I studied the stranger's face. I wasn't used to spilling my drama, but he was a random, and I needed to vent. "My husband said some shitty stuff to me too. That's why he's upstairs, and I'm down here."

He swirled his almost empty bottle, focusing on it as he spoke. "Will you forgive him?"

"We're married with kids." It was complicated. I was hurt, I was angry, and he had gone too far this time. But we weren't Gavin and Sadie; we were Papà and Mamma. "I'll forgive him, eventually. Still hurts. It's not something you forget. I wished he loved me more or respected me more, so he wouldn't say those things in the first place."

"That has nothing to do with it," he argued. "I didn't say that stuff because of how I felt about her. I said it because of how I felt about myself. I'm selfish. I, I thought I was losing her— that she didn't want me that way I wanted her." His gaze slid to mine. "Look, I'm in no place to give you advice, for all I know, your husband's a total jackass that doesn't deserve your forgiveness, but if he's like me, then he probably feels like absolute shit, regretting what he did with every fiber of his being. I didn't mean what I said. I don't know how I let myself say them. I love her more than anything. The words don't reflect that."

"But he said it nonetheless." How could you say that to someone you loved more than anything? "You said it."

"And I'd give anything to take back what I said and have her sitting where you are now, no offense."

"None taken." I watched him, seeing the anguish on his face, hearing it in his voice. But this wasn't Gavin's first offense and I was more than some passing fling— I was his wife. "Maybe instead of wanting to take back your words, you should figure out why you said them in the first place."

"I told you," he muttered. "Heat of the moment."

"The thoughts were in your head. Heat of the moment's just an excuse."

He slid his empty bottle around the counter. "Because I was afraid she would choose him and not me. I was angry. I needed a reason, someone other than myself to blame. So I made her the villain in the story."

Just like Gavin. "You're right. You are selfish."

His shoulders caved, fingers chipping at the bar. "Am I supposed to let her walk away? Because I don't think I can do that."

"Is she the one?"

He looked from the bar directly into my eyes. "Yeah. I knew it the second we kissed. It was like nothing I'd ever felt before. *She's* like no one I've ever met. I love her with everything I have."

"Hot chocolate!" The bartender slid a mug over. "Threw some whipped cream on there for ya, too."

"Thanks! I wrapped my hands around the mug. "This is perfect."

The guy next to me straightened, scooting his stool out. "I'm gonna call it a night," he sighed, dropping some cash to the bar. "This should cover yours too." He stood beside me, folding his jacket over his arms. "Sorry for the two dumbasses you had to deal with tonight," he laughed. "Thanks for listening."

"No problem." I waved goodbye, turning right back to my warm mug of cocoa.

"How is it?" The bartender asked, nabbing the cash and the empty beer bottle.

"Almost as good as the wine I wish it were!"

He laughed, then looked over, rolling his eyes. "Come on," he balked. "That's why we have a dress code!"

I followed his stare towards the entrance, where a man in a T-shirt and flannel pajama pants stood searching the bar with worried eyes. Shit. I stood, watching him scan the crowd, finding me, letting out a visible sigh of relief. Time to leave. "Thanks again!" I said to the bartender, sliding the mug over before starting back through the bar to the front entrance.

Gavin's hands smacked his temples, rubbing for a split second before shooting his glare to me. "Sofia text, asked if you were on your way back," he choked out the words.

"An hour, Sadie! With no phone. No one knew where you were. Fuck, I thought you'd taken off to the park again."

"Laurence and some groomsmen showed up to the room. I thought it'd be best to leave."

"And you thought going to a fucking bar alone was a better idea!"

I had, but now that he was saying it, probably not. "I got hot chocolate. I'm sorry I worried you. I'm going back now." I continued past him towards the elevator, hearing him running up behind me.

"Sadie!"

I didn't turn back. I didn't owe him any more apologies.

The elevator door opened, so I stepped inside, pressing the nine for our room and the twenty for the suite.

"Sadie," his voice was calmer now. "I'm sorry. I'm an ass. I don't have an excuse this time. Same shit, different day. I should have never said that to you, done any of it."

That was his apology? Same shit, different day? The elevator slowed, door opening onto the ninth floor and he stepped off, hand out for mine.

"Come back with me, Baby."

But I kept my feet firmly planted inside the elevator, arms at my sides, watching the door close, separating us. "Not this time. You broke your vows. You promised to honor and respect me, not hurt me."

The door sealed, taking me away.

NEW YORK: 5

I stepped off the elevator, already hearing the muffled yelling before I even made it to the door. I knocked hard, trying to be heard, then knocked again, finally hearing the clank of deadbolts.

"Sadie!" They all squealed, bombarding me at the door, all drunk as could be.

"What did I miss?" I laughed as the girls herded me inside.

"Four bottles of Dom!" Stella sang, dropping onto the couch next to Giorgia.

"Okay, ladies!" Sofia scolded with a smile. "It's time for bed! We need our beauty sleep! Especially the bride!"

"Excuse me!" Giorgia exclaimed.

"You know what I mean!" Sofia laughed back.

"Where am I sleeping?" I asked on my way to grab my bag.

"In my room," Sofia answered, pointing to the far door.

I went straight there, dropping my bag on the table and finding my phone, seeing the flashes from the barrage of missed calls and messages. I flipped it, setting it aside.

"You already chose a bed?" Sofia waltzed in behind me.

"Do you mind?"

"Of course not! Now, we'll meet back here tomorrow at two for hair and makeup. You'll bring Nora, and Gav can take Vinny with him."

"Okay." I settled into the sheets, finally laying my head against a pillow.

She stood there staring a minute longer, and I had a hunch she wanted to ask me where I went. Instead, she continued into the bathroom.

I was tired. Exhausted. And still dressed. I shimmied the dress off, wiggling against the sheets. Then I slipped into a sleep shirt, closed my eyes, and called it a night.

I woke, startled by a flashing light hitting my eyelids. So I peeled my mascara-sealed lashes apart, finding the source of the light- my phone screen lighting up the table under it. Already, Gavin? I swung my arm out, flipping the phone, seeing the message alerts, 12:46 A.M., 12:53, 1:27, 1:55, 2:22, 3:10, 4:04. Ugh. I shoved it into the table drawer.

"Sadie, Sadie," Sofia's voice broke through my dream, steadily growing louder. "Sadie."

I rolled over, blinking, waking to Sofia staring down at me. "What time is it?" I yawned, forcing my eyes open.

"Eleven! We've already had breakfast!"

"Oh shit!" I flung up, eyes fighting against the bright sun. The twins *had* to be up already. Gavin! I yanked the drawer open, pulling my phone, that was nothing but alerts, message after message, and a string of missed calls, from Luca. Crap. "I've got to go!" I scrambled off the bed, stepping into some leggings and grabbing my bag on my way out of the room. "I'll be back at two!"

"I'll call to remind you!" She stepped aside as I rushed past her out the door.

I hurried out of the suite to the elevator and down to the ninth floor, rifling through my bag for the key card and sliding it into the lock, stumbling into an empty room. "Gavin?" I dropped my bag, walking to the closed bedroom door, opening it slightly, finding Gavin asleep in the bed, alone. Where were the twins? I walked back to my bag, grabbing my phone and dialing Luca.

"*Sadie*!" he answered on the first ring.

"Luca! Where are you? Where are the twins!"

"We're grabbing coffee! What would you like?"

"Um, what? A mocha, I guess. Why didn't Gavin go with you?"

"Because Gav went to bed about an hour ago. We'll be back up in twenty."

He hung up, so I did the same. Gavin went to bed an hour ago? I sat on the couch, spinning the phone in my hands. I didn't want to read his messages, but I opened them anyways. As expected, there was a *where are you,* followed by *are you okay, did you make it to Giorgia's, I'm sorry,* and the last simply read *check email, please.* Email? I clicked on the email icon, waiting for it to load, and there they were, received at 5:13 A.M., 5:17, and 5:32. Jeez, he *was* up all night. I clicked on the first one he sent, reading the single line.

I hate that I hurt you.

I clicked the next one.

I don't know what to do. I hate seeing your broken heart. I hate it more knowing I'm the one who broke it.

And finally, I clicked on the last one.

I keep picturing another man yelling what I said to you and I want to kill him. How dare he talk to my wife like that, but it was her own husband. I'm sorry.

The bedroom door squeaked, opening, his swollen eyes the first thing I saw, followed by the black shadows that encompassed them. He cleared his throat, stare trained on me. "I couldn't tell if I was dreaming or if I actually heard your voice."

"I came back to help with the babies, but Luca took them to grab coffee."

He continued to the couch, dropping onto the opposite end from where I sat. "I can't believe I said that to you," his voice was hoarse, weak. "That I did that to you. I, I'm not even sorry. I'm ashamed. Fuck, I can't believe I did any of it." A tear started down his cheek, then another. "I don't break promises, Sadie, especially not vows to you." He rubbed his knuckles over his eye. "Last night, I kept thinking, what if someone else yelled that at you—I'd fucking destroy them. But it was me. The one man you trusted to not say that shit." He twisted his face away, yet I could still see the glisten of tears streaming down his stubbly cheeks. "I don't know how to fix this. I don't know how to stop it." He looked back at me, his sincere wet eyes on mine. "It's hard for me to see you walk into a room and grab every man's fucking attention. I forget about everything we have because I'm so focused on everything I might lose. And I lose myself to it. I can't believe how I treated you, Sadie. It was such a blur, but I did it. I have no fucking excuses." He looked to the window, discreetly wiping the tears before continuing. "Please tell me you're not thinking about separating, or worse." He faced me once again, tears brimming, lips quivering. "I'm so sorry."

Of course, he was sorry; he was always sorry. But that didn't negate the pain. I met his swollen red eyes on his tear-stained face, showing me the tears he usually hid, evidence of how sorry he really was. "I'm hurt, but I'm not going to leave you."

His tears broke free, flooding down his face just as a bang hit the door, and suddenly it shot open, Nora and Vinny speeding in while Luca pushed the empty stroller.

"Mamma!" They both squealed in unison, running for me.

I opened my arms, scooping them both up. "I missed my babies!" I held them tight, kissing their cheeks.

"Mocha's here, Sadie," Luca called over, setting the cup on the table. "I was thinking I'd walk the babies to see the Christmas tree. That cool?" His eyes were on Gavin, then me.

"Sure." I lowered the twins down, watching them run back to the stroller, and a second later, they were gone.

"You should get some rest, Gavin," I urged him. "We have to leave soon."

"I'm fine," he mumbled.

Only he wasn't. "You need to get some rest. Giorgia's wedding is in a few hours." He was exhausted—a week of worry, a long day of travel, and a night of no sleep.

He flashed his eyes to mine. "Will you lay with me?" he pleaded. "I know I don't deserve it, and I know you don't want to be next to me right now, but I need to feel you there."

I knew he wouldn't sleep unless I was next to him, so I stood and started for the bedroom, climbing straight into the bed. He followed, this time coming to me, nestling his teary cheeks against my chest as he draped his arm over my stomach.

"I told Luca everything," he whispered, voice shaky.

"Everything, everything?"

"Yeah, I'm sorry. I just needed to be held accountable. I don't want this ever to happen again. I love you, Sadie, and I'm sorry for treating you like that."

"Go to sleep, Gavin." I ran my fingers through his hair, feeling his tight hold relax, his breathing calm, falling fast asleep in my arms.

NEW YORK: 6

The main door boomed open, a stampede following, shaking the floor, but Gavin didn't even flinch. He was out, lost in a deep sleep, holding onto me for dear life. I didn't want to wake him, though. He needed the sleep, so I carefully lifted his arm, slipping out from under his grip and pushing a pillow in my place.

I padded out, meeting the twins playing on the floor and Luca sitting on the couch. "Thanks again, Luca." I walked straight to my phone to check the time, almost time to leave again.

"No problem. How's Gav?"

"Sleeping." But then, the door squeaked, Gavin groggily stalking out. "We have to get going." I continued to Nora, picking her up from the floor. "We've got to get upstairs." I slung my bag over my shoulder on my way to the door. "I'll see you guys later." I looked back, meeting Gavin's still swollen eyes as he watched us leave.

The suite was absolute chaos—hair and makeup people running back and forth, the girls rushing between them.

"Sadie!" Giorgia raced by, yelling over her shoulder. "Dresses are in the back. Then grab a seat for makeup!"

"Seguimi! Follow me!" Sofia hurried over, waving us to follow. "Get your gown on, Sadie. I'll dress Nora!" She smiled down at Nora. "If that's okay."

"Of course!" I grabbed the garment bag from the closet while dashing to the bathroom. I took a quick shower and brushed my teeth before unzipping the bag. Giorgia had the gowns custom made here in New York, and I had yet to see them or try mine on. I'd sent her my measurements and prayed it'd fit. I lifted the dress out, the black beading reflecting the light. The layers of black beads over black silk were breathtaking. I took my time stepping into it, tugging the sleeveless gown over my hips, my chest, zipping the side. It was elegant, sexy, accentuating my chest then giving way to a sheath silhouette, clinging to my legs, sweeping the floor around me.

I walked out, catching Nora twirling in her red gown, layers fluffing out over the petticoat, dragging across the floor as she spun.

"Oh, Sadie," Sofia beamed. "Sei bellissima! Now, hair and makeup," she instructed, waving us ahead.

I took Nora's hand, leading her to the main room to our chairs. Her chair was across from mine, complete with a booster seat, and I lifted her up before taking my place. And immediately, the team closed in. One of the women began brushing out my hair while another rubbed cream over my face.

Nora was enthralled, watching the women doing her hair and mine. She had those same severe eyes as Gavin, a stare you could feel. Not to mention she was the spitting image of him. I could see him now, laughing with her as they played at home, holding her when she cried, rocking her to sleep. He had such a loving soul with such a short fuse. And on the rare occasions when that fuse lit, all hell broke loose. Then there was the Gavin earlier, the one staring at me with tear-filled eyes, falling asleep with his arm locked over me, holding me close.

"Ready!" The woman in front of me clapped, breaking my reverie, waking me to reality.

I stood automatically, walking towards the full-length mirror, shocked and almost in tears at the reflection. I hardly recognized myself with this striking makeup, red lipstick complimenting the black cat-eye and defined cheeks, so bold, and so Giorgia. Then my hair, pulled back, long curls draping down my neck like they had at our wedding. Nora stepped up beside me, her hair styled identical to mine, her tiny hand reaching to my fingers as she twirled.

"Ready?" Sofia clapped to get the attention of the room, sending everyone shuffling around Giorgia. "It's time to head downstairs!"

We followed them down to the ballroom, slipping into a waiting room while the guests took their seats. "Get in position," the wedding planner instructed, so I led Nora back to Giorgia.

Giorgia stood in back, looking radiant, glowing. "You look incredibly beautiful, Giorgia."

"Thanks!" she chirped, shaking out a nerve as she faced the mirror.

"Now, Nora." I bent down, sliding my hands over hers. "Stay with Zia Giorgia, okay. Vinny will meet you in a minute." I gave her a kiss before stepping back in line, clutching my bouquet.

The doors opened, music filled the room, and Stella started out, leading the procession. Maria followed, and then it was my turn.

I stepped out, walking the hall before crossing through the doors to the aisle and started down, automatically searching for Gavin. He was looking at Stefano, listening to whatever was being said before flashing his eyes to the aisle, landing right on me. He stilled, his body slowing straightening, lips parting, eyes growing wide, watching me with a gaze so intense that I had to remind myself to walk, shoot, remind myself *how* to walk.

His stare dropped to my dress, raking down my curves and back up, meeting my eyes once more, his parted lips sealing into a smile. It was just like *our* wedding, walking to him, taking his hand—then Italy, the twins, our home, our life together. So many moments hit me at once. Even though he did shitty things sometimes, we still had the deepest love.

I was almost to the altar, about to veer to my side, to break our stare, but before I did. "I love you, Gavin," I mouthed over, his chin instantly trembling, his sharp inhale audible from here as he twisted his face away from the guests, discreetly wiping away a tear.

I took my place on the bride's side, watching Sofia walk the aisle, looking like the definition of sophistication, waltzing past the altar, and taking her place as maid of honor. Then there were gasps of oohs and aahs, Nora and Vinny toddling out, all dressed up. Oh, my heart. Vinny was in a black suit with a red bow tie, the same shade as Nora's dress, and my heart couldn't take it. They were too cute. Vinny took off down the aisle, practically racing, his focus on something in the front, and I looked over to Luca waving a lollipop. Nora, however, took her time. Her big eyes flashing left to right, throwing flower petals in front of her as her curls bounced against her back in sync with her flowy dress. "Nora," I whispered, gesturing her over. "Nora!"

Her eyes found mine, her little feet slowing to a stop at the end of the aisle."Nora!" I whispered sternly, both Sofia and I beckoning her over.

Then her little lips started to quiver; she was scared. She looked at us, then panned across the altar to the other side, finding Gavin. "Papà," she whimpered, looking back at me as she defiantly toddled in the opposite direction, walking right up to Gavin's leg, tugging on his pants. She was scared, and no one protected her the way her papà could.

Gavin smiled over at me, shrugging before scooping her up into his arm and pressing a kiss to her hair as she nestled against his suit jacket, tiny fingers tracing his tie.

The music roared louder, the Wedding March filling the air, sending everyone scrambling to their feet, all eyes on the bride, except Gavin's, because they were locked on me. I met his stare, lingering on his smile, then down to the tailored black suit, his jacket forming perfectly to his muscles, especially those strong arms wrapped over our baby girl, keeping her safe.

He was still the sexiest man in the room, and it wasn't because of that suit and tie or those dark eyes and five o'clock shadow on his handsome face. It was the way he held our daughter, the way his other hand rested on our son's shoulder, keeping him close. It was the way he stared at me, deep eyes speaking a thousand words from across the aisle. It was his deep love that made him so sexy, so unbelievably sexy.

I leaned forward, whispering into Sofia's ear. "Is that offer to watch the babies tonight still good?" We'd spent too long just being Mamma and Papà. Tonight, we needed to be Sadie and Gavin. We needed to reconnect, especially after last night.

"Of course!" she whispered back.

I watched him hold Nora, comfort her while his other hand wrapped over Vinny's, holding his hand. My love was almost an ache, a need to be on the other side with them, holding them, too. My family. The crowd suddenly erupted in cheers, breaking my reverie, bringing me back to reality and to the scene of Laurence passionately kissing Giorgia.

They turned towards the cheers and applause, starting up the aisle with Sofia and Pierre following. I was next, watching across the aisle as Luca lifted Vinny and Stefano took Nora, both brothers stepping back, letting Gavin forward, so he lined up with me. Then he reached his hand for mine, entwining our fingers. We followed the aisle up, eyes glued on each other, trusting our feet to guide the way, following those in front of us out the doors and into the hallway.

We stepped out, and I was being whirled around, spinning, my back hitting the wall, my husband pressed against me, hands sliding up the back of my neck, tipping my head to his, our lips colliding. Our kiss an explosion—love, heartache, need. I fell, losing myself in the dance of our tongues, the lust of our lips, the music behind us filling my ear, his tongue following the tempo, rising, falling, a passionate sonata of our love, our longing, a symphony against my lips. I threw my arms over his back, embracing the muscles that always held me so tight. I loved this man.

We lost track of time, lips smothering lips, kiss evoking more than lust, but a spiral of memories and moments. From a kiss goodnight to a kiss on the streets of Rome, our first kiss as man and wife, the mission, him with a ring down on one knee, lips locked during a slow dance in the ballroom at the gala, my soft kiss against his cut-up forehead in that hospital bed, and then our first kiss. Those two strangers, backed against a wall just like this, breaking away from a kiss so powerful, so passionate, and staring into each other's eyes, realizing that he was more than a kiss and I was more than a crush.

NEW YORK: 7

The photographer lowered the camera again, huffing under his breath. "Groomsman number four! Please look at the camera!"

Number four, that was—I looked over to the groom's side, Gavin's stare already on me. "Look at the camera!" I mouthed over. "Now!" He hadn't been able to keep his eyes off of me after our kiss. His entire demeanor had changed; all his pent-up worry had funneled into passion, and that passion was directed right at me.

"Bridesmaid number two, camera, please!"

Bridesmaid number two—that was me! I smiled back at the camera, laughing under my breath.

The photographers snapped a few more poses before one escorted Giorgia and Laurence away, and the other herded the rest of the party further down the hall. "Okay," this photographer started, pointing us to our spots. "Let's get some shots of the flower girl and ring bearer with their family."

Pierre, Stella, and Maria all stepped away, but Luca, Sofia, and Stefano stayed planted next to Gavin and me.

"Sorry," the photographer held the camera impatiently. "Only the childrens' immediate family," he clarified, but the Romanos didn't move an inch. "Just the guardians of the children," he continued.

I reached for Nora up in Luca's arms; only he gripped her tighter, then I turned to Stefano, who was holding Vinny, refusing to acknowledge me. And Sofia standing between them, her hands up on each of the babies' backs. Okay. I looked up at Gavin, whose giddy, excited smile was still on me. He didn't care about a family photo right now. He wasn't in Papà mode, he was in Gavin mode.

"Mother? Father?" The photographer groaned.

Luca stepped forward, arms wrapped around Nora. "I'm the godfather! Does that count?" he snapped. "Take the damn pictures."

I may have birthed these babies, but they were Romano property.

The photographer rolled his eyes, snapping pictures of the immediate-extended family, and we posed a while longer before finally being dismissed.

Gavin's hand immediately captured mine, locking our grip on the way to the reception. We followed the hall to the ballroom, passing through the doors into the room. "This is breathtaking!" Crystal chandeliers lit the space, candles flickered on every table, illuminating the roses and wildflowers that adorned them. It was stunning, everything, even the string quartet, strumming violins, sending sharp notes wafting through the air.

Gavin led me straight to the empty dance floor, sliding his free hand around my waist, pulling me into his chest, already swaying.

"No one's dancing," I whispered, meeting his twinkling eyes, reflecting the light from the chandeliers above.

"I don't care, Baby." He dipped his face to mine. "I've been desperate to hold you this close." His arm tightened, squeezing me in. "The last twenty-four hours have been hell, Baby. Watching you leave, then take Piccolina. That irrational fucking voice in my head convincing me you weren't coming back to me this time. That I'd gone too far. I'm so sorry. Never again, Baby. I love you, Sadie."

I rested my face against his chest, breathing him in as we swayed, but the music ended too quickly, our feet coming to a stop, his arm releasing me from its grip. Then a roar of applause started, a flash of white charging through the doors to more applause. "They're here!" I led Gavin off the dance floor, clapping with everyone else, welcoming Giorgia and Laurence into the reception.

"Champagne for the toasts?" A waiter stepped over, handing Gavin and me glasses from his tray.

Then we weaved through the crowd to Sofia and Nora. "Where's Vinny?" I searched around us, spotting him in Stefano's arm across the room, standing next to yet another floral display. "This reception is beautiful!"

"It is!" Sofia boasted, looking about the room.

Two strong arms suddenly slipped around my waist, Gavin nuzzling his face into my neck. "I love you, Baby."

"I love you, too." I wiggled out of his hold to face him directly. "Sofia's offered to watch the babies tonight."

Sofia smiled, nodding while squeezing Nora into a hug.

"Overnight?" Gavin instantly grumbled, shaking his head no. "I don't think so, Baby. What if—"

I pushed the glass to my lips, staring at him as I gulped down every, last, ounce, of the champagne. "I thought we could finish that kiss."

His eyes darkened, those pupils dilating, taking over his irises until they were pitch black. "Okay."

"Wonderful!" Sofia exclaimed.

The music became melodic, the ensemble strumming romantic notes as Laurence and Giorgia took to the dance floor for their first dance. They stepped together, holding each other close, waltzing. "So beautiful."

"Yes, you are," Gavin's whisper tickled my ear while his arms locked around my waist once again, drawing me into his chest.

"I meant the bride and groom and this accompaniment. Although, it's not as romantic as LL Cool J," I teased him, and in reply, he smacked a kiss to my neck, then another, and another.

The dance floor opened back up, and Gavin bolted, taking me with him, swinging me up into his arms.

"Mamma!" Vinny shouted, speeding across the floor.

"Sweetie!" I caught him, lifting him into my arms, Mark and Stefano following right behind. Mark. Mark! Here, in public, with Stefano. "Mark!" My squeal was out of my control. "I didn't know you'd be here!"

"I wouldn't miss Giorgia's wedding! And—" he leaned against Stefano. "This guy needed a date." He stretched his hand out, Stefano took it—he took it! For everyone to see! This was a big deal for Stefano!

Sofia appeared beside us, with Nora in her arms, and Gavin stepped forward, gesturing for Nora. "Dance with Papà," he insisted, lifting her to his chest, wrapping his giant fingers over her tiny ones. Then he spun his way to the floor, both their smiles visible from here.

"Vinny, do you want to dance with Mamma?" I wiggled him in my arms, dancing our way to the floor, too.

Gavin and Nora spun to us, the four of us dancing as one, as a family.

"Our turn!" Stefano and Mark were back at our sides, gesturing for Vinny and Nora, so we handed them over, watching the guys dancing silly, making the twins laugh.

"Will you grab me some more champagne?" I asked Gavin.

"Of course, Baby." He took off, making his way to the back, passing Luca, who was standing alone by the bar, albeit checking out every woman who walked by. So I started over, blocking his view.

"No date?" I teased.

"Of course, I've got a fucking date," he chuckled. "Eric!"

"Eric, huh?" Interesting.

"Don't get any fucking ideas," he continued chuckling. "He's my neighbor; moved in a few months ago. Eric!" His hand shot up, fingers snapping, beckoning someone over.

I saw a head weave through the crowd to us, stopping at Luca's side, a pair of sky blue eyes meeting mine. Oh, shit. He smiled, just as he had at the bar last night. So he wasn't a random, he was an Eric.

"Hey!" he exclaimed, recognizing me too.

Gavin was back, one arm draping around my waist, the other handing me a flute of champagne. Shit. I looked at Eric, discreetly shaking my head no, trying to make him understand that we'd never met. The last thing I needed was to be explaining how I knew Eric or Eric knew about us.

"Eric!" Luca flicked his wrist between us. "This is my brother Gav and his wife, Sadie."

Gavin dipped his face back into my neck, smashing a kiss under my ear, making Eric's smile grew even bigger. I'd forgiven Gavin, so there was hope for him yet.

"And there's Sofia!" Luca yelled. "Sofia!"

She waltz our way, greeting guests left and right before stepping to my side. "Isn't this so—" her eyes darted from mine to Luca's to Eric. She gasped, sucking in a sharp inhale, her stare immediately falling towards the floor, eyes blinking rapidly with her even more rapid breathing.

"And Sofia, you know," Luca spoke to Eric, but Eric's downcast eyes sunk into his cheeks, his focus solely on her, his lips twitching on the verge of saying something. Oh, shit! No! I looked between them, the tension almost palpable.

"Sofia," Eric sighed, and it wasn't a greeting. It was a desperate plea. No, no! He was the other man; he was the complication. He said she was the one, that he couldn't let her go. He was Gavin's worst nightmare, the man who chased a married woman, or perhaps she wasn't running; maybe there was no chase at all.

I glanced back at Sofia, watching her shoulders rise with her inhale, her chin guiding her face back up as she cleared her throat, flashing us a tight smile, then spinning on her heels, dashing away into the crowd. Holy shit! I whipped my face back to Eric's, his eyes closing, chin falling to his chest.

"Eric's an author," Luca continued. "Crime or some shit. He's only here for a few months, right?"

Eric's gaze was distant, on the crowd. "If I can finish the story," he answered, shrugging his shoulders. "But, I'm currently at a loss for words."

A server walked by, tray out just as my hand was, snatching up another glass and downing it. "It was nice meeting you," I called to Eric as I led Gavin away. "Good luck on your story, and remember, sometimes it's best to walk away."

NEW YORK: 8

Nora was fast asleep on my chest while Vinny was fast asleep on Sofia sitting beside me. We were the last ones standing, well sitting, and Gavin was escorting Giorgia and Laurence out.

"Ready?" Sofia whispered, rising from the chair. "The cribs are being set up as we speak."

Cribs? "How'd you get them? They told Gavin there were none available."

"I demanded them, so they made them available." She sounded like Luca at that moment. Perhaps there was a side of Sofia I didn't know yet.

I stood beside her, both of us cradling the twins while we waited for Gavin, who finally jogged back, rushing right to us. "Follow us to our room Sofia so I can grab their stuff," he instructed while draping his arm over my lower back, ushering us to the doors. "You're sure this is okay?" he asked again as we stepped into the elevator.

"Of course! I've missed them!" She kissed Vinny's hair, resting her face against his.

We headed up to our suite, and Gavin took Nora from me so I could pack their stuff. Then I loaded the bag over his shoulder, simultaneously giving him a kiss goodbye.

He started out, reaching for my hand before I closed the door. "I'll be back once I get them settled and double-check the cribs."

"I'll be here!" I shut the door behind them, catching a glimpse of myself in the full-length mirror on the wall. I'd forgotten how good I looked tonight—the gown, my curls still in shape, and the professional makeup. I wanted to stay in this gown, let him undress me, but I wasn't sure which Gavin would be coming back.

Would romantic, apologetic, lovemaking Gavin walk through the door? The one who would twirl me in his arms, sink his tender lips into my neck while his fingers danced to the back of my gown, a feather-light touch caressing me as he drug the zipper down.

Or would passionate, ravenous Gavin walk in? The one who hadn't had me in days, the one that would rip the black silk right off me, clawing the intricate beading to get to my chest, beads scattering across the floor as he ravaged me.

I ran my hands over the gown. It was too beautiful to risk its destruction, so I reached for the zipper, sliding it down, carefully stepping out, and walking it to the closet. Once again, I met my reflection, only this time in the bathroom mirror. My half-naked body front and center, my hands sliding over the lace panties, thumbs hooking over the waistband, dragging them down my legs.

I returned to the main room, hopping onto the table that faced the door, crossing my legs while waiting there buck naked, ready for romantic or ravenous Gavin.

The door jiggled, cracking open with Gavin squeezing in, stopping in his tracks, the door slamming behind him. "I was afraid you might rip the dress." I uncrossed my legs, enjoying the way his eyes turned black, so it was wild Gavin coming to play.

His hand hit his chest, unhooking the single button on his suit with ease, sliding the jacket off, letting it fall to the floor behind him. Then he reached for his tie, loosening its hold around his neck, not saying a word, but his eyes spoke volumes. His shirt was next, fingers flipping each button, tugging the sleeves down those flexed biceps, his shirt joining his jacket on the floor. He flexed his chest, his arms, a predator ready for its kill. But as much as I was enjoying this eye candy. I needed more than a snack— I needed the whole damn meal.

"Pants?"

He rubbed over his zipper, the outline of his manhood all I could see as he stepped closer, yanking off his belt. His zipper was next, then he kicked the slacks to the floor, leaving just his boxers, which he was already removing. Oh, god. I clasped the edge of the table, eyes fixated on the massive dick he was stroking. The burn between my thighs instant, the fire begging to be put out.

"Baby," his hiss steamed up my neck while his knuckles rubbed my legs as he jerked himself. "I want you on the bed." He released his arousal, sliding his arms under my thighs, lifting me, spreading my legs around his waist, his match lighting an even bigger fire.

"I want you now!" Sensual Gavin would have to wait.

But he continued walking into the bedroom, lowering me to the sheets, then lowering himself over me. "I want to give you fireworks, Baby." His arms struck down at the sides of my face, pressing into the mattress, his tight body flexed over mine. "I want to make love, apologize to you, but, I really, really, want to fuck you right now."

Thank god! "Apology accepted, now fuck me!" I arched my hips, begging.

His lips dove to my chest, peppering each breast with kisses, sucking each nipple until it ached, all the while his hand dove to my center, two fingers slipping inside me, aiming right for the goal.

I tipped my head back, my hands clutching the sheets at my sides, the first heat wave rolling, the first nerves firing off from his fingers banging against them, warming me up for the fuck that was on its way.

Fingers were gone, he was grunting, grinding, revving. "Ooh!" He was inside me, deep jolt after deep jolt, nerves combusting, the pressure turning to panic. "Gavin!" I yelped, gasped, begged.

His face sprang up, cheeks tensing with each pound, his stare down on his dick moving in and out of me. "Fuck, Baby, you, feel— " he gasped, groaned, heavy hits sending my back scraping up and down the sheet. "Soo, fucking, amazing."

Oh god! His hips paced faster, his thrusts harder, sending my hands clawing his arms, nails locking to control the surge erupting in my core. "Gavin!" The boom hit, he pulled out, flipping us over, mounting me on top, impaling me with his dick. "Fuck!" The ripples soared toe to tongue, everything quaking, spasming, the climax shattering every nerve like a glass wall.

I felt his hands on my hips, rocking me over him, his grunts distant, ringing through my head. "Fuck, Baby, Fuck, Fuck!" he yelled, hands releasing my hips, sending me collapsing forward, falling face-first to his heaving chest. "I, still, owe you an apology, Baby," he choked out between moans.

I attempted to roll off of him, only his arms clamped over me, locking us chest to chest.

"We have all night, Baby," he exhaled the words. "And I plan to use every hour of it."

"Uh, huh." I lifted my face up, resting my chin on his chest. "You do owe me a very, very, *big*, apology."

I felt the rumble of laughter under me. "Whatever you want, Baby. I can get on my knees and grovel; I can let my tongue do the talking; I can kiss every inch of you to let you know how much I fucking adore you."

"All of it," I whispered. "All of you, all of that, all night."

NEW YORK: 9

A tickle danced up my arm, Gavin's heavy breathing following his long fingers. "Good morning," I yawned, slowly opening my eyes to his face staring down at me.

"Good morning, Baby." He leaned down, pecking my forehead. "I was wondering when you were gonna wake, not that I'm fucking complaining cause I love watching you sleep."

"Creep."

He grinned, still staring with such intensity. "Sofia's on her way down with the babies."

I puckered, and his lips met mine, his scratchy morning stubble tickling me some more. "How much time do we have?"

There was a knock at the door that very minute. Of course. I laughed as Gavin stood from the bed, walking to our suitcase and tossing me a shirt and some leggings while he stepped into some jeans on his way out to the front room. I wasn't ready for the night to be over. We'd made up, over and over again, and I just wanted a little more Sadie and Gavin time. But I *had* missed my babies.

I skipped the shirt and leggings Gavin had tossed over and changed into jeans and a sweater instead.

"Mamma?" Vinny's yell echoed into the room, his feet pattering right outside, so I swung the door open, sinking straight to my knees with open arms, catching my babies running into them.

"Mamma's here! Good morning!" I kissed Nora's cheek, then Vinny's. "Mamma missed you!"

"Sadie!" Sofia clapped, addressing both Gavin and me. "I was telling Gav that I'd love to keep the twins for the day! For more Zia Fia time!"

I watched Gavin, waiting for his hesitancy, but he just shrugged, nodding yes. No drama. He must have really enjoyed last night. "Sure!" Some more Sadie and Gavin time was fine by me. "Mamma loves you!" I squeezed my babies before releasing them. "Have fun with Zia Fia!"

"Nora, Vinny! Dai! Andiamo, let's go!"

The twins took off to the stroller, Gavin following to lift them into in, and then he backed away, holding the door for Sofia to wheel them out. That was it. He wasn't giving her any rules, no warnings. Usually, he was grumbling. Now, he was smiling. Who was this man? Then he shut the door, focusing back on me.

I stood, walking towards him. "A day alone. We can stay in bed all day."

He shook his head no, taking both my hands in his, petting my fingers. "No, Baby. Last time we were here at Christmas, you were pregnant, and I promised to take you ice skating when we came back."

Ice... Ice skating! "Wait, really!" I bounced against him, my smile stretching tight across my face. "Seriously?"

"I've missed that smile, Baby. I liked your smile last night, too," his voice was suddenly a rasp. "But nothing beats your excited smile. Go put on a coat!"

You didn't have to tell me twice! I hurried back to the bedroom, grabbing my jacket from the closet. Ice skating! I'd been waiting my entire life to ice skate. I could already see myself gliding gracefully across the ice. I raced back out, coat in hand, eyes on his smile and hand in his.

We headed down the elevator and through the lobby, stepping right out into the chilly New York air. "We have to go into the park." He turned to face me, studying my reaction. "Are you okay with that, Baby?"

I nodded yes, giddily pulling him forward. I felt like a teenager going on my first date. "I miss this!" I said it more to myself as I snuggled his arm, keeping close as we crossed the street with a million other people.

"What?"

"Going on a date!" I jumped over the curb, pulling his arm with me. "We haven't done anything like this in a while!" Heck, if ever. Our dates were bars or restaurants.

He looked down at me, tight smile just as unreadable as his eyes, then he nodded his head towards the path we needed to take. He continued leading me into the park, those bad memories that once haunted me gone. My focus now on the beautiful trees and the bustling people around us. "It's right around this bend," he mumbled.

"Hey, are you okay?" He went from smiles to seemingly annoyed. "You don't have to skate if you don't want to. You can just watch me!" I flashed him a smile, winking my eye obnoxiously, but he didn't laugh.

He wiggled his hand out of mine, draping his arm over my back instead, curling me into his side. "I hate these fucking memories, Baby. I hate that one is from years ago, but the other's just from a few days ago. How am I still doing that same shit?" He was serious, guilt-ridden eyes staring down at me.

"Don't think about that right now! Let's use this time to make some new memories, like watching me glide across the ice, spinning and doing triple flips."

"Jesus Christ, Baby," he chuckled. "Take it easy. You've never been on ice before."

I looked up, meeting his smile. "No. It's you who's always on thin ice."

He laughed, pushing me towards the crowded path that funneled to the ice rink. Then he led me to an empty bench, gesturing me to sit. "Wait here. I'll grab the skates."

"You don't know my size."

"I know everything about you, Baby. Whether you've told me or not."

Great, just great. "Go!" I laughed, shooing him away.

I watched him walk over to the skate rental, that scarf accentuating the scruff on his chin and cheeks, and that heavy coat clinging to his tall, muscular body. He looked like he'd stepped right out of a magazine. And, of course, I wasn't the only one checking out my man. Every man and woman around him was glancing, gawking, stealing looks. As they should, how could you not look at him? It was fine. I didn't care. They were welcome to look, it was only natural.

"Hey, I told you to wait back on the bench!"

Bench? I looked back to the bench I had been sitting on just minutes ago, then up to Gavin, who my arms were wrapped over. How did I get—once again, my brain lost the fight with my hormones, and so here I was, claiming my husband. "Sorry." I slid my hand over the back of his jacket, resting it right over his ass, making sure my rings were visible to his annoyingly captivated audience.

"Thirteen and a half in the hockey skates, and seven in the ice skates." Gavin tossed some cash to the guy behind the counter in exchange for our skates. Then he gestured me back to the bench. "Sedersi!" he demanded, sitting while handing over my skates.

Yes, sir. I sank beside him, tugging my boots off and skates on. He finished tying the thick laces on his hockey skates, knotting like a pro, and sliding to his knees in front of me, taking control of my skates. "What are you doing!" I laughed, watching him grip the laces on the left skate, yanking hard before tying. "I know how to tie!"

He smacked my hands away, moving to the right skate, yanking the laces unnecessarily rough. "You have to tie them tight. Otherwise you can hurt your ankle."

Okay. I laughed under my breath as he tied my skates, then double-checked his work.

He stood back up, towering to the sky with that extra three inches from the skates. Jeez. I stood next, ready to go. "Shall we!" That ice was calling my name. I'd spent so many nights watching ice skaters on TV. Now, it was my chance to shine.

He took my hand, gripping with all his strength as we trudged to the rink, where he let me step in first.

My skates hit the ice, the empowerment, the pride of this moment encompassing me. I skated forward, shaking away Gavin's hand.

"Baby! Hold my hand." He skated up beside me, hand out for mine, but I didn't want to couple skate. This was my moment!

I wanted to glide and twirl, just like the figure skaters I'd watched for so many years. "No, it's my first time! I want to do it by myself."

"I bet your first time with me was much better than doing it by yourself," he teased, keeping my pace.

"Give me a minute to spread my wings." To see what I could really do! He was about to be in awe. "Let me get going!"

"Again," he chuckled. "I'm pretty damn good at getting you going!"

"Gavin!" I strode forward, gliding over the ice faster, leaving him in my dust. I was a natural! I knew I would be!

"Baby!"

I heard his faint voice, the warning, but I was in the zone! I came to the curve of the rink, kicking my left foot forward to veer. "Shit!" Too fast! My right foot stumbled, over-confiscating, tripping me up, arms flailing and failing to steady me. "Fuck!" My feet were skidding back and forth over the ice, sending me flinging backward, back crashing against the cold ice. Ouch.

"Fuck!" Gavin was immediately hovering over me, his panicked face instantly turning to a chuckle and grin. "How's that whole by-myself thing working out for you, Baby?"

Very funny. I pressed my gloveless palms to the frozen ice to push myself up. "It was slippery!"

"Well, it's ice," he kept chuckling, reaching his hands down for mine, helping me up.

"No big deal!" I steadied my skates, finding my balance. Even the best skaters fell. "I've got it now!" I skated one foot in front of the other, gliding down the ice, feet in perfect harmony. "Oh shit!" My arms were flailing, skate tipping me backward as the other veered sideways, sending me crashing down, back and ass slamming into the ice.

"Fuck!" Gavin's skate skidded to a stop at my side. His panicked face once again turning to a laugh as he hovered over. "You're gonna end up with a fucking concussion, Baby. I think we should call it a day!"

"I haven't even finished one lap!" There was a learning curve!

He held his hand out, lifting me up again. "I don't want you to end up in the hospital today."

Obviously, I wouldn't... but. "Fine." I held my hand out for him, conceding to hold his hand while we skated.

He wore the smuggest grin, pinching his lips together as we skated painstakingly slow. How was it that my giant husband was more steady and graceful than I was?

We skated a few laps, staying on our feet, and really it was simple. I'd mastered it. So I moved my legs faster, our arms stretching as I gained speed. "Shit!" My skates went wacky, Gavin jerked me straight, sending us both flying into the side railing, his arms frantically trying to hold me up as my skates took off in different directions under me.

"Fuck," he chuckled. "I don't think graceful is your thing, Baby." He leaned down, pushing a plump kiss to my frozen nose. "And I'm starting to get nervous, and I really don't want to have to deal with my fucking nerves today."

I fell into his hold, watching kids, even toddlers, skate past us with ease. It looked so easy on TV, but ice skating had literally kicked my ass. "That's fine. My ass is frozen anyways."

"Well," his hiss found my ear, that devilish grin curling up against my neck. "I'll happily warm your ass up."

I bet. "Why don't you get me out of here safely first."

He laughed under his breath as he stepped forward, guiding me over the ice to the exit, both hands helping me out of the rink like the other parents with their kids. "Clumsy and messy," he kept laughing, guiding me back to the bench.

"Excuse me?" I sat down, rolling my eyes up at his.

"Nothing, Baby. You're just cute."

"Uh, huh." I bent for my skates, but he kneeled, beating me to it, already unlacing them.

"Where to next?" I tried to contain my smile. "Back to the room? Go grab the twins?"

He shook his head no while forcing his foot into his shoe. "No, Baby. I want to finish our date."

NEW YORK: 10

Gavin took my hand, leading me across the street from the park. We'd been wandering for hours, walking every path, stopping at every fountain and bridge. "This is the Upper West Side, Baby. We can grab lunch over here. What are you in the mood for?" He stepped up onto the curb, brushing his black locks back as those deep brown eyes fell to me. I knew exactly what I wanted. I slipped my hand out of his hold, coasting my fingers up his arm. "For lunch, Baby," he spoke through that devilish grin. Why was he so sexy? "Deli?" he asked, pointing up the street. "Or Italian?"

"I had plenty Italian last night," I flirted up. So much so that even the shower hadn't washed his scent from my skin or his taste from my mouth. "A mocha would be good. I'm freezing, and I haven't had my coffee yet. I need to warm up."

"There's a place up the block." His hand was back over mine, leading me up the street, right through the door of an eccentric coffee shop. "Mocha," he ordered, swinging his arm over me while the barista made it. Then we were out the doors, walking up the street. "I gotta eat, Baby. I need my stamina."

"Yes, you do!"

"I'll just grab a sandwich." He led me up another block, then abruptly stopped. "This is where I got my tattoos." He nodded to the parlor in front of us before looking back at me. "Come on!" He was suddenly excited, rushing for and through the sticker-covered door.

"Another Romano!" Some guy yelled the second Gavin and me stepped in. "Had Luca in here a few weeks ago!"

"Yeah?" Gavin chuckled. "What'd he get?"

"An ornate cross with some initials on his arm," the guy replied on his way over to us.

"What initials?" I asked automatically before sinking back behind Gavin.

He shrugged. "Oh, fuck. Let me think. An E and a V in the top quadrants and an N and a V in the bottom."

His parents and the twins. It didn't surprise me. I knew how much Luca loved the babies.

"My own fucking brother gets my kids' initials tatted before I do," Gavin scoffed. "You have some time?"

He nodded back. "What do you want?"

"Three names across my chest, stacked right over my heart. Sadie, Vinny, Nora." He reached back for my hand, pulling my ring finger forward. "In black ink, this same font. I want a carbon copy of this style." He pushed my rings up for the artist to study my finger.

"Get in the seat," he instructed Gavin, pointing to the empty chair in the corner.

"This okay, Baby?" Gavin asked while already shaking off his coat and unraveling his scarf.

I nodded yes, enjoying my show, watching him tug his sweater and undershirt over his head, messing up his hair, making it wild and wavy before he rested back onto the chair. Damn. I pushed my drink to my lips in an attempt to distract myself from his bare chest, that now messy hair, and the fact that he was getting our names permanently inked over his heart.

The artist sketched out the names and Gavin approved, sliding his hand over to mine, intertwining our fingers. His eyes stayed on me while I watched the needle pierce his skin, inking the S of my name first, directly over the strong muscles protecting his heart. Now, I understood why the tattoo I got meant so much to him. I knew Gavin loved me, and I knew he was in love with me. But seeing my name become a permanent part of his body was incredible. A ring could be removed, this would always be there. My name would always be there.

I lost track of time, watching the needle, nurse instincts kicking in and out until finally, it was complete. My name on top, Vinny's under with Nora below his, and they all perfectly matched his name on my finger. The artist then handed Gavin a mirror, letting him check it out before coating it with ointment and bandaging it up.

"That's a wrap," the artist laughed to himself.

"Wait!" Gavin lifted his left hand, sliding his wedding band off and dropping it into my hand. "I want to get *Sadie* on my finger, same style."

The artist's stare flickered between Gavin and me. "You want her name twice?"

"You want my name twice!" I said in unison.

"I'd cover my whole body with your name, Baby. Well, maybe not my whole body."

"Are you sure?" The artist asked once more, and Gavin nodded yes, reaching for my hand again, squeezing it as the artist started on his ring finger.

"You know you're crazy, right!" I teased down to those brown eyes looking up at me.

His mischievous smile curled up. "I've been told that a few fucking times."

My gaze drifted from his face to the needle, then to his bandaged chest.

"Why are you smiling like that?" he asked, forcing my focus back on his face.

"I was thinking you might need a nurse tonight and some very special treatment."

The artist cleared his throat, the artist! Oh, god. "That's it! Anything else you want?" He laughed, wrapping the bandage over Gavin's finger.

"Nope," Gavin replied, still staring up at me. "I have it all!" He dug out his credit card, handing it over while I handed him his sweater and coat. And just like that, he was covered, as if none of this happened.

We started back outside, the sun was long gone now. "I guess I don't have to worry if you're not wearing your ring," I teased, snuggling into him. "Since you copied me and branded yourself."

He slammed to a stop, spinning me to face him directly, his hands clasping mine. "I didn't fucking brand myself, Baby. I didn't get it so chicks would know I was taken. I don't have people staring at me like they do you."

Jeez, he was delusional sometimes.

"I got this as a vow, to remind myself of this trip. So if I ever get too fucking lost in my head or in such a damn jealous rage—that I'll see this ink and remember your face as the elevator doors closed—and you, my wife, not taking my hand. To remember the way you looked at me with such fucking disgust, and the panic I felt when I thought you might not come back. I got your name so I would stop thinking about me—and think about you. This is a vow to be better, to remember that the shit I say can destroy us, and that I'm never gonna break my vows again. I don't want to keep saying sorry, Baby. No matter how much I enjoy apologizing."

Wow.

"Why are you crying, Baby?" He raised his hand to my cheek, wiping away the tears I hadn't felt.

"You surprise me sometimes." I carefully fell into his chest, wrapping my arms around his back while he did the same. "I love that you did this for me, for us." He was trying to be better. He hadn't forgotten; he hadn't blown it off. He was actively trying to better himself, for me. "I think we should head back to the room."

He chuckled, the warm exhale sending a chill down my arms. "You want me to apologize some more?"

"No. I think you need a nurse. And I know just the right treatment."

NEW YORK: 11

We made it to the hotel room, both of us slipping off our coats. "I'm going to take a quick shower. Want to join me?" I asked, hands shaking from the cold yet wiping the sweat from the heat of our many make-out sessions on the way back.

He shook his head no, pointing to his chest, right over the bandage that was under his sweater. That's right. "Okay, I'll make it fast."

I was in and out in no time, walking back out to the room. "What do you—" I yelled, only to find Gavin sitting at the edge of the bed, still fully dressed. Even better, I get a show. "Take your sweater off," I demanded, taking a step forward, unraveling the knot in my towel.

He let out a deep sigh, rolling his eyes up towards the ceiling, ignoring the towel on the floor and my naked body. "Get dressed!" He kept his eyes up, averting me. "Sofia's gonna keep the babies again tonight, and I want to take you out."

We just got back. "She's keeping them again?"

"Yeah," he sighed. "But I don't want to talk about it. I'll get too worried, so get dressed and let's get out of here!" He dropped his face back down, eyes raking over my body, and then he was up, flying out the bedroom door.

But... I wanted him... "We have time for a quick—"

"No, Baby! Once we start, I won't want to stop, and I want to give you all the dates you always miss out on."

Oh, that sounded good, too. A dinner date. Those were few and far between. I started for the closet, reaching for a sweater, only to see one of my dresses, perfect. I slipped into that instead. It was freezing, but I was skipping the tights, they only got in the way. Next, I swiped on some mascara and gloss and stepped into my heels. "Ready?" I hurried into the main room, catching Gavin fastening the last of his buttons on his navy dress shirt, almost the same shade as my dress.

His eyes went wide, once again raking over my body. "Leave!" he commanded, arm flying up, pointing me to the door. "Wait for me in the hall. Get out now!"

I laughed. "What?"

"You look so fucking sexy, Baby. If you don't wait outside, I'm gonna carry you back into the bedroom."

I started laughing, covering my cleavage with one hand while slinging my purse over my shoulder. "I'll be outside then." I walked out to the hall like he instructed, waiting a few minutes before the door finally opened behind me, and he stepped out. Holy shit. I took a step back, my jaw suddenly the weight of iron, stunned for half a second.

His dress shirt was ripping at the seams, every muscle protruding, every bump and line visible. His slacks were just as fitted, leaving nothing to the imagination. And that face, slicked back hair, sexy stubble lining his lips, his chin, cheeks, while those black eyes reflected the light above.

I stumbled back, spinning on my heels, dashing away, sprinting to the elevator, only his heavy footsteps were closing in, hands slacking my waist, capturing me. No! If I looked at him again, then I wouldn't want dinner. I'd want something else in my mouth. I shot my hand out, attacking the elevator button.

"That elevator better get here soon," his rasp streamed down my neck, scratchy lips kissing their way to my shoulder.

"Date nights are overrated," I gasped, trying to catch my breath. "Let's go back to the room!" I spun in his arms as the elevator doors slid open, and he kept me hostage, carrying me into the lift, waiting until the door was closed and it was in motion before releasing me.

"We have forever to fuck, Baby. Date nights, however, are limited." He arched his brow as his forehead tipped to mine.

"Date nights," I grumbled back. I'd been waiting for a date night. Now, I just wanted to get him in bed.

"Dinner?" He ran his fingers up and down my sides.

"Dessert," I countered.

"Restaurant?"

"Bar," I countered once again. "Copious amounts of alcohol for dinner and wife for dessert."

His lips were back at my neck. "That works for me."

The elevator door slid open, his lips retreated, both of us taking a deep, calming breath before he led us out.

We took the only empty barstools at the counter, and Gavin immediately ordered. But I wasn't paying attention to what he was saying because I was too consumed with him. The hottest man at the bar, the man, that even sitting on a stool, towered over everyone around, and that man had my name tattooed twice on him.

There was a shot in my hand; I drank it automatically, then another, and another. The room grew even darker, he grew even sexier, our kisses more frequent, getting drunk off his whiskey-covered tongue.

I downed another shot, hands falling from the glass, to the bar counter, to his thighs, watching his slow smile spread. His bloodshot eyes watched me while his hand stretched to my calf, knuckles dragging up my calf. His eyes once again doing most of the talking.

Everything was moving slower, every touch felt so much deeper, every urge inside me that much stronger.

All at once, the bar started emptying, people bumping and pushing their way out. "Where's, everyone going?"

"To the club upstairs."

A strange yet familiar voice answered. I looked over, recognizing the bartender from the other night. "Club?" Club! Dancing! I needed to dance, to feel Gavin's hands commanding my hips, to feel his erection grinding into my ass. Club! "Let's go!"

"Where?" Gavin's groggy smile met mine, his greedy hands sliding under my dress.

"The club!" I jumped up, cleavage bouncing in his face.

"Alright." He stood, eyes like lasers on me, making me stumble back, then the two of us fumbled our way to the elevator, taking it to the top level with everyone else.

The space was dark, the music pulsing, seducing us to the dance floor. He was behind me, hot whiskey breath at my ear, hands clamped around my waist, tipping my ass even deeper against his pants. I was swaying, shimmying, rubbing up and down his body. The lights, music, room—all spinning around me.

My hips rocked with the rhythm, side to side, back tight against his chest.

His face dropped to my shoulder, hands crept up my sides, tracing the outline of my chest while his kiss hit my neck. But, I wanted those lips on mine. I twirled, chest banging into his, grinding my way down, slithering to his feet, holding his legs as I worked my way up, my face brushing his zipper, cleavage following.

"Fuck!" His grunt thundered over the music, his hand seizing mine, leading me away. He stopped, falling into a chair. He was sitting? "You're too fucking sexy, Baby, and I'm too fucking drunk to control myself. I need a minute."

A minute? I couldn't stop moving! The music was coursing through me, my buzz still strong. I had to move my body—I needed to move my body. I backed over his lap, dress riding up my thighs as I gripped his knees in front of me, grinding my ass back over his pants, my hips controlled by the ecstasy, the beat, the alcohol, and the sexy man under me.

"Jesus fucking Christ," he groaned behind me, fingers clapping over my waist. But it wasn't enough to hear him; I needed to see him! I lifted, flipping around, straddling my thighs over his, watching him as I rocked my way down into his lap, my hands running up my dress as I danced for him. "Since when do you give fucking lap dances!" he groaned again, hooded stare locked on my chest bouncing in his face. Then hands hit my bare thighs, his touch like fire, searing my skin. Shit. I lowered my hips, my panties hitting his pants, rubbing against the erection trapped under them. Fuck, it felt good. I rubbed harder, grinding against him as his fingers crept up my thighs, dipping under the dress, to the wet lace of my panties. "Cazzo!" he hissed, dragging his thumbs up and down. "Come sei bagnata. You're so wet."

It was too much! His sexy face, his fingers, that Italian spilling from his lips. "I want you to fuck me!"

He sprung up, bucking me off him, pulling me into his arm, charging us towards the back of the club, down a crowded hall, smacking the mens' restroom door open, interrupting two guys snorting coke on the sink. "Get the fuck out!" he spat, kicking the door back open, leaving them grumbling as they retreated, no one fucked with a man the size of Gavin.

"This one has a fucking lock." He grinned, twisting the deadbolt.

It was a flash, him pouncing, my back banging against the wall, his mouth ravaging my cleavage, hand sliding under my dress while his other ripped at his belt. Dark, loud, our breaths steaming and screaming. My hands found his hair, his fingers found my entrance, I gasped, he grunted.

Then wet hands flew under my thighs, spreading me wide, pinning me to the wall, his dick jabbing between me. "Fuck, I love you, Baby!" He shoved inside me, a hard thrust nailing me to the wall, body crashing to mine.

"Shit." Every hit felt stronger than the last, every thrust making me quiver.

"You're, so, fucking, wet." Thrusts turned to pounds, my hips grinding as hard as he was fucking, both of us moving too fast, too hard. A surge igniting, a drug taking over me, the warmth spreading through my veins, the end coming.

"Gavin, I," I gasped, body flinging from the wall, heels dropping to the floor, hands to the dirty sink, eyes on his reflection in the mirror.

"Bend over." He pushed my back down, my ass in his hands, his dick driving back inside me. Fucking hard.

"Gavin!" I burst, elbows trembling, face falling, arms catching me before I hit the sink.

He held me up against him, one hand groping my tit. "I'm not done with you, Baby. I wanna take you back to our room."

I nodded, the rest of my body immobile. "I'm yours for the taking."

NEW YORK: 12

I stumbled out the bathroom door, leaning against Gavin, my stilettos feeling foreign on my feet. He walked straight past the dance floor, ignoring my protests. I wanted to dance.

"The room!" he shouted over the music.

"How about the chair! I can dance." I rolled my hips, body winding up and down. "You can watch."

He dug his hand over his pants, adjusting himself. "I don't want to watch, Baby." He kept charging away.

"San Diego fucking Barbie!"

Every hair prickled, that cringe-inducing voice echoing off the walls, sending my face whipping back, searching the club, spotting *him*! And his beady eyes were on me. That rat-faced mother fucker thought he had the right to look at me! He was the reason Gavin and I fought! He almost separated us! He treated Gavin like shit! He was an asshole!

I was being pulled further away; Gavin hadn't heard Adam's voice. Fuck that! There was no way I was leaving! I pulled my arm back, shaking out of his grip.

"I don't want to fucking dance, Baby! I want to—" his voice was nothing but a whisper behind me as I charged for the asshole.

Adam's eyes were on my legs, my chest, his slimy smile creeping up his face. Then I saw Luca. Luca! Luca was still hanging around this piece of trash! After everything he said to Gavin, to me! Unbelievable!

"OH FUCK! Baby!" Gavin roared in the distance.

I hadn't wanted them to think I was a bitch all those years ago, but now I didn't give a fuck! I was that bitch!

"And she's still with that fucking pussy!" Adam's eyes were behind me. On my husband! He didn't have the right to look at Gavin either.

His stupid mouth started rattling off again, yelling over to Gavin. "I owe you for fucking hitting me! You fucki—"

My arm was back, a slingshot unleashing forward, fist slamming into the brick wall that was Adam's face.

"What the fuck!" he spat back. "Get your bitch under control!"

Oh, hell no! I threw my arm back again, then jerked my knee up, only to be caught by strong arms, swinging me away just as a boom roared behind me.

I threw my face back, seeing Luca's fist still in the air and Adam falling back, skidding across the floor. He was down, this was my chance! "Let me go!" I elbowed Gavin, finally wiggling free of his grip, charging towards Adam.

"Jesus Christ!" Luca boomed, shaking the floor harder than the bass. "Get her the fuck out of here!"

I was being tossed up into Gavin's arms, flipped right over his shoulder, his hand smacking against my ass, gripping to hold me down. "Gavin!" I screamed, the rage so intense I couldn't see straight. "Gavin!" I slapped his back, batting at it, trying to kick my legs, but his grip was too strong.

He marched out of the club, into the elevator, holding me until the doors closed before lowering me down, still keeping his hold on my waist.

"Let me go!" I demanded.

His eyes were solid black, face rigid, furious. "You need to go back to the room, Sadie."

"I'm not done!" I shouted back, ready to smack the stop button. "I'm going to finish it this time!" He had no idea what was coming!

"He's gonna get handled," Gavin snapped, blocking my hand, his face set hard as stone. "But you need to get back to the room first." His hand fell to my cheek, brushing the hair out of my face, his eyes focusing on something else, on his hand and the bandage over his ring finger. "Fuck!" He rolled his eyes, inhaling heavily through his nose, lips pinching. Then his gaze met mine, tense face gradually relaxing. "We'll both go back to the room," he mumbled, keeping his hand against my cheek. "Luca can handle it." Both his hands slid down to mine. And suddenly, he was smiling, smiling? "You know," he continued. "You're a mamma now, and violence doesn't solve anything. I mean, what if you got arrested. We have babies at home."

What if? No! My words, my words! The nerve! I hated when he repeated my own words. I met his stupid grin, only now he was chuckling. This was different! "He deserved that! He's an asshole! This, was, different!"

"Of course, it was *different*, Baby." He nodded his head. "I didn't say hypocrite."

"He! It, that, different!" I scoffed. "He deserved that! You know he did!"

He squeezed my hands, dipping his face to mine. "You're sexy when you get feisty."

The elevator door slid open, and he dragged me down the hall, squeezing us by a room service cart, stopping, throwing his arm back to grab the bottle of champagne from the cart.

"Hey!" A server yelled, hustling over. "You can't take that!"

"Jesus," Gavin groaned, turning back. "How much did they pay for this?"

"A hundred bucks!"

He yanked out his wallet, tossing three hundreds to the guy. "I'm sure you can go grab them another bottle. Now, open this one, please."

The server pocketed the cash, twisted the cork, then Gavin was whirling me away, hurrying us to the room door, kicking it open.

The door slammed, rattling the room, but Gavin was unfazed, not even blinking as he pushed the bottle to his mouth, biting and spitting the cork out. He took a swig, staring at me with the darkest, most intimidating gaze. "Your turn, open up." He tipped the bottle to my lips, watching me drink. "How much do you like that dress?" He flipped the bottle back to his mouth, taking a gulp before setting it on the table.

This dress was at his disposal. "It's just a—"

"Good!" His lips smashed mine, champagne spilling from his tongue to my mouth, his fingers clawing at the fabric over my chest, bunching it into his fists, tearing it apart, ripping it from my body, catching my breasts with his greedy, groping hands. "I want to fuck these tonight. I want to fuck every inch of you tonight, Sadie." He lifted the champagne back up, taking a drink, tipping the bottle to my lips, then tilting it over my chest, the cold stream making my nipples that much harder. "I can't get that image of you hitting him out of my head—" his face fell to my chest, tongue stretching, lapping up my champagne drenched nipples. "That was so fucking hot!" He pushed the bottle back to my sealed lips.

No more. "I'm drunk enough."

His hand coasted up my cheek, fingers splayed, sliding into my hair, wrapping around the back of my neck. "Not for what I have planned." He tipped the bottle again, stepping in closer, his body towering over mine, jet black eyes focused on my lips. "Drink, Sadie."

I opened my mouth, swallowing from the intimidation before swallowing the champagne.

A boom, my body shaking, no, the floor shaking under me. Ow. Dreams turned black, black faded to reality. Ow. I blinked, eyelids stinging, struggling to open. It was cold, no, freezing. And all of me ached. I opened one eye, the other stuck with my cheek to the... bathroom floor. I peeled my face off the tile, lifting it, a jackhammer nailing it back down to the floor. Shit. Everything hurt—my toes, legs, thighs, chest, hair, mouth, everything!

I tried again, palm desperately bracing the floor, arm pushing me up. Oh, god! Too fast! I lurched forward, hugging the porcelain, dry heaving into the toilet. "Fuck." I fell back down, flat on my back, naked, aching body sprawled across the floor. What the hell did he do to me last night?

"One minute!" Gavin yelled from somewhere, then the door swung open, a half-naked Gavin barging in, rubbing his eyes before rolling them down to me. "Fuck." He bent down, dropping his hand to my thigh, making me flinch, seeing the slight bruises that matched the shape of his fingertips.

"Sofia's here, Baby." He reached his hand for mine; I attempted to lift my arm, and failed.

"I'm too sore."

He stood, walking out only to reappear a minute later with a robe in his hands. He bent down again, arms sliding under my back, lifting me off the floor and up to my feet. Then he draped the robe over me before hoisting me up in his arms and carrying me out of the bathroom.

Oh, my, god! It was mass destruction—bed torn apart, furniture flipped, lamp on the floor, champagne bottle, correction bottles scattered everywhere. "We're going to owe this hotel a lot of money."

He looked down at me, flashing a sexy smile. "Money well spent." He lowered me to the couch just as another knock sounded, and he started for the door.

"Wait, Gavin! Shut the bedroom door!" I didn't want anyone seeing that crime scene. He raced to the bedroom door, slamming it before rushing to open the main one.

"Infine! Finally!" Sofia wheeled the stroller in, lifting the twins to the floor.

"Mamma! Papà!" They squealed, with Nora taking off to Gavin while Vinny ran to me, climbing onto my lap.

"Ti vigo be-ne," he squeaked out.

"Mamma loves you, too." I kissed his cheek. His toddler Italian was so cute.

Sofia's gaze danced between us. "How was your night? Romantic, I hope! Dinner? Show? A carriage ride around the park? New York's beautiful at Christmas, romantic."

Romantic? I laughed to myself. Let's see—bar, club, dancing, fucking, fighting, and tearing up this hotel room, and me in the process. I'd always watched those sweet romantic movies, hoping to find that guy who would sweep me off my feet, one who lived and breathed romance. A well-behaved man, but Gavin was right. I didn't like well-behaved. He had altered my definition of romance, and I was perfectly okay with that.

"It was fun," Gavin replied with a wry smile. "And very needed." He met my eyes, his stare making me blush.

"Should I wait while you get dressed?" Her focus was on my robe, then Gavin's pajama pants. "It's your last day," she continued. "We had talked about taking the twins to see Mamma and Papà at the cemetery, and then Santa. Luca and Stefano will be here in twenty minutes."

How did I explain that her brother had fucked me so good and hard that I couldn't walk nor lift my children at this moment. "Do you think—"

"I'll take the twins to breakfast!" she offered, already knowing my question. "Andiamo. Nora, Vinny!"

"Mamma needs twenty minutes; then I'm all yours!" I kissed Vinny one last time, but he wasn't moving from Mamma. So Sofia walked over, plucking him from my lap, tickling him while she carried him to the stroller. Gavin loaded Nora next, and then they were out, and that door was shut. And Gavin was giving me the look.

"No! Hard no!" I tugged the robe tighter over me. "You can carry me to the shower, get me meds, and coffee."

He slipped his arms under my back, lifting me from the couch. "Not even—"

"No!"

NEW YORK: 13

I sat at the edge of the bed, legs out for Gavin, who was sliding my boots on. He was still in pajama pants, helping me get dressed first because I was helpless, which was his fault. Then he straightened back up, stretching as he faced the mirror, raising his hand to his chest, rubbing over the bandage, then peeling it off. I forced my wobbly legs to stand, walking over to see our names up close. "Maybe I should get a tattoo with the kids' names too, Grant, Nora, Vinny." I rubbed over my wrist, visualizing the names.

His eyes found mine in the reflection, staring a split second before walking away into the bathroom.

"Gavin?" Great. We were moving again. I forced myself forward, limping after him. "We could go by later today," I suggested as he flipped the faucet on, running a towel under it. I nabbed it from his hand, dabbing it over his tattoo. "Well?" I waited for any kind of reply. Why was he being so quiet? "Do you not want me to get a tattoo here? I can get it back home."

"Fuck," he grumbled more to himself. "I don't wanna sound like a selfish prick right now."

Selfish prick? "Why? Talk to me."

He lifted my left hand, sliding my rings up, smiling at his name. "This means a lot to me, Baby. The fact that my name is the only thing on your body, it's, it's powerful. And I know how shitty that fucking sounds right now because they're our children, but if you get more tattoos, then this just becomes another piece of ink. It diminishes the value." He dropped my hand, reaching for his sweater instead, tugging it over his head. "Fuck," he groaned. "I'll take you to get it today. I know how fucking horrible that sounded. I don't know what the fuck's wrong with me sometimes. Of course, you should get their names, Baby," he grumbled under his breath, eyes rolling, having an internal argument with himself while he slicked his hair. He was making this more than it actually was.

"I don't need a tattoo." I wrapped both my arms over his waist. "A necklace with their names would mean just as much."

"Are you sure?" His eyes were deep, sensitive Gavin staring down at me. The one that had lost everything, the one whose sweet possessive heart needed reassurance of my love and that he wasn't going to lose me, too.

"I'm happy just having your name. Plus, what if I met another Vinny? I wouldn't want him getting the wrong idea."

"Very funny," he mock laughed, draping his arms over me too. "You ready?" He finished dressing and took my hand, leading me out for our coats and then to the lobby.

Luca was front and center with Nora in his arms. He didn't even deserve to hold her. After everything Adam had done, he was still hanging out with him. I marched over, arms outstretched demanding Nora. "I can't believe you still hang out with him."

"I don't," Luca bellowed behind me. "I needed to get out last night. Then you fucking show up and kick his ass."

Gavin bent down for Vinny, lifting him into his arms. "Where's Stefano?"

"He's not coming," Sofia sighed, shrugging. "All I know is Mark left unexpectedly. He was supposed to stay over Christmas."

"Let's go then," Luca huffed, waving everyone forward. "Cemetery then Santa."

We followed Luca outside to the waiting SUV, loading the babies into the car before climbing in ourselves. Then we took off, Gavin and Luca immediately going off in Italian while Sofia played with the twins. So I pulled out my phone, sending Mark a text. *Everything okay?*

I watched the screen, seeing the thought bubble pop-up and then his reply. *You said it best, New York is toxic.*

Technically Gavin had said it, but it was still true. I typed back. *I'll be home tomorrow. Can talk if you want.*

He didn't reply. Whatever happened was bad enough to send him home a week early.

"Sadie!" Sofia called, focusing back on me. "I'm so sad to be missing the babies this Christmas! It'll be our first Christmas we aren't spending together."

"What about you, Luca?" I asked. "Aren't you going to Sofia's? You can't be alone on Christmas."

"Why is everybody so hung up on me being alone," he grumbled. "I'm fine."

"I, I just meant—"

"You can come to Cali," Gavin chimed in.

"Nah, I'm gonna stay in New York. I'll stop by Sofia's, maybe bring Eric."

"We, we, I," Sofia stammered, her eyes avoiding Luca's. "Family only, as always," she continued. She was worked up now, and I was the only one who knew why.

The SUV stopped, the cemetery suddenly right in front of us. The last time we were here I had to force Gavin out, but this time he tossed the door open, unloading Vinny while Luca unloaded Nora. Sofia and I followed, trailing the guys down the path to their parents. It was different this time. I didn't have to lead Gavin, and he wasn't somber, in fact, he almost seemed happy.

They all walked in front of me to the graves, so I hung back, giving them some space. The guys lowered Vinny and Nora to the ground, holding their shoulders.

"Nora, Vinny." Gavin bent down beside them, pointing to the headstones. "This is your nonna and nonno. They aren't here anymore, but they're still with us, up in the stars." He switched to Italian, rattling off while his eyes flashed from the headstones to the twins. And somehow, I knew exactly what he was saying.

"Vieni qui, Baby," Gavin beckoned me to him. "Come here, Baby."

I clasped his hand, standing at his side, spotting the wreath ornament we had placed there two years ago, and next to that was a picture of Nora and Vinny. "Where'd that come from?" I crouched down to better see the frame.

"I brought it by," Luca answered. "Thought they might want to see'em."

"They'd be so in love if they were here today!" Sofia bent down beside the twins. "I'm sure they're watching everything from above."

"Come on," Gavin called. "Say goodbye to Nonna e Nonno. We'll see them soon." He lifted a baby in each arm before smiling up at the sky. I bet they were watching everything from above, everything. Oh, shit!

I lingered behind, waiting until they were all out of earshot before stepping to the headstones, whispering against the granite. "Please don't hold last night against me, any of it." I cringed. "I was drunk; we were drunk. I don't punch people, and Gavin and I aren't usually so, um, well I'm usually more reserved, so I apologize for anything you might have witnessed. I'm typically a more well-behaved daughter-in-law. Maybe in the future, you could not watch everything. Merry Christmas." I hurried to catch up with the group.

Tomorrow we'd be back in San Diego, all this craziness would be just a memory, and Gavin and Sadie would be back to being Mamma and Papà.

VALENTINE'S DAY: 1

"Good morning, Baby," Gavin's raspy morning voice tickled my ear. "Happy Valentine's Day."

I tilted my face up, meeting his sexy smile. "Happy Valentine's Day."

"I'm gonna grab the babies. You sleep in," he insisted, lifting his arm from over me while sliding out from under me.

"Sleep in?" I repeated, rolling over onto my back while watching his naked body walk to the dresser. "It is a good morning."

He grabbed his pajama pants, turning to face me as he stepped into them. Happy Valentine's Day to me indeed. He flashed me a quick grin before disappearing out of the room.

I cozied into the pillow, trying to sleep, but the roar of giggles echoed into the room. I didn't want to sleep alone; I wanted to be down there with them. I slipped back into my pajamas and started down the stairs, following the smell of coffee. Yum! I walked the hall, stilling, staring at the three oversized vases lining the counter, each filled with dozens of oversized purple roses. "Gavin?"

"Happy Valentine's Day, Mamma!" He opened the baby gate, sending all three of them barreling my way.

"Why are there so many?" I pressed my nose to the violet petals, smelling each bouquet.

His arms snuck over my waist. "A dozen from me, a dozen from Vinny, a dozen from Nora," he gushed. "We love you, Mamma!"

I bent down automatically to pick Vinny up while he lifted Nora. "Are you okay with the flowers?"

He smiled reassuringly, smashing a kiss to my lips. "I'm at peace. It made me happy to get them for you."

He *had* been at peace lately, ever since New York. His parents' anniversary hadn't sent him spiraling this year. He was actually happy, content. All three brothers had made such strides in their healing and finding happiness.

"And," he continued. "Grant's coming over in a little bit to babysit."

Grant, what? "Really? You arranged that with him? More importantly, you want him to babysit?" I laughed. "What about Danica?"

"Don't worry about it. It's Valentine's Day. And you're finally gonna get the one you deserve."

The one I deserve? I sniffed the dozens of roses again. New York *had* really changed him. "Hotel?" I guessed, but he shook his head no.

"Lunch and a movie, Baby."

"Lunch and a movie?" That's what he'd planned? We'd never gone to a movie before. "Are you serious? A real date?"

"Yup, no funny business," he chuckled. "Just taking my girl on a proper date, a few years late."

"And you know it needs to be a romantic movie, right? No horror or action on Valentine's Day."

"I've got it handled."

"I'm sorry," I laughed, spinning Vinny and me into his arms. "Am I still dreaming? Roses, lunch, movie? What did you do?"

"Huh?"

"Did you do something wrong?" I teased. "Is this your apology?"

His eyes flashed down, gaze sliding left to right, finally looking back into mine. "No," he shook his head with a heavy sigh. "I'm sorry I'm not more romantic, Baby. I'm trying."

I was teasing, but he took me seriously, disappointed with himself. "Where are we going for lunch?" I poked his side, trying to get that smile back on his face.

"You'll see." He skirted the answer, tight-lipped smile locked.

"I need to know what to wear—dress and heels, jeans, leggings?"

He looked up, thinking. "Jeans and a sweater, casual," he answered, although he seemed to be second-guessing that. "I tried to do dinner, but Grant already had plans."

"Lunch sounds perfect!" I lowered Vinny to the floor. "But, you know what we need first?"

"A kiss." He lowered Nora to the floor, instantly leaning into me, lips puckered.

I smacked him another kiss. "And breakfast! Who wants to help Mamma make heart pancakes?"

Gavin was already downstairs, dressed and ready to go, so I changed into some jeans and a tight sweater, then threw on some makeup and stepped into my knee-high boots.

"You ready, Baby?" Gavin yelled up the stairs just as I walked out the bedroom door, seeing him and Grant.

"I am!" I shuffled down. "Hi, Sweetie!"

Gavin captured me the second I stepped off the bottom stair, swinging me up in his arms. Somebody was excited. "We'll be back later, Grant!" Gavin reached for the door, ready to go.

"And Danica doesn't mind?" I verified.

"No," he answered, arms out for the twins now running to him. "She's working until six, anyway."

"Okay, we appreciate it!" I hugged him on my way out the door, finding Gavin's supercar in the driveway. "I've missed this car." I hadn't driven in it in a while.

"It's missed you, too!" He opened the passenger door, waiting for me to get in and closing the door behind me before rounding the car to his side.

We took off. My sexy husband commanding the car. "You know after the movie we should find a nice empty beach parking lot for me to give you your Valentine's present."

"Why do you always want to get dirty when I'm trying to be romantic, Baby."

"I don't know. You, this car, and we don't have to get dirty—I can keep it clean."

His face tipped my way. "No, I like dirty."

"So, where are you taking me?"

"You'll see." He avoided my question again, zigzagging through traffic until finally pulling up to the familiar valet stand. "Look familiar?" He laughed, hopping out immediately to grab my door and then my hand.

I looked at the seaside shopping center, remembering our first outing—the ice cream, the beach, oh... the beach. I looked around, noticing the fog rolling in. "It's foggy."

"It is," his voice was suddenly low. "But that's not why I brought you back here."

"The ice cream?" I flirted, rubbing up against his arm, but he shook his head no.

"We had lunch at that barbecue restaurant, our first unofficial date. Except you paid, and that's always driven me fucking crazy. Today we're having a redo of our first date, and I'm paying."

"A redo?" Of course, Mr. Perfection thought he half-assed that date, now he had to remedy it. "Does that mean I have to order that giant sandwich, so you can take a picture of my messy face again?"

"Like I said earlier, Baby. I like dirty."

We walked straight to the restaurant, were seated at the exact same booth, and ordered the exact same meals we had the first time. That Sadie would have never believed me if I told her that she would marry that man, have his kids, and be here all these years later, with her husband.

The waitress approached with our plates, setting them in front of us. "I forgot how big this sandwich was!" This was what I really ordered on a first date? I laughed to myself.

"As I recall," Gavin whispered, fingers creeping across the table to my hands. "You were really fucking *hungry* that day."

God, I had been. Those magic fingers were one of the reasons I was here today. "I was, although you did most of the work. I think in this redo, I'll do most of the work."

He dropped his back against the booth. "Keep talking like that and we're not gonna make it to the movie, Baby."

"You've never taken me to the movies before. It's the most common date, and we've never gone."

"Sorry. I never think to do that shit."

"Me neither. If it's between a night with you or a night in the theater, I will always choose you." I picked up my sandwich, knowing what was about to happen, and also knowing how oddly happy it would make him. So I opened my mouth as wide as I could, tearing into it, instantly feeling the barbecue sauce smear across my face. And as expected, he reached down, pulling out his phone while I laughed, knowing how ridiculous I looked.

"I remember taking your picture like this all those years ago," he sighed, setting his phone on the table so he could hold both my hands. "It was the first picture of a chick I'd ever taken."

Ever? "That was the first picture of a woman you'd ever taken? Really? And you took it of my face," I laughed, pushing the napkin to my mouth. "Not of my chest, my ass, not my face with makeup—but this?" I continued laughing, wiping my sauce-covered lips. "This was the moment you chose to photograph."

He nodded silently, smiling to himself. "I wasn't taking the photo so I could get off. I took it because it made me smile, and when I looked at it later, it made me laugh. You were more than a fuck. I knew it right away."

"Well, aren't you the romantic," I teased, and he pushed himself over the table, licking my lips just as he had on that first date.

"I love you, Baby."

"I love you, too."

The waitress stopped by again, dropping the bill, which Gavin yanked over, proudly reaching for his pants. Then he flung his other hand down, wriggling in his seat, hands smacking his pants.

"You've got to be fucking kidding me!" he bellowed, slamming a palm to his face.

"Am I paying again?" I couldn't help but laugh.

He was shaking his head, brows furrowed. "It's on the fucking kitchen counter at home."

"I guess we can try a third redo on our anniversary," I laughed harder. "Guess that also means I'm paying for the movie." I watched him fume, grumbling. "I have cash for the valet, too," I added, his annoy eyes flickering across the table. "See, this time around, I'm married to a sugar daddy who always sneaks cash into my wallet."

He cracked a smile, face softening. "A sugar daddy, huh," he chuckled. "How's that working out?"

I shrugged. "He has a weird fetish for barbecue sauce-covered smiles, but nothing I can't handle."

"And," he muttered, rolling his eyes up and right back down. "He tries to give you one special fucking day and he can't even do it right."

"Oh, he can do it right, although sometimes I like when he does it wrong," I whispered over while sending my boot sliding up his pant leg. "And if it makes you feel better, my card says Sadie Romano. Your name's on the card, and your name's on me."

He slipped out of the booth, standing with his hand out. "You ready for the movie, Baby?"

"I am!" I skipped his hand and wrapped my arms over him instead. The last time we were here, I didn't want anyone to see us get close, now I wanted everyone to see.

We stayed wrapped up in each other's arms until the valet drove his car up. "What theater are we going to?" I asked as he pulled the passenger door open for me. "Oh, wait," I laughed again. "Should I drive since you don't have your license? I can drive and pay, tonight."

A laugh escaped his tight grin. "Kicking a man when he's down, that hurts, Baby." He hopped into the driver's side, revving the engine, zooming through downtown.

He parked on the street in front of a vintage theater, the kind you hardly saw anymore.

"Is there a classic rom-com playing here tonight?" I jumped out, too excited to wait for him to open my door. "Need some cash for tickets?"

He ignored me, leading us right into the theater doors, past the attendant into the theater lobby, and through a pair of doors into an empty theater.

"Gavin!" I yanked his arm to slow him. "What movie are we watching?" Again, no answer.

We were the only ones here.

He continued up the side stairs, guiding me to the very center seats. "Gavin?" I asked once more.

"Shhh," he whispered, pointing to the lights that were dimming to completely dark while the red velvet curtain raised to expose the screen. "Chocolate?" He placed a small bar in my hand, folding my fingers over it, and I knew without seeing that it was my chocolate.

"My favorite! I haven't had these in forever."

The screen started crackling to life, my face suddenly filling the screen! My face! The picture Gavin had taken tonight, no, from our first date almost exactly three years ago. "What is this, Gavin?" I asked, eyes glued on the screen, watching the picture fade to one of us on our first Valentine's, on the balcony of the hotel. "What is this?"

His arm slipped over my shoulders. "The only romance I have any interest in watching, Baby."

Music started, pianos and violins synced to a video montage of all our first moments, his photos, my photos. Then a video, me looking into the camera on the Empire State Building, and the music faded to my voice.

"Tell me when to smile." I posed against the railing, staring at the camera.

"I love you," Gavin called from behind the phone.

"Love you, too. Did you take it?"

"Yeah."

"How does it look?"

"Utter, fucking, perfection."

"Oh, god. What are you doing, Gavin!" I laughed at the camera as the video faded out.

The tears instantly welled up from both the happy and sad memories of that trip. I twisted my face up to his, catching him wipe his own tears.

Next were a series of photos he'd taken of me when I hadn't realized. Then the violin grew louder, paired with a photo of us at the gala. Followed by a compilation of photos—his graduation, him at Tiffany and Co. in New York, proudly holding up my engagement ring, moments and pictures I'd never seen.

The violins faded to The Wedding March, and there I was at the top of the aisle. I lost it, tears pouring down my cheeks as I watched the screen, as I watched myself walk to him, watched his face as he watched me. Watching the way his eyes watered the second he saw me and then once again when I took his hand.

The camera focused on him as he recited his vows. "Everything you expect from a husband. I vow to love you, protect you, honor you, respect you, and give you all of me, every day for the rest of my life."

Then the video cut to me. "My heart was yours the second I met you, and it'll remain yours forever."

Then back to Gavin, his eyes on my finger as he slid the ring on. "As a sign of my love—" He yanked my hand, his bewildered face scanning the tattoo.

I felt Gavin's eyes on me, his face now turned towards mine, pulling my hand up to his lips, kissing his name. His actions almost mimicking those in the video. I looked back at the screen, watching as the officiant declared us husband and wife, and Gavin grabbing my face, kissing me so hard. "I can't believe you made this."

Rome flashed on the screen next, the picture of me standing on the top of the steps, then us at the ruins, then a picture of me in bed sleeping. "I think that got added by mistake."

"No, Baby, no mistake. That was the night we found out you were pregnant. I couldn't sleep, so I watched you. I was so fucking proud that you were carrying my baby, well two," he sighed.

A piano ballad started up as ultrasound photos flashed onto the screen, then my messy face from Halloween, followed by a series of pictures of me and my growing belly. Followed by the picture of Gavin and me on Christmas Day at Sofia's, and suddenly, a shrill cry shot from the speakers. My eyes immediately watered, seeing the babies in the hospital, with only Gavin, before they met their mamma. My tears were working overtime. I couldn't wipe them fast enough.

I watched the series of photos and videos of the babies, even Grant. And then Gavin as Fred Flintstone popped onto the screen. "Oh my gosh!" A laugh escaped through the tears.

The music faded out to a video of Gavin with Nora and Vinny on his lap. "Ready?" he asked them, nudging them to face the camera. "Happy Valentine's Day, Mamma!"

Nora and Vinny looked at the camera, both giggling. "Happeee."

"Valentine's Day," Gavin repeated.

"Waltimes dee," Nora shouted over Vinny.

Gavin laughed towards the camera, his arms squeezing the babies tight as he continued. "Mamma."

"Mamma!" The twins squealed in unison, making me lose it again, full-blown sobbing, ugly crying.

Gavin's voice filled the speakers once more. "Happy Valentine's, Baby. We love you. Ti amo."

VALENTINE'S DAY: 2

The screen faded to black as the lights illuminated the theater, our movie was over. I wiped the remaining tears, looking up at Gavin, who had equally glassy eyes.

"I can't believe you did all this for me."

"That's why I did it!" He straightened, turning his body towards mine. "I hate that you can't believe I would do this for you. I want you to expect this from me."

"I didn't mean it like that, Gavin. I just didn't expect all this—all this thought."

"Exactly my point." His fingers found mine, roaming over my hand.

"How long have you been planning this?"

He shrugged. "A while."

"And you bought out the whole theater?" It was always extremes with him; there was never a middle ground. It was all or nothing.

"Our love story is just for us, Baby. You know I don't like to share."

I sat up, sliding over onto his lap. "I know. Thank you for today. It was incredible."

"Day's not over yet, Baby."

"But Grant has to leave," I reminded him.

He grinned again. "I have something planned for when we get home."

"Do you now?" I pushed myself higher to be level with his face.

"I'm gonna cook you dinner," he boasted.

"Um, you can't cook," I teased, brushing my nose to his.

"Neither can you," he teased right back. "But we make it work."

"Hey!" I laughed again, slapping his chest.

"Romano men cook," he declared, seriously. "It's about time I stepped up."

About time he stepped up? "Stepped up," I repeated, flicking my gaze around the empty theater. "I don't think you have to worry about stepping up. I love you so much, Gavin. You are the most amazing man, and I'm so lucky you're mine." I collapsed into him, lips clobbering his.

Our kiss went from zero to sixty in seconds, hot and heavy, tongues sweeping, dancing, lips roving, hands meeting the pace, up, down, groping, desperate.

"Stop, Baby," his command burst through the kiss, lips breaking away. "There's someone above, and they don't need to see an encore." He tipped his head to the glass window where the movie projector stood. "Let's save this for tonight, after dinner," he whispered. "You and me in the bed, nice and slow, making love."

"Making love?" I met his sultry stare. "You're taking this romance thing seriously."

"We can do nice and slow for a day, Baby," he growled. "It'll be a nice warm-up for my birthday next week."

"Ahh, I see. You're buttering me up for your birthday."

"No, this was all for you, Baby."

I dropped my face back to his chest, nestling in. "Can we watch it again?"

"At home," he let out a deep sigh. "We've got to get back." He puffed his chest, pushing me forward.

I stood, grasping his hand as tight as I could. "Thank you again. This was beyond perfect!"

We stepped through the front door, fingers aching from how hard we'd been holding each other, but I wasn't ready to let him go.

"You guys are late!" Grant playfully scolded on his way to the door, with Nora and Vinny toddling beside him.

"Thanks again, Sweetie!" I hugged him. "I love you."

Then he sank to the floor, hugging Nora and Vinny. "You two," he laughed to the twins. "Never go into your parents' room on Valentine's Day. Trust me!"

"Grant!" My cheeks burned as I laughed.

"Get out!" Gavin laughed too, holding the door open, giving Grant a wave on his way out. "Hey, forgot to tell you," he called out the door to Grant. "I got you three interviews lined up. I'll email you the details." He closed the door, addressing me now. "Okay, Baby! Can you put the twins to bed alone tonight so I can set the kitchen up?" He was so serious. Gavin was all business when he had his mind set on something.

"Of course! Nora, Vinny." I reached my hand for each of theirs as Gavin bent down in front of them.

"Sogni d'oro. Sweet dreams. Papà loves you." He gave them each a kiss before hurrying down the hall while the three of us started up the stairs.

I herded the twins into the nursery, changing, and reading to them before putting them into their beds. Then I snuck out their door, padding back down the stairs.

A wine glass was waiting for me on the bar, sitting between my roses, and I grabbed it happily, sniffing each vase on my way into the kitchen.

Gavin stood in front of the flour-covered island, rolling out some dough. He'd gone all out. "I never thought I'd see this!" I pushed the glass to my lips.

"A man cooking?" He nodded to the counter behind him, where a plate of chocolate-covered strawberries sat.

"My man cooking." I nestled into his side, watching him work.

"Here, Baby." He stepped back, placing me in front of him, lowering his face to the crook of my neck. "Here." He handed me the rolling pin, then wrapped his hands over mine, rolling the dough with me, subsequently rolling his body tight against mine. "Fuck, this is not gonna work," he chuckled, jerking his hand and body away from me while simultaneously clasping my waist, lifting me from the ground, and setting me up on top of the counter. "You can watch."

"You know I love to watch." I pushed the wine back to my lips, watching Gavin's enthusiasm turn to annoyance and his pasta turn to a mess.

"How's it coming along?" I snapped up the wine bottle, filling my now empty glass.

"Harder than I thought," he grumbled.

"Hard is not a bad thing."

He looked back, gaze falling to the bottle of wine in my hand. "You've almost finished the bottle. Slow down. You know drunk Sadie doesn't like nice and slow."

No, she didn't. "Come here!" I stretched my legs for him and he turned, stepping between my legs. "Take a drink." I pushed the bottle to his parting lips. "You're taking it too seriously. Cooking doesn't have to be perfect."

"I know that's your motto, Baby," he chuckled. "But it's not mine."

Very funny. I rolled my eyes, lifting a strawberry to his lips.

"Those are for dessert, Baby."

I ignored him, pushing the strawberry to his mouth, watching him bite over the chocolate. "How set are you on this whole making love in the bed thing?" I ate the rest of the berry.

"I thought that's what you'd want." He lowered his face to mine, tongue striking out, licking the chocolate from my lips.

"Valentine's Day is about love," I purred against his lips. "And I want to love you all over this house tonight."

"Oh, yeah."

"You haven't had me in the kitchen in a while, or by the fire, and it is a chilly night."

He leaned in closer, tongue dragging across my lips, breathing heavy. "Whichever you prefer, Baby."

"Dinner in the kitchen, dessert by the fire." My lips hit his as I spoke. "I'll be dinner, you be dessert."

GRANT'S GRADUATION

I'd been arguing with myself for days. Grant had said he was okay with Gavin going today, but I could see more in his eyes. This was his day to shine; this day was for him, and the last thing he needed on his last day on campus was to be reminded of Gavin and me.

The last two years had been so much better for Gavin and Grant because Gavin was away from the school, and the talk of Gavin had left when he left. But today would be different. Gavin had been well known at this school and he was very recognizable, not to mention he stood a foot taller than everybody else, so blending in was not an option. And god forbid someone call me a MILF in front of him, triggering his overprotective side and causing a scene. I debated asking him to stay home or wishing he'd offer to stay back, but I knew he'd never offer, and he'd be hurt if I told him to stay home. I couldn't take the twins to watch their brother graduate, but not Gavin, my husband, and technically Grant's stepdad. Gavin's graduation had been hard on me, really hard. Those snarky comments by those bitchy girls haunted me. I didn't want to hear that today, especially not while I was holding my babies and watching my biggest get his diploma. I didn't know what to do, but I did know today had to be about Grant. I couldn't let Gavin's presence or my issues interfere.

"Baby!" Gavin yelled from downstairs, letting me know it was time.

"I'm coming!" I walked out, starting down the stairs, seeing him putting on Nora's shoes below.

"You like nice, Mamma." He stood, holding her hand while watching me walk down.

"Thanks." I forced a smile. "Ready?"

He lifted both Nora and Vinny, taking them to the car. He was so proud of his family, excited to take the twins to his alma mater and show them and me off to anyone who might recognize him, which made me feel like absolute shit because once again, I wanted to hide.

"You okay, Baby?"

"Yeah," I lied, avoiding his eyes as I closed the front door behind us.

He buckled Nora while I strapped in Vinny, then he rounded the car to my side, grabbing my arm and turning me to face him, his intense, knowing stare on me. "Sadie?"

I met his eyes, knowing I couldn't lie to them. "I'm just emotional about Grant graduating." It was a half-truth.

His eyes bored into me, waiting.

"I don't want to upset Grant today. I don't want the focus to be on you and his mom."

He let go of my arm and stepped back, pulling my door open before silently stalking to his side.

"You understand, right?" I climbed up onto the seat, immediately reaching my hand to his leg.

"I understand." He kept his eyes on the road, not me.

We made our way to the school, parking in the same lot we had for Gavin's graduation, each of us grabbing up one of the twins and heading towards the crowded field.

"I can't believe I have one child graduating college and two that just turned two."

"Same," Gavin chuckled, tossing his arm over my back, then just as quickly dropping it. "So like last time, no kissing, no touching."

I hated doing that to Gavin, but today was about Grant, and he'd gone through enough. "Not around his friends."

"That mean I can sneak a kiss right now," he whispered, leaning his head down towards mine, my face jerking, smacking him the world's fastest peck.

We followed the crowd to the field, walking the aisles to find some seats.

"Sadie?" A man's voice shouted from behind us, both Gavin and I turning to see the source. Of course. Mike.

"And you were worried about who'd recognize me," Gavin grumbled, taking his usual protective stance at my side. "I'll take the babies and find seats." He reached for Nora, but I grabbed his hand, keeping him by my side.

"Sadie!" Mike greeted.

"Hi, Mike." I leaned against Gavin's arm. "This is my husband Gavin and our children." I didn't bother with their names; he didn't need to know them.

"How's it going," Mike said to Gavin, seeming not to remember him. "Can you believe the kids are graduating! Seems like yesterday we were on that freshman tour."

"It does." The last four years had gone by so incredibly fast. "It's nice seeing you again, but we better get to our seats." I tugged Gavin's hand, continuing down the aisle until we found two empty seats.

"That was fast." He sat, watching me do the same. "Were you worried I'd say something?"

"No," I answered honestly. "I had no interest in talking to him."

"I forgot about that freshman tour," Gavin leaned over, lips brushing my hair. "You know, maybe we should go revisit that lecture hall."

"Today is about Grant," I reminded him. "Besides, what would we do with these two?"

"Right," he chuckled. "Shit, that's all I can think about now. Especially with you in this fucking dress. You're like a naughty teacher."

Oh god. "Gavin!"

The graduates started piling in, and I searched the gold honor cords until I saw him, my baby boy walking across the field. I sat in a seat just like this for his kindergarten graduation, elementary, high school, and now college. The ceremony started, but I only half-listened. My mind was on Grant and our journey, all our memories together. Now watching him sit up there. He'd started school as an undergrad for business, then he switched to finance. He wanted to be an investor like Gavin. And even though he balked at having Gavin as a stepdad, he still looked up to him, and that made my heart so happy.

Gavin had stepped up too. He bought Grant the condo, invested my parents' check for him, taught him the ropes of finance, and had set him up with an interview at a local investment firm right here in San Diego.

I wonder what both our futures would have held if we hadn't met Gavin. I'd given Grant roots, but Gavin helped give him wings.

"Grant Jones." His name boomed through the speakers, sending my frantic hands clapping and my eyes flooding.

He hopped up the steps, crossed the stage, grabbed his diploma, and turned to the camera, lifting the diploma. "Thanks, Mom!" he mouthed, breaking any reserve I had, the tears unleashing.

"Here," Gavin whispered, pushing a small package of tissues to my hand. "You okay, Baby?" he asked; I nodded yes, keeping my eyes locked on Grant walking off the stage, following the line back to his seat. "You did a good job with him," he continued. "One day, Grant will realize everything you did for him, not just the big stuff, but everything you gave up, everything you protected him from, all the focus you put on him to make sure he felt complete. His life could've taken so many paths, but you kept him on the straight and narrow. You gave him two parents' worth of love while working your ass off. I can't fuc—I can't imagine doing all this alone. They should be giving you a diploma, too."

I rested my head on his shoulder, feeling his kiss on my hair. I watched the graduates take the stage before the faculty congratulated the whole class, inducing applause and graduation caps flying into the air.

"Let's go find him!"

"Give me Nora, Baby," he urged, opening his free arm.

I walked in front of them, hurrying to where we'd planned to meet Grant, and he was already approaching. "Grant!" I sprinted, capturing him in a hug. "You did it! I'm so proud of you! So, very proud!

"Thanks, Mom!"

I didn't want to let him go because I knew everything would be changing again. He was a man now, starting a career, and I saw Danica running up behind him. They'd been together three years now, and I had a hunch she was the one. I dropped my arms, stepping back, seeing the spark in his eyes when he saw her. It reminded me of Gavin at his graduation; only I hadn't beamed with pride like Danica, I sulked. Another regret I had to live with.

"Hi, Danica!" I stepped up, hugging her.

"Where are the twins and Gavin?" she asked.

I looked back, searching through the crowd. "He was right behind me."

"Over there!" She pointed to a bench in the far distance, the guilt hitting me like a brick. He was trying to keep his distance, just as I'd asked him.

"Why isn't he coming over?" Grant laughed, taking off in their direction.

"I didn't want you to feel uncomfortable if any of your friends recognized him," I told him truthfully.

He shrugged. "Everyone pretty much already knows." He hurried for the bench with us trailing right behind. "He's family," he shouted over his shoulder. "It doesn't really bother me anymore."

Gavin saw us coming, immediately flashing his eyes at me for instruction, so I waved him over, letting him know it was okay. Then he lowered the twins to the ground, and Grant and Danica immediately scooped them up.

"Grant's okay," I whispered to Gavin before turning, seeing Grant holding his little brother. "Let me take a picture!" I held out my phone. "Smile!" Then I handed my phone to Gavin. "Now one of just Grant and me!"

Danica grabbed the twins' hands, walking them over to stand at Gavin's side while I jumped next to Grant.

"Say cheese," Gavin teased.

"Cheese," Grant laughed, draping his arm over me.

Now we needed the twins. "Nora—"

Grant suddenly stepped forward. "Can I get a pic with just Gavin and me?"

I looked at him, making sure he was serious. "Gavin?" I repeated, meeting his eyes. "The two of you?"

Grant smiled again, a slight blush in his cheeks as he shrugged. "He's the closest guy I have in the family since Grandpa couldn't make it."

Breathe, Sadie, breathe. Don't cry, don't cry. "Okay." I stepped back, taking Vinny from Gavin.

Gavin walked over, looking like a dad in his slacks and that five o'clock shadow. And it didn't hurt that he was an entire head taller than Grant, if not more. They stood side by side, both smiling at me. So I snapped pictures of the two most important men in my life.

"Vinny, too," Gavin insisted, dashing to me, plucking Vinny from my arms. "The men of the family."

Make that the three most important men in my life.

"How about I take one of the entire family!" Danica offered, hand out for my phone in exchange for Nora.

So I walked over to the guys, and Gavin handed Vinny to Grant before walking away. "Where are you going?"

"Did you just want a family picture?"

Grant started laughing, lunging for Gavin's arm and pulling him back over. "Half this family wouldn't be here without you!" He shook a hand over Vinny's hair. "Don't try to bail out now."

Gavin smiled, stepping up behind me, all of us smiling at the camera.

"Perfect!" Danica cheered.

Perfect. We *were* our own little version of perfect.

"Here." Gavin handed Grant an envelope.

"What is it?" Both Grant and me asked in unison.

"Sadie said she promised you a trip to Italy if you graduated with honors."

"You remember that!" I blurted out. I'd mentioned that years ago and had forgotten about it.

"I remember everything, Baby," Gavin almost laughed, giving me a sly wink. "And he fulfilled those stipulations. There's enough for your flights and hotel, for both of you. You should book soon before you start working."

Grant stood there, looking from Gavin to me then back. "Are you serious?"

Gavin nodded. Of course, he'd remember and make this happen. I jumped against him, pushing up on my tiptoes to smack him with a kiss.

"Someone might see," he teased.

"I hope everyone does!" I kissed him once more.

"So," Grant started up. "We have an after-party right now, but are we all still on for breakfast tomorrow?"

"Yes!" Absolutely! "Have fun, and Danica, ignore any mean girls you might hear in the bathroom."

"What?" She laughed as Gavin shot his eyes down, furrowed brows waiting for more.

"Nothing, have fun!" I hugged Grant once more. "I love you more than anything. You'll always be my first love."

"I love you too, Mom."

We started off the field, walking together towards the parking lot.

"Oh shit, is that— " some guy yelled, eyes on Gavin and me as we passed. Then Grant shot his arm out, shoving the guy back as we continued walking, ignoring him.

"His mom was bangin— "

Then Gavin passed him, shoving him a little harder, sending the guy stumbling back as we walked away.

We all gave a final round of hugs; then I watched Grant and Danica disappear into the parking lot. "I feel like I've been waiting forever for this day. To get to this point."

"That's right," Gavin chuckled, knocking his shoulder into mine. "Today was supposed to be your big day of freedom. Finally free," he continued laughing, repeating my words from all those years ago.

"I am free. My freedom just wasn't what I thought it'd be. It's so much better."

We made our way to the car, strapping the babies in before climbing in ourselves, our hands automatically entwining as we drove away. "I can't wait to get the twins to sleep. Papà wants some time alone with Mamma," he rasped, hand running up my thigh.

Seriously? "Is that all you ever think about?" I was in tears from all the emotions, and he was horny.

"I'm a guy; I'm Italian. My wife is the most beautiful woman around, even when she tries not to be, because that ends up making her ten times sexier. That day with you in the lecture hall was the greatest memory I have at this place. I was fucking the girl of my dreams on a desk and fucking those glorious tits for the first time. You have no idea what that did for my ego, not to mention the many, many fantasies it spurred. So yes, Baby. That is all I'm thinking about."

SADIE'S 40th BIRTHDAY: 1

I yanked the covers up over my face, burying it away from the sun. Maybe if I hid under the sheets, then my birthday wouldn't be able to find me, and I'd stay thirty-nine. I stretched my hand to Gavin's side, which was empty. He probably took off, probably woke up, saw my transformation to an old lady, and freaked.

"Baby, are you awake?"

Or maybe not. He knocked on the door, so I peeked from the sheets. "Yes."

The door swung open with two little bodies sprinting towards the bed and Papà right behind them, carrying a tray of food. I automatically sat up, sliding back against the headboard with open arms for the twins climbing over me and the tray Gavin was setting down.

"Happy birthday, Mamma!" Gavin hopped to his side, smacking a kiss to my cheek.

"Happee beefday, Mamma!" Nora repeated, leaning up to kiss my cheek too.

"Vinny," Gavin urged. "Dillo!"

"Happee birtday, Mamma," Vinny chirped proudly. Then he and Nora fought to grab the most strawberries from the tray in my lap.

"Thank you, my loves!" This made me feel a little better.

Nora twisted back, pushing a strawberry to my mouth while I pretended to bite her fingers. This was her new favorite game.

"We picked those from the garden this morning," Gavin boasted, opening his mouth wide, gesturing for one. But Vinny got to them before I did and smashed one right into Gavin's face. "Thanks, Piccolo," he laughed, wiping the sides of his mouth. "So, what does Mamma want to do today?"

What did I want to do? I guess hiding under my sheets wasn't going to work out. I looked over to the balcony doors, seeing the bright sun outside. "Whatever I want?" I both asked and insisted. "And you won't say a thing?"

He let out a quick laugh before reaching his hand for another strawberry, popping it into his mouth. "Whatever you want, Baby."

Okay, then. "I want to spend the day at the beach."

"That sounds perfect!" He slipped off the bed, walking straight to the dresser and grabbing out his board shorts. "Let me change. Then I'll take the twins," he instructed on his way back to his closet, disappearing and re-emerging minutes later in the shorts and a muscle tee. "Meet us in the garage, Baby." He lifted Vinny and Nora from the bed, herding them out and closing the door behind him.

Wait, beach? That meant bikini. What was I thinking? I rolled off the bed, avoiding the mirror on my way to the dresser. I started rifling through my bathing suit drawer, spotting that skimpy thong bikini I'd bought for Italy, the one that Gavin had refused to let me wear. Hmm. I picked it up, dangling it over my finger. It seemed even skimpier now. But, this might be the last time I could pull something like this off, and Gavin had promised not to say a thing. Moms wore these skimpy suits all the time in Europe, and while we weren't in Italy anymore, my husband *was* European, that had to count for something. I'd just see how it fit. I tugged my sleep shirt off, wiggling on the tiny triangles in its place. Hmm. The top covered my nipples, and that was about it.

Maybe this was a little too much for Mamma. No! This was happening, dammit. Forty had nothing on me! Age was not winning today. I needed to see Gavin's jealousy, and I needed to see his greedy eyes on me, reminding me that age was just a number. I found the skimpy bottoms, stepping into them while twisting towards the mirror, studying my exposed ass. It, didn't, look, bad. Actually, I looked damn good. I could do this! I grabbed the sheer white cover next, draping it over the suit before stepping into my wedges. Mamma was taking a break today, and Sadie was stepping in.

I took my time down the stairs and out to the garage where Gavin was loading the twins into the stroller.

"Ready, Mam—ma." He stilled, stare raking down, then up my body, eyes squinting to see under the sheer cover, brows furrowing at the sight. His lips started moving, but no words came out. His head shook side to side, his right hand smacked his left, spinning his wedding ring like a madman. That tattoo had really made a difference, it had slowed down his knee-jerk reactions, and his short fuse was gradually getting under control.

"Ready?" I walked past him to the edge of the garage, knowing good and well his eyes were on my ass.

"Sadie!" he groaned, feet stomping.

I turned around to face him, watching as he furiously spun his wedding band, staring at my name under it. "Yeah?" I asked, hiding my smile.

His jaw set like stone, face tensed, chest rising with his deep inhale. "Don't you think you'll be a little, fuck- a little cold?"

I looked up at the blazing July sun. "No."

His face dropped towards his chest, exhaling through his nose. The struggle evident. "I think it's too hot, not good for the twins," he grumbled under his breath. "We can just hang out here today."

"If you want. I shouldn't be at the beach too long. I'll meet you back here later."

"No," he snapped. "You're not fuc—going alone. We'll all go."

I continued down the driveway, listening to Gavin's annoyed grunts behind me. I shouldn't enjoy his misery, but... I needed to be shallow today. I couldn't think about forty or that he was only twenty-six.

We made our way to the sand, finding a spot on the beach where Gavin parked the stroller, lifting Nora and Vinny out. He set up our chairs and towels, then dumped the twins' sand toys out for them, all the while I disrobed.

The twins started digging in the sand while I rolled my stomach down over the towel, putting my back on full display. I closed my eyes, immediately feeling a pile of sand dump over my ass. "Hey!" I twisted my face back, meeting Gavin's smug smile as he dumped another bucket over my body.

"Sorry. You're in the play zone."

Two can play at this game. I arched my ass up and back, right in his face as I slid to my knees. "I was going to the water anyway." I stood, rubbing my ass to get the sand off, a little more seductively than necessary. "Can you handle the babies for a minute?"

He didn't respond, but him stabbing the shovel into the sand gave me the answer I was looking for. "Thanks!" I started down to the water, absorbing the warm rays while wiggling my toes in the shallow tide.

"It's cold!" A guy shouted in my direction, making me turn, finding two of them standing there, eyes on me.

Oh, god. I didn't want to get hit on today. I wanted slightly jealous Gavin, not crazy jealous Gavin. And what the hell was wrong with me? Forty hits, and suddenly, I'm trying to piss off my husband and get hit on, in front of my kids. I was losing my mind. I needed to dive into the waves, let that icy water slap me in the face.

"You going in?" One of them was still talking to me, probably talking to my ass. What the hell was I thinking!

"Mamma!" Nora's squeal sent me spinning around. "I pooped! I pooped."

Oh my god! The guys instantly took off, and I dropped to the sand, catching her in my arms, and she was clean. Gavin's laugh followed.

"Gavin! Seriously!"

His hand was out to high-five Nora. "It's nice having minions to do my *dirty* work! Papà owes you a biscotto. Good job, Piccolina! Now, you gonna actually swim, Baby? Or stand here giving your husband a heart attack?"

"I'm done." I followed them back to our spot, and Gavin clasped my waist, pulling me onto his lap.

"So," he sighed. "You hate when I get jealous, but then you do shit like this, purposely."

"No," I interrupted him.

"Purposely," he reiterated. "To get me jealous. What's going on, Baby?"

"Nothing." I nestled into his chest, watching the twins playing in the sand at our feet. "I, I just—"

"Wanted to show your ass off to a bunch of strangers? Wanted to let some douchebags stare at your tits?"

I flashed my eyes to his, and he threw his hand up in apology, then pushed it to his face, sliding his glasses up so I could see his eyes as I continued. "I don't want any more birthdays!" They were my biggest enemy. "I wanted to still feel hot."

His laughter was immediate, chest bouncing me from the force. "Still feel hot? Jesus Christ, you didn't travel in a time machine sixty years. You went to bed and woke up. You've been forty for what a few hours. I swear chicks are so fucking weird sometimes."

"You wouldn't understand."

"No," he chuckled, arms locking tight over my waist. "I get mad when I get insecure, you get naked, and I'm not sure which is fucking worse. But, Baby," he whispered, lips nibbling at my ear. "You look fucking incredible. If you want to flaunt your sexy ass, then go. Just make sure to flaunt that diamond too, and the name under it. Blind those fuckers with it."

I wiggled my rings as I laughed. "Blind them with the diamond."

"That's why I bought the biggest one they sold." He ran his finger over my ring. "So assholes a mile away could see you were taken."

"I think I'll stay right here." I cuddled into him, using his chest as a pillow. "I've had enough attention today."

"That's too bad," he growled. "Because I had planned on giving you my attention all night long."

"Acqua! Acqua!" The twins started yelling, waving their arms towards the water.

That sounded good. I pushed off Gavin's lap, his hand smacking my ass on the way up.

"Lots of attention tonight," he rasped before following.

He reached for Nora's hand while I took Vinny's, then Gavin reached for mine, all of us walking as a family to the water.

"Hold on," he insisted, releasing my hand and bending to the sand, handing Nora and Vinny a rock while he grabbed a stick. Then he started dragging it into the sand, popping back up next to me, waving his hand down at the inscription, *Gavin loves Sadie*.

"I love you too."

SADIE'S 40th BIRTHDAY: 2

I padded down the hall to our room, shutting the door quietly behind me. "Babies are asleep."

"What the fuck!"

"Excuse me!" I walked into the bathroom where Gavin was hunched over his vanity, water droplets still clinging to his back, dripping down to the towel loosely wrapped over his hips.

"This can't be fucking happening! Is this a gray hair?" he barked. "Look at this shit!"

What? I walked over, and he leaned his head down, pointing to a single strand over his forehead. I rubbed it between my fingers. It wasn't painted on, and it wasn't sand, nor was it blond—it *was* gray. In the midst of black waves, there was one gray strand. Suddenly, my smile was bigger than it'd been all day.

"I'm only twenty-six! Why am I getting this shit?"

Gray! Gray! I didn't even have gray hair yet. I pinched it tight between my fingers, yanking it out.

"Shit!" he yelped, whipping his head away. "Why the hell did you do that? Twenty will grow back in its place!"

"I know!" That's exactly why I did it. "This is the best birthday present you could have ever given me." He was the perfect yin to my yang, always making me smile, whether he tried to or not.

He met my eyes, knitting his brows as his head slowly cocked to the side. "I swear, Baby. You are fucking crazy today. You're happy about this?"

"You going gray before I do? Yes!" I nodded. "Very." He would always be fourteen years younger, but he didn't have to look it.

"I'm not fucking going gray! It's one hair!"

"And tomorrow, there'll be twenty," I teased him. "And while you're sleeping, I'll rip those twenty out, and then there will be—"

"You have fucking lost it, Baby." He chuckled, shifting his body to face mine. "I didn't realize this age shit still bothered you so much."

It didn't, it did, it mostly didn't, but today, when I had to face forty, it did. I looked back up at his hair, then his face. I didn't look any older today, but he did. His face had matured. That stubbly beard and the dark around his eyes gave him an older, sexier look, and now a smidgen of gray in that black hair. How had I not noticed this? I followed the stubble of his chin down to his chest, to my name inked over the strong muscle. I continued down the trail to his towel, clinging to his manhood.

"Are you done?"

"Huh?" I blinked, finding his face.

"You know I can take the towel off if you'd like. It is your birthday." He flicked the towel knot, sending the whole thing unraveling, falling to his feet. Oh, fuck. I pounced. My kisses smothered his chest, his stomach. My fingers strangled his firming dick, rubbing him hard.

"Shit," he moaned as I stroked. "I thought going gray was a bad thing, fuck, I'll take it if this is how you react."

I kissed my way up to his neck, hand abandoning his erection to trace the muscles up his stomach.

"Baby, it's your birthday. Let me do the work."

That sounded good, too. "Did you like my bikini?"

He nodded. "Yeah."

"I was thinking of wearing it again tomorrow."

"No," he sighed, reaching his hand for my face, his thumb strumming across my bottom lip. "I'm burning it tomorrow."

I stepped back, tugging off my T-shirt before kicking down my leggings, leaving me in only the bikini I hadn't yet taken off. "So then I guess you need to get it off me?" I danced to the bad, crawling up the sheets on all fours. "I think from now on only you get to see me in this. I don't need any other guys' eyes on me." I straightened up on my knees, facing the wall, hearing his footsteps behind me, his presence growing nearer.

I hooked my fingers through the bikini top, yanking it over my head. At that exact moment, the bed dipped and warm hands slid around my sides, thick fingers grasping my breasts.

"Tell me what you want, Baby," his hiss streamed down my neck, sending my core into a frenzy. "You want me to fuck you like this? Or do you want to watch yourself?"

"What?" I whispered back to him, meeting his lips as they drug a kiss over mine.

"You want to feel sexy tonight, Baby? Then ride me in front of the mirror, see what I see." His hands slid to my waist, turning me around to face him while he scooted to the edge of the bed, laying down, his hands reaching for mine, pulling me over him. "You are so fucking sexy, just as you were yesterday, and just as you'll be tomorrow," he rasped, fingers tickling over the thong before curling under it, rough knuckles gliding over my clit. "Fuck, I never want you wearing this shit again."

I looked straight ahead, meeting my distant reflection, watching through the mirror as his hand tightened over the bikini bottom, ripping it off, tossing it to the floor. It felt like I was watching someone else, watching the naked woman in the mirror. I watched her thighs spread wide, mounting over the man under her. Her hips rolled with her tight stomach, her pussy hit his dick, the two became one as she sank down, taking him completely. "Ahh... god." I watched her rock over him, grinding her hips in circles, side to side, front to back, taking him deeper, her body flush against his. I felt the heat, heard her gasp, moan his name. The intense pleasure sending her hands coasting up her smooth skin to her tits, clutching them as she bounced over him, breasts flailing with the motion, her thighs quickening now. Her body was on fire, her own hands fueling the heat, groping her tits as she rode his dick harder.

"Fuuck!" he groaned under her, his fingers clawing into her thighs, my thighs, awakening me. "Keep, your eyes, on the mirror, Baby!" Only then I was being lifted while he sat up, scooting to the edge of the bed, reversing me onto his lap, both of us now staring at her in the mirror. "I like to watch too, Baby."

TONSILS

"The tonsillectomy will take about forty-five minutes," Dr. Earp started, addressing both Gavin and me. "Then we'll grab you, and you can wait with Nora in recovery while she wakes from the anesthesia. And if all goes well, she'll be discharged this evening."

Oh no...

"If?" Gavin spat out, glare on the papers in the doctor's hands, the *'what if'* papers that every parent had to sign. Gavin had been holding it together as best as possible this morning, but I knew he was a ticking time bomb.

"She'll be fine," I assured him, reaching for his hand and locking it in mine. "Dr. Earp's the best E.N.T around, and we're lucky to have him here at Hope."

Gavin shook his head. "I think you need to be in there, Baby! She's only three and a half!" He started to fidget, pulling at the sides of his collar, flipping his palm to his neck, scratching at the skin.

"You know I can't." I reached for his other hand, pulling it away from his neck. You couldn't bring emotion into an operating room.

"The anesthesiologist is on his way in," Dr. Earp added, rising from Nora's bedside. "I'll see you soon, Nora!"

Her big dark eyes darted from him to Gavin. "Papà you stay with me," she squeaked out, stretching her tiny hand for his.

He nodded, pulling her fingers to his lips, pressing a kiss to her knuckles. "Papà non se ne sta andando. I'm not leaving."

A knock hit the door before it swung back open. "Nora Romano," the anesthesiologist confirmed while pushing in his cart, followed by two nurses. "We're ready for you."

Gavin's hand tightened over hers, leaning in closer to her side. "I want to stay until she's under. I promised her."

"Gavin." I tugged his arm, forcing him to look at me. "You won't be able to handle it, please."

"It's up to you," the anesthesiologist replied. "We'll start the mask in here, so she isn't afraid. Then we'll wheel her over to the operating room." He rolled his cart to her side, unraveling the mask while the nurses powered on the machine and clipped a heart rate monitor over Nora's finger.

"Nora," the anesthesiologist called. "This is a space mask; isn't it cool!"

"Gavin!" I had seen this scene a hundred times before with other parents. Nobody was ever prepared for it. "We need to leave! Let them do this." We'd discussed this part, and I knew Gavin wouldn't be able to handle seeing her fade to sleep. I couldn't even handle it, and I'd witnessed it a thousand times.

"Mamma," Nora whimpered, shooting her arm towards me, so I walked to Gavin's side, placing my hand over his and hers.

"I'm not leaving her, Baby!" Gavin's eyes stayed on her. "She needs her papà."

Okay. I nodded to the nurses, giving them the go-ahead before leaning down to Gavin's ear. "You need to prepare yourself."

"I'm fine," he belted right back.

The machine whirred louder, almost as loud as my heart thumping out of my chest.

They closed in on my baby girl, her eyes on me, then Gavin, then to the stranger lowering a mask over her face.

"Mamma! Papà!" she screamed, tears filling her eyes, streaming down her cheeks. "Papà, no! Papà! Papà! No!"

"It's okay, Piccolina," Gavin whispered back, his voice cracking, his composure faltering.

She tried to pull her hands away, her eyes on Gavin's, her screams turning into hysterical wails as the nurse fastened the mask to her face. Then her gasping cries slowed, her heavy eyelids dropped over her wet eyes, her body went limp, the struggle over. She was out.

I hated this, cries to silence.

"Piccolina?! Piccolina!" Gavin whimpered.

The nurses immediately kicked up the brakes on the bed while the anesthesiologist secured the mask.

"Piccolina!" Gavin was shaking, his hand locked onto hers, but her fingers straightened, no longer holding his grip.

"She'll be back in recovery in about an hour," one of the nurses informed us as they began pushing the bed out, but Gavin's arm blocked them. "You're going to have to let her go," the nurse demanded.

"Don't tell me what to fuc—" he started, then his gaze fell to Nora, his lips starting to quiver, nostrils flaring, his eyes brimming with tears. "Ti voglio bene, Piccolina. Starai bene. Papà sarà proprio qui. You'll be okay. Papà will be right here."

I grabbed his shaky hand, forcing him to release her, the two of us watching them wheel her away. Then Gavin was gone, charging out with me scrambling after him. "Gavin!"

He spun back, holding up his finger, gesturing for me to give him a minute before he took off in the opposite direction.

I wiped the remaining tears from my cheek on my way to the waiting area, bumping into May as she turned the corner.

"I was just coming to find you!" She smiled sincerely. "You okay?"

"Yeah, not really."

"I was going to bring flowers, but figured Gavin would send them away. Speaking of which, where is he?"

He was either hiding his meltdown from me or saving me from being the brunt of a rage-filled outburst. "The restroom," I guessed, dropping into the first seat while May sat beside me.

"How about a stuffed animal?" she squealed, jumping right back up. "I can get one from the gift shop."

I nodded yes even though we had a bag full of presents and an entire family room filled with new toys for her. She took off while I stared up at the clock, then the floor, the clock again. Time was moving too slow. I glanced back up to count the minutes, seeing Gavin approaching in the distance. I stood, needing him to hold me, and his arms immediately flew open, enveloping me in a tight hug.

"Are you okay, Baby?" He held me tighter. "I'm sorry I left. I needed, needed a minute alone." He nestled his face down against my shoulder, his cheeks wetting my hair. "I didn't expect that to be so intense." He stepped back, sinking into a chair, pulling me onto his lap. "Luca's a fucking mess."

Poor Luca. He'd had his fair share of hospital waiting rooms, and I tried to tell him he didn't need to be here, but he insisted. He had to make sure Nora was okay.

"Luca also said Grant just got to the house. They're both keeping Vinny busy."

Grant, my heart stung just hearing his name. We only had a few more months with him before he moved to Texas. I'd spent the last two decades only an arm's length away from him, and now he'd be a plane ride away. I buried my head into Gavin's chest, letting his arms comfort my heavy heart.

"Mr. and Mrs. Romano?"

Gavin jumped up, sending me stumbling forward as he took off towards the nurse.

"Nora's in recovery. She's still sedated but should be waking up soon."

"Take me to her!" Gavin demanded.

"Of course." She started down the hall. "Surgery went better than expected."

Gavin didn't bother walking with me; his antsy feet were practically stepping on the nurse's heels as she led us to Nora's room.

She pushed the door open, gesturing us in. "You can sit with her on the bed if you'd like."

Gavin walked right over, kissing Nora's forehead as he settled onto the edge of the bed next to her, carefully draping his arm over her shoulders, drawing her into him. "Papà è qui, Piccolina. I'm here," he whispered. "Sei al sicuro tra le braccia di papà, you're safe in my arms."

Nora rolled her face towards him, nestling against his chest, sensing her protector was close.

"The doctor will be in shortly," the nurse added before stepping out, closing the door behind her.

"How does she look?" Gavin asked, gesturing to Nora.

I stepped to her side, checking her pulse, then running my hand over her forehead. "Okay," I assured him. "But, Gavin, when she wakes, she might be panicking, be prepared." I took a seat at the bottom of the bed, watching Papà's arms wrapped over our baby girl, his love almost palpable. Then I saw a tear streaming down her cheek, then another, and another. "Gavin, get ready."

He looked down just as Nora's eyes shot open and she screamed, tried to at least. Her arms then went flying against Gavin, tears gushing down her cheeks as her chest puffed heavily.

"It's okay, Piccolina. Papà's here, Mamma's here, shhh. It's okay, Tesoro mio."

Her crying grew louder, the panic taking over Gavin's face, his eyes calling to mine, but I was already scooting up her side. "Nora," I whispered, leaning over her so she could see me. "Mamma's here. Do you see Mamma?"

She flashed her tear-filled eyes to mine, her screams quieting, but she was starting to hyperventilate.

"Mamma is here with you, and Papà is here with you. Do you see Papà?" I smiled, and she twisted her face to Gavin's. "And pretty soon, we'll go home and see Vinny! Would you like to see Vinny too?"

She was gradually calming down, the hyperventilating turning to soft whimpers.

"And guess what! Zio Luca and Grant are waiting for you, and they brought you a new toy! Would you like a new toy, maybe some ice cream?"

She nodded yes, a smile replacing her tears as she looked back up at Gavin. "Papà," she screeched, reaching her hand up to his face, grabbing at his chin.

He cradled her tightly in his strong arms, the same way he had cradled me earlier in the waiting area. He was our rock. Both his girls knew they were safe in his arms and that Papà would always protect us.

ROMANO FAMILY CHRISTMAS

"Gavin?" I hopped down the last step, peeking out the front window, the sun was setting, yet they still weren't here.

"Family room, Baby," he called back, so I followed his voice down the hall, seeing him adjusting the stockings on the mantel, with two little helpers flanking his sides.

"They should be here soon." I walked up, admiring his handiwork.

He turned around, his big natural smile taking over his entire face. "Any minute!"

"So, what's the count?" I eyed the row of red stockings.

"Seventeen!" Nora squealed.

"Seventeen! But the rest of the family won't be here until the twenty-sixth."

"They still get stockings!" Gavin scoffed playfully. He was so excited for the family to come out. "I got ten to fit here, then put all seven kids on the wall."

"Seven kids?" I looked over at the stockings, laughing under my breath. "Grant and Danica are on the kid wall? He's twenty-three!"

"He's your, our kid," he chuckled before bending to scoop up Nora, letting her hook a candy cane into her stocking. I remembered our first Christmas, him lifting her like that when she was just a baby, now the twins were almost four.

A sudden chill rippled down my back as the slightest rumble vibrated under my feet, whispers mixed with the wind, the sound intensifying with each passing second—Italians. "They're here."

Gavin and the twins bolted down the hall, except the door was already swinging open, shaking the house from the force.

"Buon Natale! We're back!" Luca dropped his bags to the floor, arms wide for the twins, who jumped right into them, followed by Gavin, who gave him a side hug.

"Welcome!" I started over, happy to finally have them back. "Merry Christmas!"

"Ẹ kú Ọdún Kérésìmesì!" Crystal greeted, walking in behind Luca and capturing the twins. "Merry Christmas, Vinny and Nora!"

Sofia followed them in, carrying Matteo in her arms. Matteo! I started for them, but Gavin got to her first.

"Come to Zio Gavi!" He reached for the baby, making him giggle. I missed hearing those sweet baby giggles.

"How was the flight?" I snuck by Gavin to hug her.

"Turbulent," she sighed, exasperated. "I still feel sick. Nora! Vinny!"

The twins jumped to Sofia while I swung back to Luca and Crystal, hugging them before they continued to the family room.

Eric stepped in next, shutting the door behind him, and as always, smiling ear to ear. "Sadie!" His arms flew open.

"Eric!" I leapt into his embrace. "Congrats on the book!"

He blushed, smile growing wider, gaze on something behind me. "What can I say," he gushed. "I've got the best muse."

I followed his stare to Sofia talking with Gavin, then saw Luca standing in front of her, staring at us.

"Don't say that shit," Luca huffed. "I'm flattered, but you sound like a fucking creep."

Eric half-laughed. "Sofia is my muse, Luca. Not you."

"Whatever." Luca rolled his eyes, turning to join the girls in the kitchen.

Eric and I followed them in, sending Matteo lunging out of Gavin's hold the second he saw Eric, his hands frantically waving for his daddy.

"Come here, little man!" Eric lifted him up. The two of them looked so much alike. Matteo had Eric's blue eyes and his smile, but the Romano hair.

"He's starting to talk," Sofia cooed to him, dancing her fingers over his tummy, making him wiggle and giggle. "He said Mamma the other day. And he's walking, well, attempting."

"Mamma!" Vinny repeated, jumping for my arms.

"So," Crystal lifted Nora onto her lap. "What's the plan for tonight?"

"Christmas lights," Gavin answered from behind me, one hand falling to Vinny's back.

"You get the P.J.s?" Luca asked, looking between Gavin and me.

"Me?" I shook my head no, gesturing to the twins. "The *elves* might bring them by when we're gone tonight."

"P.J.s?" Crystal laughed. "What am I missing?"

This was her and Eric's first Christmas here, and it was going to be fun. "The elves, might, bring us all matching Christmas P.J.s to wear tomorrow morning."

She whipped her face to Luca's. "You wear Christmas pajamas, Polpetto? Are they black?"

"They," I laughed, answering for him. "Are usually red and green."

She belted out a laugh, rolling her face right back to Luca's but not saying a thing.

"Stop smiling like that," he huffed, rolling his eyes.

"I'm not smiling," she replied, fully smiling.

"Let's get all your stuff upstairs!" Gavin announced. "Then we'll head out to look at lights."

"This is exciting!" Eric bounced Matteo. "I used to look at Christmas lights back in Virginia when I was a kid. I'd take you back there one day, little man," he laughed to Matteo. "But your mamma's on all the wanted posters." He started laughing while Sofia rolled her eyes, nudging him towards the hall. Eric had brought out a new side of Sofia, as had Matteo. Just as Crystal had done with Luca, and Mark with Stefano. As they always say, that's amore.

Gavin herded everybody upstairs, so Mamma raced to the closet, piling all the presents under the tree before meeting the family at the front door. Oh! I almost forgot! "Wait! Before we go!" I hurried to the kitchen, plucking the carton from the fridge and a handful of red glasses. "I thought I'd make tonight even more festive!" I returned, waving the plastic cups.

"What is it?" Gavin reached for the carton, snatching it from my fingers. "Eggnog?"

"Spiked!" I corrected him.

"Egg, nog," Sofia repeated, pushing her fingers to her lips. "I think I'm going to be sick!"

"It's not that bad!" I laughed, watching her face pale from the sight. "It's festive, eggnog!" I hadn't actually ever tried it, but everyone talked about it.

"I'll take some!" Crystal held out her hand, so I pulled a cup, holding it while Gavin poured. Then we all watched as she took a sip. "Oh, shit!" She choked it down. "That's strong!"

"I made it myself!" I held out another cup for Gavin. "I poured half the eggnog out and poured half a bottle of rum in." I pushed the cup to my lips, sipping it. Holy shit! "Agh, agh. Okay, so it's mainly just rum." I coughed, then coughed again. It was gross! Why would anyone drink this?

"I'll give it a go!" Eric handed Matteo to Sofia, hand out for the cup Gavin was pouring, then he downed it. "Not bad!"

Luca snapped his fingers next, gesturing for Crystal's cup, but she shook her head no, sipping it herself. So he waved his hand to Gavin. "Season's greetings!" He lifted the cup in the air, then pushed it to his mouth. "Fuck," he spat. "The rum's good, but that egg shit is nasty."

"Sofia?" Gav shook a cup in her direction, making her almost gag, shaking her head no.

"Come on, Babe!" Eric pushed his empty cup in front of Gavin for a refill. "One sip, and then you can say you've tried it!"

Luca chuckled. "Funny, that's what I told Crys—"

Crystal's hand shot up, smacking the back of Luca's head. "Fuck," he groaned. "Sorry, Baby. I'm getting there."

"It's taking a little longer than I thought," she rolled her eyes to his. "You need to get another tattoo, *filter*!"

Luca kept smiling. "Hit me again, Baby." He threw his hands around her back, clutching her ass, in plain view.

"Okay!" We needed to get outside! "Everybody out!" I opened the door, ushering everyone to the front yard. "Nora! Vinny! Time to go!"

Gavin bent down, arms open, but Nora veered right around him. "Zio Lewcha!" she squealed, running for Luca, who scooped her up, lifting her onto his shoulders.

"Piccolo!" Gavin stretched his arms for Vinny, who ran to him. "Want Papà to carry you too?" Vinny nodded, so Gavin lifted him up onto his shoulders too.

Then Sofia helped Eric lift Matteo securely onto his shoulders, and Eric joined the guys while Sofia, Crystal, and I walked behind them, watching our men with the babies they loved.

The twins and Matteo were all oohs and aahs as we walked up the street, wide-eyed and giggly as we passed the decorated houses. And the guys holding them were smiling just as big. I was a lucky woman, we were lucky women. I shook my now empty cup, feeling the lightness in my step as we started the trek back home.

I swung the front door open, tripping in with it. Wow, that *was* a lot of rum. I held the door, well, fell against the door, letting everyone pass. "Let's go check out the tree before we go to sleep!"

The guys lowered the twins, who immediately took off running, screaming as soon as they saw the family room.

"The elf came!" Nora squealed, running back to grab Luca's hand, yanking him towards the tree.

We trailed behind them, sitting on the couch while Luca took the floor with Nora, helping her hand out the gifts.

Eric opened his box first, lifting out the red and green pajamas. "Awesome! You'll wear these too, Babe?"

"Of course!" Sofia scoffed as if it was a crazy question. "Matteo has a pair too!" She held up the matching baby onesie, and Eric's eyes went soft, almost glassy.

"Now!" I clapped, getting the twins' attention. "Time for bed!" Gavin picked up Vinny while I went for Nora, but she climbed into Luca's lap, arms up around his neck.

"Zio Lewcha put me to sleep tonight!" she asked and demanded him.

"Always!" He wrapped an arm around her, pushing himself up, carrying her behind Gavin.

I walked over to her in Luca's arm. "Goodnight, Nora. Mamma loves you." I kissed her, then moved to Vinny. "Goodnight, Vinny! Mamma loves you!" I kissed him and then Gavin before they started away.

"I'll put Matteo down too!" Sofia stood, taking Matteo from Eric's arm to follow the guys up.

Tonight had been a perfect night, and the buzz was making it even better. "More eggnog?" I asked Eric and Crystal as I made my way to the kitchen to pour myself another glass. They both shook their heads no. "Just the rum?" I offered, and both of them nodded yes. Sounds good to me too. I pulled the rum and some glasses out, hearing the heavy pattering bolting down the stairs, then meeting Gavin's sexy smile as he passed the counter. "More rum?"

"Sure, Baby," he answered on his way to the fireplace, starting a fire.

I walked his glass over, handing it to him. It really felt like Christmas, except, I reached for the remote, powering on the T.V. and cranking the volume up on the Christmas Carol channel, music immediately flooding the room.

I was warm inside and out. "It's beginning to look a lot like Christmas," I sang, stepping into Gavin's arms, lifting on my tiptoes to meet his lips. "I love you, Santa."

"Love you too, Baby. I see you bought some mistletoe." He nodded to the leaves on the mantel.

"I did, and some whipped cream." I smashed his cheek with another kiss. Mamma and Papà always had fun on Christmas Eve.

"We should head to bed too," his whisper was more a rasp, pushing his lips back to mine.

"Presents first and more eggnog!" I wiggled out of his grip, dancing my way over to the closet and pulling the door open, grabbing out the first round of wrapped gifts.

"Rum?" Luca was in the kitchen behind the counter, lifting the bottle. Our personal bartender, how fitting.

Then the song changed, the drums hitting, The Little Drummer Boy roaring through the speakers.

Eric walked to the bar counter, nodding his head to the song, then tapping his hands like drum sticks against his cup before holding the cup out to Luca. "Pour... the rum—a—rum—rum," he sang to Luca.

A laugh burst from my lips, a tear following from the fast laughing fit.

Luca stood there, stone-faced, shaking his head side to side. "See the shit that happens when we come to Cali for Christmas!" he yelled over to Gavin.

"What?" Eric laughed, shrugging. "The little drummer boy." He looked from Luca to Gavin. "The song playing."

Luca raised the bottle, pouring rum into Eric's cup while glaring at him.

"Polpetto!" Crystal sang, lunging for the counter next to Eric, raising her glass too, smiling ear to ear. Then the chorus hit again. "Pour... the rum—a—rum—rum," she sang, giggling. Luca shook his head again, trying to fight his smile, but we could see it. He was close to breaking. So, I stepped up next to them, bumping Crystal, trying not to laugh, but I heard my giggles echoing around me.

"Don't do it, Sadie!" Luca warned, dropping the bottle to the counter, rolling his eyes at all of us. "Gav get a hold of your tipsy elf."

I squeezed in closer to Crystal, both of us laughing so hard we were crying, holding our glasses up to Luca, his stern face cracking. Then Eric threw both his hands to the counter, palms drumming away, belting out— "I played my drum for him—"

Crystal and I fell against each other, singing in unison. "Pour—the—rum—a—rum—rum, rum, a rum, rum."

"Then," Crystal sang. "He smiled at me." She leaned over the counter, smacking Luca with a kiss, finally breaking him, his smile instant. "You know Polpetto—" she pulled at his jacket, tugging him towards her. "The lyrics before that are, to lay before the king."

"Damn straight, Baby." He tipped the bottle to her glass again. "Bottoms up."

The clattering of heels sent all of us spinning towards the hall to Sofia jetting into Eric's arms. "Matteo's asleep!"

"Good," Luca huffed. "Now handle this one." He eyed Eric.

"Oh," Sofia sighed. "I love handling him."

"Ew, abbastanza, enough!" Luca rolled his eyes again, tilting the bottle towards her.

She waved it off. "I still feel sick from the plane, and tired." She stifled a yawn, sending my eyes automatically to the clock. It *was* almost midnight New York time.

"If you're tired, then let's call it a night." Eric stood, draping his arm across her back, leading them away.

"Goodnight!" We all called.

Luca dropped the bottle again, rounding the counter while Crystal flipped around, back resting against the bar as he stepped in front of her, hands flying to her waist. "What about you, Baby? Ready to lay before the king?"

"So now you're singing," she teased him. They were so cute together, a perfect match.

"Baby, every time you fall on your knees, I hear the angels' voices."

Oh god... okay. I stepped away, immediately smacking into something hard, landing in Gavin's arms.

"It's just us now, Baby."

I looked back to the empty bar. We *were* alone. "Help me with the presents?"

He stilled, quiet, so I did the same, finally hearing the doors upstairs shut, inducing Gavin's devilish grin. Then he charged for the lights, knocking the switches down, the room going dark, lit only by the tree lights and fire. "This is my favorite part of Christmas." He stepped behind me, breath like a whisper against my ear, hands caressing my arms, my shoulders. "How about you sit on Santa's lap, Baby." His hand slid down my arm, up and under my shirt, a rash of goosebumps following his touch.

"Your family's upstairs." I swallowed a gasp, staring at his hands under my shirt, groping my breasts.

"They won't be coming back down." He pressed in harder, letting me feel he was ready. "It's just you and me, Baby." His teeth grazed my ear, nibbling down my neck while his hands flipped, bunching my shirt in his fingers, slowly rolling it up my body.

"We do have that mistletoe." I spun in his arms, hands falling to his belt, and the dick making its escape under it. "Would you like me to kiss you under the mistletoe?"

FIVE-YEAR ANNIVERSARY

I'd been waiting all week for tonight, scratch that, all month! Today was our five-year anniversary. We'd been married half a decade, and they'd been the best years of my life. Grant flew in to watch the kids because Gavin was surprising me tonight, and the only hint he gave me, was to wear something fancy.

I grabbed the garment bag off the door, unwrapping the dress it held. I never splurged on myself, but this was different. I fell in love with the gown the second I saw it, so I'd closed my eyes and handed over my credit card. The dress was the same shade as both the roses from our wedding and the amethyst bracelet Gavin bought me on our honeymoon. I opened the zipper, slipping into the purple silk, watching it seal to my body like plastic wrap. Gavin said fancy, but I knew my husband and knew how much he liked to see my curves. Last, but not least, I stepped into my heels. Perfect.

"Mamma!" Nora yelled the second I stepped into the family room, running over with awestruck eyes. "You look like a princess, Mamma!"

My eyes strayed beyond her to the black suit and the incredibly handsome man wearing it so well. His eyes were on me too, dark and deep as they ran the length of my gown, then met my eyes. I didn't expect him to be in a full suit with a jacket, the sight alone driving my heart and hormones over the edge.

"Ready, Baby?" He bent down, arms open, beckoning the twins. "Listen, ascolta lo Grant! Papà ti adora!" He kissed Nora's cheek, then Vinny's before straightening, sending them my way.

"Just like what Papà said," I laughed. "Listen to Grant, and Mamma loves you!"

Grant walked over, grabbing the twins' hands. "Have fun, you two."

"Thanks, Grant!" I stepped towards Gavin, his arm draping across my back, ushering me towards the garage door.

"You look beautiful, Baby."

"Where are you taking me?" I let his heavy-handed arm guide my way to the car door.

"To dinner." His smile turned mischievous, watching me as I got situated in the seat before closing the door and heading to his side.

"And?" I knew there was more. He'd been too excited.

He shrugged, starting the engine with one hand while his gaze fell to my chest. "No necklace?"

My hand rose to my bare neck. "I don't have one that matches the purple," I answered automatically, seeing the pop in his eyes. I knew that look, and that look meant I'd be getting a matching amethyst necklace for Christmas. "By the way, Mr. Romano, you look very handsome." I stretched my hand to his thigh, his cheeks immediately blushing. "You didn't bring a bag, so I'm guessing we're coming home tonight."

"You sound disappointed," he chuckled. "And who says I didn't bring a bag." This car had no backseat and no trunk, and there was no bag.

He dropped his hand over mine, driving with only his left, taking us down the familiar route, one we drove on special occasions. He parked at the valet, hurrying out to get to my door before anyone else had the chance.

"Dinner at our favorite hotel?" I took his hand, stepping out and into his arms. "You didn't buy out the whole restaurant did you?" I teased.

"No." He shook his head, but that mischievous grin was still plastered cheek to cheek. "And if I did I wouldn't tell you." He led me through the hotel lobby to the restaurant, nodding directly to the hostess, who immediately walked us back to a table overlooking the moonlit waves. Gavin then pulled out my chair, just as he always did, and I sat, watching him do the same. It'd been five years, and he still opened the car door for me and pulled out my chair.

Almost immediately, a waiter was at our table filling the wine glasses and just as quickly disappearing. "He forgot the menus!" I looked back, about to wave.

"I already handled it, Baby." Gavin's hand caught mine, pulling me back to face him. "Don't worry about it." He smiled, dark eyes reflecting the candlelight while the glow illuminated his grin, making him look mysterious and so sexy. I was so used to seeing Gavin as husband and papà that I forgot how handsome and rugged he was. I forgot how thick his black hair was, how deep his dark eyes were, how sexy that stubble emphasizing his full lips were, and how muscular his body was.

He chuckled, running his finger over my rings. "What?"

"I'm lucky," I replied honestly. "And I'm hoping to get lucky." Again, I replied honestly, giving him a wink.

The waiter returned to the table, placing our dishes in front of us.

"So, what did you order?" I looked down at the plate, chicken, salad, and bread. Huh... the bread was usually in a basket, and the salad always came separately. This didn't look like their typical plating either; it looked more like a banquet plate rather than a— "Our wedding."

"Yeah," Gavin sighed, nodding. "I never took a moment to eat, one of the many things I didn't get to fuc—to do that night. I'm sorry I rushed it, Baby. I was so anxious for you to say yes and so excited to be in Italy with you as mia moglie."

He recreated our wedding reception dinner. I stretched both hands for his. "Our wedding was perfectly us, well perfectly you," I laughed, teasing him.

"Baciami!" he demanded, leaning over the table, lips already puckered. "Happy anniversary."

I met his chaste kiss before we broke to eat. Romantic Gavin was one of my favorites, but he rarely came out, at least not like this.

We continued eating, stealing glances at each other every few bites.

"Dessert, Baby?" He arched his brow while dropping his napkin to his plate.

Absolutely. "I thought you didn't get a room?"

He burst out laughing, shaking his head at me. "Not that kind of dessert, Baby. Actual dessert."

"That's too bad." I slid my foot out of my stiletto and straight to his leg, dragging up his pants.

"Every time I try to be romantic, you try and get me into bed," he chuckled.

"Cause and effect." I slipped my foot back into my heel.

He signaled for the waiter, and the guy rushed over, refilling our wine, grabbing up the plates and leaving just as another stepped up, placing a chocolate cake down.

No... I flashed my eyes to Gavin then back to the two-layer chocolate cake complete with strawberries. It was a smaller yet identical version of our wedding cake. "Is it?"

He nodded. "Same bakery."

Of course, because Gavin was always all or nothing, he never half-assed any detail. I ran my finger along the chocolate icing, giving him a playful smile. "Do I get to smudge it on your nose like I did at our reception?"

"You can put it wherever you want, Baby."

I stretched my finger to his lips, watching his serpent tongue shoot out, licking its way up my finger, leaving both my hand and my thighs wet. Then he stuck his fork in the cake, slicing a piece and pushing it to my lips.

"Want to take a walk after this?" He dug his fork back into the cake, devouring the bite himself.

A walk... a walk that would lead us to a dark corner, a wall hidden in the shadows, an empty beach. "Yes!"

He took one last bite before standing, taking my hand in his and pulling me up to face him. "Sei bellissima stasera, amore mio. You look beautiful tonight, my love."

He led me out through the lobby, out the doors to the dark moonlit terrace, following the same path we had at our wedding, all the while his hold on my hand growing tighter. Then he turned, the dark suddenly light.

"Oh, Gavin!" I stilled, eyes and heart overwhelmed by the display.

Then he spun me into his arms. "Will you dance with me, Baby."

The quartet started strumming, perched on the stage just as they had at our reception. "Always." I clasped his hand, letting him lead the way while I stared around us, taking it all in. We danced past the bouquets of violet roses and daisies lining the dance floor, illuminated by strings of twinkling lights strung above us.

"All I wanted to do that night was dance with you, Baby," he whispered against my ear as he waltzed me across the dance floor. "And now we have the whole floor and the whole night to ourselves. No interruptions, no place to be." He twirled me out then in, wrapping one hand over mine as his other pressed into my back.

"This is the greatest anniversary gift you could have ever given me, Gavin."

"Traditionally, the five-year anniversary gift is wood, but I figured I've already gifted you that quite often." And, there was my Gavin. "But I do like tradition, Baby, so I'll make sure you get that wood tonight."

I laughed, smiling up at my husband. He was too good to be true sometimes. "I *am* a fan of traditions."

He tightened his hold, pulling me in even closer to his chest as the band played on.

"Gavin."

"I know, Baby." He grumbled, hand releasing mine to adjust his pants. "Your tits are pressed right into me. I can't help it."

What... I laughed again, looking up only to see his eyes staring down my dress. "I was going to say I love you."

"I love you too, Baby." He dipped his face to mine, our lips meeting for a peck, but as always, we couldn't stop.

The music slowed, violin taking control, our tongues meeting its pace, slow, sensual, filled with longing. The cello joined, sending our lips pacing with its deep notes while we moved as one across the dance floor, his hands now clasping my back, mine cupping his face, keeping our kiss tight. We were slaves to the melody, the overtly romantic, slow pace we weren't accustomed to.

My eyes closed, skin burning from his touch, my lips hungry, and my mind lost in these last five years as my feet followed his. We had so many memories, both good and bad. Gavin was a complicated man sometimes, but at the end of the day, he was my Gavin, and I would take the lows to get these highs.

He broke the kiss, but not our dance. "Baby, we have a room."

I laughed. "Are you already done dancing?"

"No," he whispered back. "Not yet."

We danced a while longer until Gavin finally stepped away, meeting my eyes. "Let's head upstairs, Baby."

I nodded yes, looking around the dance floor one last time before his arm draped across my back, guiding me past the bouquets.

We walked in silence through the lobby to the elevator, down our floor, into our room, to a rose-petal-covered bed. "Champagne, Baby?" He tipped the bottle, filling the flutes. "Another regret," he sighed, gaze flicking from the bottle to me. "Was that I never got to have you on our actual wedding night." He walked over, circling me as he sipped. "I never got to watch you step out of your dress." His fingertips coasted across my back, sweeping my hair over my shoulder. "So now—" he trailed his fingers down my back to the zipper. "I'm gonna unzip you, Baby, and then make love to you the way I should have that night." His chest formed to my back, his hand the only thing between us, dragging the zipper apart, guiding the dress down my curves, my legs, letting it fall to my feet. His hands gripped my hips, his heavy breathing hissing in waves up my neck. "Give me a minute, Baby," he warned, body flexed hard against my back, fingers gripping even harder. "I need to calm down. I want to make love to you, not rip you apart."

"I guess I should have worn panties," I whispered over my shoulder.

"That's not fucking helping."

I stepped forward, swiveling on my heels to face him, wanting him to see all of me. "Your turn," I demanded, reaching to the single button on his jacket, unhooking it, and pushing the jacket off. I started for his shirt next, only to catch his rising zipper. How was I supposed to go slow when that giant erection was right in front of me.

"Baby," he muttered, raising his hands to his shirt, too impatient to wait for me. So I started at the bottom, releasing each button while he started at the top, meeting me in the middle. My hands took back control, sliding the shirt over his shoulders, pressing a kiss to his chest as I drug the sleeves down his arms. I peppered kisses down his stomach, my hands and mouth meeting up at his belt, kisses following the trail as I undid his belt, his zipper.

I looked up; only his eyes were sealed shut, shallow moans escaping his lips as I teased his pants. "You are the sexiest man I've ever seen," I breathed with my kiss. His leaky tip was at lips, my tongue in motion, licking it dry as I worked his pants to the floor. But he wanted to make love, so this play had to wait. I straightened, stepping away, traipsing to the bed, stare on him as I lowered my back down over the petal-covered sheets.

His jaw was set, lips still sealed, exhales audible. He was fighting to control himself. He slid my heels off, lifting a foot to his lips, smashing a kiss to my ankle, then nibbling his way up my leg. "Sei cosi sexy, Baby." His hiss hit my inner thigh as his stubbly chin grazed my center, a precursor to the sharp tongue that followed.

A lick, a kiss, a flick, calm tongue turning to a tornado. His mouth was in a frenzy, fast and furious one minute, soft and teasing the next. A heavy breath, a hard suck, a whipping attack on my clit. "Ooh!" I slapped the sheets, bunching the rose petals in my fingers. I loved his tongue, but I loved his dick even more. "Gavin!"

His kisses started up my stomach, greedy lips owning my breasts while his hand slipped between my thighs, hooking under my leg, the strike so close I could already feel it. "Gavin," I pleaded, arms wrapping around his back, urging him inside me.

He entered slow, no strikes, no pounds, agonizingly slow and cautious. Making love was a beautiful concept, but for my impatient, impulsive, hungry, rather starving Italian husband, making love was almost cruel. It wasn't natural him; he had to force himself to slow. "I married *you*, Gavin, this isn't you," I whispered, meeting his heavy gaze. "I want you to fuck me, make love Gavin style."

His eyes lit and darkened at once. His body retreating, emptying me, only to pound right back inside, sending my eyes rolling back and my arms flailing, rose petals flying around the room as he rammed. "Guardami, Baby!" he belted out, panting with his hard thrusts.

I opened my eyes, staring up into his. This was the very definition of making love because this man loved me more than anything.

We moved as one, rolling in the sheets, legs every which way, his grunts meeting my moans, his flexed arms controlling my body as he fucked the shit out of me.

"Fuck!" he yelped, body moving at the speed of light, my body imploding at the same speed. "I'm gonna come, Baby."

"Harder!" I yelled, capturing his arms as he battered that bundle of nerves, hitting the target until I burst. "God, fuck, Gavin! I, love, you!"

SEPTEMBER

"This is a bad fucking idea!" Gavin groaned, pacing the bathroom floor, abruptly slamming his palms against the vanity counter.

"Gavin! I, we, had no choice. You know that." I started walking towards him, then thought better of it.

"This is bullshit!" he spat right back. "I'm putting my foot down this time, Sadie!" He spun around, resting his back against the counter, glowering at me. "It's fucking dangerous, and all kinds of shit happens these days!"

I rolled my eyes, tired of having this same fight over and over again. "Dangerous? It's kindergarten, Gavin."

A soft knock rattled the door before it flung open, with Vinny and Nora rushing in.

"I'm ready, Papà," Nora squealed, twirling endlessly in her uniform dress.

"Well, you can take that off!" Gavin instructed, pointing towards the door.

"Why, Papà?" Nora's eyes grew wide.

"Gavin!" I warned. He wasn't handling the thought of separation well. He could protect his babies when they were with him. Now they'd be out there on their own, without Papà.

"Five and a half is a little young to be starting school," he grumbled, rolling his eyes obnoxiously, pouting like a kindergartner himself.

The twins didn't go to preschool since we both stayed home, but kindergarten was mandatory, and we couldn't wait until they were ten, like Gavin had tried to convince me.

"Can we go now?" Vinny pleaded. "I want to see my new school!"

"Yes!" I ushered him to the door. "Let's go!"

We shuffled down the stairs, the kids running straight to their new backpacks, proudly hitching them over their shoulders.

"I have a meeting with the principal tomorrow," Gavin sighed as he grabbed his keys and reluctantly opened the front door.

"Why!" I guided the kids to the car. "Go ahead and get in," I instructed, closing Nora's door and rounding the trunk to Gavin's side, waiting for an answer.

"I want to go over their security protocol, and I have questions regarding a few of their policies with bullying and shit."

I stifled my laugh, continuing around the car and climbing into the passenger seat, pulling his hand into mine. "Gavin, they're only going to school for four hours a day. Not to mention we've enrolled them in the best private school in all of San Diego."

He nodded, lifting my knuckles to his lips, kissing them before twisting back to face the kids. "Pronti?"

"Si, Papà!" The twins yelled back in unison as Gavin started up the engine.

The kids were smiling and giggling the entire drive while Papà braced the wheel at ten and two, eyes locked on the road.

We finally arrived, parking and walking the twins to their classroom door, helping them hang their backpacks on the post, then stepping away, watching them take off excitedly.

"How are they already five?" Gavin mumbled, draping his arm over my shoulders, curling me to his side. "It feels like we just brought them home from the hospital. It's not supposed to go this fast."

I had been the brave one all week, acting indifferent to them starting school, but now it was sinking in. I'd be home alone, no more cuddles in the morning or family beach walks. My babies *had* just come home from the hospital, and they *had* just been toddlers yesterday, and now they were starting school.

"Hey," Gavin whispered, flicking a tear from my cheek with his thumb. "I thought you were okay with this."

"I am." I sniffled back the tears.

"What's that kid doing!" Gavin huffed, body stiffening, nodding his head over to the playground.

I followed his glare to Vinny standing with another boy, who looked like he was laughing at Vinny. Then I spotted Nora marching right up to them.

"Vai via stronzo!" she shouted, slapping her hands against the boy's chest, shoving him away from Vinny.

"That's my girl!" Gavin boasted.

Oh my gosh! "Gavin! She can't curse or hit at school!" I started towards her. "Say Sorry, Nora!"

"She said it in Italian, Baby," Gavin called, racing up to my side.

"Doesn't matter!" How was he smiling about this! "I'm glad you're talking to the principal tomorrow because I have a feeling we're probably going to get called in."

"Let me handle it, Baby," he insisted. "Piccolina, vieni qui!" Gavin was stern, and she flashed her eyes over first, then walked to him, smiling as big as she could.

"Yes, Papà?" She wrapped her tiny arms around his leg, hugging them while looking up at his eyes.

I cleared my throat, reminding him of what he needed to do.

"Yeah, yeah," he sighed, bending down to her eye level. "No hitting, no kicking, and no Papà words. Capisci?"

"Sì, Papà!" She smiled, grasping the pleat of her dress, twirling in front of him, putting on quite a show before waltzing away.

Gavin straightened back up, crossing his arms over his chest like some tough guy. "There, handled."

Uh, huh.

The bell sounded, the playground suddenly chaotic, everyone darting towards the classroom doors.

"Have a great first day of school! Mamma loves you!" I squeezed my babies, then Gavin squeezed them, and we stepped back once more, watching them make their way to their door.

Nora reached for Vinny's hand, leading him to the classroom, walking right to the front of the line, pushing herself and Vinny into the first spot. The girl standing there yelled at them to go to the back, but Nora ignored her. The little girl protested again, turning Nora's eyes brown eyes black, the exact way Gavin's did. Oh no. Nora turned around, shoving her shoulder against the girl while whispering something that caused the little girl to step back, sinking her face down into her shoulders.

"Gavin," I whispered, tugging his shirt so he'd drop his ear down to me. "We should probably research some back up schools."

"Why?"

I looked at Nora, watching her smile at her new teacher with those big eyes and that deceptively sweet smile. "Because Nora is a Romano, and I don't think she's all you. I think she has some Luca too."

He nodded with pride. "She'll teach Vinny the ropes."

Lord help us.

We gave a final wave, waiting as they marched into their class and the door shut before we turned away with the stream of parents. I continued walking, only to realize Gavin wasn't beside me; he was still standing at the now locked gate, his back towards me.

He turned around, giving me a glimpse of his tattoos peeking out from under the sleeves of his shirt. "I don't know if I can do this," he called over, slumped shoulders guiding him away. "The house is gonna be so quiet."

Quiet wasn't a bad thing. "That all depends on you."

"What?"

I glanced around, making sure we were alone. "The harder you fuck me, the louder I get. So the house can be as loud or as quiet as you'd like. We have the entire house to ourselves, the bed, the tables, your desk."

His devilish grin curled up, his brown eyes went black.

"Of course, we could just grab breakfast instead."

"Oh, I'm fucking gonna get my breakfast, Baby. Don't you worry."

Now it was a race. Hustling to the car, driving home, leaping from the car doors, Gavin throwing my back against the front door, hungry lips crashing into my neck, his words a hiss against my ear. "An empty house."

We were in our own world, hands fast and flying, bodies entwined, spinning into the house, lips smacking, tongues messy and urgent.

"An empty house," I repeated, stumbling for his office, only he pulled me to a stop.

"I want you outside, Baby," it was a growl, a demand, his lips back in the crook of my neck, nibbling to my shoulder.

"It's too bright outside!" I stared out at the blazing sun.

"I know. I want to see every inch of you, Sadie."

Sadie...

He continued down the hall, dragging me with him out the door.

"We could do some gardening when we're done."

He stilled, turning to face me. "Will you do something for me?"

"Depends." I felt so small under his intimidating gaze.

"Will you put on your sports bra and those booty shorts you run in?"

A laugh escaped my lips. "You want me to put clothes *on*?" I didn't actually want to garden right now.

He dropped his hand to my waist, fingers roaming my curves. "I always dreamed about fucking you when I first saw you bent over in your garden. I fantasized about taking you right there in the grass."

"Ahh, so you *do* want Mamma to do some gardening."

"No, I want Sadie. I want to fuck you, exactly as I'd pictured doing it."

"You fantasized about it?" I pictured him stroking his dick to me. I gulped, instantly dashing away, hurrying back down the hall and up the stairs, taking them two at a time to get to our room.

I dug through my drawers, finding the exact sports bra and shorts I'd worn the first time I'd met him. And I changed in record time, sweeping my hair into a ponytail on my way down the stairs.

He was standing where I'd left him, gaze locked on me, closed-lipped smirk curled wickedly up his face.

"I'm Sadie," I flirted, passing right by him. "Nice to meet you." I walked straight to the daisies, bending over seductively to all fours, ass arched in the air.

He charged, shaking the ground under my knees as he stormed forward, dropping behind me, hands gliding up my thighs. "Fuck, Baby." His greedy exhales hit my back, his knuckles now bumping my ass as he ripped at his belt, the clank piercing my ears, the metal hiss of the zipper following. Then a palm smacked my ass, that hand then snaking up under my shorts.

"No panties," I breathed back.

"Wait," he growled, fingers running up and down my wet center. "You weren't wearing any fucking panties the day I met you?!"

"I'll never tell."

Fingers instantly struck inside me, his arm cranking them deeper, finger fucking me from the back.

"Fuck," I whimpered, arching against those talented fingers.

His other hand pressed over my back as he bent over me, pumping his fingers even faster. "Tell me now! Were you wearing panties under these shorts." His knuckles hit my ass again, rubbing up and down my shorts while he stroked himself in rhythm with his fingers fucking me.

"No, nothing. Just these little, flimsy shorts," I lied.

Wet fingers tore the shorts right off, his hips squared up behind me, his dick shoving between my thighs. "I've wanted to fuck you like this for so fucking long!" He bucked his hips, driving himself deep inside me, sending my fingers desperately bunching into the grass, ripping the blades.

God! He hit deep, every nerve going haywire, pressure mounting from all sides, surges erupting like volcanoes, the heat overwhelming.

"Fuck, fuck," he wailed, chest falling flat against my back, fingers wrapping over my sports bra, clutching my breasts.

"Harder!" I tipped my head back, feeling the instant yank of my hair, his hand twirling the ponytail into his fist. "Gavin!"

He pulled my hair tighter, my chest arching, face to the sky as I screamed.

"Say, my name, again, Baby," he huffed, ramming with all his might, breaking me, sending my quaking arms collapsing to the ground, my body falling with them.

"Gavin," I whimpered into the grass.

His body fell over mine, his chest heaving forcefully, smothering me, pushing me deeper into the grass. Then with a grunt, he pushed up, flopping to my side. "Fuck!" He clasped his chest, holding with his heavy breathing. "You have no idea how many fucking dreams I've had about this, Baby."

I rolled my face to the side to see him, and he instantly cracked a smile, then laughed. "Why are you laughing?"

He stretched his fingers to my cheek, sweeping them across my skin. "You had dirt on your face when I first met you, too."

Too... "Lovely," I laughed sarcastically, plucking off a blade of grass from my cheek. "And yet you came back the next day."

"And every other day after that." His fingers continued tracing over my face.

"So does this mean I can take a little nap, like the old days?" I laid flat against the grass, letting the sun stream over me.

"After."

"After what?" I closed my eyes, tilting my face towards the sun.

"Now I want to see you." A dark shadow cast over me, a heavy body climbing over mine, hands attacking my sports bra, flipping it up for the face already smothering my chest.

"But I'm covered in dirt," I laughed, batting away his wild hair tickling my face.

"Dirty Sadie is my favorite."

The jolt sent my back flying off the grass. "Fuck!" He was inside me, clobbering my sensitive nerves.

Suddenly my legs were up, breasts bouncing violently, and the louder I moaned, the harder he pounded, and the deeper my nails dug, the faster he fucked me. I was at the mercy of his insatiable appetite, giving myself over to his greedy hands having their way with my nipples, my clit, my legs, groping me in rhythm with his thrusts. Fuck! I looked up, the sun illuminating his body. "Your shirt," I gasped. "Take your shirt off."

He huffed, jerking up, hips still rolling as he yanked his shirt over his head, exposing every strong muscle he had. I was mesmerized, watching each flex, each movement as he rocked over me, each bead of sweat streaming down the lines of his muscles. Then I followed his eyes as they ran over my body, watching me shake and bounce from his own force.

His face suddenly came crashing down, lips smacking mine, our tongues like glue, couldn't separate them if we tried.

"Oh, Gavin!" Oh, oh, oh...

"Fuck," he let out a deep groan, jerking fast as he came inside me. Then he collapsed at my side, opening his arm for me to cuddle into.

"Baby."

I heard a whisper, then felt a tug on my hand. "We have to go, Baby."

I blinked, opening my eyes to the blazing sun above and the scratchy grass under me, and the fully dressed man standing at my side.

"I brought your clothes from upstairs."

"What time is it?" I yawned.

"Noon."

"Noon!" I jumped up, losing my balance, wavering, his hands catching me, wrapping around my waist to steady me. "Why'd you let me sleep so long?"

"It's not every day I get to watch my wife sleep naked in the grass. Well, maybe it will be now."

"Creep!" I fell into his chest, holding him just as tight.

"Just more than a crush, Baby," he teased back, pressing his lips to mine while pushing my clothes into my hands. "Twins will be waiting."

I took the clothes and hurried inside, changing and meeting him at the car, zooming off to the school.

We parked and started for the gate, but Gavin let go of my hand. "I'm gonna go talk to the principal, Baby. Need to reschedule that meeting."

"Why?"

"I have *other* priorities right now." He grinned, giving me a wink before veering away while I continued to the gate, taking my place in the clutter of parents.

"You're the twins' mom, right?" A woman asked me, causing a handful of moms to turn around towards us.

Oh, no. Please don't let this be about Nora. "Yes."

She gave me a pitiful half-smile in return, reaching her hand to my hair. "You poor thing. You've got grass all in your hair." She plucked a blade, waving it.

Oh, my, god. I looked to the ground, peeking for Gavin from the corner of my eye.

"And your shirt's on inside out," she continued.

Oh, my, god. Gavin! I slowly raised my eyes back up, finally seeing him making his way over.

"It's okay, honey," another woman sighed, resting her hand on my arm. "We've all been there. Motherhood is rough. And twins, must be exhausting."

I looked over at Gavin, his sexy satisfied grin covering his whole damn face. "Rough," I repeated with a laugh."It is, but I wouldn't want it any other way."

The gate suddenly swung open, an ambush of parents ensuing, but Gavin and I stood back, eyes locked on each other.

"You've still got grass in your hair, Baby."

"So I've heard."

"Mamma! Papà!" The twins screamed, breaking our reverie, focusing now on our babies, who weren't babies anymore, running towards us. Gavin was right. Time wasn't supposed to go this fast. The last five years felt more like five weeks. Another chapter closed.

GAVIN POV
Chapters

For more Gavin:

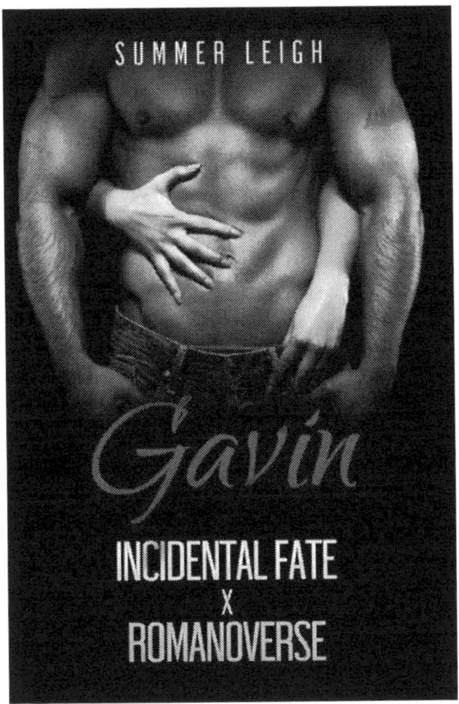

GAVIN POV: 24TH BIRTHDAY

My phone thudded along the bedside table. They never fucking remember the time difference. It might be nine in New York, but it was only six a.m. here. I shot my hand out, smacking it off. Fuck, now I was up. I leaned up, checking the bassinets to make sure the phone hadn't wakened the babies, nope. I fell back down, smashing my arm over my eyes to block out the incoming sun. My chest was empty, where was she? I flipped, meeting her naked back, that skin calling my fucking name.

I thought last year was the best birthday I'd ever had, but today I had my babies, and my girl. This was fucking everything. Twenty-four was a magic number. I pressed a fingertip to her back, except she didn't even flinch. This last month had been the greatest and most torturous. I got my babies, I got my wife home safe, *and* I got no action. She was out of commission until she recovered, and the only time her tits, hands, or mouth were free was when she was passed out. And then, on top of that, she slept fucking topless, so she could feed the babies easier. It was the biggest fucking lesson in patience and sharing I'd ever had. But today was my birthday. I could be selfish, right? Wake her from the sleep she barely got, tell her I needed attention too. That the babies had taken turns sucking on those tits all night, and now it was my turn. I just needed to feel her, fuck, I just needed her.

I pressed another fingertip to her back, then another, running them up and down her skin. She shivered, and like I'd hoped, rolled over, sending those swollen fucking tits bouncing against the sheet inches from my face. Fuck, my fingers stretched, wanting to fucking grab the shit out of them, smother my face, my dick with them. But I didn't want to seem greedy. I knew she was still recovering, and it hadn't even been a month, but I wanted to fuck those massive tits so damn bad.

I traced her dark nipples, two bullseyes that I had no fucking restraint against. I didn't want to wake her, but Papà was hungry too. I looked up, watching the quiet breaths escape her parted lips. God, I was fucking selfish. I stopped touching; her eyes instantly batted open.

"Good morning," she squeaked, giving me a groggy smile. "Happy birthday."

"Good morning, Baby." Fuck, that morning smile of hers and that messy hair in her face was so fucking sexy.

"I'm sorry I wasn't able to get out and get you a gift," she yawned, her eyes following my fingers retracing her tight nipple.

Just say it. Tell her that for your birthday, you want to fuck the shit out of these tits. That you've been waiting patiently for almost a month. "Baby," I started, meeting her tired eyes. She'd been up all night with the babies. What the fuck was wrong with me? Who gave a shit if it was my birthday? She'd barely been home a month. She'd been working twenty-four-seven, caring for my fucking babies while recovering herself, and instead of letting her rest, I'm trying to get my dick on and in her. "Get some rest, Baby." I dropped my fingers from her tit and pulled the comforter over her, ending my torment.

I threw my legs off the bed, stalking into the bathroom. I hadn't jerked off this much since high school, but her hands were always full, so mine were all I was left with. Fuck it. I wasn't even in the mood anymore. I walked back out—holy fuck. My feet stopped a few feet from her naked body perched on the edge of our bed, legs crossed. "Do you, d-do you need some help, Baby?"

"Do you?" She smiled back seductively, shifting, giving me a better view. "It's your birthday, Gavin. I won't take no for an answer. Whatever you want."

I was sprinting, zero fucking control, scooping up her tits like they were water in the fucking desert. "But you should rest, Baby." Fuck, my dick was fighting my pants, painfully fucking throbbing for her.

She sent her hands diving for my waistband, her nails dragging over my stomach on their way down, smiling when she saw my dick. Fuck! She stretched those fingers over every inch of my dick, thumb rubbing my head, damn I missed being touched. Her hand was softer than mine, stroking me from the left, giving me a whole new fucking sensation. "Oh, fuck!" It was wet, hot, her lips plunging down my pipe, making him fucking disappear. Cazzo! Fuck! I had a month of deprivation, now she's swallowing me whole.

Her head bobbed at my waist, but I didn't want head, fuck I did, but I wanted her tits first. "Baby." I threw my hand to her hair, stopping her, watching those eyes flash to mine, lips still wrapped around my dick. Fuck. "I want to fuck these first." I pinched her nipple, keeping my eyes on her retreating mouth, then her hands clutching her tits, presenting them to me, it was my fucking birthday.

My hands hit her shoulders, her tits trapped my dick, and for once, it actually looked small, lost between those giant fucking milk tits.

"I thought maybe you'd want to have me instead," her voice was just a fucking whisper, making me stop mid-fuck to make sure I was hearing her correctly.

"What do you mean, Baby?"

"It's your birthday. You can have all of me if you want."

"Six weeks." The doctor said six weeks!

She batted her eyelashes while licking her lips. "Can you be gentle?"

Fuck no! I've been waiting way too long to be fucking gentle! I was capable of a lot of shit, self-control was not one of them. I wanted to fuck the shit out of her, leave her shaking, unconscious from the orgasm. *No baby, no way in hell can I be gentle right now! We'll have to wait*. "Y-yeah."

She dropped her tits, leaving my dick cold while she rolled down onto the bed, lifting her knees, pussy right in my face. Jesus fucking Christ. Gentle. Control, your, fucking, self. You're not a fucking animal. I jumped over her, shooting my fingers up her thigh.

"Ooh!" she moaned, and I hadn't even touched her yet.

"Baby, if you want me to be fucking gentle then you need to be quiet."

She tilted her head back against the sheets, eyes closed, nodding back to me with a heavy breath. That was really not fucking helping.

Slow, gentle, you got this. I smacked my whole fucking hand against her pussy, her wet, drenched pussy. I hadn't had her in forever, and I wanted, no, I fucking needed to feel her, taste her, inhale her. My head was between her thighs, feeling her tighten as my lips sank to hers. Fuck, I missed this. My tongue flicked her clit, she shivered. I hissed, she squealed. I licked her pussy clean, she whimpered. I slipped a finger in next, dipping into her pool, too tight for a second finger, her gasps becoming screams. Her legs trembled against my face, her whines getting louder, then a yank at my hair, her fingers pulling me away.

"Gavin," she begged, slithering her hips under me. Fuck she was already gonna come. Wait for me, Baby. I slammed my dick down that waterslide, forcing my way into that tight pussy, sending her flying up the bed.

"Gentle!" she yelped.

"Fuck!" Gentle, fuck. What the fuck did that even mean! I'm Italian, for God's sake! I slowed, biting my fucking tongue, my dick so fucking greedy, screaming for more. I rocked in short bursts, her pussy welcoming me back home, inch by inch taking me until I was balls deep. Fuck. Fuck. My dick wanted to slam, to pound, to juice him until he spewed. I closed my eyes, counting to ten, slow the fuck down! I didn't realize how badly I needed to be one with her. My whole body was on fucking fire. "Fuck, I, love, you, Baby."

"Gavin," she whined. "Faster."

My eyes sprung open to hers, her hands squeezing her overfilled tits, teasing her fucking nipples. Holy shit! My dick was locked and loaded! I grabbed her hands over her tits, squeezing them both as I shot off inside her. Fuck, fuck! There was no better fucking feeling.

I stayed over her, not wanting to pull out. Our touch was fucking powerful. I could feel my heart recharging from the connection. "Baby," I whispered to her closed eyes. She was quiet, too fucking quiet. "Sadie?" I sat up, and she opened one eye, then another. Phew. "You okay, Baby?"

She nodded, a tear falling from her eyes down to the sheet under her. "I've missed you." She sniffled, crinkling her nose with a smile. "I've missed being touched by you."

Me too, Baby. I lifted her back from the bed, sitting her up, sitting down beside her. "Get on my lap."

She jerked back, eyes wider than normal, face fucking horrified. "No! You'll destroy me!"

"I just wanna kiss you."

"Oh," she laughed, throwing her shaky leg over my lap and her hands to my face. "Today's special," she teased my lips. "You're twenty-four, on the twenty-fourth, and the babies are twenty-four days old!"

"Twenty-four's a new favorite number." I missed that smile too. Fuck, it felt good getting back to my girl.

"New? You have more?"

"Eighteen." I looked into her beautiful tired eyes. "The best day of my life. The day you took my name, the day I got to call you mia moglie. The day that changed my life." I went for it, nailing her mouth with my lips. I could go a month without fucking her, but I wouldn't last a day without kissing her.

GAVIN POV: SADIE TRIP: 1

She flashed her big eyes up as she leaned in, hovering those lips an inch from mine. "You sure you're going to be okay?"

Nope! Absolutely fucking not! You haven't left my side since the hospital, and I'm two seconds away from losing my fucking shit. I nodded, biting my tongue. "Yeah, Baby. We'll be fine. Call me the second the plane lands."

Her glossy lips hit me, holding them to my mouth as she took a deep breath. "I love you, Gavin."

"Love you, Baby. I'll pick you up tomorrow." I licked my lips, savoring the fruity-smelling shit she left on them. I can't believe she was fucking leaving us.

She flashed me her nervous smile before looking back over her shoulder. "Mamma loves you, Nora and Vinny! I'll be home tomorrow. Take good care of Papà for me."

"You're gonna miss your flight, Baby." Actually, how about you do. Stay in the car, and I'll take you back home.

Nope. She got out, closing the door, taking off into the airport. Fuck! My blood was fucking boiling, urging me to take off after her and drag her back. She'd never left me like this, flying away to another fucking state where I couldn't protect her or keep her safe. But she wanted to go, shit, she needed to go. The babies were already a year and a half old, and she'd barely done any work for Hope. She was too fucking excited for me to bring her down with my shit.

I could rally, push my irrational fucking anxiety to the side, and man up. "Cosa dovremmo fare?" I called back to the babies. "What do you want to do? Zoo?" I saw Sadie's white tank and that leopard print bra, fuck I missed that bra. Then her face in the mirror, watching me f— "Fuck, no zoo! No zoo!" I drove home, ignoring the empty seat beside me. I needed to be rational, goddammit. She'd be in the air for a couple hours, then at the hospital for the rest of the day, then in her hotel room, then meetings tomorrow morning, then back home. No big deal. Unless some asshole hit on her at the airport, or one of those guys at the hospital got fresh with her. Dammit, rational, be rational. She's fine; she'll be fine. No big deal. I was suddenly pulling into the driveway, not even realizing we were home.

I carried the twins in, letting them cruise the hall. This big ass house felt empty right now. "Andiamo fuori, let's go outside." I needed fresh air to clear my head. I elbowed the back door open, Piccolina took off into the yard, but Piccolo wasn't moving. "Vai a giocare, go!"

He slumped forward out the door, looking back at the house. "Mahmah," he called, tilting his head around for a better view.

"She'll be back soon, Piccolo. Come play with Papà and Nora." I carried him to the playhouse to meet Nora. "How about for our special Papà night I make spaghetti! Real authentic spaghetti, not Mamma's American spaghetti," I laughed.

"Mahmah!" Vinny wailed, racing back to the house.

"No, fuck." I wasn't saying she was here. I grabbed him back up, carrying him right back over to the playhouse. He still looked so fucking lost. I wrapped him up in my arms. I miss her too, buddy.

We needed to get our minds off Mamma. I released him, throwing my arms up in the air, roaring at the two of them. "Papà's gonna get you!" They took off running around the yard, those cute fucking laughs shooting off as I chased them.

We ran and played in the backyard for hours. It was time for something new. "Okay, now what? How about the park?"

They followed me to the garage, and I loaded them into the stroller, checking the flight status once more. It'd been over three hours and her flight status now said delayed. That was it, no fucking explanation as to why or where the fuck the plane was.

I stomped to the playground, parking the stroller and checking my phone once more.

"You've got your hands full!" Some chick yelled over, waving towards my fucking kids. "They're gorgeous, look just like you."

Dammit, Sadie! Text me that you landed, Baby. I need an update. It's been too long. I unbuckled Nora, lowering her to the ground, Vinny next.

"How old are they?" That chick was still talking to me, looking right at us.

I stared at the phone screen. This wasn't gonna fucking work. I couldn't watch them both. "You wanna swing?" I lifted one in each arm, plopping them into the swings so I could focus on my phone.

"Must be nice having such a strong daddy. My ex could barely lift my son." That chick was next to us again, putting her own kid on the other swing. Why was she following my fucking kids? Moms around here did weird shit.

"So, are you a stay-at-home dad?"

Still nothing on my screen. Where are you, Baby? You should be there by now. Two more fucking minutes, and I was calling the damn airline. This was just fucking unacceptable.

"Let me guess, you're Greek?"

Greek? What the—I looked at this chick now, wearing fucking workout gear but standing around not doing shit but insulting me. "Italian." The fucking nerve.

She laughed. "That was my second guess. The thick black hair threw me."

Following my kids around, and now fucking insulting me. When I came here with my girl, none of this shit happened. No one talked to me.

"So, do you live around here? My place is just up the street."

Now she wanted to know where we fucking lived as if I'd tell her how to find my kids. The phone buzzed in my hand, fuck. I practically dropped it, throwing it to my ear. "Baby?"

"Hi! We just touched down. The flight was delayed."

No shit. I'd been checking the tracking every five minutes for the last three hours. "I'm glad—"

"Oh shoot! I've got to go! I see my driver."

What? That's all I get! One fucking minute of your voice. "Okay, Baby. Call me later."

"I love you."

I love you, too. "Ti amo."

She hung up. I tucked my phone into my pocket before tugging the babies out of the swings, setting them free.

"Wife? Girlfriend?" The chick was near me again, stretching her legs on the playground steps, her form all fucking wrong. Who would throw their leg up like that?

"Wife." I followed the babies around to the slide, and she somehow managed to be there with her kid too.

"She must be a *very* happy woman."

Happy? What? Happy because she was gone? Happy to be away from me? From us? Happy to be in another fucking state?! What the hell was this chick's problem. "Andiamo!" I waved the twins over. I was done here.

"Is that Italian?" She stepped in front of me, testing my fucking patience. Who the hell was she to question my Italian? Of course, it was Italian! The fucking nerve of some people. I grabbed the babies, tossing them into the stroller, wheeling them away.

"I'm here every day around this time!" She was still yelling at me.

"Thanks for the fucking warning!" I hustled back down the street and over to ours, driving the stroller back into the garage. "Okay, how about Papà starts the pasta. No more adventures today."

I carried them into the family room, scattering all the toys around before hopping over the couch to the kitchen. I had made a list of to-do's back when Sadie was pregnant and cooking authentic Italian was one of them. It was also the only one that I hadn't gotten serious about, until now.

I gathered everything on the island, then heard a yelp, a scream. "Shit!" I raced around the counter, bypassing the baby gate and hopping over the couch, grabbing Nora's hand, forcing her to release the wad of hair she'd ripped from Vinny's head. "No, Nora!" I hugged Vinny, then hopped back over the couch. "Okay." I skimmed the recipe on my phone, measured the ingredients, mixed, and rolled. The counter suddenly looked just like it did when I was growing up, flour and dough covering the entire surface. Perfetto!

Even the babies were quiet, giving Papà all the time he needed. I glanced back, seeing Piccolina flipping through a book. Good. I turned back to the stove, bending to grab a saucepan. Fuck, Vinny! I jumped back up, scanning the room. Where the fuck was Vinny! "Vinny!" I raced over, he had to be in here, there was a fucking gate! "Nora, where's Vinny?"

She pointed over to the couch. "Vinyee bye-bye."

Fuck! I raced down the hall, catching a flash of black hair in the living room. Fuck! I ran in, finding him on the floor, holding a wedding picture in his hand.

"Mahmah." He tapped the glass with his finger.

"I know, Piccolo." I lifted him up, walked him back to the family room, double checking the lock before heading back into the kitchen. Okay, I tossed the tomatoes into the saucepan, then grabbed up the garlic.

"Bye-bye, Vinyee."

Not again! I jumped back to the counter, watching Vinny climb up and over the couch. Where the fuck did he learn—shit. "No, Vinny!" How was I supposed to get anything done with these two! I tossed the remote up, turning on some cartoon they both seemed into.

I hurried the sauce, boiled the noodles, running back and forth to the babies before finally loading them into their high chairs. I did it! "Pasta di Papà!" I presented them with their bowls. "Mangia!" I made my children an authentic Italian dinner. It'd only taken me two fucking hours, and I was fucking wiped out, but I did it.

Nora picked up the bowl, giving it a big sniff while looking up at me. That's right. I made that! She smiled, shooting her hand up, sending the bowl flying across the floor.

"Shit!" Tomato fucking everywhere, hours' worth of cooking on the floor. She didn't even take one fucking bite.

Come on, Vinny, my boy. Romano men loved Italian. But Vinny just looked it over, scrunching his face as he pushed the bowl away, completely fucking rejecting it. "Piccolo, come on." I swirled the noodles, pressing the loaded fork to his mouth. "Try it!" At least fucking taste it!

"Mahmah!" he screamed, tears pouring from his eyes as his hand hit the pasta away. "Mahmah!"

Fuck. No big deal. I could handle this. No fucking big deal. I could fucking handle this.

GAVIN POV: SADIE TRIP: 2

"Eight, nine, ten, fuck!" I dropped the bar to the floor, forgetting the babies were asleep, but it was too late. The weights were crashing down against the mat. I turned, catching my reflection in the mirror. I looked like a wild ass cage fighter with all this sweat dripping down my chest, swollen arms locked in a flex from the lifts, but at least I felt better. At least the noise of my own grunting and rep counting drowned out the silence of this giant fucking house, and the weight on the bar forced me to concentrate on my form, taking my mind off missing her.

I grabbed my phone up again, nothing. All I'd received tonight was one fucking text, a simple, *Heading to dinner*. No, I miss you, no, I'm thinking about you, no, I'm okay, nothing. And who the hell was she heading to dinner with! Some fucking doctors, probably. She knew not to drink, right? God, what if she was drunk. I was trying to give her space, trying so damn hard to be supportive, but there was only so much I could handle before losing my shit. I smashed the towel to my face, wiping the sweat before sliding it over my chest, then slamming the lights off. I still had to deal with cleaning the house.

Any other day I'd hear that boy band shit and find her dancing away in here while she cleaned up the day's mess, twirling around the fucking kitchen with a big ass smile across her face. How did she fucking do it? I was exhausted. The last thing I wanted to do was clean up all this shit. I was breaking after one day, and she was still dancing around the kitchen with a smile after twenty-one fucking years of parenting and working her ass off. She was amazing.

I walked past the toy-covered family room, heading to the kitchen. There was shit everywhere; marinara sauce all over the floors and cabinets, the island was covered in flour, and the dirty pans were still on the stove. Fuck it. I was calling it a night. I hit the lights off, walking right up the stairs to our room, cranking on the shower.

I kicked off my shorts and stepped in, turning the water warmer, dunking my face under the showerhead. This was usually the moment she would join me. She always played coy, but I knew she was always fucking watching. She'd pull the glass door, step in behind me, press her tits into my back, razor-sharp nipples slicing against my skin. Then she'd wiggle, knowing how much that fucking got me going. I'd turn around, watching her smile as I bent to grab her. "Fuck." I slammed a palm to the glass, the other to my dick, stroking fast, wishing it was her wet pussy milking me, almost seeing her sliding up and down the wet glass, tits bouncing, water splashing, screaming while I fucked her, my name spewing from her lips while I spewed inside her. "Fuck, fuck!" I rinsed my hand.

Maybe I was thinking about this all wrong. I always focused on the losses, not the gains. We'd never had phone sex. I'd never watched her through a screen. Never saw her naked body teasing the camera, a live movie just for me. I snatched a towel, smashing it over my body on the way to the bed, falling face-first to the sheets. I didn't want to deal with blue balls all night or this empty pit in my stomach from missing her. I needed to sleep.

I threw my hand to her side of the bed, which was cold. Cold and fucking empty. I had just fucked her in these sheets this morning. How were they already so fucking cold! There was no way I could sleep without her head against my chest, without her arm weighing me down, or without being able to breathe her in. Tits, Gavin. Think about her tits. They'll calm you down.

My phone rattled the table, vibrating back and forth. Baby! I slammed it to my ear. Finally! "Hey, Baby."

"Hi. I'm sorry for calling so late. I hope I didn't wake you."

No, I was just imagining how fucking good your tits would look through the camera. "It's okay, Baby. I was just about to go to bed. How'd it go today?"

"Good, the team here is onboard, and they already have investors lined up. That's who we met for dinner."

Investors! She had dinner with sleazy fucking investors and out until fucking midnight!

"The investors were women, Gavin."

"I didn't say anything, Baby." Shit, was I thinking out loud.

"You didn't," she laughed. *"But I know you."*

Then you'd also know how much I fucking miss you and how bad I want you next to me right now. Speaking of which. "How are you feeling, Baby?" Say horny!

"Exhausted and, well, exhausted I guess."

Fuck, that wasn't sex talk voice. She sounded wiped out. I'd have to table it, something to look forward to next time. "Get some rest. Call me in the morning."

"Oh, okay. Gavin, I love you."

"I love you too, Baby. Sogni d'oro."

I should've felt better after talking with her. I didn't. This would get easier. I just had to get used to this feeling and relax, trust that she'd be okay without my protection. I closed my eyes, but my brain was wired. I needed a distraction. What did men do when wives were away? Watch T.V. all night? Get trashed? Binge on porn? Or, did they not even fucking care and pass out without even noticing the empty space next to them. Work, work would distract me! I took off to my office. There was a new IPO this month, and I didn't trust the underwriter on this one. I could use this time to reread the prospectus.

I flipped open my laptop, but my focus was on the walls, the shelves. Whose bright idea was it to cover this room with pictures of her? Every memory was in here. I logged into the investment portal, catching the scratches on the wood under the laptop, the claw marks from her nails dragging across the desk. I could hear her whining and screaming as she came. How was that animal who destroyed my desk the same one in these photos? The girl laughing at me with a barbecue sauce-covered face, or the beautiful woman in white staring at me from the wall, or the one holding her pregnant belly, looking like a fucking angel. I was the luckiest fucking man. I rested my head back against the chair, getting lost in the analysis, feeling the weight of today hitting me, closing my eyes for a minute.

I'd spent the night selfishly bitching about her leaving me, but I woke with fucking gratitude she was coming home to me. Then I looked around the house, realizing what I was welcoming her home to and getting my ass into gear, scrubbing the house from top to bottom before the babies woke.

Then Piccolo helped me make pancakes, and since he made them, he actually ate them. Then we all practiced some Italian for Mamma. Mamma! God, I couldn't wait to see her. Now that I could fucking think straight, I had a slew of questions for her, specifically the terms they'd presented.

"Who's ready to get Mamma! Andiamo!" I carried the babies out, walking on fucking air to the car.

I drove up to the arrivals terminal, scanning the crowd, spotting her hurrying through the doors. Baby. I veered the car to the curb, shoving my door open, racing to her.

"Gav—"

I smashed my lips to hers, catching her in my arms as she stumbled backward. I knew I was smothering her, but I didn't care if she couldn't breathe, she could have my air—all of it. I wasn't fucking letting go.

She relaxed, falling into my hold, sliding her hands to my back as her tongue shot into my mouth. "Babies," she breathed.

"They fell asleep on the drive here." Fuck. I didn't want to stop. I didn't want to pull away, but the babies *were* still in the car behind us. I stepped back, pulling her door open, reaching for her hand, grabbing those tiny fingers in mine, feeling that heat spread through my veins. I could fucking breathe again. I hopped into the car, my smile so damn big it hurt.

"You seem so happy," she sighed as she buckled in.

Hell yeah, I was fucking happy! Mia moglie was home! Mamma was back! My heart was whole again, and I just kissed the most beautiful fucking woman on this planet. I blinked, trying to clear my now blurry eyes. God, I was such a fucking chump sometimes. I was way too fucking big to be crying. I flipped open the console, grabbing my sunglasses out, sliding them on to hide the tears.

"You look handsome," she whispered, probably trying not to wake the twins. "How'd it go while I was gone?" Now she sounded nervous, probably afraid her asshole husband was gonna unleash, and ruin the excitement she was trying to contain. But that wasn't me, not this time.

"Great, Baby!" Except for the fact that our children are fucking savages, the house was a disaster, I couldn't sleep, and I hated every fucking minute that you were gone. "I made spaghetti, we played, went to the park, had pancakes. It was nice Papà time. How was your trip?"

"Fine," she shrugged, staring out her window.

Something wasn't right. She was giddy as fuck when she left yesterday; now she was. "What happened, Sadie!"

"Nothing." She was lying.

"Sadie!" I hated when she fucking did this. "Baby, did someone do something?"

She looked back at me. "I missed you and the twins. I could barely get through dinner. I couldn't sleep. I was almost sick this morning."

What was the right response? Selfish, happy as fuck husband who'd hoped she was as miserable as he was or supportive husband. "It'll get better, Baby," I mumbled. "Next time will be easier."

"I love what I do, Gavin. It means a lot to me. But I love you three more, and being home with my family means more to me. I don't want a next time."

"Thank god!" I groaned before I could stop myself. "I mean, we were fine, Baby, so whatever you want to do."

She still looked sad. I couldn't read her. I didn't know what I was supposed to say. You know what—fuck it. "Baby, I was so fucking miserable! The house was fucking wrecked, I slept in my office, and Vinny wouldn't stop calling out for you. We missed Mamma!"

She finally smiled. "That makes me happy." It was her real happy smile, and I was tempted to pull over just to kiss her again. I wasn't whole without her. I'd gone years with a void, my reflection just a fucking shell of a man, until her. Now my reflection was full because she was a part of it. There was no Gavin without Sadie.

GAVIN POV: 25TH BIRTHDAY: 3

She slammed me into the chair, tits and pussy hanging out of that black dom shit she was wearing. "What lesson would you like to teach me first, Mr. Romano?"

I have a lot of fucking lessons I want to teach you. First, I want that red lipstick staining my dick. "Voglio quelle labbra su di me. I want those lips on me."

Her eyes widened, lips parted. Italian drove her crazy. Keep opening your mouth, Baby. "Inginocchiati!" I spread my knees for her to kneel, stretched my hand to the black straps suffocating her massive tits, slipping a finger under to feel that hard nipple, yanking her down by the straps.

She fell to her knees, palm rubbing my jeans, stroking the fucking dragon, but he was awake, hard the second I saw her on my desk wearing nothing but black strings. Her fingers fumbled with the zipper, I lifted my ass, letting her yank the jeans down, and I expected her hand to start, but her face dove, hot tongue and wet lips kissing my dick. "Fuck." There was no greater fucking view than watching my girl's face in my lap, hair falling over her eyes as my dick disappeared into those red lips. Fuck, almost as warm as that pussy, and almost as tight. Her hair was in my hands, but she didn't need my guidance, she knew exactly what to fucking do. "Fuck, Baby." Those lips were tighter, exhales blasting out her nose, sucking my dick into her throat.

Then fingers gripped my sack, fuck! "Baby, I'm, I'm—" She hollowed out her fucking cheeks, flashing her eyes at me, that mouth about to be filled with my cum. "Fuck!" I held her head, staring into her eyes as I spewed, load after load. Damn. I fell back against the seat, watching her face, that tongue still spinning, working its way up to my tip, slurping over my head before she pulled her mouth away, that red lipstick smeared over her lips, and all over my dick—a beautiful matching set. I needed to remember this, needed to cement this fucking image.

She stayed on her knees, eyes up on me, submissive, silent, waiting for direction. God, I loved birthdays. "Can I fuck you in that outfit?" My hands were back to the x's covering her tits, rolling over the flesh escaping from the sides, hearing her whimpering gasps, her breath hitching as I traced her skin.

"The panties detach," she purred like a fucking kitten, more hair falling over her eyes as she arched towards my touch.

"I want them off."

She squeezed my knees, pushing back up, bumps and curves sliding up my legs. She stood before me, hooking her thumbs under the strings, making me lunge, slapping her hands away. I wanted a taste of her too.

I tore my shirt off, falling to my knees now, her thong bunched in my palm, revealing a freshly shaved pussy, my favorite fucking dessert. I gripped her hips, holding her straight while I kissed her stomach, dragging my tongue until she split, where the desert became the ocean. She was always so fucking wet for me. I shoved my face between her thighs, each inhale fattening up my dick. My tongue was out, licking her lips, swirling in the juices, turning her drip into a downpour. Now, it was time to feel her shake, hear her beg. I flicked, tongue zeroed in on the knot, her clit made her crazy.

She gasped, as expected, thighs trembling. That's all it took, one flick, one stroke, one hiss. So I gave her relief, dragging my lips down her pussy, smacking right back into her clit, making her jerk, hands attacking my hair. She was begging for relief, but I was a fucking monster, no mercy tonight.

"Shit, shit, shit," she squealed, ripping my hair from my head, driving me crazy. "Gavin!" My name, making me double down, calling in for the finale. I ate her pussy hard, sneaking two fingers after me, dipping them into the rushing water, plunging inside her, finger fucking her the way she liked. "Oh, my, god!" she wailed, writhing, ripping more hair, trying to escape from my hold. This game was my favorite. I dug one hand into that plump ass cheek while sliding my fingers out and shooting my tongue up her pussy instead. "Fuck! Gavin!" That whiny scream was begging. I held the fucking power.

I pulled back, looking at her heaving chest, and parted, gasping lips. "Take all this shit off, Baby. Now!" My dick was calling the shots, ready to fuck.

It took her a second to come to, that fuzzy look in her eyes slowly sharpening, groaning in frustration. Then her hands were up on the strap shit, while I sank back into my chair, licking my lips as she stripteased the lingerie off. Her tits came bouncing out, nipples tight, wanting to be sucked, bit. Her lips parted again, messy red lips, and she arched her chest above me, making her tits seem that much fucking bigger.

"Come closer," I demanded, guiding her onto my lap, her legs instinctively straddling mine, shoving those tits in my face, my mouth clamping over a hard nipple, tempted to fucking bite. Instead, I sucked, lapping each one up like a wild dog. "I want you to fuck me," I spoke to those hazy eyes, her body lifting on command, dragging her pussy up my dick, staring at me as she sank down, taking all of me in one fall.

"Fuck!" Both our yelps filled the room, then she slowed, hips barely rocking, mouth parted, hissing out her moans. She always fucking did this when she rode me, too fucking deep, too intense, but dammit, I needed her to move. "Fuck me, Baby!" I sucked a nipple between my teeth, forcing her awake, her hips rocking harder, taking my dick for a tight fucking ride.

Her hands slid over my shoulders, nails slicing into my skin, legs squatting, pussy sliding up, down, smothering my dick, milking him hard. "Fuck!" I let those tits smack my face, pussy doing all the work, now it was time to fuck her. "Bend over my desk, Sadie."

She popped up, spinning, bending over the desk, ass in my face, begging for my tongue. This ass had been calling my name since the minute I saw it in her garden. This ass was untouched, unowned, the last piece of her to be claimed, and I wanted fucking ownership. I gripped her thighs, lifting her, that wet pussy ushering me in.

She was tight; I had to work for it, shoving, ramming, the feeling fucking indescribable. "Gavin!" she belted out, arms stretching across the wood, nails screeching as I destroyed her g-spot.

"I need you to come for me, Baby." I stared at that ass, my dick plowing under it.

She rolled her hips back, screaming I was too deep, but pushing for more. "There!" she squealed. "Oh, god!"

Fuck, I was gonna come too. I bent over her, dropping my hands to find her tits, pinching her nipples. "Vieni per me. Come, Baby."

"Gavin!"

My dick was too fucking hard, she felt too fucking good, and those whiny screams were driving me fucking crazy. "Come now!" I slid my hand down her stomach, latching to her clit, rubbing while I fucked her.

She tightened, sucked in the loudest inhale, exhaled the loudest moan, clenching those thighs as she squirted.

I yanked out, sliding my drenched dick to her ass, no time for lube, this would have to do. I pressed against her sealed entrance. "This is what I want."

She was quiet, fuck, I wasn't going to last long, just the thought of owning this piece of her was getting me off.

"You're too big," she whimpered, voice shaky.

"Trust me, Baby." I ran my hands up and down her ass cheeks. "I won't hurt you."

"Okay."

Okay? Okay! I smashed my dick harder, rubbing her juice over her ass, coating before tipping deeper, but she was locked. "Fatti penetrare. Relax, Baby." Fuck, I was out of time, but I needed to slow, ease her into it. I sank my hand into her soaked pussy, coating it, sliding it up to her ass, inching my wet finger in.

"Ooh, ooh." She relaxed, letting out little moans.

I slid my finger out and my head in. Fuuuucccck! I needed to ram, god, she was so fucking tight. I worked harder, losing my fucking mind. My dick had never been so strangled, fighting for his fucking life in there. This was mine. No dick had penetrated this ass, until me. I'd fucked every inch of her, all of her.

"You okay, Baby?" Fuck, I watched her ass taking me, this was like mind, body, and spirit shit. I was on the next fucking level, cum mounting like a hose under pressure. "Oh, fuck!" I nutted, spewing deep—a high like I'd never felt, the intensity leaving me fucking shaking. "Fuck, fuck." I dropped my lips to her back, pulling out, flipping her over to face me. "You okay?" I asked, she nodded yes. No words. Fuck. "Did I hurt you?"

"No," she mumbled, shaking her head.

Fuck I hated when she was quiet. "Let's get upstairs, Baby." I bent, hooking my arm under her legs, flipping her up into my arms.

Her face dropped against my sweaty chest, still so fucking quiet. Did I cross a line? She said yes, right? Fuck did she? Or was I hearing shit. She wanted this too, right? She hadn't said anything before when I played back there. She said okay. I kicked the bedroom door open, taking her straight to the shower, backtracking to the tub, and elbowing the water on as I lowered her in. "I'll be right back." I raced down the stairs, grabbing some wine and the birthday cake, rushing back up.

She was lying back in the water, eyes closed, water waving around her thighs. I felt that heat in my gut, that worry, something was wrong. I stepped into the water, resting back against the opposite end. "Wine, Baby?"

Her eyes opened, hand immediately reaching for the bottle. "This isn't going to be an everyday thing, right?" Those big eyes were on me as she pushed the bottle to her lips, taking a long sip.

"The wine?" I grabbed up her foot, rubbing. "It already is an everyday thing for you, Baby."

She didn't laugh. "Are you—" she took another sip from the bottle, still staring at me. "You're, you're still satisfied with me, right? Is the sex not—"

What? Shit! "Yes! Of course, Baby! This has nothing to do with that. I love fucking you." Why would she think that? She wasn't even responding; her eyes were thinking something.

"No man's ever touched you there. You let me have it, let me fuck you, gave it to me, trusted me. It's just a—"

"Possessive thing?" She laughed, swirling the bottle in her hand. "Well, it's yours now. You're the proud owner of my ass. Congrats." Her teasing smile curled into her cheeks. She was so damn beautiful.

"Come here." I opened my legs, and she sat up, sending the water waving around her as she flipped, resting her back against my chest.

"Cake?" I drug my finger across the frosting to her lips, her tongue rolling up my finger, sucking her way down to my knuckle. Fuck, my dick wanted more from her. I looked down, only to see her soft nipples tighten before my eyes.

She laughed. "There's nowhere left for him to explore." She sat up, twisting to face me, water dripping over her wet tits. I hadn't fucked those yet tonight. Then she raised her hands to them, tiny fingers tweaking her hard nipples. "It's still your birthday," she offered.

"Keep touching yourself."

She scooted to the opposite end of the tub, spreading her thighs, left hand trailing down her tits to her pussy, rubbing her clit, moaning at contact. Then her right hand started on her tits. Fuck, this was a good show. My hand was on my dick, jerking to her fingers disappearing inside her. She let out a quiet moan, then another before closing her eyes, both her hands working her pussy now.

"No, Baby! I want you looking at me!" I demanded, her hazy stare shooting over to me, focusing on my hand.

Her lips parted. "My fingers feel too small after having your giant dick in me."

Oh, fuck! She never talked like that, and I was about to come just from hearing it. She sat up, then stepped out of the tub, tossing a towel to the floor, dripping her way to the sink, bending over it.

Holy fuck! I hopped out, charging up behind her, meeting the reflection of her dirty glare. "You have two options, Mr. Romano. Fuck me hard in the front, or fuck me gentle in the back. But choose fast because it's almost midnight, which means your birthday's almost over."

Incidental Fate Book 6: More Moments, More Time.

Preview Chapters

Follow the Romano family up to the twins' high school graduation. Stories include: Grant's Wedding, Ten-Year Vow Renewal, Homecoming, Dani, and more!

HOMECOMING: 1

I pulled the zipper up Nora's back, then stepped beside her, the two of us almost the same height now, and she was almost as curvy, especially in this red gown. "Well, what do you think?"

"I love it!" she squealed, immediately twirling to check the back of her dress.

Good lord—when did this happen? When did my little girl become a woman? I stepped back, giving her space to pose in front of the mirror, watching her whip her long black hair over her shoulders and back.

"Baby?" Gavin's yell echoed into the room.

I froze, eyes flashing to the bedroom door—watching in suspended horror. I thought he was still working. I hadn't prepared him for this.

Our bedroom door swung open, Gavin stepped in, smiling when he saw me; only then his gaze drifted to Nora. He stilled, cheeks blistering red, eyes matte black. "What is this?"

"My homecoming dress, Papà!" Nora gushed, hands sliding over her curves while she posed.

"Homecoming!" he repeated, not moving an inch.

She looked over her shoulder, shrugging. "I told you I was going to homecoming this weekend!"

"Homecoming is a fuc— homecoming is a football game, Piccolina! I said you could go to the football game!"

"It's also a dance, Papà!" She spun towards the mirror, adjusting her dress and posing some more.

"No!" he spat, stomping forward. "And there's no way in hell you're wearing that dress out of this house!"

"Papà!" she snapped back. "Mamma loves the dress!"

"Piccolina!" he roared, exhaling through his nose.

She whipped around, dark fiery eyes challenging his. "It's Nora! I'm fourteen now! Stop calling me that! I'm not a baby anymore!"

"Nora," he groaned through gritted teeth, fingers flexed at his sides. "You're too young to go to a dance! You're too young to wear shit like this!"

"Too bad! I already have a date!" she boasted, her dark eyes meeting his once more, refusing to back down.

Here we go. I took a step back, knowing too well what happened when Gavin and mini-Gavin squared off.

"A date!" he yelled, flashing his eyes back to me, but I shrugged. She hadn't told me about a date.

"Yes," she replied so matter of fact. "He's a sophomore," she boasted, digging an even deeper hole.

"No!" Gavin belted out, pacing. "You're not allowed to date! You have to get my, our permission, and the answer is no!"

"Ti odio! I hate you!" she yelled at him while rushing to me, throwing her arms around my waist. "Mamma."

"Let me talk to Papà," I whispered. "He just needs some time to calm down."

She dropped her arms, dramatically wiping her tears as she stalked to the door, ignoring Gavin, while even more dramatically slamming our door shut.

"What the fuck was that!" Gavin screamed, charging at me now. "Did you buy her that?"

"Calm down," I warned him. "You said she could go to homecoming. I thought you were okay with this."

"Okay with that!" he bellowed, waving his hands over his body. "When did she— why didn't you warn me?"

"When did she... become a woman?" I laughed up at his panic-ridden face. "Over the summer. She's in high school now." Nora had gone from skinny little girl to curvy woman over the past few months, and I'd wondered when Gavin would finally notice.

"And those—" he waved his hand over his chest. "She's way too fucking young for any of that shit."

"She started developing—"

"Started?" he snapped at me like I had something to do with it. "No! That shit needs to be finished! That's plenty! That's all she fucking needs."

"Well, if they're anything like mine—"

"Yours! Absolutely fucking not!" He wheeled around to face me, stare falling to my chest. "I swear to fucking god, Sadie—Piccolina better not get your tits."

I laughed. "I can't control that. It's genetic."

He stalked back and forth a few more times, running his hand through his hair. "I'm not ready for all this. I'm not ready for that," he sighed, waving towards the door. "Every sleazy fucking guy in Cali's gonna come after her, just like they do with you."

"Nora's pretty tough. She's all Italian, and she's all Romano. I'd be more worried about the guys than Nora."

He walked over, taking my hands in his. "She was just in kindergarten," he mumbled, pulling me into his arms, resting his face on my hair. "She doesn't even want me calling her Piccolina. And what was that *I hate you* bullshit?"

"She's mad." I stifled my laugh, looking up at the man she got her personality from. "And she has a bad habit of being mean when she's angry. I have no idea where she gets that from."

"Very funny." He pressed a kiss against my hair. "So, what do I do?"

"Go talk to her. But remember, she reacts the same way you do, and you can't fight fire with fire."

A knock hit the door, sending Gavin stepping back, releasing his hold of me just as Nora stepped in.

She had changed into a T-shirt and leggings, looking so much younger than she had only minutes ago. "Papà," she squeaked. "I'm so sorry for saying I hate you. I love you more than anything. I was just hurt that you thought I looked ugly in my dress."

"What!" He tripped over his feet running to her. "Picco—Nora, no, you looked beautiful, too beautiful."

Her bottom lip quivered, she batted her thick lashes, her eyes welled up. "It's okay if you don't want me to go, if you're too... embarrassed. I'll just stay home, be alone that night." She stepped into him, wrapping her arms around his back while managing to squeeze out a single tear—which she made sure he saw.

"No, Piccolina!" Gavin fell right into her trap. Because while Nora was a mini-Gavin, she was also a mini-Luca, clever and smart as hell. "Of course, I want you to go!" he frantically shouted. "Jesus, I would never—"

"Thanks, Papà!" She wiped away her crocodile tears. "Francisco will be here at six to pick me up!" She flashed me a quick smile before releasing Gavin and dancing her way out our door.

Gavin stood there for a minute, looking side to side, brows furrowed. "What the fuck just happened?"

I laughed, walking over with my arms open for him. "She knows how to work her papà, and she's good at it!"

"Wait, did she just say Francisco was picking her up?"

"Gavin, breathe!"

"No one is picking up my figlia! Especially no one by the name of fucking Francisco, sounds like a player."

"Relax, he's a sophomore," I assured him, trying and failing to calm him. "Probably all gangly and awkward with a face full of pimples."

He smiled back at me, nodding okay, then abruptly turned and threw our door open. "There's no way in hell he's picking you up or driving you home!"

"Ti odio!" Nora screamed before slamming her door.

"Then hate me! I'm your papà, and it's not happening!"

HOMECOMING: 2

Gavin had been quiet most of the morning, keeping to his office downstairs, which was fine by me after all the drama the last two days. In fact, I was more than happy distracting myself with laundry until it was time for me to start Nora's hair and makeup.

"Mamma! MAMMA!" Nora's scream rattled the house, sending me flying out my bedroom door, rushing down the first few stairs.

Oh my god. "Gavin! GAVIN!"

"You're always screaming out his name!" Luca roared, dropping his bag to the floor. "Fratellino must be doing something right!"

"Luca!" I warned.

"I mean wrong," he chuckled, throwing his arm up in defense. "Dai, Piccolina! Give Zio Luca a hug!"

"What are you guys doing here?" I made my way down the last of the stairs just as the office doors swung open.

"Luca! Stefano!" Gavin shouted with a smile.

"We're going to a dance!" Stefano answered me.

"Mamma!" Nora bellowed once more.

"Gavin?" So this was why he'd been so quiet.

"We're gonna chaperone, Baby!" He wore the proudest, smuggest smile I'd ever seen.

Oh, no. This was a little too much, even for Gavin.

"You can't just show up!" Nora screamed. "They won't let you in!"

"Who's running it?" Luca shot back, looking between her and me.

I shrugged. "Probably the PTA moms."

"Moms." Luca smiled, Stefano smiled, Gavin smiled. Like dominos, one curling up right after the other. "I don't think we'll have a problem."

Still as cocky as the day I'd met them, and the older they got, the more attractive they became. They still had that same power over women and men, and they knew it.

"Zio Luca! Zio Stefano!"

It took me a minute to register that it was Vinny shouting. His voice had gone down two octaves. Nora wasn't the only one growing up; while she grew curves this summer, Vinny had grown six inches.

"Vinny!" Stefano pulled him into a hug.

"Vinny!" Luca roared next, stealing him from Stefano.

"This is so unfair!" Nora whined. "Why can't Francisco just drive me!"

"Who the fuck is Francisco!" Luca barked.

"Luca!" I rolled my eyes at Gavin, shaking my head.

"My date to the dance, and he's a sophomore," Nora bragged, oblivious to the fact that she was bragging to the wrong crowd.

"Where does he live?" Stefano asked, all three Romano men tensing up.

"I don't know," she huffed.

"Good fucking answer!" Luca belted out.

"Luca! Enough!" I warned him, yet again.

"No date!" Luca boomed, completely ignoring me. "Not happening!"

"I told her," Gavin assured him.

"What about Vinny!" Nora screamed back, pointing an accusatory finger at him.

"I don't have a date." He stepped over to the mens' side while Nora moved closer to me.

"No, you don't have *a* date—you have lots of dates! You're a player!" she yelled. "It's not fair! Vinny can date all the girls at school, but I can't even go on one date."

My Vinny was hardly a player. He might look like the Romano men, but he was still just a boy, my baby boy, and he wasn't good with making decisions. He was shy, liked to process. Picking a date for a dance was probably too overwhelming.

"I'm not a player!" Vinny scoffed.

"I know, sweetie," I cut in, but he kept talking.

"Luca said to sample the menu before I order a dish." He nodded to Luca. "So, I'm sampling."

Oh, my, god! This was my fault! Who in their right mind would choose Luca as a godfather? Why? "Vinny," I emphasized, feeling Nora's tug at my arm. "Sampling is not good. Girls don't like to be left half-eaten—" Oh, my, god! I cringed the second the words flew from my mouth while the guys burst out laughing.

Luckily, Vinny wasn't old enough to understand the double entendre, at least, I prayed he wasn't.

"Don't worry, Sadie," Luca chuckled. "I told him that too. Never leave a job unfinished. Satisfaction is always guaranteed with a Romano."

Oh- my-god. "Gavin!" I pleaded, begged, demanded.

"Knock-knock!" There was a guy in the open doorway. "I've got a one-hour delivery for Sadie Romano."

Me? I stepped forward as he handed a box over to me. "Bottles of wine?"

"There's a card too!" The guy pointed before taking off.

I carried the box of wine inside, plucking the card out, reading it. *Sorry in advance. Had to call in backup. Knew you'd be pissed. Please try to understand, Baby. Love, Gavin.*

I looked at Gavin, who mouthed, sorry. There was no going back now. Nora was stuck with three chaperones taking her to her first dance. Poor Nora.

"Come on, Nora." I urged her to follow me up the stairs. "Let's get you ready." I started up, looking over my shoulders at the men downstairs. "Best behavior tonight, boys!"

HOMECOMING: 3

I brushed Nora's jet black hair, flashing between her smile in the mirror and her hair in my hands. "How about we pin it up on the sides and curl it?"

"Okay, Mamma!" She was jittery, bouncing in the seat. "Oh!" She reached for her phone, accepting the video call. "Hi, Zia Fia!"

"Giorgia's here too!" Sofia yelled through the screen. "Wait, Sadie, are you doing Nora's hair?"

"Yes," I laughed back. "And her makeup."

Giorgia pushed her face into the camera so we could see both sisters. "Why?"

"Because she's only fourteen! And she's gorgeous! She doesn't need a professional team—she doesn't even need makeup at all!" Nora was stunning, and if Gavin thought it was bad now—he had no idea what was coming.

"True, sei bellissima, Nora," Sofia gushed.

"Can we call you two back later?" I talked down at the screen, meeting their disappointed faces. "We'll call back and send pics! I promise!"

"Fine," they grumbled in unison before hanging up.

"Now, back to work."

I curled and sprayed, pinning her hair up. I was usually the one in front of the mirror doing my hair and makeup, stepping into a tight dress while Nora sat on the floor watching me. But I wasn't the princess anymore; she was. I finished her hair, then started on the makeup, some blush and mascara, and a little gloss.

"It looks so good, Mamma!" she squealed, clapping her hands, bouncing in her seat. I'd never seen her so excited. She could barely contain the smile on her face, whereas I could barely contain the tears.

"Dress time!" I walked over, grabbing the dress off the hanger and helping her step into it, then zipping it.

She gasped, twirling her way to the mirror, just like she used to when she was little. Now, she was a beautiful woman. "I'm so excited!" she squealed again, posing left and right.

The makeup made her eyes pop, the hair pulled up and curled made her look five years older, and the red dress that had no choice but to cling to her curves made her look like a woman.

She stepped into the heels next, making her two inches taller, eye level with me now. Where had my baby gone?

"Ready?" I asked, blinking back the tears as she rushed over, practically knocking me down to get to the bedroom door. I take it that's a yes. I followed her out, seeing the guys waiting in the entryway.

Their stares all jumped to her, watching her cascade down the stairs.

"Jacket!" Stefano demanded, flicking his wrist for her to go back upstairs.

"No!" Luca snapped, shaking his head. "We stay home tonight! Sadie, go make popcorn. Family movie night! Nora, pajamas, take that shit off!"

"Best behavior!" I repeated to all of them.

Gavin was still silent, his tirade faltering, his shoulders caving, eyes deepening, staring at his Piccolina. I knew this day would come, the day when Piccolina became Nora, and Gavin would have to deal with losing his daughter to another man. Only I think Gavin had thought it'd be further in the future. He wasn't good with loss, even the tiniest bit.

"Papà!" She hurried straight into his arms. "What do you think?"

His eyes roamed her hair, her face. "Sei la ragazza più bella del mondo."

"Thanks, Papà! I do feel beautiful tonight!" she gushed, giving him one last hug.

"Ready?" Vinny shouted from upstairs, taking the steps down two at a time.

He had his hair gelled, matching his black suit. How did my little guy become a six-foot giant overnight? And so handsome, just like Gavin.

"Vinny," I sighed, trying not to cry as I jumped over to his opening arms.

"I know, Mamma, no sampling," he laughed, pressing a kiss to my hair.

The guys started cracking up again, so I shot them a look—shutting them up. "Picture time!" I insisted, pulling out my phone while pointing the kids to the stairs.

Vinny stood beside Nora, towering over her, draping his arm over her shoulders, both of them giving me their best smiles.

"How is this happening?" Gavin whispered in my ear.

Suddenly the doorbell rang, and Luca swung it open.

"Yeah?" Luca gruffed.

"Come in, Francisco!" Nora yelled, pushing past Vinny and the uncles.

Francisco walked in, finding Nora, his smile curling right up.

"No!" Luca yelled. "Absolutely fucking not! You better put that damn smile away."

"Luca!" I warned, shaking my head, again.

"I'm Francisco," he announced, reaching his arm out to shake the guys' hands.

So much for gangly and awkward. He was almost as tall as Gavin and not one pimple on his tan skin.

"What up, Vinny!" He smiled, waving his hands up and down in a bow-down gesture. "No date?"

"Many," Vinny boasted.

Oh, my, god! Where did my sweet baby go? Many?

"Zio Luca!" Luca spat, shaking Francisco's hand a little too firmly. "Ever heard of the Italian mafia?"

"Do mafias still exist?" Francisco chuckled.

"Lay as much as one fucking finger on her, and you'll find out," he growled, glare matching the sinister tone.

"Stefano," Stefano grumbled, pushing his way forward to shake Francisco's hand.

"Which means—" Francisco spun towards Gavin. "You must be, dad?" He stuck his hand out to shake Gavin's, but Gavin just glared at his hand, shoving his own into his pockets, rebuffing Francisco.

"Touch my daughter, and you fucking die."

"Gavin!" What was happening! "Stop!" I warned him on my way to Francisco. "It's nice to meet you."

Poor guy. He was the first date, A.K.A the first threat.

Francisco laughed towards Gavin. "I have to touch her to dance," he joked, to the very wrong crowd.

"We'll be watching you, kid," Luca's voice was a scary whisper. "In case Nora didn't tell you, we're all fucking going to the dance."

Poor Nora.

"That's fine." Francisco turned back to face her. "I'm good just staring at her all night! You look hot, Nora."

Luca jumped forward, hands up. "Oh, you better—"

"Luca!" I snapped once more, warning all three of them. "Time to go!" I insisted, looking back at Nora, seeing her eyes narrow, darken, fixate on Francisco while that smirk of hers curled up at the edges—staring at him the exact way Gavin... stared at me. Oh, shit! Nora was Gavin's mini, and I'd never thought about the passion before because she was too young. But she was looking at Francisco like trapped prey she was about to devour. I wasn't ready for this! We hadn't even had the talk with her yet. Gavin would go ballistic if I even brought it up.

She stepped down from the stairs, walking straight to Francisco with the same confidence Gavin always had, meeting his eyes directly as she smiled, holding out her hand for him before waltzing out the door. She wasn't shy, and she didn't play coy. She was Italian, a Romano.

"Go!" I practically yelled at Gavin. "Watch her!"

"Wait, you're okay with this now, Baby?"

"Yes! Gavin, watch her like a hawk!" I held the door for them, letting them all shuffle out.

Nora had Gavin's insatiable passion, and Vinny was a player—where did I put all that wine?

I heard the front door boom below, feet stomping up the stairs, bedroom doors slamming shut, so everyone was home. I lifted my foot to the bath faucet, shutting the water off while finishing my third, fourth, perhaps eighth glass of wine. I hadn't heard a peep from Gavin all night, which was either really bad or really good.

I stepped out, skipping the towel, opting for my silk robe, sliding it on as I walked out the bedroom. It was silent. No loudmouth Italians, no screaming kids. What was going on? I hurried down the stairs, finding all the Romano men on the couch, scrolling on their phones.

"What's going on?" I asked.

"We're looking up all-girl schools!" Luca shouted back without bothering to look up.

Oh jeez. "The guys were that bad?"

"Guys," Gavin groaned, face down on his screen. "Baby, it was Nora!"

"Nora tried to take down every chick who even looked at Fran-dick-o," Luca huffed. "She was fucking ferocious."

"Territorial is an understatement," Stefano mumbled.

"Oh." I giggled from the wine. "So baby girl Gavin is a tad jealous, a little possessive. Humph, did not see that one coming."

Gavin's face shot up, giving me a mocking smirk before noticing the wet silk robe glued to my skin.

"Well, you guys have fun. I'm going to finish my bath and the rest of my wine." I turned as Gavin hopped over the couch, tripping to get to me.

"You guys got this?" he yelled over his shoulder. "I'm gonna finish my bath and the rest of my wine."

Romanoverse

Sadie, Gavin, and the twins can be found throughout the Romanoverse spin-off series.

LUCA (3-book series): Women were just a number until he laid his eyes on Crystal. This man falls hard and learns a few lessons along the way.

SOFIA (2-book series): Sofia finds unexpected love in a man her opposite, a man who also isn't her husband. She does the unthinkable and cheats, only to realize how cheated out of love she'd been.

STEFANO (2-book series): He's dedicated his life to representing his name and family, at all costs, including hiding who he truly is. One man will change all that.

GIORGIA: A dark night leads Giorgia to finding her knight in shining armor, but nothing is that easy when you're a Romano with three overprotective big brothers.

GAVIN: Read Incidental Fate Book 1 through his eyes.

Summer Leigh is a new adult, and contemporary romance author. Her debut 6-book series Incidental Fate spawned two spin-off series: Romanoverse, an 8-book interconnected family series, and Romanoverse Heirs, coming 2022.

You can connect with her and get updates on new book releases via Facebook, Instagram, and her website.

@AuthorSummerLeigh

www.AuthorSummerLeigh.com

Made in the USA
Columbia, SC
07 July 2023